The China Connection

A Novel

Timothy Trainer

The China Connection
A Novel

Timothy Trainer

Published by
Joshua Tree Publishing
• Chicago •
JoshuaTreePublishing.com

13-Digit ISBN: Print Edition: 978-1-956823-26-4
13-Digit ISBN eBook: 978-1-956823-29-5

Disclaimer:

This is a work of fiction. Names, characters, places, and events are the product of the author's imagination or have been used fictitiously. Certain long-standing institutions, agencies and public offices are mentioned, but the characters involved are wholly imaginary. Any resemblance to actual persons, living or dead, events, locales or organizations is entirely coincidental.

Printed in the United States of America

Table of Contents

Character Names in Order of First Appearance

PROLOGUE

US West Coast (Saturday, May 16, 1998)

Customs agent Jake Evans assembled a nine-man team and conducted a pre-dawn briefing. He explained that this would be a document collection operation. Nevertheless, he and his fellow customs investigative agents put on their protective vests with bold lettering on the backs to identify themselves as customs agents. They also made sure that they had handcuffs and that their pistols were ready for use in case of any unexpected resistance. On paper, they expected a routine mission.

The ten agents were divided into three SUVs. Three joined Jake in the lead vehicle, and the remaining six divided into three, each in the other two vehicles. They headed off toward the Long Beach area, away from downtown Los Angeles. Sunrise Imports, the target, was a few blocks away from the Long Beach container terminal. Like many others engaged in the import-export business, Sunrise located itself near the container port.

One of his junior agents drove to Sunrise as Jake reread the information he had in a folder on his lap. Ray Jackson, the customs attaché in Hong Kong, had transmitted information back to his colleagues in the US. The details Ray had sent had gotten the attention of several people and were forwarded to the US Attorney's office in Los Angeles. Jake and his team were quickly mobilized because the information suggested that possibly life-threatening products were entering the country, justifying the team's actions being put on a fast track.

While Jake read through the file that he had in his lap, another agent, sitting behind the driver, checked a street map of the area, acting as the second pair of eyes to ensure that they were going to the correct location and address.

"We're getting close," Jake observed as he looked up from the file. Jake got on the radio to communicate with the other vehicles. "We're going to make a left in a moment. When we do, I want you two to pull to the curb and stop. We'll do a slow drive by the address and look to see if there's any activity."

The street was lined mostly with three- to five-story-high office buildings along both sides of the street. It was still early enough for there to be only intermittent traffic.

Jake leaned forward to look into the passenger side mirror, seeing no one behind them. "Slow down. We can take a few seconds to look at our target address," Jake instructed. The agent driving reduced speed to about fifteen miles an hour. The target address looked slightly larger than a ranch house. It sat on the north side of the street, facing south. The entry into the business was a double glass door about ten feet from a driveway. One single-lane driveway led to the back, where there appeared to be several parking spaces.

"Did anyone see any windows on the west side of the house as we approached?" Jake asked no one in particular. No one provided an affirmative answer. The front of the structure had three windows about three by six in size, probably one in each of the offices located in the front of the structure. A few minutes later, they drove by in the opposite direction and, again, noticed no windows on the side facing the driveway.

"We have to assume there are windows facing the back," Jake said. "Anyone notice any security cameras?" In unison, Jake heard three "nos." With an outstretched arm, he motioned for the driver to pick up speed and meet up with the other two vehicles parked at the curb at the next corner.

At the corner, Jake had his driver make a U-turn and park along the curb. "Everybody awake out there," Jake said into his radio. "All ears," was the response he heard back from the other two vehicles.

"There's a single-lane driveway leading to the back where there are several parking spaces. I want both of you to pull into the driveway. Whoever pulls in first, pull up to block it to prevent anyone from driving out. Keep the back of the place secure in case anyone tries to exit from the back," Jake instructed. "I want you guys in the second vehicle to pull into the driveway and come inside with us to see what we can find. Clear?"

"Copy," Jake heard from the other two vehicles. Jake gave his driver a nod, and they started back toward Sunrise Imports. As they reached Sunrise, Jake's driver pulled up and parked along the curb facing the oncoming traffic. They waited a few seconds for the next SUV to turn into the driveway and stop. The three agents got out and disappeared behind the structure.

Jake waited, listened, and watched as the third SUV pulled into the driveway. "We've got the back, two cars parked," Jake heard over the communication line. Jake nodded as he and the other three in his vehicle exited and walked toward Sunrise's entry.

Knowing there were cars parked in the rear, Jake pounded on the frame of the double glass doors with the heel of his right fist. He leaned in toward the glass door, trying to see if anyone was approaching. The other six agents stood at both sides of the door and had a hand on their holstered pistols. Jake waited about ten seconds, then pounded on the frame again.

Lights flickered before coming on, and someone appeared, walking haltingly toward the door. Jake saw a distorted figure through the frosted glass and listened as the door was unlocked. A petite black-haired woman, looking to be in her forties, opened the door slowly and intended to open the door only a couple of inches to see who was pounding on the door while standing behind the door.

Jake pushed the door wide open and into the woman behind it before she had any chance of closing it. The other agents were through the door in seconds, striding past Jake and the woman. Jake pulled out a folded document from an inside vest pocket.

"We have a warrant," he said to the woman still standing by the door and saying nothing with a blank shocked look on her face. Her eyes followed the agents who entered, then returned to Jake standing in front of her.

"How many people are here?" Jake asked.

The woman focused on Jake. "Only me and the manager."

Jake could hear some sounds, noises from the back, but didn't know what it was. It was too loud for a copy machine. It had made some whirring and ripping sounds. The sound started again but stopped after just a second or two.

"Take me back to where you and your manager are working," Jake ordered.

Jake and the woman left a small reception area that didn't have any chairs for anyone. There was a counter about fifteen feet from the entrance that was about eight feet long with a desk and chair behind it. Four black metal filing cabinets lined the wall. He followed her into a hallway that opened up into offices on both sides of the hallway. One door opened into a small office area behind the wall to the reception area. It had a couple of copy machines, a small table with a coffee pot, and more metal filing cabinets.

Jake walked by the first office facing the street and saw two of his agents searching through the drawers in a desk. Two more agents were going through files in the second office facing the street. The third office was the last office facing the street. Jake's driver and one other agent were there with the manager. Jake's driver stood between the manager and a shredder.

"He was shredding papers when we walked in," Jake's driver said.

PART I

Six Days Earlier

Chapter 1

Arrival

Hong Kong (Sunday, May 10)

Aaron's eyelids were half closed. He felt every minute of the sleepless hours on his just completed San Francisco to Hong Kong non-stop flight. With each labored step, he seemed to be getting farther behind Kellie. Her steps were quick, not sluggish like his. Other passengers who had disembarked their flight marched past him. Aaron kept grabbing the shoulder strap of his bag, adjusting it for better balance as he pulled a wheeled carry-on piece behind him. No doubt, Kellie had slept much better on the flight than he had.

He glanced at the signage in English and Chinese. There were large banners hanging from the ceiling at regular intervals informing travelers of the coming closure of this old Kai Tak Airport in two months. But Aaron wasn't interested in that.

Kellie continued her quick pace ahead of him. He could see her head bobbing up and down with each step as she was inches taller than most of the women ahead. He focused on the signs in English. The crowd of passengers around him grew as he passed the gates of arriving flights. With each step, Kellie was creating more space between them, and he could barely make her out ahead.

They had agreed beforehand that they would get through immigration separately. There was no reason for both of them to suffer through a long wait if there was one. The first one through would wait in the luggage claim area. Aaron slowed as he approached the backed-up lines for immigration clearance in the bright, massive arrivals hall. As a frequent international traveler, he hoped that Hong Kong Immigration was more efficient than he had experienced in other countries.

Aaron glanced at his watch and then looked at the long single-file lines for each of the immigration officers checking passports. He dropped his head and closed his eyes momentarily before looking up again. His hope for quick clearance evaporated. It could be a while—perhaps hours—before his head and body would enjoy the feel of a soft hotel room pillow and mattress.

His search for Kellie among hundreds—no, maybe a thousand—people in the vast immigration area seemed futile. She blended in easily with most of those surrounding him. In a crowd like this, her height didn't help. And with so many Hong Kong locals and other Asians waiting in the lines, Kellie's long black hair simply helped her fade into the crowd.

Kellie's black hair, brown eyes, and understated Asian facial features were inherited from her father's Asian familial background. Her above-average height was something she got from her mother's European ancestry.

Aaron tilted his head from side to side. Occasionally, he stood on his toes to try and see how long the immigration officers were taking with each traveler. Thankfully, many seemed to be getting their passports back after a brief glance by the immigration officers. Ten minutes into his wait, he looked behind him. There were more people behind him than in front of his goal. That perked him up. He rolled his shoulders to loosen up, then reached into his trouser pocket to get his passport.

As he waited his turn, he looked at the pages of his passport, flipping through it. He half-smiled to himself, impressed with all the stamps on the pages representing his travels. When he was done admiring his global travels, he looked up to see that there were only two people ahead of him. He readjusted the strap on his shoulder and grabbed the handle of his wheeled carry-on.

The immigration officer waved him forward and picked up Aaron's passport and customs declaration form. Usually, a US passport led to quick entry. Just as Aaron had done a few minutes ago, the immigration officer flipped through the pages, not stopping to see where Aaron's travels had taken him. Instead of returning the passport, the officer closed it, inspecting its overall condition. The officer reopened the passport's cover and examined the page with Aaron's photograph.

"Mr. Foster, have you changed the photo on the passport?"

The British-accented English from the Hong Kong immigration officer amused Aaron for a second. He hesitated. "No, no, I haven't done anything. Maybe the edges are worn from all my traveling."

The immigration officer ran his index finger around the edges of the passport. He looked at the pages more carefully.

"What kind of work do you do in the United States?"

"I'm a lawyer," Aaron answered accurately but not completely.

"Are you traveling with anyone?"

"Yes, my friend," Aaron responded. Kellie would've playfully punched him if she'd heard him say that.

"Please wait," the officer instructed. The immigration officer stepped out the back of his enclosed booth.

Aaron took in a deep breath and exhaled. The energy that had run through his body a few minutes earlier was now replaced by exhaustion. *How long is this going to take?* he wondered. He saw the immigration officer talking to an older man in uniform. He watched them as they both looked his way. He saw the older officer take his passport and declaration form. As he looked their way, they looked back at him. The older officer waved him to come to them.

The younger officer returned to his enclosed booth to get back to the long line of waiting travelers.

"Mr. Foster, follow me, please," the older officer directed.

The two men walked along a wall behind all the immigration booths. Though Aaron wasn't extremely tall, not quite six feet, he was several inches taller than the immigration officer he was following.

The officer stopped and opened a door to a small room, motioning Aaron to enter. Aaron stepped in, just clearing the door, and stopped to wait for the next instruction. His eyes assessed the room instantly. The room might have been about nine feet square. There were no windows, but there was a mirror about two feet square on the wall opposite the door. Aaron immediately concluded that this room was intended to intimidate. But it wouldn't intimidate any real criminal who had experience being on the wrong side of the law. Aaron wasn't a criminal and felt assured that there was nothing to worry about.

Aaron was motioned to sit facing the immigration officer. Aaron placed his bag on the floor next to his chair, and he positioned the wheeled piece of luggage against the wall. He eyed the officer's name on his uniform. Officer Wong took his time. Aaron remained silent. It was better to wait and let Wong speak first. As the duration of the silence grew, Aaron realized that Officer Wong was waiting for him to speak first.

Officer Wong put Aaron's passport and customs declaration form on the small table, then reached into his pants pocket and placed a pack of cigarettes next to the passport, pushing the cigarettes toward Aaron.

"Don't smoke," Aaron said. He sat back, extended his arms, and clasped his hands on the table.

Officer Wong looked directly at Aaron. Aaron returned the glare. The fifteen to twenty seconds of silence felt a lot longer.

"Mr. Foster, I'm Officer Wong. We're concerned that you or someone may have tampered with the passport."

The corners of Aaron's mouth began to rise.

"Is there something amusing or funny about this?" asked Officer Wong with some irritation in his voice.

"I'm sorry, no. This is my first time in Hong Kong, and I'm not used to hearing the British accent from someone who looks like you," Aaron offered.

"You're not the first person I've heard that from," Wong replied flatly. Wong picked up the passport and opened it to the page with Aaron's photo. He inspected the page and felt around the picture and put the passport back on the table. "I understand you are a lawyer. What law firm do you work for? We have dozens of large British firms here."

"Actually, I don't work for a law firm. I'm a government lawyer," Aaron answered.

Wong's eyebrows rose as if to prompt more information.

"I'm a lawyer with the US Customs Service," Aaron said finally.

"Is this an official trip?" Wong asked.

"No, this is just a week-long vacation for me in Hong Kong. If it was official, I would be using my government passport." Aaron didn't mention the fact that his official government passport was in his trouser pocket.

Again, Wong picked up the passport. To Aaron, it appeared that Wong just wanted to have something in his hand and something to look at. "Is there a particular focus of your customs legal work?" Wong asked as he aimlessly flipped through the passport pages.

Aaron wanted to just grab the passport and leave but knew he was stuck for as long as Wong wanted to keep him. *Play along politely,* Aaron said to himself.

"No, I work on whatever issue or case my boss puts on my desk. Sometimes personnel issues, sometimes it's about tariff classification issues, and there are rare instances when I might help with a copyright or trademark case," Aaron explained.

Wong nodded in affirmation as if he understood exactly. "Sometimes, we have nervous travelers because they know they're doing something illegal. Sometimes we have people who are very calm and relaxed even though they're committing serious crimes, and other times, we bring people into this room and even when they've done nothing wrong, they sweat, anxiously wondering why they're here. In your case, I think we have a situation where my young officer was being very careful and, seeing some fraying on the edges of your pages, thought that you may have tampered with the passport. I think we can attribute this to being overly cautious. Hong Kong has been a little different since our handover back to China recently. Everyone is being careful," Wong explained.

Aaron nodded, signaling his understanding.

Wong pulled a small drawer open and pulled out the stamper and stamp pad so he could properly stamp Aaron's passport for entry into Hong Kong. "It's a long way to travel for just a week. I see from your declaration form and the local address that you chose a nice hotel for your stay. A great view if you are high enough. I apologize for this delay. Working for customs, I'm sure you understand," Wong said with a friendly smile. He reached out and placed the passport in front of Aaron.

"Yes, of course."

Wong got up and opened the door, giving Aaron a nod.

Aaron was ready to run out the door. Instead, he pushed himself up slowly to his full height. He then bent down to grab his bag and his luggage. As he reached the doorway, he turned to Wong and nodded without a word, then looked for the signage pointing to baggage claim.

Wong stood in the doorway and watched Aaron walking away, then turned and went to the mirror. As if talking to himself, he said aloud, "Aaron Foster, Marriott Hong Kong. Let our customs know."

After several minutes of walking and following signs, Aaron arrived in the baggage claim area. He checked his watch. It was nearing two hours since his flight had touched down. His delay meant that none of the monitors displayed his flight and baggage carousel numbers. He went to one end and started looking for Kellie.

He was passing the third carousel when he spotted Kellie curled up in a chair with a sweater draped over her shoulders. She had collected their two lime-green pieces of luggage and used them as a barrier in front of her.

"You awake?" he asked as he tapped her shoulder.

Kellie moved the long black hair covering her face and slowly unfolded her legs and sat upright. She looked at her wristwatch before finally looking up at Aaron. "What the hell took you so long?" she asked just above a whisper. Her throat was dry.

"I'll explain later. Let's just say that immigration took an interest in me."

They gathered up their luggage and made their way through customs without any delay. As soon as the doors opened to exit the air-conditioned terminal building, the heat and humidity embraced them. They scanned the walkway for any signs for taxis. Kellie stopped to put her sweater away. She unzipped an outer pocket of her carry-on bag and stuffed the sweater into it. A few minutes later, they were in an air-conditioned taxi, making their way to Hong Kong Island.

The lights of Hong Kong and Kowloon's buildings danced on the water of Victoria Harbour. Aaron sat staring out at the spectacle of lights that he had only seen in magazines and brochures.

"What country you from?" the driver asked.

"Mei guo," Kellie answered without hesitation.

Aaron turned his head and looked at Kellie. He didn't speak Chinese, but he did understand that "mei guo" translated to the United States. As they rode from Kowloon to Hong Kong, Aaron longed for a good night's sleep.

Chapter 2

Rise and Shine

Hong Kong (Monday, May 11)

Aaron's head snapped toward the sound of the ringing phone. Sleep had his eyes glued shut. His arm reached blindly out in the direction of the ear-splitting sound. His forearm knocked the phone off the bedside table. The ringing stopped when the receiver fell out of its cradle.

"Hello? Hello? Anyone there?"

Aaron could hear the voice. He twisted his body and reached to the floor to pick up the receiver. Receiver in hand, he plopped his head back onto his pillow. "Who is this?"

"It's Roger. Rise and shine, young man. You have to get on Hong Kong time. You can't sleep the day away."

"What time is it?"

"Time to get up and meet me down in the lobby lounge. Make sure you bring your Sleeping Beauty along."

Aaron propped himself up on an elbow and looked around for a clock. Over Kellie's shoulder, he saw it: 7:30. She was on her side looking at him with eyes that were slits. "Okay, at least one of us should be down within thirty minutes. I need to wake up and take a quick shower."

Roger hung up the hotel's house phone. He wandered back into the expansive lobby lounge area. The tall, wide glassed area invited the morning sun. He chose a table by the massive windows that allowed him a view of the streets below and the wide lounge area leading up to the lobby, the doors, and the corridor where the elevators were located.

Roger's habits prevented him from concentrating on the newspaper's headlines and articles. After reading a sentence or paragraph, he surveyed the lounge for the changes among hotel guests and any local friends and guests who might have arrived.

He was reading his third article when he glanced up and saw Aaron walking hesitantly into the lounge. Roger stood and waved.

Aaron squeezed between a few chairs and tables to make his way to the far side of the lounge.

"Good to see you, Roger," Aaron said as he shook Roger's thick hand. "Looks like Hong Kong's been good to you."

"Nothing to complain about. It's never cold. There's a constant rush of energy and no shortage of work to be done."

"So, the work and the pay are both in your favor," Aaron said, his eyes darting to Roger's midsection. "I guess that means that your retirement isn't really about retiring."

"Well, the work is interesting, and yes, I've grown just a bit since you last saw me several years back," Roger acknowledged, patting his midsection. "I was presented with an opportunity to pad my old-age pension by coming back or, more accurately, staying here," Roger said as a way of a short-cut explanation.

"Don't forget, I saw you very briefly some months back when you were rushing between meetings back in DC just as you were retiring," Aaron reminded him.

"I'd forgotten about that. That trip was a bit of a blur. I was going from one office to another and one building to another. Before that, how long had it been?"

"Several years."

"Yeah, you were doing pretty well in the agent's training course down in Glynco before you opted to do your lawyer thing," Roger recalled. "How long has it been since you switched over to doing that?"

Aaron tilted his head back slightly, thinking back to his career change at customs. He had originally been hired and sent to Glynco, Georgia, for training to become a criminal investigative agent. "I'd say seven years," Aaron calculated.

"What, exactly, are you doing?" Aaron asked, flipping the conversation to Roger's new pursuits.

"It's all about exports, young man. It's all about the bottom line, right? In the big scheme of things, Hong Kong or China, it's all one and the same, and the game is all about money. There's also a strange relationship with Taiwan. In the end, you realize they can ignore a lot of the political bullshit when they focus on the money," Roger explained.

"You didn't do the traditional customs work, so what's the gig?"

Instead of an immediate answer, Roger picked up the go-cup of coffee he had brought with him and took a sip of the cold brew that was still left in the cup. It gave him a chance to survey the lounge. His eyes studied the people. "My employer is a parent company. I'm not sure how many companies belong to the group, but there are several located in the region. They liked the fact that I had been the customs attaché here. I made some interesting contacts, as you might guess, when I was working on cases. I was to come back after I retired. A government pension isn't going to be enough for me to live the lifestyle I've become accustomed to," Roger said with a wink.

"I was thinking we might," Roger's voice trailed off as he turned his head to see a tall young woman approaching. Given her concentrated look at his table, Roger realized she had to be with Aaron as she smiled and nodded to Roger as she approached. He pushed himself up out of his chair, tugging at his sport jacket to try and straighten its creases.

Aaron stood and smiled. He pulled out a chair for Kellie.

"Kellie, this is Roger Steeg. One of the instructors I had back in my customs training days," Aaron said.

"Kellie Liang, a pleasure to meet you, Roger."

"Likewise," Roger responded. He saw her Asian features balanced with a little of the European. But he noticed her height more than anything. He guessed that in heels, she might be looking him straight in the eyes at nearly six feet.

"This is a work trip for you, Kellie?" Roger inquired.

"Nothing heavy duty. I work for the Pacific Rim Trade Consortium. I'm meeting with some locals who are either part of the Consortium or want to be part of it," Kellie explained.

"Aaron's just extra baggage on this trip," Roger chided.

"Something like that," Kellie said, smiling. "What are you boys up to? Are you taking Aaron away for the day?"

"I thought I'd show him around. It'll be part of his continuing education." Roger watched as Kellie and Aaron looked at each other momentarily.

"Sounds like a great idea. That'll give me time to make calls and arrange a few of the meetings I need to have while we're here. It doesn't matter how hard you try to schedule things before you arrive—there are always last-minute meetings to arrange," Kellie said, smiling to both men.

They lingered for another twenty minutes. When Kellie stood to excuse herself, Aaron and Roger got up, taking the cue that it was time to leave. Aaron and Roger watched Kellie head back toward the elevator bank.

Roger glanced over at Aaron as Kellie disappeared behind the elevator doors. "She's a prize," Roger commented.

"She is that," Aaron agreed. "She's smart and has a quick wit. She's willing to take some risks and not afraid of change."

"And she's attractive on top of all that," Roger said.

"Yes, yes, she is," Aaron said with a wide smile, still looking toward the elevators.

Roger waited a few seconds before saying anything.

"I know you're a headquarters guy, so I'm going to take you over to look at the container terminal area. You'll see what a busy container terminal really looks like," Roger explained.

As they walked toward the exit, Roger scanned the room again. Walking a step behind Roger, Aaron didn't see Roger's self-assuring smile when they exited the hotel.

Cheng Gao had slipped in unnoticed and found a place to sit and observe Roger and his friends from several tables away. Wearing wire-rimmed glasses and trying to look studious, he had been looking at a newspaper and held a mobile phone to his ear for most of the past thirty minutes. Cheng's bosses knew Roger well from Roger's past work. They wanted to know more about his new role in Hong Kong.

* * * * *

Back in the room, Kellie pulled a typed sheet of paper from her small briefcase. She sat at the desk in the room and took a breath before picking up the phone's handset. She put herself into a Chinese mental mode for the call she was about to make, then called the Conrad Hotel.

"Can you connect me with Mr. Lai Guang?" she asked in Cantonese, stating the last name first as it's customarily done in Chinese.

"One moment," she heard back in Chinese.

"Hello?" a man's voice answered in Chinese.

"Mr. Lai Guang?"

"Yes," he said hesitantly as he reacted to a strange voice.

"This is Liang Kaili," Kellie said, using her Chinese name and saying it with her last name first.

"Ahh, so happy you have arrived and called. I was hoping to hear from you so we can meet. It was kind of you to inform me that you were coming to Hong Kong. As I stated in my response to you, I'm here for several days, and meeting you is very important," Mr. Lai responded happily, recognizing the name immediately.

Kellie could hear the bit of aging in the man's voice. There was a similarity to her father's voice. "Our hotels are connected through the shopping mall. I can walk over to your hotel, and then we can find a place to talk, if that is acceptable to you," Kellie offered.

"Yes, very acceptable. Shall we meet in my hotel's lobby area in thirty minutes?"

"That would be perfect," Kellie answered. This would give her time to navigate the massive Pacific Place complex. The complex was a maze that included a multi-level mall that had direct access to three large hotels, including the Conrad and Marriott. She'd need to find a map to orient herself.

In the Marriott's lobby, Kellie found a detailed map of the various levels of the mall and the different levels that connected to the three large hotels. The Marriott was at one end of Pacific Place. The two other hotels were toward the other end of the mall complex and connected to the mall complex at higher levels than the Marriott.

As she strode through the mall, she felt both strange and at home. Because her black hair and brown eyes added to her Asian features, she was the one who always looked out of place in the United States. She was used to being the one who was different. Striding through this complex, she realized she was just one of thousands. The only thing that made her different here was she felt a little taller than most of the women she was passing by, a little something from her mother's side of the family. Otherwise, she felt an unexplained sense of belonging in this environment.

She slowed her pace as she passed people walking in groups of two or three. This was only the second time in her life that she was absorbing English and Chinese simultaneously and understanding what was being said in both languages. Unconsciously, she smiled. Her father had been a taskmaster forcing her to speak Cantonese. He never gave in to her tantrums at learning the difficult language and required her to use only Chinese to speak to him at home.

Walking through the mall, she remembered her first trip to Hong Kong when she was eight or nine years old. Her Chinese was limited at that age, but her father was persistent. He was getting tired of her tantrums, so he arranged the trip. He took her for walks to nowhere in particular while they were here. They would find a spot and just stand in pedestrian walkways. Or he'd find a park bench, and they would sit, sometimes for hours. Her father would tell her to close her eyes and listen to people walking past. She heard and understood a lot of the Chinese spoken, and she was amused by the accent of the locals in Hong Kong when they spoke English.

Her father's strategy worked. She thought it was magical to be able to live in a world of two languages. After the trip, she stopped protesting when her father insisted on her Chinese language lessons with him. She wanted Chinese to be as natural to her as English. Though her reading and writing skills still had much room for improvement, her father's insistence on speaking Chinese with him at home meant that her level of fluency was like a native speaker.

As she rode the escalator up toward the Conrad Hotel, she looked down at the crowds below. To her, it was a natural meshing together of cultures and languages. She wanted to be in the middle of it.

Kellie refocused on meeting Mr. Lai as she entered the Conrad.

Mr. Lai double-checked a photo as soon as he saw Kaili enter and headed toward her as he replaced the photo in his inside jacket pocket. To him, she had never been called Kellie and was unaware of her American name. His cousin, Kaili's father, had always referred to her as Kaili in all phone and written communications.

Kellie saw the older man approaching just steps after she entered the hotel. She slowed and watched him approach.

"Kaili?"

"Yes. Mr. Lai."

"So nice to meet you again after so many years," Guang Lai said. "Of course, you were very young, and possibly, you will not remember a dinner we had when you were here with your father."

She had no memory of having met Mr. Lai. But he was right. There had been a dinner with some people her father had described as old friends and distant relatives. She had been the only child at the table.

Guang Lai made regular trips from Taipei to Hong Kong. To him, it was a two-hour commute by air to oversee his business interests in China. At first, he made infrequent trips to Hong Kong, but during the past twenty-five years, the commute had become more routine to meet with his business associates.

Kellie assumed that he was in his sixties, like her father. Even in low heels, she was taller than her distant and older cousin. Unlike her father, Guang had a full head of black hair, graying only at the temples, and she noticed that he had a very erect way of walking and standing, reminding her of the way military men would walk and stand.

"Would it be acceptable to find some other place to talk, less formal?" Guang asked though he was wearing a suit and conducting himself in a formal manner.

"Of course," she replied.

Guang led the way back into the maze of mall shops. He chose a coffee and tea shop that had a mix of patrons who appeared to be local and Western tourists. It was mid-morning, after the breakfast time rush. They settled at a table against the wall.

"On the phone, I was impressed with your Chinese, but if you are more comfortable speaking English, we can use English," Guang offered.

Kellie looked around the shop first. It seemed to have more foreign tourists than locals. "It depends upon what we're going to discuss," she answered in Chinese as a signal.

Guang smiled. "Your father is so proud of you. There are some sensitivities involved, and I now understand that you have grasped them already. Just now, your eyes told me that you are thoughtful and cautious. We shall proceed this way."

After having drinks placed in front of them, Guang continued. "You are in a unique position to provide us with some, shall we say, vision as our business group expands the portfolio. In fact, through your father, we have been impressed by your insights and your advice." Guang paused, seeing Kellie's smile leave her. Her face had lost any expression.

Kellie leaned back slightly, having bent forward to hear Guang. She smiled at the kind words Guang had said, but she was now a bit confused. What insights had she provided? What had she said to her father that he might have mentioned to Guang or anyone else? For a moment, she wasn't listening as her mind searched for recent conversations with her father, coming up empty. She refocused on Guang.

"Our meeting is important because you should not come to our next meeting and be surprised by the people involved. When I say we are all Chinese, it is meant in the broadest terms possible," Guang explained. "We may come from different places geographically, but we all have this one thing in common. While you are coming from the West, you possess elements of the East. You have been offering and you can continue offering something special just as we can offer you something special."

Listening to Guang, who was still a stranger, Kellie sensed that he was telling her something extremely important without divulging anything. She understood the Chinese, but now she worried that she had missed the message—something was lost in translation. Were there nuances to the language that she hadn't learned? Was there something her father was supposed to tell her that he had failed to say before she flew to Hong Kong?

She struggled to understand how she had provided any advice. There were no China-related business conversations with her father that she could recall. She wondered what she had said to her father that sounded like business insights or advice. She reached down into her small handbag, moving things around as if looking for something, buying time as her mind raced. A blank.

She had always been cautious in discussing her work in Washington. Her time as a staffer on a US Senate trade committee had been a short stint of only a couple of years. There had been several sensitive issues relating to China, but she had been careful not to divulge things to her father or anyone else who had no need to know. She was always aware of security issues that could arise and jeopardize her position.

"Is there anything I should know before this meeting, or are there specific questions I should prepare for?" Kellie asked.

"There isn't anything specific, but keep in mind some things you have already provided about exporting to the US," Guang said. He reached into his inside jacket pocket and handed over two pages. "Look at these. They don't involve you but give you an idea about what our trade targets are."

Kellie unfolded the two pages. One page had a map of Africa, and the other a map of Central and South America. Each had city designations along the coastlines. She didn't understand what she was supposed to gain from these, but one thing she was sure about was that the city designations didn't correspond to the country capitals.

"I'm not sure what this means," Kellie commented.

"These are major ports. That's the importance of the map and what you need to know from our perspective. The only other thing I can say is that you may be asked about things you've already contributed to us," he advised.

Kellie felt her heart rate increase, and she felt warm as her anxiety level rose. She was convinced that she was going to go into a meeting completely unprepared for whatever was headed her way.

Kellie leaned in over the table. "These two pages have nothing to do with the United States, and I have nothing to do with Africa or these countries in Central and South America. This," she said as she held the pages over the table, "doesn't help me." As soon as she finished, she knew her tone had been too abrupt.

Kellie saw Guang's brow furrowing and his upper lip tensing. "I'm sorry. I didn't mean to be impolite," Kellie said. "I'm worried that I might not be able to meet the expectations of your business colleagues."

Guang relaxed. "Don't put too much pressure on yourself. The meeting will be managed, and I will be there next to you," Guang said.

"When is this next meeting?" Kellie asked.

"The day after tomorrow. We'll meet and go to the meeting together," Guang recommended and saw Kellie nod in agreement.

* * * * *

Roger's driver, Jie Jia, whom Roger introduced as JJ, maneuvered the Camry through traffic to cross Hong Kong Harbour onto the Kowloon side.

"Wow, I'm impressed. You have a company driver," Aaron said enviously.

"Yes and no. He's a driver whom I found, and I pay. I didn't want to have a driver who was a real company person to keep tabs on me. I met JJ a few years ago through some other contacts. I'd call him, and he'd drive some friends around if I had visitors from home or if we just needed an extra car for some reason. When I came back and needed someone for myself, I negotiated a nice fee allowance for him. I like to think I've done right by him in that way."

"No complaints, right, JJ?"

"No complaints," JJ repeated.

JJ pulled up in front of another hotel.

"I guess I thought we might be headed to your office."

"I don't like being tied to one spot all day," Roger answered. Roger grabbed a small case and led Aaron in and to a bank of elevators. Roger pressed the button for the 26th floor. He led Aaron into a sparsely filled restaurant, taking a table by a large picture window.

"Interesting view," Aaron observed.

A young waitress smiled in Roger's direction, and Roger put up two fingers. She understood Roger wanted coffee for both of them. From the

26th floor, the broad window provided them with an expansive view of the container terminals half a mile away.

"One of the biggest and busiest in the world," Roger remarked. He opened the case he'd brought with him from the car. "Here, use these," Roger said as he handed Aaron a pair of binoculars.

Aaron looked toward the container terminals and saw containers stacked row upon row. Many of the rows were ten containers high, and some were twenty. The various colored containers made the place look like a colorful work area. The long arms of cranes reached high into the air to latch onto the highest container and move them from ship to shore or vice versa. Someone had to be a well-organized choreographer to arrange the movement of the thousands of containers from trucks to the piled containers, then onto the ships. Aaron surveyed the terminal area through the binoculars and realized that there were acres of land paved over for the containers and cranes.

"Have to admit that even during my days as an agent, I didn't see something like this. That, Aaron, is volume from the mainland. Things come from every direction through this terminal. It means there's no time to worry about what's in those containers," Roger added.

Aaron turned his head away from the view of the terminals to look at Roger. "That can be a problem. No, let me rephrase. That is a problem, and we both know it."

Roger nodded and noted the serious tone in Aaron's statement. "I wanted you to see that," Roger nodded toward the window and the view beyond, "because it's hard to grasp the challenge if you don't see that operation and what goes on over there. You can see it from this distance because if you get too close, things might get unpleasant."

"Meaning?" Aaron needed more to understand.

"Meaning there are shipping companies that make money from moving goods. There are people who work in these terminals who don't want anyone interfering with containers and trucks. Anyone who starts to make waves trying to stop containers and shipments might find themselves locked in a container at best or threatened, beaten, or worse. This place—I mean Hong Kong and China—is both a treasure trove of riches and a powder keg that could blow up any time," Roger said as he watched Aaron peering through the binoculars toward the container facilities.

"How often do you go into the container terminal?" Aaron asked, handing back the binoculars and letting Roger replace them in their case.

"Rarely. I stick out there like a sore thumb. I prefer to do what I do from a distance."

"It sounds like you're the maestro, the conductor. How many people are under your supervision?" Aaron asked.

"No one is really under my supervision. And no, I'm not a conductor. I'm a go-between, an advisor of sorts. Most of the time, I'm not that busy, but I need to be available 24/7 in case of any snafus."

"Am I understanding this? You get paid well but have no real office. You don't supervise anyone, but you have a driver and spend your day doing, well, what exactly?" Aaron wondered aloud.

"I'm on call around the clock, and I had better answer the phone or the knock on my door when my employers need me. They'll take care of me as long as I make myself available to them."

Roger's cell phone began to ring. "Just as I was saying," Roger said as he slouched down so he could reach into his pants pocket to grab his phone. He flipped the phone open to take the call. "Steeg here."

Roger listened expressionless at first. "When did this happen?"

Aaron couldn't help but listen to Roger's half of the conversation. He sipped his coffee and found this interruption a bit entertaining.

"Who chose Mexico?" Roger inquired. He listened for a couple of minutes before speaking. "What you're telling me is that there were several bad decisions made and a shipment was seized. It doesn't matter that the numbers aren't bad. There are other reasons to be concerned. Okay. I'm meeting with someone right now. We'll discuss this later." Roger ended the call.

"This is the kind of thing that pops up. Our guys, well, I mean your guys seized a shipment of stuff at the southern border that had arrived in Mexico and headed to the US," Roger explained. "I can't fix it, but I'll try to get them to avoid these issues going forward."

"Roger, the more you describe your arrangement, the less I want to know about it. It's like that saying if it's too good to be true, you know the rest. You just retired from a job that required you to question things, and I'm still in a position that requires me to wonder when something either sounds or looks too good to be true," Aaron noted.

"Point taken. You ready to go? Let me give you a pleasant vantage point of this place. This was the work part of the day. Now, we can take some time to enjoy the good weather."

Roger threw down enough Hong Kong dollars to cover the check. JJ drove them back to Hong Kong Island and dropped them off. Roger bought two tickets for the tram to go up to Victoria's Peak. The ride up was not rushed, and Aaron watched the view change every few seconds as the tram clambered toward the peak. Aaron's back was pressed against the seat because of the steep ascent to the peak.

The vegetation along the tram route obscured the views Aaron had hoped for as he got glimpses of the city below.

"Don't worry, you'll have a panoramic view once we're at the top," Roger said, watching Aaron twist in the seat to get the view below.

After exiting the tram, Roger led Aaron to an observation deck atop the Peak Tower. On the observation deck, Roger and Aaron were fully exposed to the sun. It was a cloudless sky. The only thing that hindered the view was the haze that drifted south from mainland China's factories, expelling polluting particles that blanketed the region.

Aaron absorbed the view of Hong Kong below as thousands of buildings jammed together stood tall and stretched skyward. It was hard to believe that there was any space for streets, parks, and pedestrians. The hillside prevented any good views of the container terminals on the Kowloon side, where they had been just a little while ago. The wake and waves created by the dozens of various boats, ships, and ferries produced a zigzag of water designs. It was hard to believe they could operate without colliding.

"Because of the buildings, you can't see the hydrofoil terminal down below. You can get to Macau in roughly an hour," Roger said. "We'll have to have an evening with you and Kellie so you can have an experience riding at forty miles an hour, skimming the water."

"From here, it looks like you could get lost in that maze below or over there on the Kowloon side," Aaron said after gazing out over the skylines on either side of the harbor.

"No doubt about that. This place is what some might say is a labyrinth, and it can work to your advantage or not," Roger said as he started walking to exit the observation deck. "Let's get out of this sun and find some shade."

Roger found a bench partially shaded and sat.

"You keep saying things that make me wonder about this place. Earlier, you said this is a treasure trove and a powder keg," Aaron said.

"There's a new free-for-all going on here. When the Brits gave Hong Kong back to China, they were under some false belief that all is or will be fine. Us, we Americans, aren't so sure about that. For now, everything is as it has been, but how long will that last? The mainlanders have a new prize to exploit. There are others like the Japanese, Koreans, and others in the region wondering what's going to happen. In addition to the regional players, a few of the world's power players are invested in this place. But China is at the controls. And remember, in a few months, Macau will be China's, too.

"Even before I retired and more recently, I've noticed when I go to places, there are some interesting people here who aren't tourists and business types. It's a gut feeling and one I'm not ignoring. Nothing official, but I think this place is crawling with people from different places gathering info. Information about who's doing what or who's going to be doing something," Roger explained.

"You mean spies?"

"That's my gut feeling," Roger confirmed, shaking his head. "But a lot of it is local or people trying to seem like they're local."

Aaron looked around at the crowds of people. Everyone, whether Asian or European, appeared to be tourists with their cameras and phones out. He wouldn't be able to tell if anyone he saw was anything other than someone on vacation.

"Maybe that explains my delay at the airport," Aaron commented.

"Why? What happened?"

"Immigration inspected my passport and thought it had been tampered with because of the frayed edges by my photo. Then, an older immigration officer quizzed me in a room. I explained that I worked for US Customs, and he wanted to know if I was here on official business. I told him I wasn't," Aaron explained.

"They'll know where you're staying," Roger advised. Roger made a mental note of Aaron's encounter with immigration.

"The local immigration folks are taking a greater interest when they come across someone like you. Don't worry, you may be low priority, but you just made the cut to being on the radar. You're not a high priority or anything, but they know you're here, and they know where you're staying.

"You do have one other problem," Roger added, looking away before continuing. "You've been seen with me. Now you just went up a notch on that radar screen because someone likes keeping tabs on me, a retired US Customs attaché who's back in Hong Kong working in the private sector. For some reason that I can't understand, there's some interest in keeping tabs on me."

"How would they know about me and you?" Aaron asked innocently.

"I hate to break the news to you, but there was a young man trying to fade into the scenery this morning when we first met at your hotel. Unfortunately for him, I've already seen him once or twice before keeping an eye on me. By now, he's informed his bosses about my meeting with you. If anything is cross-checked, the powers that be will figure out that you, a customs guy, met with me, a retired customs guy, and put the pieces together. Congratulations," Roger commended Aaron with a bit of sarcasm.

"Shit," Aaron said. As he digested this bit of information, he hoped that Kellie was still an unknown because she had joined them later. If Roger's "spy" was watching, Aaron hoped that Kellie was seen as someone Roger didn't know until they met at the hotel.

"Now that you've got an update of sorts, I'll take you back to your hotel. I've got some things to do. As much as I'd like to, I can't be your tour guide all day, every day," Roger said.

"Understood," Aaron said, mulling over the last few minutes of conversation.

They took the tram down. As it descended, Aaron was able to admire the view but also continued to think about what Roger had said. In this place, it wouldn't matter how hard he tried; he knew he'd never be able to know if anyone was following or watching him.

JJ was parked by the tram station and waiting for his two passengers. It was a short ride to the Marriott, where Aaron exited the car.

Roger rolled down his window. "Dine out," Roger suggested. "A little local atmosphere will do you some good."

Aaron nodded and watched JJ pull away. He watched as Roger rolled up his window and put his cell phone to his ear. Dine out? Aaron wondered if that suggestion was simply so he and Kellie would get out of the hotel to explore the surrounding neighborhoods or if that was because whoever was watching Roger's movements would have arranged for someone to be looking for him in the hotel. He also wondered if he should say anything to Kellie. Why would he? Roger was just giving him a heads-up. There was no reason to say anything that might worry Kellie.

* * * * *

Aaron opened the door to their room. The afternoon sun lit the room, and the expanse of the harbor displayed itself through the windows.

"I wasn't sure if you'd be back already," Aaron said, seeing Kellie at the desk. "You had a meeting, right? Did it go well?"

Kellie, sitting and facing the desk and window, turned in the chair to look Aaron's way. "Everything's fine," Kellie lied. "I have to be at a day-long meeting."

"When?"

"The day after tomorrow," Kellie answered. "I'm just prepping some notes for myself." As she said that, she looked down at the sheet of paper covered with her doodling. There were no notes. She crumpled it up in her hand and dropped it into the wastebasket by the desk. She decided there was no reason to mention her anxiety about the meeting because of the things that Guang had said.

"You didn't know about this until now? Not much notice."

"You know how it is when you're on the road. Some things are scheduled, and other things just pop up at the last minute. Besides, I thought you liked a little chaos and unpredictability," Kellie said with a smile.

"Hopefully, we'll still have some free time. Roger wants us to have a night out. He said something about taking the jetfoil to Macau one evening. He also said we should dine out."

"He's right. We shouldn't be anchored to the hotel when we have time to ourselves," Kellie agreed.

"If you've still got some work to do, it's early enough that I'd like to pop to the gym."

"Go," she insisted. Kellie looked at the hotel-provided writing pad and stared at the blank sheet of paper. Insights? Advice? Vision? Those things that Guang had referred to meant nothing to her. With her elbows on the desk, she rested her head in the palms of her hands.

Aaron changed into workout clothes and shoes, grabbed a towel, and left the room without noticing Kellie arched over the desk. He spent over an hour working out. It was part of his regular routine. He didn't consider himself a gym rat, but when he decided to become a criminal agent, he became a serious fitness person trying to maintain his exercise routines as a law student and even now as a lawyer. Although work no longer allowed for the kind of workouts he had engaged in when younger, he still made time to try and keep fit.

When he finished, he draped the sweat-dampened towel around his neck and over his shoulders and went back to the room. Kellie was still planted at the desk and working. After a shower, he put on the bathrobe hanging on the bathroom door and sat in a chair by the bed.

Within minutes, his eyes were closed, and his chin was resting on his chest. He was asleep.

Kellie heard the change in his breathing. She looked at him, checked her watch and decided that she needed to put an end to her self-imposed frustrating efforts at making notes. They needed to get out of the hotel, walk around, and get some fresh air. She knew that they'd both be asleep early if they didn't fight off the jet lag at the end of their first day.

She pushed the writing pad away and closed her laptop.

"Hey, wake up. It's time to go out and see the nightlife," Kellie said, shaking Aaron gently on the shoulder.

Aaron took in a deep breath and opened his eyes. Just as Kellie started to step away, he caught her by the wrist and pulled her onto his lap.

"Not now. Food first, then play if you're still awake," Kellie teased.

Thirty minutes later, Aaron followed Kellie out of the hotel and into parts of the shopping mall that Kellie had wandered through earlier. She led them down to the subway and onto a crowded subway car.

They rode one stop and exited. Though she had never been here before, Kellie took the lead.

"Are we going anywhere in particular?" Aaron asked.

"Not really, but we need to be somewhere lively."

"Well, you've succeeded," Aaron said as they joined the throngs of people wandering the shops and restaurants along Nathan Road. The busy energy of the people on the street was contagious. Aaron was having one of those "it's the same but different" feelings. It was like being in crowded New York City, but there was an atmosphere he had not experienced anywhere else. It was a different vibe that he couldn't describe. It felt different.

Aaron and Kellie tried to walk side-by-side holding hands, but the crowded sidewalk made that impossible. Aaron let go of Kellie's hand and fell in behind her.

As he walked, he leaned forward. "You're in the lead, so you choose where we get something for dinner." He saw Kellie nod her acknowledgment.

Aaron was barely a step behind her. As he followed, he realized that this had become the norm with them. She took the lead, made decisions, and he followed.

Chapter 3

Counsel

Hong Kong (Tuesday, May 12)

A shaft of bright sunlight was on Aaron's face. It woke him. The sliver of sunlight found the opening between the drapes that had been pulled closed. He turned carefully to get out of bed to block the sun, but his movement caused Kellie to roll onto her back and see him stand.

"Sneaking off?" she asked.

The phone rang. They looked at each other. Neither one seemed eager to answer.

"It's probably for you," Aaron said.

On the fourth ring, Kellie answered. Aaron sat near the foot of the bed, facing Kellie.

"Hang on, I'll put him on," she covered the mouthpiece. "It's Roger."

Aaron rolled his eyes and then took the receiver from Kellie's hand. "I didn't expect a wake-up call today."

"Hope I'm not interrupting anything. I figured it was late enough to call. I know this is a vacation for you, but I want to pick your brain for a few minutes today, figuring you're here, and I might as well take advantage of you. I want to make sure that my instincts and yours are on the same page."

"I think I can fit this into my busy schedule. Where and what time?"

"I'll pick you up in an hour if that works," Roger suggested.

"Yep. See you then."

"You're abandoning me," Kellie teased. "Last night, you dozed on the subway on the way back and were barely awake to walk back to the room. I thought you were the world traveler and could handle the jet lag."

Aaron crawled toward the head of the bed. His hands and knees straddled Kellie, still under the covers.

"He said I have an hour. Plenty of time."

"For what," Kellie said with a wide smile. "You think I'm going to let you have a quickie? I can't have you meeting up with your friend wondering why you have a funny-looking grin on your face. Nope. I can't let that happen." Still smiling, Kellie's quick hands tapped Aaron's cheeks.

"You need to get dressed," she urged.

Aaron crawled off the bed slowly and started toward the bathroom.

"What does Roger want?" Kellie asked.

"He didn't say exactly, just that he wanted to pick my brain about something."

"It'll be a short meeting," she said, smiling.

"Thanks for the confidence booster," Aaron said, chuckling. "I'm sure I won't be gone as long as I was yesterday."

Aaron was ready and down in the lobby in plenty of time to see JJ drive up to the front of the hotel. Roger lowered the window and waved Aaron out.

"Good day, Counselor."

"Am I your legal advisor today?" Aaron asked.

"Yeah. You come at a price I can afford. Just wondering, do your clients always follow your advice?"

"Remember, I'm a government lawyer. I suggest a way to resolve an issue and rarely am I the only person involved in giving advice. And, since I'm the bottom rung of the ladder, there are several people above me who have input, and their inputs are more important than mine," Aaron reminded Roger.

"Today's your lucky day. You're the only person I'm talking to, and only your opinion matters."

JJ had driven around the Pacific Place complex, making a complete circle.

"What're we doing? Driving in circles," Aaron asked when he saw them pass the entry toward the hotel lobby.

"No, JJ's just making sure about our friends who like keeping tabs on me. I told him to do it. Now that he's confident that we're alone, he'll take us to the office."

JJ drove across the bridge and stopped at the same hotel where they had been the day before.

"Nice office," Aaron said, shaking his head.

Instead of going up to the twenty-sixth floor, Roger guided Aaron toward the lobby coffee shop, finding a place to sit where he could watch the entrance.

"What's the deal? Do you get a free coffee after so many meetings here?" Aaron joked.

"I have a rotating system. Since I know I have people wanting to keep tabs on me, I have three or four places over here near the container terminals that I pop into if I need to have a business meeting. So far, I haven't noticed any other regulars who follow me around," Roger explained.

After they had their coffees delivered, Roger placed his chair closer to the wall and leaned against it.

"Let me ask you. If you wanted to make a lot of money in the export business in a rather short period of time and didn't care whether it was legal or not, what would you do?"

Aaron straightened in his chair, staring straight at Roger. He was taken by surprise.

"That's not legal advice you're asking for. You want me to answer that?"

"Yes, I do," Roger said. "All kidding aside. I'm serious."

Aaron hesitated. "You want me to recommend an illegal business racket?"

Roger said nothing. He sat and looked at Aaron with the slightest nod to proceed.

"Low risk, of course. That means I'd stay away from things, like drugs, that can get me a lot of jail time if I'm caught or big money fines. I'd also export to countries that aren't very good at finding the stuff I'm exporting."

"That's rather general information, Counselor," Roger noted. "What would you stay away from?"

"Roger, I feel like I'm helping break the law, not follow it. Remember, you and me, we're the good guys, right?"

"This is related to the call I got yesterday," Roger said.

"Why don't you tell me about that?"

"I will in a few minutes, but first, you keep going."

Aaron looked around the lobby area as he thought for a minute. A strange thought hit him. Was Roger recording this conversation? He decided not to ask. "Stay away from drugs of any kind and cigarettes. I'd avoid things that can cause people serious injuries, meaning no medicines and auto parts critical to the car's operation and safety, like the braking system. And I'd definitely stay away from the weapons trade."

"Okay, that's a nice short list to start. What about countries?"

"What about them?" Aaron asked.

"Where would you focus, specifically?"

"The world is a big place. No reason to take risks with the US or Europe. There are a few other places to stay away from. The rest?" Aaron shrugged.

Roger moved his chair and sat up. "To make you comfortable, you and I are on the same page about this. My advice to my new bosses was exactly or close to what you just said. It's amazing how some smart people who are running businesses can be so stupid.

"A shipment went to Mexico. They got stopped trying to truck it into the US," Roger added.

"What was it?" Aaron asked.

"I'm getting this second-hand. There were a few thousand pairs of high-top sneakers without any labeling or branding. The problem was that there was a false wall in the truck and there were separate bags of branded patches that would be applied to the sneakers at a warehouse after passing through US Customs. You know what anybody would think once they find that false wall."

"Smuggling," Aaron said. "Interesting thing is that the way you describe the sneakers, we wouldn't touch them if they're plain generic without the labeling or the brand patches on them."

"Say that again," Roger prompted.

"They didn't have to hide the patches. The sneakers were fine, just generic without any of the patches," Aaron explained. "I guess the truck might be ours now because there's clear evidence that it's used for smuggling."

"The truck didn't belong to us, but I guess that Mexican company isn't too happy if they lost the truck to the US government."

"How many of these seizure calls have you gotten since you started this job?"

"Only a couple," Roger answered.

"Risk versus reward. I'm guessing you have no clue how many shipments like this have been made."

"True. They only call me when there's been a problem," Roger said.

"Then the only thing I can say is it must be worth the risk because the money is still coming to the business," Aaron concluded.

Roger took in a deep breath and exhaled. He picked up his coffee cup and just held it in his right hand. "If they're going to play this game on the wrong side of the legal line, I hope they don't go too far over. I hope they stick to things like sneakers, and they don't get too greedy or stupid."

"You need to be careful. You know better than most how things can spiral out of control," Aaron warned.

"What I don't understand is, why not focus on where the easiest money is and forget the risky places? They can ship the crap to Mexico or Canada, but don't try to cross into the US. It's like talking to the wall."

"Greed makes people do risky, stupid things," Aaron repeated.

* * * * *

"Honey, I'm home," Aaron announced as he entered their room. Seeing Kellie at the desk, he rushed toward her and embraced her from behind as she sat in the chair. He stepped around and gave her a kiss on the cheek.

"Have you been planted in this chair while I was gone?" Aaron asked.

"I did what you did yesterday. I checked out the hotel gym. Do you have anything left in your brain now that you're done with Roger? Did he pick it clean?"

"Nothing difficult. It's like having a client that doesn't want to listen to common sense advice."

"His new employer," Kellie guessed.

"Yeah. I hope he knows these people well enough to keep himself out of any trouble. It's clear they have the money and pay him well. Well enough that Roger's got a thousand-dollar phone to be at their beck and call. He's a big boy. I'm sure he can take care of himself. Enough of that. What are we up for this afternoon?"

"I thought we'd walk over to the tram station and go up to the Peak," Kellie suggested.

"Dress lightly. It can get a bit warm and sticky out there."

They decided to walk through the park that was situated between the hotel and the tram. The afternoon sun disappeared behind a bank of dark clouds. They hadn't thought they needed an umbrella. It was as if the clouds had stored rain for days and could no longer hold back the weight of all the water. The biggest raindrops Aaron had ever felt pelted him. They didn't need to say a word to each other as they both turned and ran back to the hotel.

Fifteen minutes later, they were standing in the lobby, dripping, and creating puddles where they stood. Their clothes clung to their skin. The rain was already letting up.

A young man in a hotel uniform was standing a few feet away. "It's rainy season. It rains like this almost every day, so you should always take the umbrella from your room," he said as he passed by, amused by the soaked guests.

"I hadn't really planned a second shower. I need to get out of these soaked clothes," Kellie said. She reached back to gather up her long black hair and wrung out the rain.

"I'm sure I can think of something else we can do in our room," Aaron suggested with a smile.

Chapter 4

New Connections

Hong Kong (Wednesday, May 13)

Aaron grabbed the pillow and covered his head when music from the clock-radio alarm went off. He had switched it from a buzzer to a radio station playing music when he set it the evening before.

He peeked out from under the pillow and saw that he was alone in bed. When he glanced at the clock, it was a few minutes past seven.

He rolled over and sat up. The room was dark, with the blackout drapes pulled closed. He saw light under the bathroom door and heard water running.

"Did I wake you?" Kellie asked as she opened the bathroom door, wearing a bathrobe.

"No, the alarm."

"I kept tossing around thinking about today's meeting, so I decided to get up and get ready," she explained.

"This last-minute meeting seems to be bothering you. Do you know who you're meeting with or what you're discussing?"

"I'm not sure who will be at the meeting or how many are attending. I'm making a lot of assumptions. There must be an export angle that involves the US. More likely, they're interested in exports to the US. They probably want to know how my organization can help either directly or indirectly. Otherwise, why would they want me to attend?" Kellie said as she started dressing.

"Are you wearing your mature pair of glasses today?" Aaron joked.

Kellie smiled and pulled out a pair of black-framed glasses, a pair Aaron thought of as ugly but one Kellie preferred in certain situations. It was part of her "business" look. She was assuming that she would be entering a room filled with older conservative men, and that required her to think about how she wanted to present herself. She also chose shoes that had an inch-high heel so that she wouldn't be too tall. She didn't want to tower over older, shorter men. That had occurred far too often before when dealing with Asian men and led to awkwardness when dealing with some of their fragile egos.

Aaron, still sitting in bed, watched as Kellie pulled her long black hair together. It flowed to the middle of her back. She captured any loose strands and created a low bun above the nape of her neck. She had hung her black pantsuit in the clothes closet. She paired that with a red button-down blouse. Kellie wasn't one for much makeup, and she didn't stray from her routine for the day's meeting.

"Do you know where you're going?"

"I'm going to meet up with Mr. Lai, the person I met with the other day. He'll get us to the meeting," Kellie answered. "I'll call if it seems things will go longer than expected, but I have no reason to think I won't be back here by five or six." She walked over to Aaron's side of the bed, giving him a peck on the cheek before leaving.

* * * * *

Kellie strode through the mall, retracing the route she'd taken previously. Except for some cleaning crew staff in the mall, the only other people seemed to be making their way to one of the connected hotels or the subway station. It was too early for any of the mall shops.

She arrived at the Conrad Hotel lobby and saw Mr. Lai standing and waiting. "Good morning, Mr. Lai."

"Oh, hello. I didn't see you. I was watching for you, but I guess I wasn't paying enough attention."

Guang's reaction confirmed her decision to dress the way she had. The thick black-framed glasses and the other choices she had made meant she didn't stand out too much.

"Shall we go? We'll go by taxi," Guang said.

The pair rode through the clogged streets of Hong Kong Island. It seemed that the driver changed lanes constantly, squeezing into spaces to get one or two cars ahead in the early morning traffic. The driver steered toward the bridge to get on the Kowloon side.

"I tried to prepare for today, but I'm not clear on what I need to know for this," Kellie said in Chinese.

"We're meeting with representatives from two different organizations. Their names are very similar. One is the China International Transport Network, and the other is the China International Production Network. Perhaps you will understand that there is some overlap with their similar names and, collectively, they are called ChiTran," Guang explained. "But they are two separate business operations. One produces while the other engages in the logistics of land, sea, and air transport of the products. The managing structure includes an interesting group of people who are part of ChiTran. I want you to be able to assess these individuals yourself, and then, if you have more questions, we can discuss that later."

Kellie wrote herself notes despite the constant jostling movement of the taxi in traffic. The taxi made good time after getting through a bottleneck at the bridge to cross over to Kowloon. When Guang had stopped explaining and sat back, she took that as a hint and put her small notepad away. Kellie glimpsed at her watch: 8:45. The taxi stopped in front of a nondescript sandstone-colored office building. It wasn't one of the newer modern buildings. After Guang took care of the fare, she followed him into the lobby.

As they waited for an elevator, Kellie looked at the building directory. Curiously, none of the company names that Guang mentioned appeared on the directory. They exited at the 12th floor. Guang led them to a locked double-door entry and pressed a buzzer to be let in. There was a moment of hesitation before the sound of an electronic release allowed Guang to open the door.

They had barely cleared the door when a young woman seemed to come out of the woodwork to greet them. "Mr. Lai, Miss Liang, please come this way," said the young woman in Chinese as she motioned them to follow.

Kellie realized that a few feet inside the entry door, there was a dark wooden wall about ten feet wide that opened on each end to allow this young woman—or anyone else behind it—to come out and meet people entering. Kellie looked around the small reception area and saw only a couple of wooden straight-back and uncomfortable-looking chairs for any guests who might be waiting to meet anyone.

The young woman marched down the wide hallway. As Kellie got closer, she could hear voices, but nothing in English. Everything was spoken in Cantonese. It was one thing to have conversations with her father in Chinese or occasional exchanges as she had experienced in the past, but she conceded that the day ahead would be long, mentally tiring, and a test of her abilities. Could she engage in a day-long business meeting in her semi-native language? She wasn't sure, but she was about to find out.

Guang stopped before entering the meeting room. Kellie was a couple of steps behind him. She looked easily over Guang's shoulder. She could see part of the large corner conference room that had thin curtains to shield the room from the sun on two sides. She saw a couple of groups of three and four people talking among themselves. From where she stood, she saw no other women, and most of the men looked to be in the age range of her father and Guang. There were a couple of men who stood out only because they seemed twenty years younger than everyone else.

Kellie tried to make out the conversations going on among the groups of men in the room, but given where she was standing, she couldn't hear well enough. On the far side of the room, a man with his back to her was in an animated conversation as he repeatedly pressed his right index finger into the palm of his left hand, making a point about something. The two men whose faces Kellie could see were not smiling. Whatever that conversation was, it didn't appear to Kellie as if the topic was making them happy.

"Ahh, Mr. Lai, so happy to see you," a woman's voice brought Kellie's attention back to Guang and the people immediately in front of her. This woman seemed to come from nowhere. She was petite and dressed elegantly in a dark-blue skirt and white blouse with well-coiffed graying hair. She wore a matching blue jacket, giving her a very smart overall look. Kellie thought that the woman, like the men, wore conservative colors. Kellie guessed that even in her heels, she was barely over five feet tall.

"As you requested, Mr. Lai, you'll be sitting next to Ms. Liang instead of at the head of the room with us," Ms. Tai said softly to Guang.

Guang shook his head in acknowledgment. If Kellie had heard what had just been said, she might realize that Guang had never explained his position within the group that was meeting. Guang turned so that the two women were face-to-face.

"Liang Kaili," the woman said as she reached out to shake Kellie's hand. "I am Tai Shu," the older woman said in Chinese. "It's nice to see that we have another successful woman joining us and especially one who is so young. It is an exciting day for me."

"Thank you so much for having me today," Kellie responded, making note of the older woman's use of Chinese names by putting the last name first. Her thoughts were racing at the mention of her "joining" this group. She wasn't joining anything, she thought. She was simply attending a meeting. She felt that she was at a major disadvantage. The hints that Guang had dropped at their meeting and now the mention of being part of this group, whatever it might be, started to cause a knot in her stomach.

"Please come in. We've designated a seat for you down there," Shu pointed to the far end of the conference table. She backed away and turned, allowing Kellie to walk toward her seat.

The tables and chairs were arranged in a rectangular shape. The center opening was only about five feet between the tables running lengthwise in the room. Kellie walked the length of one side, nodding to each of the men as she passed. On the far side of the room and a couple of seats from her chair, she saw another woman, younger than Shu but older than her.

Kellie pulled out a notepad and placed it on the table before settling in her chair. As she lowered herself into the metal-mesh chair, she looked past Guang and at the woman sitting next to him, who was, in Kellie's eyes, tiny in the chair. The woman on the other side of Guang had narrow shoulders, and her short black hair framed her face and gave her a boyish look, and the makeup couldn't hide the beginnings of crow's feet at the corners of her eyes. The small frameless lenses of her glasses made her look very bookish. Kellie wondered if her feet touched the floor, given how small she appeared.

It made Kellie feel just a bit better that there were at least a couple of other women in the room. She wiggled a bit in the chair to get comfortable on the seat pad. Expecting a long day in the chair, she was glad it had armrests. She adjusted the chair slightly lower to be more comfortable writing on the table.

Guang turned to her, smiled, and nodded to her as if sensing that she was now settled.

Kellie wanted to ask Guang about what she'd overheard about his place next to her instead of the head table, and she hoped to be introduced to the woman next to Guang, but the chance faded when she heard Shu.

"Now that everyone has arrived, I believe we should take our seats so we can begin our deliberations," Shu announced.

Settled, Kellie glanced at Guang. He nodded to her and then looked down at the conference table. Kellie followed his eyes and saw a large brown envelope with her name written in Chinese characters. She moved an arm toward the envelope but was stopped by Guang as he reached out and lightly tapped her hand.

"Later," he said quietly.

Kellie looked straight ahead to the front of the room. Shu sat next to an older gentleman, who looked to Kellie to be in the sixty to seventy age range.

"We shall begin," Shu said. "First, I am very happy to recognize Ms. Liang Kaili. As a few of you know, she has provided helpful advice to us. When we heard about her plans to travel to Hong Kong, we hastily arranged this meeting so that we could both meet her and have a face-to-face discussion."

Kellie, now known to everyone in the room as Liang Kaili, listened and was surprised that Shu was still speaking. She was conscious of everyone, except Guang, looking at her when her name was mentioned. She expected Shu to yield the floor to the man at the front of the room. Kellie's hands were clasped on the conference table. Her knuckles and fingertips were white from holding her hands together tightly as she worked on breathing normally despite her nervousness. Shu's mention of Kellie's advice put her on edge. First, Guang and now Shu spoke of her advice, but she had never provided advice to them. She had never contacted anyone in the room except a short note to Guang about the dates of her Hong Kong trip.

"We apologize that this meeting was arranged without the usual period of advance notice and hope your prior plans were minimally disrupted," Shu was saying when Kellie returned her attention to what was being said.

"I want to remind everyone that you may take written notes, but you are not to record any of our discussion on any device," Shu warned. "There should be a copy of our discussion topics in front of you."

Guang moved the envelope intended for Kellie and exposed a sheet of paper. He slid the paper so that it was almost directly in front of her. She tried to read the Chinese characters. Since her Chinese reading skills were less fluent than her speaking ability, she was able to read only half of the document. She hoped that the discussion to come would let her make notes to herself so she could link the writing to the discussion.

"We shall address our Africa and South American strategies first as these should not take much time," the older man sitting next to Shu finally said.

Guang leaned toward Kellie. "He is Qian Rong. He and Shu are part of ChiTran's executive management team."

Kellie realized that everyone was introduced in the Chinese style with their last names first. As an American, she was naturally putting names in the order she was used to.

"As everyone knows, we must keep people employed, provide salaries, and keep products moving. We cannot sell everything we make within our domestic market because so many people are still making a very limited wage in China," Rong said. "During the next several years, we believe that we have an opportunity to exploit international rules so we can sell all that we produce. We know that our government is negotiating China's entry into the World Trade Organization. That will take time. But we have many national markets in Africa, Asia, and South America, where some of the rules will not take effect for several years. This is our time to export. This is our time to profit and establish our markets."

As Kellie listened in Chinese, she scribbled notes on the agenda sheet in English. She was hearing the words but not interpreting what they meant. She didn't have the time to digest all the nuances of what Rong was saying.

"Are you saying that for those two continental markets, we are unrestricted?" asked a man sitting off to Kellie's left along the window row.

"That's Hsieh Liwei. He's at the management level under the two at the head of the table," Guang whispered to Kellie.

Kellie had seen him as she waited to enter the room earlier. He was the one jabbing his finger into the palm of his hand, speaking to a couple of others emphatically. She had thought of him as a bit taller than average. He had a handsome face, square-jawed, and like all the others, black hair. She guessed that he might be in his forties, but she was never good at guessing ages.

Kellie sat back and took notes sparingly as a lengthy discussion followed about production in China. The two-way conversation between Liwei and the two at the head of the table returned to exports.

"They can't stop us," Rong said. "It doesn't matter what we send and what ports we send things to because we have placed facilitators in a number of these places. It's like printing money. For us, Africa and South America are money-making places. They are easier markets to ship our excess production. Nothing will be stopped at the ports unless we do reckless things ourselves."

"What does he mean by 'facilitators'?" Kellie leaned and whispered to Guang.

Rong saw Kellie lean toward Guang. "A question, Ms. Liang?" Rong asked.

"I apologize, but I wanted to know what was meant by your reference to facilitators in various places."

"My apologies for creating the confusion. Our network includes Chinese business associates in various countries to help us distribute our goods in different countries. They make local contacts, and they do what is needed to permit our goods into these foreign markets," Rong explained.

"Thank you, and I apologize for the interruption," Kellie said. She waited for the discussion to resume before she wrote herself some notes. She was careful not to write for long. Her interpretation of what had been explained was that there were probably large amounts of illegal payments being made to government officials, and there were lots of other favors being provided in one form or another. She didn't want to put all of that in writing.

Rong's explanation—or, as Kellie decided, his concession of reality—caused her to sit up and listen more carefully.

As the morning wore on, Kellie realized that the Africa and South America strategies were simple. ChiTran would put as much product as possible into these countries without any regard for quality, and they would all fill their bank accounts, including the accounts that were in foreign countries. The strategy being discussed meant that the local businesses on these two continents would be destroyed by both the volume and low prices of Chinese goods.

The exchanges between the head table and others in the room were simple to follow, and there was no debate about how they would go about their business practices. Instead, they seemed to be going over agreed tactics and strategies.

There was no midmorning break. Instead, tea and coffee were brought in, and they worked straight through until there was a lunch break. As soon as people started to get out of their chairs, Kellie reached for the envelope that had been placed on the conference table between her and Guang earlier in the morning.

"Not yet," Guang said. "We'll linger here a moment and let the room empty." She and Guang swiveled their chairs to angle them toward each other. Anyone looking their way would see two people appearing to be huddled in a private conversation.

Kellie watched as everyone filed out of the room, including the woman who had been sitting next to Guang. She wanted to know who she was. She noticed that Guang would occasionally whisper something to her, and she would jot down notes.

Once the room had emptied, Guang picked up the envelope. He pulled out the documents, including one that looked like a passport. "This is your Mainland Travel Permit. It'll make it easier for you to enter China if the need arises," Guang explained. He offered it to Kellie.

She opened the document and noted that it had her Chinese name, Liang Kaili. "How did you get the photo?"

"Your father provided me with several," Guang answered.

"What about this address? This shows that I was born in Taiwan," Kellie said, concerned about the obvious lie.

"Don't worry. Everything is fine. If anyone does check, all the records will support what's on the document. It's a real address and your birthday and name are accurate. We just made some minor changes that are easy for you to remember," Guang tried to reassure her.

"Why? Is this necessary?"

"We want you to have it," Guang said, smiling. "Now, it'll be rude if we don't join the others for some lunch."

"What do you mean? Who wants me to have this?"

"Your father and I discussed this. We agreed that this would be both safe and convenient for you." Guang rose to leave. Only Kellie's eyes followed him at first, watching him rise. As she stood, she realized that seeing the Mainland Travel Permit and trying to understand it caused her to forget about asking Guang a question that lingered in her mind. If he usually sat at the front of the room, the only thing that could mean was that he was one of the ChiTran executives. She thought it strange that he hadn't come out and told her.

Standing by her chair, she took a deep breath, convincing herself that everything would be fine. She dropped her notepad into her small bag and placed the envelope on the seat of the chair, and headed down the hall where everyone else had gone.

Kellie welcomed the midday break. A room down the hall from their conference room was set up with a buffet along one wall and several round tables. Because they arrived a few minutes late, she was glad that she was able to sit with Guang.

Kellie sat down and let her arms hang, trying to relax her shoulders. She closed her eyes.

"Kaili, are you all right?" Guang asked.

"I'm fine. It's a mixture of a little jetlag and the high level of discussion. I'm just relaxing for a moment," she said. Jetlag had nothing to do with this. She needed the mental rest. This was a level of intensity in Chinese that she wasn't used to. Following the discussion and writing notes at the same time were mentally tiring her, especially since she needed to turn the Chinese discussion into English notes.

Half an hour later, everyone was back in the conference room. Kellie felt mentally fresh after some tea and a few nibbles of food.

"Let's now turn to our US, Europe, and Japan strategies," Shu began. "The freedom of exports we exercise in the regions discussed this morning is not available to us in these developed markets. As you know, the US threatened us with penalties on China-made goods a couple of years ago for some of the alleged illicit goods reaching the US. We need to be careful if we want to continue cultivating the US market. We'll face the same threats and restrictions in Europe and Japan. Do you think this is true, Ms. Liang?"

Kellie had been jotting down keywords in English as Shu spoke. Her head snapped up when she heard her name. She saw all the heads turn from looking toward the front of the room to her. She put down her pen, saying nothing for a moment. She had been listening to statements, not questions, so she was caught by surprise.

"Yes, it is likely," Kellie said. She cleared her throat. "As I'm sure you know, the US, Europe, and Japan have better systems in place at their borders. They work harder to prevent illicit goods from their markets, or maybe, it is better to say they are better at identifying things that appear suspicious. In fact, the US has sent some of its officials abroad to provide education and training to other countries."

"Can you give us specifics?" Hsieh Liwei asked.

Kellie fidgeted with her pen for a moment. "Customs has been working with people in Europe and Canada about some of these things for some time. But I doubt you need to be very concerned because, in the short run, even the US has limits on its number of capable people for it to be very effective against illicit imports from China."

"But, do you have specifics?" Liwei pressed. "Your statement is just a general comment. There are several in this room that know what you've just said. What's the actual number of people in the US who would be involved, and what foreign countries will they target for detecting illicit goods? What kind of illicit goods are they concentrating on?"

Kellie felt her body temperature rise. She didn't have any exact numbers to give to the group. Her information was second- or third-hand since she had received it through contacts on Capitol Hill and people she contacted at other government agencies. She could feel the stares. She needed to flip this discussion.

"I'm sorry, but I'm confused. I would understand if you wanted to learn about the rules so that your goods would meet US requirements for toys, medicines, cars, and industrial equipment. But you want information about how illicit goods are prevented from entering markets. How much of your exported products are illicit goods? What do you consider as illicit goods? Perhaps I don't understand," Kelly put forward to the assembled group.

Liwei was sitting erect in his chair with arms folded in front of him. Slowly, he turned his head to the front of the room.

Kellie looked to the head of the room as everyone else had turned to Shu and Rong.

Shu began, "Ms. Liang, we hope you will understand that we have multiple obligations, and one of them is to help the government. We have many people who need to work. This means there are times when we produce things in accordance with Chinese rules. Sometimes, things made within Chinese rules may not comply with foreign rules. It's hard for us to meet the rules of outsiders. If we unintentionally violate some foreign rules, we don't see this as a violation as they are not our rules.

"I will keep this simple. ChiTran is involved in many different products made in various parts of China. We maximize production, and we ship to every market where we can enter our goods. We want to grow, but we want to avoid big mistakes that lead to barriers," Shu added.

This was beginning to feel like a ping-pong match where everyone's eyes and heads followed the ball back and forth across the net. The ball was back on Kellie's side of the net, and everyone turned their heads toward her.

"I'm sure you know that it would be inadvisable to export medical products, auto parts, or electrical goods that have not been properly tested or meet the US standards. Detection of these kinds of things that could harm your customers, the consumers. If you're caught, your company will be put under a microscope. Of course, that's an extreme situation," Kellie explained.

"Would you be able to provide a detailed list?" Liwei wondered.

"If you mean an itemized list, I wouldn't dare to create a list of possibly thousands of items. I could leave something off the list. I don't want to be responsible for making that kind of mistake," Kellie conceded.

"What kind of a list could you make," Liwei continued pressing.

Kellie pursed her lips. Just for a moment, she stared straight back at Liwei. His questioning was starting to anger her.

He stared straight back. He read Kellie's reaction. His arms still folded, he hinted at a smile.

Kellie shifted her line of sight back to the front of the room. "Ms. Tai, since I am not satisfying your colleagues with my responses, if Mr. Hsieh or another of your colleagues could provide a list of products you are exporting to the US, I can identify which ones pose the greatest threat of detection for violations in the US. Then ChiTran makes the decision what to do."

Liwei leaned toward a younger man sitting next to him and whispered and followed that up with a written note that he gave the younger man. The note was passed to Shu and Rong.

Shu and Rong were also whispering back and forth, considering Kellie's proposal. Kellie watched them. As Shu and Rong whispered to each other, Shu looked at Liwei as if signaling him.

"We know from information that Ms. Liang has provided earlier that we must be consistent in our shipping patterns. Deviation makes Americans curious, and curiosity means more invasive investigation of our shipments. According to Ms. Liang, using consistent shipping routes and creating a good record with customs will work in our favor when we have goods suspected by customs of possibly violating one of their rules," Shu explained.

Kellie was sitting forward. With her elbows on the table, her chin rested on the steepled and interlocked fingers of her hands. Her brow crinkled, listening to Shu. What did Shu mean? How had she, Kellie, provided or said any of these things to this group of people? As Kellie looked intensely at Shu, trying to read something from the older woman's expression, she found the effort useless. She didn't know the older woman well enough to interpret any expression on her face.

"I must confess my disappointment and share this with everyone. We've been hearing about the wisdom we would receive from our new colleague, but to be kind, she has provided nothing that was unknown to us before this meeting. We have been told about her contributions to our trading activities, but she has disappointed us today," Liwei stated.

Shu and Rong glared at Liwei while others looked around the room as Liwei spoke.

"You've made your point," Shu said as a way of stemming a confrontation.

Shu moved the meeting along, taking attention away from their guest. Kellie was glad to be off the hot seat, but she was troubled by the things she was supposed to have said to this group through someone else. *Who, when,* and *where* were unanswered in her mind. How had she communicated anything to anyone in this room through someone else?

* * * * *

Kellie checked her watch: 5:45. She was mentally exhausted. With elbows on the table, she leaned forward. With everyone looking toward the head of the table, she massaged her temples. She hoped no one noticed.

The older man at the front of the room, Qian Rong, was wrapping up, summarizing the second half of the afternoon's session. Kellie had not concentrated as much on the discussion about Europe and Japan. Realizing that Rong was bringing the meeting to an end, she placed her small bag on the conference table, putting her writing pad and the folded envelope into it.

As she looked around to make sure she had everything, she could hear chairs moving, briefcases or bags being clasped, and people talking. She paid no attention to the background noise.

"Excuse me, Ms. Liang."

"Yes," she said, twisting in her chair toward the voice behind her, not realizing that she was reacting to someone speaking English.

"Mr. Hsieh."

"I hope I did not make you too uncomfortable earlier," he said in flawless English. There was barely a hint of any accent.

Hsieh Liwei stepped back a couple of paces, giving Kellie space around her chair. As she rose from her chair, she gave Guang a quick glance, but he was in a whispered conversation with the woman on his other side.

"You can call me Lee. That's the name I used when I studied in the US years ago."

"If you don't mind, I'll use your Chinese name," Kellie offered.

"I know it has already been a long day for you. But if it is possible and you have time, could you join me for a more casual discussion? I'm happy to continue in English if that would be easier for you."

"I appreciate the offer of continuing in English. That will make things a little easier for me. Yes, I'm happy to join you," Kellie answered with a smile. Liwei's friendly approach was welcome after his earlier questioning and probing. She convinced herself that during the formal part of the meeting, he might have felt a need to be more aggressive.

"I have a car being brought around, and it'll be out front in a few minutes. I'll be back in a moment to walk down with you. Excuse me."

Liwei rode the elevator down and dashed outside to speak to his two young underlings. "We're heading to Tai Po with an extra person. You know what to do when we get there." When he saw the two young men nod, he turned and rushed back into the building.

Kellie watched Liwei leave the conference room. She leaned down and tapped Guang on the shoulder. "I'm sorry to interrupt," she said in Chinese. "I'm leaving with Hsieh Liwei. He asked if I could join him for further conversation in a more casual setting," Kellie explained.

Guang's expression wasn't what Kellie expected. He seemed unhappy hearing what she had said. Guang's eyes darted toward the door, seeing Liwei reappear. "Be cautious," he warned.

"Ms. Liang, are you ready?" Liwei asked as he walked toward her.

She said nothing. She put the strap of her bag on her shoulder and turned toward Liwei, who stepped aside to let her pass.

Outside the building, a black Mercedes sedan was parked at the curb. Shing Fang, a young man in his mid-twenties, was behind the steering wheel and had the window open and saw Kellie and Liwei. He was quick to get out and open the back door for the two of them.

Kellie nodded and said, "Xie xie," thanking the young man and noticing the young man's scarred cheeks. Once in the car, Kellie slid across the seat. She and Liwei were joined by another young man who sat up front next to the driver, saying nothing. All the windows were tinted.

Liwei looked into the rearview mirror and made eye contact with the driver. The car eased into traffic.

"Have you been to the New Territories?" Liwei asked.

"No," Kellie answered simply without turning her head away from looking out the side window. She didn't understand why he asked about the New Territories.

She saw the crowded apartment buildings, stores, and warehouses giving way to wider vacant spaces. "I'm sorry, but I thought we were going to a teahouse or someplace nearby," Kellie said.

"No. We're going to a place I have in the New Territories. It'll be quieter and more comfortable there," Liwei explained.

Kellie pushed herself up straighter in the corner of the back seat, less comfortable than she'd been just a minute ago. She had no cell phone to call Aaron.

"I need to make a phone call," Kellie said as she watched the city fade farther into the distance.

"You can make a call once we get to my place," Liwei said.

They rode for the next forty-five minutes with little conversation. Kellie noticed that they had left the congestion of Kowloon far behind.

The hills and mountains were a lush deep green color. Looking off into the distance, it was like a beautiful mountainous landscape painting. She took in the views of the rural areas they drove past. She tried to relax but couldn't. She wondered what Guang meant in warning her to be cautious.

Though her eyes looked out, her ears were sensitive to any sounds of movement in the seats. Nothing warned her of any movement by Liwei toward her.

"Everything turns to this deep green this time of year when the rainy season gets started," Liwei said as if reading her mind.

"We're about halfway between Kowloon and Shenzhen. I'm sure you're aware that Shenzhen has become a major manufacturing hub at the border. We have some operations in the Shenzhen area," Liwei explained.

"I'm aware of it, and Guangzhou, not far away, is also a growing city down here, near the border," Kellie said, acknowledging Liwei's comment.

The driver slowed and flipped the turn signal on and turned onto a secondary two-lane road. They were still in what looked like a rural area. They didn't go very far off the main road they had been traveling. The driver slowed to turn. Where the driveway met the road, there were two cylindrical stone sculptures that looked to be four to five feet tall on either side of the driveway. Each of the cylindrical sculptures had snake carvings as if they had come up out of the ground to wrap around the stone.

Kellie noticed a large expanse of land behind the house. The slow slope of the land was lush with tall grass as it rose toward the forested hills that were a couple of hundred yards behind the house.

The car pulled into the driveway toward a house that would be considered large anywhere in the world. A stone wall that was no more than a foot or two high marked the property's width on both sides of the house but didn't extend along the front. The wide green spaces around the house and the sculptured stonework at the driveway entry screamed privacy and affluence.

The two young men got out and opened the back doors.

"Do you live here with your family?" Kellie asked, assuming there had to be several people living in such a large house.

Liwei led them into the house and its large entry foyer. The tiled floor caused their footsteps to echo throughout the house. "This is a business getaway. It's convenient when I need to be in Kowloon or Hong Kong. I don't have to go all the way back to Shenzhen, and I don't have to stay in the congested city." Liwei said nothing about family.

The open foyer let her see an expansive sitting area that had two long leather sofas and high-backed leather chairs. It was a masculine room. There were simple, light-colored sheer curtains over the windows and a few items on the coffee and end tables. An area rug covered the floor between the sofas and chairs.

Without asking, she walked over and sat in the corner of one of the leather sofas. Liwei took a spot on the other leather sofa facing her. The space between them seemed vast, with a large square glass table between them.

Kellie was curious. Liwei had surprised her with his English capability. He was self-assured and confident. He had not tried to engage in small talk during the ride to the house to fill the time with chitchat. Most men would have asked a lot of questions or told her everything about themselves, but he hadn't.

"I hope you're comfortable. I've arranged for some refreshments," Liwei said.

"I'm fine. This is an impressive place. Perhaps it could use a few decorating touches, but it's much more comfortable than the conference room we spent all day sitting in."

"Yes. I'm hoping that we might discuss some of the things from earlier today. We, meaning ChiTran, are still learning some of the ropes, as you might say," Liwei explained. "You should understand that ChiTran, as a Chinese company, must do its part in keeping our large population busy with work. Otherwise, the government would be concerned that too many idle people could lead to less-than-favorable social activities.

"Sometimes, this leads us into production and export situations that are interpreted by foreign governments as breaking international rules. That's not our real intent," Liwei added. "Ms. Liang, you have advised us about consistencies of shipment and how to minimize our production mistakes so that we are on good terms with Americans, but we need more specific guidance from you."

"Liwei, can you tell me when I provided this advice and who told you the advice came from me?"

Liwei had been sitting back relaxed but moved his body forward, sitting closer to the edge of the sofa and leaning forward.

"What is the name of your firm?"

"I work for the Pacific Rim Trade Consortium. It's a group of companies that want to promote regional trade," Kellie answered.

"You are involved in details and in advising foreign companies how to import into the US, yes?" he inquired.

"Only in general ways. I don't get involved in anyone's detailed business activities," Kellie tried to clarify.

"Do you know anything about the way customs officers work?"

"I know a little, but not a lot," Kellie said. As the words passed her lips, the fog of confusion lifted slightly. It was Aaron. He was the source. Her source of information. But how did these tidbits make their way to ChiTran?

"Mr. Lai professed your value to us. We believe what he says because of the investment he makes in ChiTran and because of his senior position within ChiTran. He said something else that I hope you can confirm. If we overwhelm the Americans with lots of products, it would be difficult for them to check everything."

"There's some truth to that. We're the biggest market for goods from lots of countries, and it's impossible to go through every shipment arriving in the US every day. Can Hong Kong check everything that arrives and goes through its port on a daily basis?" Kellie countered.

"Then it is very possible that even products that might fail to meet all the American standards could enter the American market?"

"Of course, it's possible," Kellie agreed.

Liwei nodded in agreement with her.

He and Kellie turned to the approaching footsteps. The young man who had been the other passenger in the car brought a tray of tea.

Liwei suspected that Guang had overstated Kellie's value to ChiTran but couldn't be sure. He was still fishing for something more specific, something beyond what he already knew. As he picked up his cup of tea and sipped, he watched Kellie over the rim of his cup as she sipped her tea.

Kellie had taken a few sips of tea. She closed her eyes and rotated her head, trying to loosen her neck muscles. "I apologize for being so tired. I'm suddenly very drowsy. I should get back to my hotel."

"I understand. But before you make the journey back, it would be good for you to finish your tea," Liwei suggested.

Kellie sipped her tea. "I'm sorry, but I'm feeling very tired, drowsy," she said.

Liwei, sitting forward, waited a few minutes. Then, he stood and walked over to Kellie and helped her stand. Instead of helping her walk, he picked her up, cradling her across the front of his body and carried her upstairs to one of the bedrooms. Kellie didn't resist when she felt his arms lift her off the floor. She closed her eyes. She was overtaken by whatever had been put in her cup.

After putting Kellie in bed, Liwei came down and saw Kellie's bag on the floor next to where she had been sitting. He sat down and rummaged through her bag. He pulled out a folded envelope and its contents. Liwei smiled as he stared at the Mainland Travel Permit. He put it down and rubbed his chin, thinking that this provided him with an unexpected opportunity.

Turning his attention back to the bag, in one of the inside pockets, he found her hotel room key card. It was still in its little folder with the room number written on it. He took the key card and walked into the kitchen. The two young men who had been in the car earlier were sitting at a small table drinking tea.

"Take the other car and see what you can find in her room. Any documents, folders, notepads—things like that. I don't need her computer. Just papers. And grab some of her clothes," Liwei instructed in Chinese.

Chapter 5

The Wait

Hong Kong (Wednesday, May 13)

Aaron stood at the window in his room, looking out at the lights sparkling on the water. He had enjoyed a day of leisure in the hotel. He had done some reading by the hotel's pool, gone to the gym, and done more reading.

He checked his watch again: 8:45. He looked at the phone on the desk. He had expected Kellie back hours ago. This wasn't like her. He thought that she would've called if she was going to be late. She had said she would if she was unexpectedly delayed. Even if she couldn't call using her mobile phone, she would've borrowed a phone or found a landline phone to use.

He hadn't eaten earlier, thinking they would go out when she got back. Now, he was too worked up to eat anything. He thought about calling Roger, but how could Roger help? That made no sense. The only thing he thought he could do seemed far-fetched. Should he call her office in the US? Would they be open? Was it too early in the morning? Hong Kong was an easy twelve hours ahead of the east coast. He couldn't think straight.

If he did call Kellie's office, who would he talk to there? He went and sat at the desk. He slid the small notepad by the phone toward him and started writing names, trying to remember the name of one of Kellie's colleagues he had met. John? George? Greg? He had no last name. He concentrated on the names and decided that it was Greg.

Aaron searched his luggage. He had a thin address book that included Roger's contact details, and it would have Kellie's office information. When he found it, his index finger jabbed at the push-button numbers on the desk phone.

"Trade Consortium," a female voice answered.

"May I speak to Greg, please?" Aaron asked, hoping he had recalled the correct name.

"Let me see if he's in this morning." The phone was silent. Aaron didn't know if she was trying an extension or if she was physically walking to see if Greg was in his office. "I'm sorry. Who should I say is calling?"

"Aaron Foster, a friend of Kellie Liang," Aaron waited.

"Hello?"

"Good morning, Greg. Sorry to bother you, but I wondered if you could assist me with something. I traveled to Hong Kong with Kellie. I was hoping you might be able to tell me who she may have been meeting with today. She left for a meeting first thing this morning. I haven't heard from her at all, and I'm a little concerned. It's unlike her to not check in."

"Aaron, I'm sorry to say that I don't really know anything about her trip other than I knew she was going. If you can hang on, let me poke my head in with our director and see if he knows anything. If so, I'll let you speak directly to him."

Aaron was back on hold. He looked out at the array of neon-colored lights flashing in the night sky as he waited.

"Aaron, I'm connecting you with George, our director."

Before Aaron could say anything, Greg was off the line.

"Aaron, good morning. How can I help you?"

"George, appreciate you taking my call. As you know, Kellie is in Hong Kong. She had a short meeting two days ago and had an all-day meeting today. I haven't heard from her at all today. She's very good about calling if she's going to be delayed. You know it's twelve hours later here than in DC. This is a bit unusual, so I was hoping you might be able to tell me whom she might have met with so that I can be sure she's all right."

"Hmm, I understand. If I knew, I would tell you, but I don't know her meeting schedule. We had sketched out her possible meetings, but nothing was concrete. She told me that there were only two or three possible organizations that she identified, and she had reached out to them, but meeting arrangements were still in flux. Given the somewhat loose schedule, we agreed that this was a combined business and personal trip. She agreed to take personal vacation days to cover the time she's away if meetings didn't materialize."

"Then, you have no information about the meeting she attended today."

"That's correct," George confirmed.

"You don't think there's a chance that someone else at the office would know?" Aaron asked.

"I doubt it. We're a small organization. I'm the most likely person she would have told about things like this. As you probably know, she has a lot of freedom and latitude when it comes to China-related matters."

"All right, thanks," Aaron said. He hung up. He wondered what kind of business trip this was. He suspected that she had not planned to be gone all day and into the night. Otherwise, wouldn't she have given him a name or a number so he could contact her? His thoughts were racing in several different directions. A lot of things didn't make sense.

Aaron hadn't moved from the desk. His finger was punching the numbers to call Roger, then stopped. The only other thought that popped into his mind was to call Kellie's parents. They lived near Philadelphia. The time difference was the same as with Washington, DC. What would he say: "Hello, I think I've lost your daughter in Hong Kong" or "Hello, I think your daughter is missing somewhere in Hong Kong"? That wouldn't be a great way to start a conversation with her parents.

Fidgeting sounds by the room's door interrupted Aaron's jumbled thoughts.

Finally, Kellie's back. He pushed himself out of the desk chair and marched toward the door. It began to open before he reached it.

The two young men Liwei had sent saw Aaron stop a few feet from the door as they pushed it open. They hadn't expected anyone to be in the room. They stopped for a split second, then rushed toward Aaron.

Aaron, surprised at seeing two men, hesitated for an instant, stopping his forward movement. That hesitation gave the two men, one behind the other, the time and space to charge at him in the short and narrow room vestibule area. The first man went for Aaron's throat and face. Aaron, backing up, raised his left forearm, blocking the first man's outstretched right arm.

The second attacker kicked the door closed and had time to unsheathe a knife on his belt and maneuver around and behind Aaron now that he had backed up into the main part of the room where there was space.

As the first attacker's left hand came at his face, Aaron turned his head while blindly swinging with his right. Aaron's right fist connected with the side of the head, causing the first attacker to step back, unable to connect with his left.

Aaron tried to turn around but couldn't.

"Stop!"

Aaron heard the angry voice in his ear. Aaron's eyes were fixed on the man in front of him, but he felt something on his neck. The man in front backed off, but the man holding the knife had a firm grip on the waistband of Aaron's jogging pants. He could feel the man's heavy breathing behind him.

The man who held the knife stepped backward, pulling Aaron with him. Both men stepped backward. The man had moved the knife, and Aaron felt it on his back. The point of the knife at his kidney.

The man behind him said something in Chinese. Aaron watched as the man he had punched checked the desk and its drawers, then went to the wardrobe closet. He found Kellie's briefcase. He then crouched down and took a quick look under the bed. He took a quick look in the bathroom, then came out and took one more look in the wardrobe closet. He pointed at something. Aaron didn't know what he was pointing at.

The nudge from behind and the increased pressure of the knife on his back were enough for Aaron to take steps toward the closet. When he was close enough to see what was causing interest in the closet, he understood. The safe. He interpreted the hand gestures and opened the safe. It was empty.

The man doing the searching threw suitcases on the bed. Some of Kellie's clothes were still in her carry-on bag. He turned and went to the bank of drawers in the closet and grabbed what was obviously Kellie's and threw them into the bag. He grabbed up more of Kellie's toiletries in the bathroom and dropped them in the bag.

Watching what the man was doing, Aaron realized if they were filling the carry-on bag with things she'd need for days, he shouldn't expect Kellie's return anytime soon. He squirmed to get loose despite the tight grip on his waistband from behind. The young man filling the bag walked over and slapped him hard across the face, causing Aaron's body to twist. As his body twisted, he felt the tip of the knife slice into his back.

The man who had slapped him picked up the carry-on bag and Kellie's briefcase without saying a word. The knife-wielding man turned Aaron around, positioning Aaron to stand facing opposite the room door and started backing Aaron toward the door. Aaron heard the door being opened. The man holding the knife jabbed him in the back a second time and shoved Aaron forward, away from the door, toward the window. The two were out of the room, pulling the door shut behind them before Aaron could turn around.

Aaron heard the door slam shut. He turned, flung the door open, and jumped out into the hallway and saw the second man's heels as he went into the stairwell. Aaron ran down the hall, caught the door as it was closing, and pushed it wide open. He heard nothing when he entered the stairwell.

The two young men raced down one flight of stairs, entered the corridor one floor down, and walked toward the elevator bank located at the midway point of the corridor. They were breathing heavily but needed to slow their pace, hoping that they didn't look suspicious to anyone who might see them. They saw another exit sign at the opposite end of the corridor, walked to it, entered another stairwell, and walked down the stairs.

Hearing nothing, Aaron decided the thugs had headed for the elevator below. He turned back into the corridor and ran back to the elevator and pressed the button. His right fist drummed on the wall as he waited for the elevator. He took little comfort in seeing it empty and punched the down button for the lobby several times.

Aaron rushed out of the elevator and into a crowd of people near the reception desk. The lobby was crowded with young people and businessmen. He realized people were staring at him and assumed it was his jogging pants. He couldn't see what some of them saw, bloodstains on the back of his shirt. When he reached the hotel's large glass entrance doors, he stopped, looked out, then turned to look back into the large lobby lounge area.

Aaron's body jerked to his right, feeling a tap on the shoulder.

"Sir, are you all right? Do you need any assistance?" a young bellman asked.

Aaron looked at the uniformed young man blankly for a few seconds. "No, I'm fine. Really."

The young man's approach caused even more people to look Aaron's way. As he looked around, he was now the focus of attention. He turned and walked back toward the elevators. He kept looking over his shoulder to see if he could spot his intruders anywhere. They had vanished.

On the ground floor, the young man with Kellie's briefcase and carry-on bag stepped back and let his empty-handed partner ease the door open and look out into the open spaces of the ground floor. The stairwell opened near a corner of the long reception area. The two young men had taken their time coming down, careful not to make any noise as they descended the bare concrete staircase. The empty-handed young man took the briefcase so that they each had something in hand. He led the way out of the hotel at a leisurely pace, mixing among others in the hotel reception and lobby area.

Back in his room, Aaron realized they were gone. He felt sweat rolling down his neck. Standing just inside the door, he leaned against the door and took several deep breaths trying to calm himself. After a minute, he went into the bathroom. He pounded the counter with his fist. In front of the mirror, he twisted to look at his back. He saw two holes in his shirt and bloodstains in two places on his back. He pulled up his shirt and looked at his back. It appeared his shirt had helped stop the bleeding, and the two puncture wounds did not appear to be serious. Not wanting to call attention to his situation, he hoped both wounds would heal without any need for medical attention. His mouth was dry.

Aaron splashed water on his face and ran his wet hands through his hair. With arms extended and a hand on each side of the sink, he leaned over the sink and let the excess water drip off his face.

In addition to the two knife wounds on his back, his left cheek was burning from the hard slap. Coming to his senses, Aaron rushed to the desk and wrote: "One man about five feet eight, fit. Round scars on both cheeks, slightly bigger than the end of a cigarette. Nickname 'Dimples.'" He looked at his watch. What seemed like thirty or forty minutes had taken less than fifteen. The mental rewind and playing it over were in slow motion, while the real-time event seemed to be in fast-forward when it was occurring. He noted the time in his notes.

Now what? he thought. Debrief. He sat at the desk, grabbed a bottle of water from the room refrigerator, uncapped it, and drained half the bottle by the time he stopped swallowing. He closed his eyes as he sat. The adrenaline rush was gone. He put his head on his forearm that rested on the desk.

He got Roger's number and called.

"Steeg here."

"It's Aaron. I need your help. I've been mugged, and Kellie's missing."

"Whoa, whoa, whoa. Stop! Where the hell are you?"

"I'm in my room."

"Where were you mugged?" Roger asked.

"I was mugged in my room." Aaron heard Roger laugh. "Hey, I'm serious!"

"I don't mean to laugh, but if you were on this end of the phone, that would sound a bit strange and funny at the same time."

"You've got a strange fucking sense of humor!"

"I'm sorry, Aaron. What's going on?"

"First, Kellie's been gone since early morning to a meeting. She thought she would be back no later than five or six this evening. It's not like her not to call if she's going to be late. I had no problem with her being late, but the part that started bothering me was when she didn't call at all. The second thing is the mugging. They had a room key card. I thought it was her, but as soon as they saw me, we got into a tussle. The third thing is that they weren't here to rob me. They grabbed her briefcase and whatever was in it then one of them started throwing clothes and her toiletries into her bag. No demands for my wallet, its contents, my watch, nothing like that."

"Wow. You're in a respectable place. The only way they had the key card is because it's Kellie's. The fact that they didn't care about robbing you is interesting. They aren't after your money, but they wanted her briefcase and some clothes. Somebody wants something, documents, information. Does she have anything sensitive that you know about?"

"Nothing I can think of," Aaron answered.

"What do you know about the meeting she was at? Do you know who she met with or the organization?"

"I've got nothing. I called her boss in DC earlier in the evening, and he had nothing to give me. He said she was finalizing things when she got here. I thought about calling the police but hesitated."

"What would you be able to tell them even if you did call them?" Roger asked.

"That's why I haven't called them. The only thing I'm sure of is that I could identify one of the two guys who was here. Other than looking Chinese and fitting in with half a billion others, he did have very distinctive scars on both cheeks."

"Do you think they expected you to be there?"

"No. When they saw me, there was an instant of hesitation," Aaron explained.

"It's interesting that they didn't take you. Did they say anything? Communicate in any way?"

"They spoke Chinese to each other. The guy with the knife in my back said just a couple of words in English. Otherwise, I was able to understand their instructions through hand gestures."

"Knife? Are you all right? Are you hurt?"

"I'm fine now. I've got a couple of superficial knife wounds on my back. They don't look serious. I'm hoping all that's needed are a couple of large band-aids."

"The question is, what do they want from her or intend to do with her? Since they've taken clothes for her, there's no plan to let her come back immediately, but it appears they have no plan to harm her," Roger said as he was thinking out loud. "I can come around and bring you over to my flat for the night."

"Glad I called you. Your logic is better than mine right now. I won't get any sleep here knowing that some knife-wielding crazy could walk in any time. But I don't want to be gone if Kellie comes back."

"Aaron, she won't be back tonight. Remember, they took her clothes. More importantly, when that guy with the knife goes back to his boss and reports to him that they left a witness in the room alive and kicking, it might be reason enough for you to have an unexpected overnight visitor," Roger warned.

"You've convinced me. It's not a good idea to be here."

"I'll be there in thirty by cab to get you. Grab a few things and get out of the room," Roger advised.

Aaron's shoulder bag was on the lobby floor. He had put on a polo-style shirt over the T-shirt and wore his sneakers without socks. He was planning to be back at the hotel sometime in the morning. He watched a parade of taxis, most of them shiny recent model Toyotas.

He noticed a taxi pull up that had dents in the front fender and passenger door. He shook his head and saw Roger step out and wave him over. Given the evening he was having, riding in a beat-up vehicle seemed right for the night.

"How are you feeling?" Roger asked.

"Exhausted."

"Any pain, soreness? We can stop somewhere if you need some meds."

"No, let's just go."

Aaron didn't have a clue where Roger lived. They crossed over to Kowloon, and he noticed the driver take a turn that allowed him a glimpse of Nathan Road. He tried to track the turns and figured that they were a couple of streets away from Nathan Road but parallel to it. This was not the bright, neon-lit area like his hotel. This was an area of residential high-rise apartment buildings. The streets were narrow. Thousands of people were crammed into these older high-rise apartment buildings.

Aaron's body was thrown forward, using his left hand to prevent his face from hitting the back of the front sea. He'd have to check if his back was bleeding again after the sudden forward thrust of his upper body.

"Sorry, sorry!" the driver yelled. He had suddenly pressed the brakes.

Roger was fine. "I tend to keep one hand on the headrest of the seat in front of me because of these sudden brakes." Roger paid the fare and led Aaron up.

"This ain't the Marriott, so be warned."

Aaron could smell cooking grease wafting through the corridors along with a mix of other fragrances, none very inviting.

On the fifth floor of the building, Roger opened the door and let Aaron into a small one-bedroom flat. It was one open living area, and it was clear that Roger didn't waste time on housework. A six-foot-long counter with one gas burner, toaster, small microwave, and a sink made up the kitchen at one end of the living area. A window at the opposite end was large, almost the whole width of the living room. Aaron saw a pillow and sheet on the sofa against the wall and concluded that would be his bed for the night. A narrow coffee table was placed in front of the sofa. One additional chair facing away from the kitchen counter with a small table defined the end of the kitchen area. A doorway opened to the one bedroom.

"You may have missed it, but if you need the facilities, it's back there by the door into the apartment."

"Got it," Aaron said.

"There's a couple of sodas and beer in the fridge if you're thirsty."

Roger's phone rang. He checked the time. It was late. "I'm getting too old for calls at this hour."

"Steeg."

Aaron sat on the sofa and let his head rest on the back of it. His eyes closed, but he could still hear Roger's side of the conversation.

"How many times do I have to say that you should not ship that kind of stuff to the US?"

Aaron opened his eyes and watched Roger, who had the phone to his ear and his left hand on his hip. Roger's lips were pressed closed, and even in limited light from a lamp, Aaron saw Roger was getting red with anger. Aaron had seen that expression before.

"We'll talk tomorrow morning. Where do we meet?" A minute later, Roger flipped the phone closed and stood shaking his head.

"These assholes! Somebody decided to try and get some electrical devices into the US and guess what happened?"

"Wild guess. They were seized," Aaron said.

"Yeah." Roger opened his small refrigerator, tossed a can of beer to Aaron, and popped one open for himself.

* * * *

Liwei was walking toward the kitchen located in the back of the house when he heard the vehicle engine in the driveway. He flipped the switch, turned on the large ceiling light, and stood by the granite countertop of the kitchen island.

Tengfei Meng and Shing Fang, both dressed in all black, came in through the back door. They saw the light come on when they parked behind the house.

Tengfei, though only in his late twenties, was the older of the two young men by a couple of years. He entered the house first carrying the briefcase. Tengfei put the briefcase on the granite countertop and pushed it toward his boss.

Liwei looked at his two young minions. "Is this all that you brought back?" Liwei asked, looking at the two young men he had tasked. "Did the two of you have a fight? Shing, what happened to your face?"

"Yes. This is it. We had to work faster than we expected," Tengfei answered, giving the cheek-scarred Shing Fang a quick glance.

"Explain," Liwei prompted.

"There was a man in the room, so we had to control him before we could look around the room. I'm sure he expected the woman who's upstairs to be coming through the door. Shing Fang was hit by the man, but we were able to get him under control," Tengfei explained.

"How did you leave him?"

"I used my knife to convince him to settle down, and he did. I didn't do anything stupid. Shing Fang did a quick search of the room. We saw the briefcase and grabbed it, threw some clothes into this other bag, and got out quickly. The safe was empty. We didn't take anything off the guy in the room."

"Did he scream? Was any furniture broken? Any noise that people in other rooms might hear?" Liwei asked.

"No broken furniture, no other loud sounds to alarm anyone," Tengfei assured.

"Okay. Tengfei, go up and make sure she's still asleep. Shing, are you okay? The one side of your face is very red."

"I'm fine. He surprised us, but we kept everything under control," Shing Fang said. "If there's nothing else, I'll go to bed."

Liwei watched Shing Fang leave the kitchen, and then he turned his attention to the briefcase. He opened it and found notes Kellie had written to herself in preparation for the meeting. He checked the small pockets on the inside of the briefcase and found Kellie's US passport. This was his second surprise. His first was what he found in the bag she had with her from the meeting, the Mainland Travel Permit.

Liwei found the existence of the passport and Mainland Travel Permit a bit confusing. The Travel Permit showed Kaili Liang as being born in Taiwan, but her US passport indicated her US citizenship, US birthplace, and her legal American name. He decided she could explain that if he really needed to know.

Liwei had greater concerns about the unexpected man in Kellie's hotel room. Liwei marched out of the kitchen and took the stairs two at a time and knocked on one of the bedroom doors.

Tengfei opened it.

"How was this man dressed?"

"Something like a T-shirt and jogging pants. Very casual," Tengfei answered.

Liwei turned and went back to the kitchen. He decided it was either a husband or boyfriend, but as he thought about it, he was certain that Kellie was not wearing the kind of rings that indicated she was married. He went up to the bedroom where he had laid her down and left the door open, having enough light from the hallway instead of any need to turn a light on in the bedroom. He checked both hands. No rings of any kind. He wondered who the mystery man was. That would be another piece of information to get from Kellie, but it wasn't a priority.

Chapter 6

Inquiries

Hong Kong (Thursday, May 14)

Aaron tossed and turned on the sofa with the hint of dawn. He was on his side, facing the back of the sofa. Without any curtains or blinds on the wide expanse of window, Aaron was awake but hadn't opened his eyes. Roger's bedroom door was open. Aaron heard the snoring sounds of a man still deep in sleep. None of that mattered. All he could think about was Kellie.

Aaron sat up on the sofa and looked out the window to the building across the street. He realized people could see into the flat, so he stood up, grabbed his trousers and pulled them on. He then tiptoed over and pulled the bedroom door closed. Back on the sofa, he looked around and saw a cordless phone on the small table next to the lone chair in the room. He searched his bag and pulled out his small address book, flipping through the pages till he was on the page he wanted.

Aaron stared at the number for Kellie's parents. He had no choice. Who else could he call? Who else might have any idea whom she was meeting? He pressed the numbers for the US country code and then the phone number.

"Hello?"

"Mr. Liang, it's Aaron. I'm in Hong Kong with Kellie."

"Yes," Mr. Liang said, drawing out the response. "Is something the matter?"

Aaron heard the slightest hint of Mr. Liang's accented English. Decades living in the US had polished his English. "I'm not sure. It's now early morning here, as you know. Kellie went to a meeting yesterday and never returned to the hotel last night." Aaron hesitated. Should he say anything about the two men who came to the hotel? No, that would invite questions, and he had no answers.

Aaron continued, "I'm worried about her because she never called, and you know that's not like her. I don't know whom she was meeting with or where. I have no way of contacting her. I did call her office in Washington, but no one there could help me with any information. I decided to call you in case Kellie said anything to you about her meetings here before we left."

"Thank you for calling me. No, we didn't really discuss her trip in any detail, although she mentioned it. I did say that if she had the time, I knew that my cousin from Taiwan might be in Hong Kong on some business and suggested she make an effort to meet with him. But I do not know if that occurred. May I suggest something?" Mr. Liang offered.

"At this point, I'm open to any suggestion," Aaron responded.

"I will try to contact my cousin. If he's in Hong Kong and has any information, I will tell him to contact you directly. That will make things easier and more efficient. Give me a phone number where you can be reached."

Aaron didn't know what number to give him. The Marriott or Roger's cell phone? He didn't know the number for the cordless phone he was using. "Mr. Liang, I'm going to give you the cell phone number of a friend here in Hong Kong. He's local."

Aaron read off Roger's cell phone number and hung up. He was more hopeful after talking to Kellie's father. At least it wasn't a complete dead end, unlike the call to Kellie's office.

Aaron walked over to the so-called kitchen, looking for coffee. There was no coffee pot on the counter. He looked in the cabinets above and below the counter. Aside from a few dishes, a couple of pots and pans, silverware and beer glasses, Roger didn't have much of anything. There was nothing to suggest a pantry with instant coffee or any other food. The guy must eat out for all his meals, Aaron concluded.

It was only 6:45 in the morning, but he put his shirt and shoes on and decided to go out looking for coffee and something to eat. Now, he was hungry. He realized he had been too concerned about Kellie to eat last evening. And after his encounter with those thugs, he forgot completely about food. If he was going to think straight and help Kellie, he needed to eat something. Down the stairs and out on the street, it hit him that he had no key and didn't know if the door automatically locked when he closed it.

* * * * *

Guang was an early riser. The *Asian Wall Street Journal* spread out on the desk had his attention. The *Financial Times* and the *South China Morning Post* awaited his eager eyes.

He liked being lavish when traveling. His suite had a dedicated bedroom with two double beds and a separate living room with sofas and chairs in case he decided to invite anyone to come for any business conversations. During this trip, he was being generous. He was letting his daughter from the mainland share the room.

The cell phone vibrated and danced on the desk. He snatched it up and answered. He listened, then sat back in his chair. His empty right hand went to his forehead as he listened.

"I know who Kaili was with when she left our meeting," Guang said. "You say you received this call earlier from . . ." Guang reached out for the notepad on the desk and wrote. "Don't worry. We'll find her and have her back very soon. I'll call you at the end of my day to give you an update." Guang disconnected and put the phone down.

"Who was that?"

Guang turned in the chair to see Meilin, his mainland daughter, leaning against the door frame between the bedroom and living room of the suite with her arms folded. Meilin was part of Guang's mainland China family. His regular trips to Hong Kong and across the border into Guangzhou Province meant a lot of time away from his family in Taiwan. Guang was rich compared to many in the mainland when he first started traveling to the mainland. When he was confronted with the fact that his mainland girlfriend was pregnant, he had the financial ability to take care of his girlfriend and the child. Unlike many of his friends, he wasn't disappointed that he had a daughter. He decided he had the resources to give her the knowledge needed to make her successful. It had paid off. Meilin was bright, thoughtful, and good with details. He cultivated her talents so that she could help look after his mainland and Hong Kong business interests.

Over the years, Meilin had become a strong business agent for Guang. They collaborated on every detail when it was about business, but Meilin had an impenetrable wall when it came to her personal life. As she grew older, especially after having had medical issues in her twenties, she fended off Guang's questions about her personal life, and over the years, they learned to engage in small talk when not discussing their common business interests.

Guang was just as committed to his wife and two adult children in Taiwan. The difference was that he wanted someone on the ground watching over things in China and Hong Kong, and Meilin was better suited for that than his children in Taiwan. He was, however, very careful about keeping the two worlds separate and apart.

Meilin repeated her question. "Who was on the phone?"

"My cousin, Kaili's father. He got a call from Kaili's boyfriend a short while ago. She never returned to the hotel last night. It never occurred to me that she had traveled here with anyone, especially when she left with Liwei after our meeting."

"Liwei may be older now, but he may be hanging on to some of the habits of his youth," Meilin commented.

"What do you mean?"

"Kaili is an attractive woman. She seems to be intelligent, and she's a challenge for him," Meilin answered. "She won't be intimidated by him and that might strike him as an interesting pursuit."

"I didn't know that you had these insights about Liwei. I'm afraid to ask how you might have these opinions," Guang said. "Kaili's father gave me a phone number to contact her boyfriend. His name is Aaron Foster."

"What do you have to say when you call? You saw her leave with an associate," Meilin said curiously. "I might be able to help. He has a large house in the Tai Po area. He doesn't stay here in the city when we have these meetings. He doesn't like to go all the way back to Shenzhen. At least you can tell him that."

"Just knowing that he has a house in the Tai Po area isn't that helpful. That area is growing and is more confusing to all of us than it was in the past."

"I've been there, his house, I mean. But it has been a while, and as you say, the area has grown more crowded," Meilin offered. "I remember Liwei saying that he liked it there because there was plenty of space around his house, a bit out of the congested area."

"When I make this call, can I say that we might have an idea of one possible place where she might be? Would you be willing to help find it?" Guang asked.

"I can try. What other option do we have?"

"You're right. This is the only option," Guang agreed. For a moment, he stared down at the notepad, looking at the numbers he had written down during the call with his cousin. He pressed the numbers and waited.

Roger rolled onto his back. His eyes closed, he felt for his cell phone on a small bedside table. "Steeg, here."

Guang hesitated, expecting to hear something else.

"Anyone there?"

"Sorry, sorry. I must have the wrong number," Guang said haltingly in English.

"Wait, who are you trying to call?" Roger asked, his free hand rubbing his forehead.

"Mr. Aaron Foster."

"He's here. Just give me a minute while I go to the other room." Roger swung his body around and pushed himself out of bed.

Roger saw the bedding piled up on the sofa, but Aaron was gone. "I'll have to have him call you. He's gone out for the moment. Let me jot down your name and number, and I'll have him call as soon as he gets back."

Roger was still trying to focus as he finished writing down the name and number when he heard the hard knocking on the door. Roger, still just in his boxer shorts, looked through the peephole and opened the door.

"Where the hell did you go?"

"I was hungry and wanted some coffee," Aaron answered.

"You just missed a call. I didn't know you gave my number to someone."

"I called Kellie's parents earlier, and her father said he'd have his cousin call me."

Roger handed Aaron the scrap piece of paper with Guang Lai's phone number. He held out his cell phone for Aaron to take.

Aaron pressed the numbers. "This is Aaron Foster," he said as soon as the call was picked up on the other end.

"Mr. Foster, my name is Guang Lai. I am a cousin of Kaili's father. I met with her on Monday and yesterday. Kaili's father phoned me and explained that she did not return to her hotel after yesterday's meeting."

"That's right," Aaron replied. "She hasn't phoned or contacted me at all. What time did the meeting end? Did she leave with you or someone else? Do you have any idea where she might be? How can I find out if she's all right?" The questions flowed out of Aaron. He looked over at Roger, who was motioning with his hands with his palms pushing downward to slow down. Roger then made a time-out signal with his hands. Aaron understood.

"I think we should meet. I cannot answer all your questions, but someone else who was at the meeting might be able to help."

"Where and what time?" Aaron said impatiently. "Wait, I'm going to let you give the meeting information to my friend who answered the phone when you called."

Roger took the phone and listened. "No, we have another meeting at that time. How about noon in the lobby at the Marriott? Let me get your cell phone number, and I'll call you when we get there. Hopefully, my other meeting won't be long, so we don't keep you waiting." Roger jotted down the number and hung up.

"We have a meeting? I don't have anything," Aaron said, agitated.

"We both need to meet with this man, and I already have a meeting at ten, remember? JJ will drive us. You and JJ can wait in the car while I have my meeting, and we'll go straight from there back to the Marriott."

* * * * *

Roger had JJ stop curbside long enough for him to get out of the car. JJ knew what to do. He'd try to find a place to pull over somewhere within a block or two and wait for Roger to call for a pick-up. Aaron sat up front with JJ.

As JJ pulled away from the curb, Aaron eyed a black Mercedes with tinted windows parked just a space away from the building entrance. The young man leaning against the front fender looked toward them for a few seconds as JJ pulled away. Aaron thought he recognized the well-dressed young man in the suit. It was only a second or two, but the dimpled or scarred cheeks were familiar. Aaron turned in the seat to look back at the man leaning on the Mercedes.

"JJ, can you go around one more time and come by the front of the building?" Aaron asked.

JJ gave Aaron a glancing look and shrugged. "Okay." It took several minutes for JJ to go around the block.

"If there's space, can you pull up near the Mercedes parked in front of the building where we dropped Roger?" Aaron said.

JJ came around and turned onto the street, running in front of the building. There wasn't space behind the Mercedes, but JJ found a spot a couple of car lengths past the Mercedes, giving Aaron another chance to look at the young man who hadn't moved. When JJ had the car nearly stopped, Aaron jumped out of the passenger seat. He ran toward the young man. Seeing the dimple-like scars as he got to the young man, he grabbed a handful of the young man's shirt at the neck.

JJ shifted the car into park, flung his door open, and jumped out, barely avoiding an oncoming car. He ran and grabbed Aaron's left wrist. "Let him go now," JJ commanded in a firm low voice. "You can't do this on the street!" JJ's mouth was only a couple of inches from Aaron's ear, and his grip on Aaron's wrist was firm and strong.

Aaron opened his hand, releasing the young man, Dimples.

In the few seconds that the altercation had occurred, several passersby took notice, and a couple of them were on their cell phones.

JJ grabbed Aaron by the arm and pulled him toward the car. "Get in. We need to move right now," JJ said.

"But he's one of the two men who came to the hotel and attacked me," Aaron said.

"Nothing good happens if you get arrested," JJ remarked. JJ started the car and got them out of that space and out of sight as fast as possible. He drove several blocks away from the building before making the turns that would take him back in the building's direction. He looked for somewhere to park, out of sight of the people who may have witnessed Aaron's assault.

Parked, the two men sat without exchanging a word for several minutes.

"Thanks," Aaron said finally. "You're right. I wasn't thinking clearly. What I did back there was stupid."

JJ said nothing, just nodded as if to acknowledge Aaron's appreciation and to agree with Aaron that what he'd done was stupid.

"Do you spend the whole day in the car?" Aaron asked, trying to return to normalcy after another several minutes of silence.

"Maybe four hours," JJ said. "Roger, he meets people or talks on the phone a lot, but he is free a lot, too," JJ explained. JJ's English was much better than Aaron's nearly nonexistent Chinese.

* * * * *

After exiting the car, Roger took the elevator up to the 12th floor. He had been here before. He heard the clicking sound of the door being unlocked just as he reached for the handle. A young woman was waiting for him on the other side of the door and led him into a large conference room where he found Mr. Qian sitting.

"Mr. Steeg, good to see you," the older man said from his chair, not bothering to get up. Rong didn't need an interpreter. His English was very good. Like many other educated Chinese, he had studied English for many years and spent some time in English-speaking countries. Nevertheless, he was discriminating in using his English with those from English-speaking countries. He preferred to let people assume that he didn't speak or understand English well, seeing that as a benefit.

"I hope you're well," Roger said in greeting.

"Yes, but we aren't here to discuss my health. I'm sorry that the call you received last evening irritated you. The numbers of our shipments being detected and seized by your former employer are increasing."

"That's because some of your companies aren't following the advice I've given. Some of your senior managers must think they can just ship garbage and everything will get through. Unlike some parts of the world, the customs officers in the US do try to do their jobs. I've repeated myself often about sending any medical or electrical products. If you haven't met the standards and you're caught trying to smuggle them in, you're risking future shipments."

Rong listened intently. The muscles around his eyes had made him appear to be squinting as Roger spoke.

"I suppose the one good thing about these questionable transactions is that those set to receive the goods are the ones whose names are on the documents as importing them. We're not there to suffer any additional negative consequences," Rong answered.

"I'm not sure I understand. Does that mean you'll continue to look for ways to send these kinds of products to the US?"

Rong knew better than to tell Roger the answer was yes. "Of course not. I'll send down instructions that we need to be more sensitive and aware of how the goods are made and sent to the US. We may need to redirect some of these things to other markets."

Roger was sitting forward in his chair. His elbows were resting on the conference table as one hand rubbed the knuckles of the other. He looked at Rong, trying to understand what Rong really meant.

Rong saw that Roger needed more reassurance. "You are worried. We are, too. We can't have barriers to our goods entering the US market. Not only will I issue instructions to my managers, but I'll make sure that we get more input from others about how to avoid mistakes like this in the future."

"Can you tell me what was in the shipment that was seized?" Roger asked.

"There were a few thousand residential smoke detectors. They were exported originally to Mexico. The trucking company hid them in a secret compartment to take them to the US, but your customs inspectors detected the false section in the truck."

As Roger listened, he took in a slow deep breath, preventing himself from reacting to the information Rong was sharing. He was glad that the smoke detectors were found. This was a dangerous game someone was playing. Smuggled smoke detectors meant they weren't likely to provide the best protection, and that meant a house, apartment, or business office building could go up in smoke and take people with it.

"Look, greed must be balanced with common sense. You could have sold them in Mexico. They had already made it past customs in Mexico, so why get so greedy?"

"Someone thought the profit margins were better in the US," Rong said.

"Most likely, they'd also be better off in Canada, and they would have gotten past customs there just as easily," Roger said. His remark was meant to mask how disgusted he was with what he was hearing. He wanted Rong to understand that there were alternatives to the US market for these kinds of products.

"I understand. We'll work on adjustments. Your advice is very valuable to us. I'm glad we've brought you back," Rong said, smiling for the first time during the meeting. "I will discuss the possibility of your direct introduction to some of our managers soon. Do you have other questions? If not, we are done for today, yes?"

"Yes," Roger said as he rose from the chair. Seeing Rong nod but saying nothing, Roger shook Rong's hand and headed for the door and down to the lobby to call JJ. Roger shook his head as he stood, waiting for the elevator. He wondered why he was working for ChiTran. The money? Wanting to stay in Hong Kong? Traveling Asia? Helping ChiTran do the right thing? He didn't have an answer.

At the ground floor, Roger waited inside, out of the sun and humidity that was ever present during the day. It took longer than usual for JJ to drive up, and when he arrived, Roger plopped into the backseat.

"You took your time getting here," Roger commented. He noticed the momentary look between Aaron and JJ. "Did I miss something?"

"Nothing," Aaron said.

"Uh-huh." Roger decided not to pursue it. His eyes went back and forth between the two sitting in the front.

Aaron turned a little sideways in his front seat. "All good now? Were you able to solve their problem?"

"No. They got caught trying to smuggle some smoke detectors into the country," Roger answered.

"Interesting. When did this happen? Did they show you any of our documents?"

"They didn't share any documents. But I understand the goods were sent via Mexico and trucked up. Why?"

"It's just that the scenario sounds familiar. One of my colleagues called maybe a week or ten days before I came to Hong Kong. We were looking to get the agents involved in a trafficking case, same products, same routing. We decided we had a shipment of counterfeit or substandard home smoke alarms," Aaron explained. "They may have let the shipment through to find out who was importing, where they were going. You know the drill."

"Yeah. I do."

"We didn't publicly disclose some of the details about the seizure. There was something else that you might be interested in knowing."

Roger stared at Aaron. "Well, are you going to spit it out, or do I have to guess?"

"In each of the large boxes that had the individually packaged detectors, there was a little surprise inside, you know, like a box of Cracker Jacks. There were a couple of small boxes containing thousands of pills. The pills were in clear plastic bags to be repackaged for sale."

"Did the lab test the pills? Do you have any clue what they are?" Roger asked.

"We suspect they're fake versions of a cholesterol drug that's become a hot item. Once they're packaged and offered on the internet, somebody's going to be rolling in the dough."

Roger shook his head. "I'm glad the shipment was snagged. We both know what the absolute worst outcome could be if all this shit got into the market. From one problem to another," Roger said, shaking his head. He turned his gaze to the harbor, and JJ crossed the bridge and headed to the Marriott. "Sounds like things are going to get more interesting."

* * * * *

Aaron was opening the door before JJ was at a full stop in front of the hotel entrance. Roger got out of the car, reaching into his shirt pocket for the slip of paper with Guang Lai's number and dug into his pocket for his phone. He walked through the glass doors that Aaron held open.

Roger was on his cell phone as he walked past Aaron. "Mr. Lai? We just walked in. How can we find you?"

"I see you, and we're coming toward you," Guang said as he and Meilin went to meet the two Americans.

Aaron and Roger dwarfed Guang and Meilin. Guang led them down into the lobby seating area. Roger took up the rear as the four walked in a single file. Roger glanced around the massive area as he always did. When they left the office building and started heading to the hotel, Roger caught JJ's look into the rearview mirror and saw the subtle nod. Roger was hoping that within the next few minutes, he would see his minder show up.

Guang marched toward a table for the four of them as close to the lobby periphery as he could find. The lobby's open space was fine, but he didn't want others to overhear any of their conversation. There were just enough people to create the buzz of a big room.

Roger liked where Guang was leading them. He would've made the same decision about a table location and appreciated the older man's strategic decision.

"May I sit there?" Roger pointed to the side of the table, giving him the best view of the lobby possible.

"Yes, of course," Guang said as he situated himself in the chair that had the large glass panoramic window behind him. He sat across from Aaron as Meilin sat facing Roger. Looking at both men, Guang guessed that he was sitting directly across from Aaron.

"You are Mr. Foster? I think Kaili's father said you are her boyfriend."

"Yes."

"Who's Kaili?" Roger asked, looking at Guang and then at Aaron.

"Kaili is Kellie's Chinese name," Aaron said. "She has two first names. One that she uses everywhere except here. For her Chinese family, she's Kaili."

"What do her parents call her?" Roger was curious.

Aaron looked at Roger. "Not sure. Can we move on?"

Roger got the message and shrugged, "Yeah, sure."

"This is my mainland daughter, Meilin. She works with me and takes care of many of my business interests here and in the mainland," Guang explained.

As Guang introduced Meilin, Aaron looked over at Meilin. His brow furrowing and ready to say something, but Roger put a hand on Aaron's forearm, saying, "I'll explain later."

"I'm an old friend of Aaron's," Roger offered. "I was the US Customs attaché here until a few months ago, but now I . . ."

"I think I know who you are and who you work for," Guang interrupted. Guang didn't say anything about his own connections to ChiTran and Mr. Qian.

Aaron ignored the look between the two men. "What do you know that will help us with . . ." Aaron paused. "Where do you think Kaili could be?" Aaron decided to use the Chinese name.

Guang began to explain. The pace of his English was slow, deliberate. "Kaili was fine throughout our meeting yesterday. One of our corporate people pressed her with lots of questions. I think she felt some stress. When the meeting ended, this same gentleman asked if she would join him to continue their conversation in a more casual place, not a conference room."

"Do you know where this casual place is?" Aaron pressed.

"I do not know, but Meilin says she might know, but she can't be sure." Guang looked to Meilin.

"I can't be sure, but Liwei, the gentleman who asked Kaili to leave with him, has a house in the Tai Po area. I've been there only once, and it was years ago," Meilin explained.

"Wait, wait. You said this man wanted to continue the discussion at a casual location. Wouldn't a more casual place be a coffee shop, a hotel lounge like this or something?" Aaron asked, leaning in across the table. He looked at the two across from him. "But you think he took her to a house?"

Neither Guang nor Meilin answered.

Roger broke the momentary silence. "Tai Po. Isn't that in the New Territories?"

"Yes," Meilin said softly, her eyes darting between the two Americans.

"Is that the only possibility?" Aaron asked.

"Oh no. There are many possibilities, but this is the only place we are aware of as a possibility," Guang said. "Liwei could have taken her anywhere, but the house is a good start. It's away from the city but also not across the border."

"She can't cross the border. As far as I know, she doesn't have a visa to enter the mainland. I didn't get one. We had no plans to cross the border," Aaron said.

Guang sat listening and simply nodded, hearing about the visa. He wasn't sure if he should say anything about the Mainland Travel Document he gave Kaili, allowing her to cross the border. It might unnecessarily provoke questions and an unwanted outburst from the two Americans. He decided to keep that to himself.

Looking at Meilin, Roger asked, "If you've only been there once, and it was years ago, would you be able to direct us there, or could you ask someone else for an address or directions?"

"I'm good with many kinds of details. I think I can help you find this house," Meilin offered.

"But hasn't there been a lot of development in that area? Won't that make it more difficult for you to find this place that you've been to only once and years ago?" Roger asked.

"Yes, it might be more difficult, but if I go, I might recognize things that will cause me to remember," Meilin replied.

"In the dark," Roger wondered.

"It'll be more difficult, but when I was there, it wasn't in a crowded area. He likes space, so the house was not in the city but on the outskirts. It's big, has a long driveway," Meilin explained.

Roger and Aaron sat looking at Meilin, then at each other. They didn't have any other options.

"If this is the only known possibility we have, we need to check it out as soon as possible, later today or tonight. Meilin, you'll have to guide us the best you can. I'd suggest you wear all dark clothes and comfortable shoes," Roger said.

Roger turned to Aaron. "Time to resurrect and put to use a bit of that training you had down at Glynco."

Aaron nodded in agreement.

Roger then looked to Meilin. "I need to make some arrangements. I'll call you in a few hours and let you know our next steps. Where are you staying so I know where to pick you up?" Roger asked.

"I'm nearby at the Conrad. Call my father's phone. We'll wait together to hear from you."

Aaron knew that Roger was in his element. Roger was putting an operation together, and he would position the right people in the right place to get this done. At least they had a lead.

Roger and Aaron stayed at the table and watched Guang and Meilin leave. "I've got a call to make. Sometimes you can't wait for the cavalry to come and save your ass if you call at the last possible minute," Roger said as he started pressing numbers on his phone.

"Ray, it's Roger. I need your help. We have a soon-to-be member of the family missing. She came here with a family member a few days ago and didn't come home last night. Can you tag along with me on a lead?"

"Roger, I'm up to my eyes in shit today. We've got a three-person delegation starting some talks with Hong Kong government folks tomorrow. They're here for a couple of days, and I need to have some things put together for them and then meet them early tomorrow."

"Is that a yes?" Roger pressed, giving Aaron a wink as if he was just joking around.

"I'm tied up, Rog."

"I know you. You'll have all this crap put together so that you don't have to work late. And I know you'll push it off onto your assistant," Roger continued.

"What's the deal?" Ray asked, relenting to Roger's wishes.

"We need you to come along. JJ will have the car, but I'd like you to drive your pickup and bring a full tool kit," Roger prodded.

"How many people?"

Roger closed his eyes, thinking about the answer. "Five, maybe six. We have you, me, JJ, another member of the family, and our guide."

"That's five. Why six?" Ray asked.

"We have to be ready for the unexpected."

"Is this going to get me into deep shit with my bosses?" Ray asked.

"Not if we do things right. They'll never know."

"What time am I seeing you, and where?"

"Use your special sign, put it on your dashboard and park near the Conrad entrance, and wait for us to pull up there to pick up one of the crew," Roger answered. "We'll see you around 4:30."

"Who the hell was that?" Aaron asked.

"Ray Jackson. He took over as the customs attaché when I retired. Good guy. He's tough and smart, just like me. He's fitter than any guy I know. He was a college running back until he blew out his knee. The way he looks, I think the guy works out about two hours a day. He's got muscles everywhere, but a hell of a nice guy. He comes to me a lot about what's going on, and I try to help him. While he's got about eighteen years in with the agency, he's still new to this particular job."

"What's the deal about the family?" Aaron asked.

"Now he knows you're with customs and that the person in trouble is your future lifelong soulmate. Enough reason for him to drop things to help out. Of course, the fact that I'm asking doesn't hurt either."

Aaron shook his head and laughed. "He doesn't know me, but he's going to drop everything and do this?"

"Yeah. Ray and I have a good working relationship. Just because I'm no longer with customs doesn't mean I've forgotten where I came from. And he knows that sometimes it's in his best interest to oblige me."

"That's reassuring."

"While we wait to get the pieces in place to try and find Kellie, I need your help with something. Remember when I told you about being on someone's radar screen here? Just keep looking at me while I tell you where to look. Don't turn your head or anything until I get up to go to the men's. Just watch me walk out and then take the opportunity to identify the guy who's following my every movement. But just to help you out a little, he's wearing wire-rimmed glasses, has a book in front of him. He's wearing a gray sport coat and a light-blue button-down shirt. No remarkable facial features, just blends in with everyone. He's alone at a table. Once I pass him, get up, and go sit down at his table before he has a chance to leave. Wait for me to come back."

Aaron waited till Roger was a couple of paces away from their table before turning to locate the man Roger had identified. He spotted him immediately.

Roger took his time, choosing a path between occupied chairs. He seemed to walk as if begging for attention from the people he walked past, smiling and nodding to strangers who would look toward him.

Gao Cheng's full attention was on Roger. He didn't see Aaron get up, and he didn't notice him until Aaron grabbed a chair to pull away from the table so he could sit.

Gao's head twisted toward Aaron. "Who are you? What do you want?"

"Don't worry, he's not leaving. You're going to keep me company until my friend returns," Aaron said. "I guess you know him well. You've been following him for weeks, right?"

Cheng closed his book slowly. He pulled a handkerchief from his pocket and started wiping his lenses. "He's a person of interest," Cheng said in English, his voice firm. He stuffed the handkerchief back in his pants pocket.

"Why all the interest?"

"We see him with other people of interest."

"Am I a person of interest, too?" Aaron asked.

"More of interest now than an hour ago."

"Then you know who we were meeting with."

"Yes. I know the man you met with, and we are familiar with his business enterprise."

"And who might that be?" Roger said as he approached Cheng Gao from behind.

Cheng Gao snapped his head up to the side when he heard Roger's voice ask the question. He had concentrated on Aaron's presence too much.

"ChiTran is a major exporting company. My superiors are concerned about some of their activities. They may be causing us to have problems with the Americans," Cheng volunteered.

Roger sat down, clearing his throat. "The older man we were just meeting with is also with ChiTran?"

Cheng Gao nodded his confirmation.

Roger decided to be blunt. "You're watching me for your people. Is that Customs and Excise?"

Cheng folded his arms and remained silent.

Roger already knew the answer but wanted to find out if his young minder would verbally confirm it. He didn't.

"You know who I am. What's your name?" Roger queried.

"Gao Cheng." Cheng said it with his family name first.

"Mr. Gao?" Aaron asked.

"Yes."

"Gao Cheng, I'm going to call you Chuck," Roger said. "Chuck, my friend and I have a problem, and that's why we were meeting with that other gentleman and his daughter. My friend here, Aaron Foster, arrived in Hong Kong a few days ago with his girlfriend. She went to a day-long meeting yesterday in Kowloon and never returned from her meeting. She's missing after meeting with ChiTran executives in your territory."

Cheng's expression didn't change.

"You don't want this problem to become your problem or a problem for your superiors," Roger warned.

"It sounds like a police matter, not for Customs and Excise."

"Do you want this to become a police matter?" Roger asked. "Before you answer that, maybe you should check in and find out and make sure you tell them who is telling you this. I've got a history of being reliable," Roger added. "One last thing, Chuck. I want your cell phone number."

Cheng's eyes darted back and forth between Roger and Aaron. "Why would I do that?"

"It's easier than if I call my contacts at customs and ask them for your number," Roger answered.

Slowly, Cheng leaned forward and pulled a pen from his jacket pocket and a piece of scrap paper. He wrote his number and slid the paper across the table to Roger.

"Good talking to you, Chuck. You have a good rest of the day. Aaron and I need to try and find our missing person," Roger said as he pushed himself out of the chair. Aaron did the same. As they walked away, Roger summoned JJ for a pick-up.

"Why don't you go up to your room and get changed? Put on dark clothes and your running shoes. That'll eliminate one stop later today. JJ and I will wait in the car," Roger suggested.

* * * * *

In his flat, Roger changed into all-black clothes and comfortable rubber-soled shoes. He sorted through a cardboard box in the corner of his bedroom and found a small video camera. He plugged it into the wall so it would be powered up for the evening. Next, he located an adapter for the camera in case it needed to continue powering up in the car.

"What's your operational plan?" Aaron asked as he watched Roger's preparations.

"We want to get to the Tai Po area before dark and give Meilin a chance to identify this house while we still have light. If we're lucky and she can identify the place, you, me, and Ray can scout around before it's completely dark. JJ can stay with Meilin while we look around. Then we find a place nearby to wait for it to get dark before we move in on the house," Roger explained. "If we're lucky, Meilin has a great memory, we find Kellie still there, we come back, and we'll all live happily ever after."

"It's all starting to sound too good to be true," Aaron remarked.

"Yeah, it does," Roger agreed. "Here, take this." Roger handed Aaron a small backpack. "I'll give you the small video camera. Depending on what happens, you can capture some things on it so we have evidence."

Roger's cell phone rang. "Damn. It's Ray. Never good when he calls before the agreed meet time."

"Roger, I'm just checking if we're still green-lighted."

"Yeah, you had me worried. You usually don't call unless there's a problem. We're good. See you very soon."

"I have the toolkit fully stocked," Ray said and ended the call.

Roger went through a short checklist, writing down what he needed to take and who would do what in case the house was occupied by several people, including Kellie. He had a small bag with ropes, some zip ties, and several pairs of gloves. He threw several bottles of water into the bag and handed the video camera to Aaron.

Roger hesitated. "Am I forgetting anything?"

"Yeah, you'd better call and let Meilin know we're on the way. Otherwise, we'll be twiddling our thumbs for a while when we get to her hotel," Aaron advised.

Roger made the call to Guang's phone and told him that they'd be there to pick up Meilin shortly. Given the late afternoon time, traffic would be getting worse.

"Time to go and meet up with Ray and pick up Meilin," Ray instructed.

JJ drove in the mid-afternoon traffic and the usual congestion. "JJ, Meilin, and I will be in the car. I'll have Ray stay back a little. That double cab pickup he drives around is noticeable here. It attracts attention because of its size, but we need to have the extra space. Aaron, you'll ride with Ray. It'll give you two time to get to know each other."

JJ drove through the slow traffic as the buses and cars jockeyed from lane to lane. The hotels and shopping at Pacific Place attracted a crowd. As JJ pulled up toward the Conrad Hotel, Roger saw Ray's black double cab truck already parked. Ray had maneuvered and backed into a spot he could easily vacate.

Roger and Aaron got out of the car. When Ray saw them, he got out to greet them.

"Ray, this is Aaron Foster."

Ray had a strong grip when he shook hands with Aaron. Aaron thought he was in good physical condition, but seeing Ray made him realize that he would have to live in a gym to be anything like Ray. Aaron thought Ray had to be wearing a shirt that was a couple of sizes larger than a normal person would need just so his muscled chest would fit into the shirt. The muscular upper arms were like those of a weightlifter, but Ray had a trim waist—no body fat. The man was impressive, Aaron thought.

"I'll show you the toolkit," Ray said as he walked to the rear of the truck and unlatched the tailgate. The toolkit looked like a small version of a metal footlocker. Because he had backed into the spot, the three of them blocked any clear view into the toolkit. It had a few knives with sheaths that could be put on a belt. Ray took a knife and gave one to Roger. He opened a compartment in the locker and handed Roger a Glock 27 pistol and took one for himself. Both men released the magazine and checked that they were full.

Ray picked up a stack of neatly folded balaclavas, not taking them out of the box but showing them to Roger and Aaron. "We'll wear these if we find the place and enter. We don't need anyone identifying us."

"I sure as hell hope we don't need to use these," Roger said just above a whisper as he let the weight of the Glock rest in the palm of his hand.

"You want anything else out of here?" Ray asked.

"Not right now. We can take the balaclavas out later."

"Of course," Ray said. "We don't even know we'll find the place, right?"

"Aaron's going to ride with you, and I'll be in the car with JJ and our guide. Don't be right on our tail. Your truck is an attention grabber. I'll call Meilin, and we'll get going," Roger suggested.

Ray and Aaron climbed into the truck and waited. Ray kept a steady watch on the hotel entrance.

"There she is," Aaron said.

"You're kidding. She looks like a little kid," Ray observed. He watched as she got into the front passenger seat of Roger's car. As JJ pulled away, Ray put his truck in gear and was ready to follow.

"How long will it take to get to this Tai Po area?"

"Given the time of day, this could take a bit of time. It could be an hour or hour and half. We're getting into the rush congestion, and we've got some distance to cover. That's compounded by the fact that our guide may not really know where this place is located. We might take some wrong turns, need to backtrack, and get lost. Who knows? We could end up coming back without ever finding this house," Ray offered.

"Understood. Is your toolkit passed down from Roger?"

"I think it gets updated and restocked by each of us who comes into this job, but we have to be careful. We don't tell people about the toolkit, and we definitely don't tell people what's in the toolkit," Ray said with a quick glance at Aaron.

"I appreciate you doing this," Aaron said.

"Roger said you're a customs guy. Since it's coming from him and he says we need to do something, that's enough for me. Until you prove otherwise, you're one of the good guys on the team."

Unlike Kellie's observations of the landscape and scenery, Aaron rode without noticing the landscape. His mind was preoccupied. He hoped he'd see Kellie by the end of the night. He wondered what he would do if they didn't find the house or if they found it without her there. He shook his head.

"Are you all right?" Ray asked, noticing Aaron's head moving out of the corner of his eye.

"Yeah," Aaron said just above a whisper.

Ray kept a constant distance behind JJ, allowing for a car or two between them but never falling too far behind. They'd been on the road for about seventy-five minutes when he saw JJ pull off the road and turn his emergency blinkers on. Ray drove past and turned into a small parking area in front of a little store about a half mile past JJ's location.

Ray's cell phone rang. "What's up?" he answered. He was looking down the road in JJ's direction but couldn't see the car due to the curve in the road. "Will do," Ray said and headed back on the road, keeping the phone line open and handing the phone to Aaron.

Ray circled back in JJ's direction and about a hundred yards past where JJ was stopped. Ray made a sharp right turn onto a road that was a lane and a half wide, except that Ray's truck took up the whole road, making it difficult for two-way traffic. He slowed after making the turn. He was moving at about ten miles per hour and looking into his rearview mirror, waiting to see JJ's car make the turn behind him. Aaron leaned forward and looked into the passenger side mirror. When JJ turned onto the road, Ray veered over to the left as far as possible to let JJ pass.

"Stay back, and we'll go on ahead and see if Meilin recognizes anything," Roger said over the open phone line.

Ray stopped and idled on the side of the road. "Let's wait and see what happens for a few minutes," Ray suggested.

Despite a wide view of the road and terrain in front of her, Meilin leaned slightly forward in the front seat of JJ's car, concentrating and looking at both sides of the road. She remembered the turn off after they had passed it a few minutes ago, but this wasn't the only road that veered off from the main road. The elevation of the road on the passenger side and the slight drop-off on JJ's side had caught her attention a few minutes ago.

"This hasn't changed at all over the years," Meilin said as she kept sweeping the area with her eyes on both sides of the road. "You should go a little faster," she said as she saw some markers at the end of a driveway they were approaching. She sat back and stared at the cylindrical concrete markers. "I think that was the house," she said. "It looks much bigger than I remember. Maybe he added to the house. I'm sure about those markers at the end of the driveway."

Ray and Aaron listened to Meilin on the phone.

JJ kept driving. He and Roger started looking for a place where they could park and walk back to the house.

"Ray, JJ will look for a place where we can park our vehicles and make our way back to the house. If we can't find a place, we may have to consider a bit of a longer hike than anticipated," Roger said over the phone.

JJ drove about a mile past the house. There was nowhere to park two vehicles without it looking suspicious. "JJ, turn around and let's head back to the main road," Roger instructed.

Hearing Roger's instruction, Ray got his truck turned around and waited for JJ to come by. When he saw JJ appear in the mirror, Ray put his truck in gear. He watched as JJ stopped behind the truck and ran up to say something.

"Back to where you stopped earlier."

Ray led them back to where he had pulled in and stopped. There was a small parking lot, and the only thing that might raise any suspicion was the oversized American pick-up.

"Unfortunately, we're going to have to walk back to the house," Roger said, disappointed. "The house sits on the north or northwest side of the road. Across the road from the house, there's a very gradual slope and no houses. There's enough shrubbery on the opposite side for us to use as our cover. We grab whatever we think we'll need and get there before it gets dark, then wait until it is dark to approach the house," Roger suggested.

Speaking in Chinese, JJ turned to Meilin. "We're going to be parked here for a while. You should go into the store and buy some water and some snacks so that it doesn't look too strange that we've pulled in and parked without anyone going out or getting anything."

When Meilin got out to go to the convenience store, Ray went to the back of the truck and got the balaclavas, zip ties, ropes, and flashlights. He and Roger had the hardware they needed, and Aaron had the video camera in his bag. They hoped that they were sufficiently equipped.

Before Meilin got more than a few steps away, Roger stopped her with a question. "What makes you sure that's the right house?"

"The snakes," Meilin answered. "We've driven by many places, but I remembered when I saw them. It is not just the round, tall stone, but it's the snakes carved into the stone that convinced me."

"We need to give ourselves time to walk up there before complete darkness. It's nearly two miles of walking, so we need to start moving," Ray suggested.

"JJ, maybe you should stay with the vehicles just in case anyone wonders what's going on, and you'll be able to handle that," Roger decided.

Ray, being the fittest, took the lead in a single file along the road. Meilin followed Ray, with Aaron and Roger walking in the rear. They walked as far off the driving lanes as possible, but the cars swooshing by were only a few feet away as there was no sidewalk. The road was not paved with pedestrians in mind. Because they were all wearing black clothing, a couple of cars blared their horns at the last second as drivers weren't expecting to see anyone walking along the road.

Ray took up a brisk pace, and Meilin found herself jogging at times as her short stature meant she fell a little farther behind with each one of Ray's longer strides. For only four people, they were strung out farther than they should have been. When it was time to cross the road, Ray checked his watch. Seventeen minutes had passed since they started. He estimated that they'd covered the first mile. It would take at least that long to get to the covering brush as the narrower road where the house was located had a slight uphill incline.

Aaron felt comfortable, but he could hear Roger's labored breathing as they started up the slight incline. Aaron slowed to let Roger come within a stride. "Are you all right?"

"Yeah, I'm fine. I hadn't really planned on a forced march," Roger answered. "One thing about Ray, when it's time to be on mission, he's completely into it, no holds barred."

As the house came into view, Meilin ran up to Ray. "Up there," she said, pointing.

Although the sun had already set, Ray decided it was still too light. He nodded and led them off the road. Just as Roger had described it, Ray found some shrubbery and a nice patch of grass for them to stop and sit. They were across the road from the house and about thirty yards from it. They'd sit and wait till it was completely dark.

"How do you want to do this?" Ray asked as he squatted and looked at Roger. Roger got down on one knee, then Meilin and Aaron got down on a knee.

Roger explained. "There's a long driveway that runs along one side of the house. Ray, go to the back of the house and see if you can peek into the windows and see anything. If there's a back door, try it to see if it's open. I'll stay at the front of the house, with Aaron and Meilin following me. I'll position myself so I can see you along the back. If you find a back door and it's unlocked, bend down and flash your flashlight once at ankle level. Flash twice if it's locked.

"Once I've seen your signal, I'll flash my light once when I start to the front door with Aaron and Meilin accompanying me. Any questions?" In the fading light, Roger had trouble seeing any head nods. No one spoke. He assumed there were no questions.

Roger, looking at Meilin and Aaron, said, "Put the balaclavas on when we reach the end of the driveway. If anyone is in there, Meilin, we'll need you to be our interpreter. Are you ready?"

"Yes," whispered Meilin.

Before making any move toward the house, Ray handed one of the balaclavas to Meilin. "Put it on," he directed. He watched as Meilin pulled it over her head. The open part of the balaclava was much too low, and her eyes and nose were covered. Ray pulled it up and gauged the size it needed to be for her.

Meilin pulled it off and handed it back to Ray. He tied the excess into a knot and let her try it on again. "Don't pull too hard," he instructed. He watched as she got it to fit, exposing her eyes and mouth. He tugged on it slightly to cover the lower half of her nose. "This way," Ray said. He didn't want anyone to be able to recognize her. "This is medium size for a man," he added. "You're very small. Now that it's fitted for you, leave it."

Ray and Roger waited another fifteen minutes when the evening sky had darkened. There was no residual light along the horizon from the setting sun. Because the moon was just beginning its ascent, it wasn't a concern. Dressed in black, pulling on the balaclavas and black gloves, Ray and Roger were hard to see as they walked out of the shrubbery and across the road and toward the driveway.

Aaron couldn't hear their footsteps. He could barely make out any dark silhouettes moving along the road despite being only a few feet behind Roger. The only light Aaron could see came through two windows on the front of the house they had targeted, one up and one down.

When they reached the driveway, Ray sprinted up the driveway to the near corner of the house. Roger followed and stopped when he got to Ray. Roger simply nodded, and Ray crouched to make his way along the side of the house to its rear. Roger stayed put where he could see the front and looked straight back along the driveway for any signal Ray might give with his flashlight.

Ray stopped by the window that was casting light outside. He glanced into the window, but a thin sheer curtain made it difficult to see what was in the room. He glanced again before crouching low and glanced from the other side of the window. He assured himself that he saw no one in the room and continued to the back of the house. He saw a vehicle and used his flashlight to make sure it wasn't occupied. The vehicle's backdoor was about five feet from the corner of the house. He grabbed the doorknob with his gloved left hand and turned it slowly. He was a little surprised when it didn't stop. It was unlocked.

Ray walked over to the corner of the house and flashed his light a few inches above the ground.

Roger, seeing Ray's signal, turned to be sure that Aaron and Meilin were just a few steps behind him, crouched by the driveway. Roger flashed his light at knee height, signaling Ray to enter the house.

"Meilin, I'm going to pound on the front door. If anyone comes to the door, I'll push them back into the house, and you need to come in right away," Roger instructed.

Ray snuck into the house and was in the unlit kitchen. He moved stealthily. Each step was slow and silent. He stayed near a wall and moved toward the front but stayed away from the room that was lit and stopped to wait for Roger to knock.

Aaron and Meilin waited at the corner of the house while Roger went up to the door. Roger knew that Ray was already inside the house. He stood at the front door, took a deep breath, then pounded on the front door.

Shing Fang, dressed in jeans, a T-shirt, and socks, was sitting on his bed. His feet on the bed, knees up, and his back against the wall, he was playing video games on a laptop. His head jerked up toward the bedroom door when he heard the knocking. Liwei had not told him about possible visitors. He put the laptop on the bed, swiveling to sit on the side of the bed. For a moment, he wondered whether to answer the door.

Roger waited, turned his head so that his ear was toward the door, and listened for any footsteps. Nothing. Roger made a fist with his right hand and pounded the door with the heel of his fist.

Shing Fang hurried down to see why someone was pounding on the door, still wondering why Liwei had not told him to expect visitors. He flipped on the light switch at the bottom of the stairway. That sent light through the transom window above the front door. He unlocked the door and started to open it.

Roger shoved the door open with force as soon as he saw it move. The door slammed into Shing Fang's face, forcing him backward, and he fell as his socks slid on the slick, polished floor. The door opened a vertical cut on Shing Fang's forehead. Blood ran down onto his nose, dripping off it.

Roger was in and standing above Shing Fang before he could move to stand. Ray moved forward as soon as he saw Shing Fang get to the door, knowing that Shing Fang had no idea that anyone else was in the house. When the door opened and slammed into Shing Fang, knocking him to the floor, Ray was standing over Shing Fang.

"Check upstairs," Roger said, and Ray was taking the steps two at a time.

Meilin and Aaron ran in and closed the door. Aaron had a video camera in the palm of his left hand.

"Shit, it's him," Aaron said. He forgot about the camera in his hand and started to lean down to grab Shing Fang but was stopped by Roger's outstretched arm.

"Take it easy," Roger urged. "Who is he?"

"Dimples," Aaron said. "Look at him. Two scars on the cheeks. He was one of the guys who mugged me at the hotel last night. He knows something. He's the one who packed up Kellie's clothes and grabbed her briefcase."

"Then he has information he can give us. Get him on tape."

Aaron was breathing heavily but stepped back and started taping and making sure he captured a good face view of Shing Fang.

"No one but us," Ray said from the top of the stairs. "I think the kitchen in the back of the house where I came in is best. Take him there."

"Who are you?" Shing Fang said in Cantonese. Meilin didn't translate it.

Roger reached down and grabbed Shing Fang's muscular right upper arm. Roger pulled the young man to his feet and pushed him forward toward the kitchen, following Ray's lead.

Meilin and Aaron followed. Meilin recognized the layout of the ground floor. She also recognized Shing Fang.

Roger dropped the small backpack he had onto the floor and pulled out short pieces of rope and a handful of zip ties. "Bring a chair and tie him to it and bind his arms."

Aaron put the video camera on the kitchen island as he and Ray followed Roger's instructions.

"I'm not sure why we're doing this," Aaron said as he zip-tied Shing Fang's hands behind the back of the chair.

"Sometimes a little intimidation goes a long way," Ray answered.

"Meilin, come over next to me while we talk to this young man," Roger instructed.

"I can tell you his name," Meilin offered. "He's Shing Fang. He drives and does errands for Liwei."

"That's fine, but let's let him confirm things," Roger said. He began the questioning through Meilin.

"Name?"

The young man's eyes studied the obscured faces of the four people in front of him. He saw nothing but eyes and mouths exposed. Tied up and having no advantage, he finally answered. "Shing Fang."

"Do you own this house?"

"No."

"Whose house is it?"

"It belongs to Hsieh Liwei."

"Will he be coming here tonight?"

"I don't know."

"Where is he?"

"I don't know."

Meilin had removed the glove from her right hand unnoticed. She took two quick steps forward. Her right hand stabbed at Shing Fang's throat, but it was a controlled move, hitting his throat without damaging it. Shing Fang's head went back then down toward his chest. He was coughing, trying to get air. "Your answers better become more helpful, or things will get much worse than that," Meilin warned in Chinese, knowing that it was an empty threat.

Shing Fang tried to smile as a way of taunting her. He was still trying to get air and coughing.

Roger, Ray, and Aaron stood staring at the tiny woman. She had moved in too fast for any of them to react. None of them knew what she had said.

Meilin stepped back next to Roger. "Sorry, but I had to do that. We can't spend all night with him," Meilin explained.

"Was . . ." Roger paused and looked at Aaron, then continued, "was Kaili here last night?"

"Yes."

"Where is Kaili now?"

"I don't know."

"You need to do something to convince him you're serious," Meilin said to her three American companions.

Roger gave Ray a nod. Ray said nothing but stepped forward and positioned himself so that he could easily put his fist into Shing Fang.

"We don't want to hear you say, 'I don't know.' If you continue to answer this way, my friend here is going to demonstrate how unhappy we are," Meilin said as she translated Roger's words.

"Where did Liwei take Kaili?"

"Maybe the mainland."

Ray's fist hit Shing Fang's left cheek hard, sending him sideways in the chair onto the floor.

Ray grabbed the chair and pulled it upright with Shing Fang still tied up.

"When was the last time you saw Liwei and Kaili?"

"This morning."

Aaron whispered in Roger's ear. "Ask him if he drove an older man to a meeting. I thought I saw him outside by the car in front of the building where you had your meeting."

"What? Why didn't you say something earlier?" Roger wasn't happy to learn that bit of information until now. "Did you drive Mr. Qian Rong to a meeting this morning?"

Meilin hesitated, looking up at Roger. "I know Mr. Qian. He was at the same meeting as Kaili."

"Ask him," Roger insisted.

Shing Fang confirmed that he had driven Mr. Qian. Something was wrong, and Roger stood with hands on hips looking at Shing Fang. "This guy's just a gofer," Roger said, sharing a thought with the others.

"What did you do after you finished driving Mr. Qian?"

"I came here. I've been here since I returned."

"What did Liwei say about what he and Kaili would do or where they would go today?"

Shing Fang shrugged. "He wants to show her some of his operations. She said something about lists. I wasn't part of their conversation."

"Where are Liwei's operations?" Roger asked.

"Liwei has a lot of business going on in Guangzhou Province. He has an office across the border in Shenzhen," Meilin explained.

Aaron stopped filming and put the camera on the kitchen's granite island. "Kellie, or Kaili, doesn't have a visa for China."

"No, but she does have a Mainland Travel Permit," Meilin said.

"What? How? She told me she had nothing to get her across the border," Aaron insisted, staring at Meilin.

"I don't know that this guy has much more he can tell us," Ray interjected.

Roger nodded in agreement. "This thing seems to be very contained within a small group of people. Meilin, ask him who Liwei works for."

"I can answer that. Liwei is part of the China International Production Network."

Roger looked away from Meilin and at Shing Fang. *This is a fucking mess,* he thought. China International Production Network was part of ChiTran, and he worked for ChiTran. What did Rong know that he failed to mention earlier in the morning? Did Rong know about Liwei's abduction of Kellie when he had met with the older man in the morning?

"Meilin, ask him, when will Liwei or someone come back to the house?" Roger prompted.

"I stay here till someone calls and needs me. Maybe it's Liwei or it's someone else, but I don't know when," Shing Fang said. Blood had dried on his forehead and nose, and there were drops of blood on his shirt and pants. His left cheek was swollen and red from Ray's fist.

"If we're done with him, what do we do with him?" Aaron asked.

"Leave him the way he is. He won't die in the next day or two if he stays tied up. We'll come back to check, see if anyone's come back. If someone calls and he doesn't answer, somebody might show up and untie him," Roger said.

"What about food, water, and bathroom?" Meilin worried aloud.

"He should be okay for thirty-six to forty-eight hours. I promise, we'll come and check on him. Now, we know how to find the house," Roger answered.

"Will he be able to get loose?" Meilin asked.

"No, I bound him tight, and he was still bound to that chair after I knocked him over and pulled him back up," Ray said.

"We'll get out of here and reassess the situation," Roger said.

Ray went and made sure the front door was closed and locked. He turned off the lights that Shing Fang had turned on when he came down. The four of them exited the house through the back door that Ray had used to enter. Light from the kitchen spilled out through the window.

"Give me a few seconds to make sure everything is still quiet out front. Wait here," Ray suggested.

They removed the balaclavas and gloves as soon as they were in front of the house. They walked about a hundred yards when Roger called JJ to come get them. They crammed into one car for the short ride back to Ray's truck.

Chapter 7

Dilemma

Hong Kong (Thursday, May 14)

"I can't give you any time in the morning. I'll be with the visiting delegation. So, if there's anything more we need to do, let's do it tonight," Ray insisted as he looked at Roger in the front seat of his truck. They were parked near Roger's flat.

"It's late."

"It's getting later by the minute, so make a decision," Ray barked.

"All right. I'll call my customs shadow, and we'll meet with him first. I think I need your take on exactly what is said at that meeting. I still want to meet with Meilin's father, but I can meet with Meilin and her father later. I can give you a recap of that conversation tomorrow or when you have time. You have any suggestion or preference on where we meet my customs shadow?"

"I'd suggest a seedy bar in Tsim Sha Tsui that has a few booths if you know one," Ray suggested. "We won't be seen there, and we can block him in during the conversation."

"Good idea. There are a few I've passed just a few blocks from here," Roger said. Earlier in the evening, Roger had put Cheng Gao's phone number in his pocket. He pressed the numbers on his cell phone and waited. It rang several times before it was answered.

"Chuck, this is your favorite American calling," Roger said, smiling at Ray.

"Who?"

"Roger Steeg. We met formally at the Marriott earlier today." Roger waited for a response.

Cheng Gao had drifted off to sleep on his sofa after a couple of beers. He swung his legs around to the floor and sat up. "Yes, yes."

"Meet me in an hour," Roger said, then explained that Cheng should take a taxi to the intersection of Hanoi, Hart, and Mody roads and hung up.

Roger turned to Ray. "I'll have JJ drive Aaron over here with the video camera and let JJ go for the night. When Chuck gets here, Aaron and I will take him to the bar. Hang back a few minutes and make sure he didn't contact anybody to follow."

After leaving Shing Fang at the house, JJ had driven Meilin and Aaron back to Hong Kong while Roger rode with Ray. His first stop was dropping Meilin at the Conrad Hotel, where she would wait for Roger or Aaron to call but was warned it could be hours. JJ sat up when he felt the vibration of his phone. It was time to swing back around to the Marriott entrance and take Aaron to the meeting spot.

"Tired?" Aaron asked as JJ drove him back to Kowloon.

"Not tired. I'm worried."

"Worried about what?"

"Different people, new people, coming from different places. This is a very strange situation. It feels different from Roger's usual work," JJ offered.

Aaron wouldn't disagree with that. It was different for him, too. He rode the rest of the way without saying anything. He watched as JJ made a few turns and stopped behind Ray's truck. "Thanks."

"Maybe I'll see you in the morning," JJ said. He drove off, leaving Aaron standing behind the truck.

"Time for us to take a walk," Roger said as he and Ray exited the truck. "You've got the camera, right?"

"Got it."

Roger explained the plan to Aaron. The three men, still wearing dark clothes, walked a few blocks to the intersection that Roger had designated as the meeting point. There was still time to kill. Ray chose the darkest spot near the intersecting streets for his position. He found a closed and darkened storefront with a small canvas awning and leaned into the doorway, hoping that any headlights from oncoming cars wouldn't expose him.

Roger chose separate places around the intersection for him and Aaron to wait. When Cheng arrived, they would meet him and take him to the bar they had chosen. They would also divert his attention to prevent him from seeing Ray. After standing around for ten minutes as cars drove by, Aaron and Roger saw a car slowing and noticed it was a taxi. It stopped where Aaron stood.

Cheng opened the back door, paying the fare before getting out. Aaron waved Roger over. "Good to see you, Chuck," Roger said. Cheng said nothing. He was a very lean young man and stood a couple of inches shorter than Aaron. He wore a dark sweater over his buttoned-down white shirt.

"Did you call your office or your supervisor or bosses?" Roger asked.

"No, no one."

"Good. Let's go somewhere and talk." Roger led the way. Cheng followed, with Aaron walking behind him.

They walked a block to a bar that had a neon light in the shape of a martini glass flashing and entered. The dimly lit bar wasn't very wide, with the bar itself running along one side of the room, and about six feet away, several small two-top tables were placed along the opposite wall. At the far end, where the bar ended, there were five booths.

"Hey, big man, good to see again," a middle-aged Chinese woman said as Roger entered, followed by Cheng and Aaron. Roger smiled and waved at the woman behind the bar. There were no customers at the bar, but two young women wearing very short skirts, revealing tank tops, and spiked heels sat together at one of the two-top tables by the wall, looking at the three men.

Roger chose the last booth and motioned Cheng to slide in so that a wall was behind him, and he faced the entrance. Roger sat next to Cheng, boxing him into the corner. Aaron slid in across from them. A few seconds later, the woman from behind the bar appeared.

"Drinks?"

"Four beers and keep the girls away. Thanks," Roger said.

"Why meet so late?" Cheng asked when the barmaid had left.

"We have something to show you, but we'll wait for our drinks," Roger answered. He saw Ray entering and waved.

After Ray settled in next to Aaron and the beers were delivered, Aaron put the video camera on the table.

"We have a video of one of the men who made our friend go missing." Roger started the video camera and adjusted the volume so Cheng could hear what was being said above the background music in the bar.

"Stop! Who was that?" Cheng asked. He saw an arm and hand flash by Shing Fang's face.

"That's not important." Roger continued the tape till it ended. Aaron had kept the camera focused on Shing Fang and never turned it toward anyone wearing the balaclavas.

"Do you recognize him?" Roger asked.

"No. I'm sure I would remember the scars."

"What about the names Qian Rong or Hsieh Liwei?"

"Qian Rong is familiar. He's very high up in a trading company."

"You said you were watching me because I'm a person of interest, and that's because of other people who are interesting to your bosses, right?"

"Qian Rong and the man you were meeting with, Lai Guang, are connected. It's a Taiwan–Mainland connection through ChiTran. They meet in Hong Kong and are shipping high volumes of products out," Cheng said.

"What's the problem?" Ray jumped in and asked.

"Hong Kong is being blamed for the poor products that they're making in the mainland and shipping from here."

"Now you have another problem. You just heard this guy on tape say that Hsieh has taken an American citizen across the border to the mainland. We want her to be let go," said Roger.

"Not our jurisdiction if she's in the mainland," Cheng answered.

"That's true, but if you know Qian Rong and now you know Hsieh Liwei and how they are using Hong Kong to ship goods, you can make their lives more complicated by increasing inspections as soon as they cross the border or before their containers are loaded onto ships," Ray added.

"I don't make these types of decisions," Cheng insisted.

"No, but you can say that you've learned something based on your surveillance of me. Maybe you'll even get credit for the good work," Roger suggested.

"I can talk to your bosses," Ray added. He pulled his official identification out of his pocket and put it on the table.

Cheng slid it closer to look at Ray's identification. "You're the American customs officer here?"

Ray nodded to confirm Cheng's question. "I'll check with my Hong Kong Customs contacts to be sure you report what we've shown you."

"Can I have the tape or a copy?" Cheng asked.

"We'll get you a copy," Roger assured him. "Take a break and follow someone else tomorrow," Roger said as he stood up to let Cheng leave.

They gave Cheng time to get outside and get a taxi before they got up to leave.

"How do you want to play this out? Do you want me to bring it up with the small Washington delegation that's here? Hong Kong Customs is already on the agenda," Ray offered.

"We have a couple of friends at customs, so why not tighten a few loose screws on ChiTran? People at ChiTran know that some of their companies and associates are involved. They're messing with us by taking Kellie across the border, and we know they're trading in some dangerous stuff. Yeah, raise it with the delegation, and if you're at these meetings, take your customs guys aside and have a heart-to-heart chat," Roger said.

Listening to the back and forth, Aaron wondered if Roger was putting himself in a losing situation. He now understood that Roger worked for Mr. Qian and ChiTran but was working against his employer by agreeing to have Ray make this a government question.

Roger threw down enough Hong Kong dollars to cover the beers that were never consumed. He considered it payment for the use of the table and having the girls kept away.

* * * * *

"Do you need to call your cousin?" Meilin asked.

"Yes, but I'm trying to decide how I explain the situation," Guang answered. "He knows his daughter is missing. I don't want to tell him that we found the house where she was taken, but now we don't know where she is. I suspect that Liwei has taken her across the border, but this is not a certainty."

"They must be across the border. Liwei's operations are all there, not in Hong Kong. He tries to make it sound like he has all these different facilities, but he has only one place where he has different lines of products. To impress everyone, he makes it sound like the different things he's doing in one facility are taking place at many different facilities," Meilin explained.

"You seem to know a lot about Liwei."

"He's easy to understand. And, in some ways, he's still a competitor. I like to know what others in the consortium are up to."

"At least I can tell Kaili's father we believe she's in the mainland, who she's with and what she's doing. This should do away with any concerns he has. I'll just say she'll be there for a few days," Guang said. "The important thing is that we buy ourselves time."

* * * * *

Early the morning after drugging Kellie at his house, Liwei had carried her down to the car. She was leaning into the corner of the back seat with a small pillow for her head. She was still out of it from the sedative that she had drunk in the tea she was served. He sat behind Tengfei, who was in the driver's seat. It was shortly after dawn when they left the house and headed toward the border. Liwei put Kellie's documents in his pocket. He and Tengfei crossed the border regularly. They weren't strangers to the Chinese and Hong Kong immigration officers at the border.

When Liwei found Kellie's Mainland Travel Permit, it was an unexpected gift. Initially, he thought he'd have to keep her at the house. But with the Travel Permit, he could take her to one of the employee apartments he had. He could hold her Travel Permit and passport for a few days so he could wring more information out of her before letting her go back to Hong Kong.

Tengfei slowed as traffic backed up to enter the mainland. When it was their turn to have their documents checked, Tengfei lowered the driver's side front and back windows. Liwei handed over documents for himself and Kellie.

"Very late night. She's still not awake," Liwei said to the Chinese immigration officer who glanced at the Mainland Travel Permit. With Kellie's head leaned back and turned away from the immigration officer, he couldn't see her face but waved them across, having seen Liwei and Tengfei a number of times.

Tengfei drove north of Shenzhen's central downtown district. Shenzhen was a growing city attracting thousands of people to its expanding industrial areas. The people were arriving for new work faster than the city could accommodate everyone.

Liwei used his ChiTran connections to his advantage. The money was there for him to grow north of the city center in the Longgang district. He had enough land there, about fifteen acres, to put up a few cheap housing buildings. He maintained on-site living quarters for over a hundred employees.

There were a few walled-off living quarters that might be generously called apartments for his first-line foremen since they had private bathing, sleeping, and sitting areas within the larger employee residential buildings. Each of these had a private phone line to the main company office, where Liwei kept his office. These phones connected to the general office, nowhere else. Anyone wanting to call someone outside the office needed to use a personal cell phone. Most of the employees didn't have the money to buy a phone.

For the rest of the workers, the living quarters were more like military barracks. Making living quarters available ensured that employees were on-time and didn't have to commute through the chaos of the growing city and the unplanned roads that seemed to appear overnight in some industrial areas, creating traffic chaos. The men and women who worked for Liwei lived in separate buildings.

The complex was surrounded by an eight-foot-high chain-linked fence to keep people out. There was one gate entry for trucks and other vehicles and two pedestrian gates. Although Liwei made sure there were "No Trespassing" signs around the facility, he didn't maintain security. That, he believed, was an unnecessary expense. Inside the fence, trees and shrubs were planted along the whole perimeter to add some greenery. A few feet from the tree and shrub line, there was a sidewalk that ringed the perimeter with benches placed at various intervals. There was no mistaking the complex for a park, but Liwei attempted to eliminate the harsh look of a workplace for his employees living on the grounds. He believed these little things improved productivity and enhanced his bottom line.

Liwei's operations assembled parts into residential and business safety products like smoke detectors, carbon monoxide detectors, fire extinguishers, and other home safety products. He also dealt in lots of leather goods with an assortment of bags, everything from purses and wallets to school backpacks. In one far corner of the fenced area, there was an "off-limits" building. This was the only place where Liwei maintained security, but there was nothing to identify the type of activity that occurred in the building.

Liwei's personal office was outside the fence in a five-story-high office building, but a five-minute walk through one of the pedestrian gates put him into his production facility. He had Tengfei drive through the gate and stop by the closest building that housed his workers.

"Tengfei, go in and tell Yuming that she needs to vacate her room for a few days so a guest can stay there. Make sure she understands what I expect. I know there are some empty spaces she can take. She doesn't have to move everything. Just have her move some things quickly. We'll put Kaili there. I'll stay in the car with Kaili. Let me know when you're ready for us," Liwei instructed.

Tengfei left the car. Liwei turned toward Kellie in the back seat and patted her cheek. She had slept soundly during the drive. Liwei was wondering how much sedative Shing Fang had put in the tea. Kellie hadn't shown any signs of the drug starting to wear off when he carried her down to the car. The car's movement in turns or hitting a few bumps along the way did nothing to rouse her from her sleep.

Liwei tapped both cheeks with his hand. Kellie moved her head but didn't open her eyes. He was sitting back comfortably in the car when, ten minutes later, he saw Tengfei walking to the car and giving a thumbs up. Liwei got out and walked to Kellie's side of the car so he could swing her legs out and carry her in. He reached in to pull her forward.

"No, no," she said, opening her eyes and seeing Liwei just inches from her face.

Liwei stepped back. "It's all right. I was going to help you out of the car."

Kellie squinted. The bright morning sun was hard on her eyes. She looked around, saw the interior of the car, Liwei standing by the car's open rear door, and another man waiting slightly behind Liwei.

"Where are we? What's going on?"

"I wanted you to see my facility," Liwei answered.

"But where are we?" Her head was still foggy. She remembered it was later in the evening when she had entered Liwei's house.

"Why don't you freshen up, and we'll show you around, and then we can talk after that," Liwei suggested.

Kellie felt groggy. She scooted to the edge of the seat and got her feet on the ground. She pushed herself out of the car and stood. Looking around, she thought for a moment that she had been dropped into a prison facility. She used the car door's frame and armrest to hold herself up. For her, Liwei's attempt to place shrubs and trees inside the fencing made her think she could be in a minimum-security prison. The buildings and the fencing looked like an updated version of World War II prison camps she remembered from movies, documentaries, and pictures in history books.

Kellie looked around. "I don't care that this is all yours. Tell me where I am!"

"We're in Shenzhen," Liwei answered.

"How did you get me across the border without documents?"

"We got your documents, and we brought some of your clothes."

Kellie's eyes darted to Tengfei and back to Liwei. "How? The only way to get my clothes was to go to the hotel, and the only way to get my documents was to go through my personal bag." She was fighting through her mental fog.

"I sent Tengfei here and someone else to get your things," Liwei said casually.

"Who the hell do you think you are? And did your boys meet my friend?" Kellie moved slightly toward Liwei and straightened herself so that she was nearly eye-to-eye with him.

Tengfei took a step toward his boss, who put out a hand at his side to stop Tengfei from coming closer.

"There was a minor difference of opinion, but it's my understanding that everything is fine," Liwei explained.

"Does he know where I am?" Kellie asked.

"My associates don't speak much English, so they didn't stay to engage in a conversation about your whereabouts," Liwei said.

Kellie's eyes opened wider, then glared at Liwei. She realized Aaron had no idea where she was and, since she hadn't told him anything about her meeting, would have no way to figure out where she could be. She stood by the open car door, her mind racing as she thought about how Aaron might try to locate her. Would he call her family, reach out to Roger, call the police, who else?

"Can you walk?" Liwei asked in Chinese.

The question broke her train of thought.

"Yes, just give me a moment." She wanted the anger to subside, and she needed to quiet the many thoughts colliding in her head.

Liwei motioned for Tengfei to get Kellie's bag out of the trunk.

Kellie walked to the back of the car. When the trunk lid opened, she gave Tengfei a shove to his shoulder with both hands, causing him to hop to his left on one leg to keep from falling to the ground. When he regained his balance and was back on both feet, she saw him take two aggressive steps toward her when Liwei stepped in to prevent Tengfei from retaliating.

Kellie lifted her carry-on bag, putting it upright in the trunk before grabbing the handle. She gripped the handle and swung it in Liwei's direction, barely missing his chest as he saw what she was doing in time to take a step back and lean away from her. She smiled at him as he straightened up, but her eyes looked at him with contempt for what he had done by bringing her to his facility.

Kellie stood, holding the bag in her hand. "Now what?"

Liwei motioned Tengfei to take her bag.

"I think I've shown that I can manage it myself."

Liwei nodded his agreement. He finally found his voice again. "There's a phone inside. Have someone call the office when you've freshened up, and I'll come to show you around," said Liwei, ignoring her anger and questions.

Kellie followed Tengfei into the employee dormitory and the private apartment. "Use the phone on the desk to call the office when you're ready," Tengfei said and left Kellie standing in the room.

The so-called apartment was in the corner of the building and had two windows that provided enough natural light that she didn't need to turn on the lamps or ceiling light. Kellie stared at the phone. It was a dated telephone. At least it had push-button numbers rather than a rotary dial. She picked up the handset and heard a dial tone. She needed to find phone numbers before she could call anyone. She placed the one bag stuffed with her clothes, her briefcase, and the small bag she had with her at the meeting by the door. She paged through her address book and realized she didn't have the number to the Marriott, and she never asked Roger for his number. She'd have to think of another way to contact Aaron. But first, she needed to know how to use this phone.

Kellie left her room and went out into the open area of the living quarters and saw a young woman tidying up. "Excuse me," Kellie said in Cantonese.

Yuming Pei, who had just been told to give up her apartment for this stranger, stopped and turned. Although she was only twenty-five years old, Yuming was one of the experienced workers and had worked her way up over three years. Her short black hair framed a round face with small eyes. She was several inches shorter than Kellie but looked athletic in her black pants and bright-orange polo-style shirt.

Yuming took a couple of seconds to give Kellie a good look. She was used to seeing foreign businessmen arrive and visit the facilities, but not women. She quickly saw some of Kellie's Chinese physical features, but she looked different. Kellie's height and slightly Western facial features made her look foreign in Yuming's eyes.

"Can I help you?"

Kellie introduced herself in Chinese. "I want to make a phone call from that room. Are there special numbers I need to dial to call Hong Kong?"

"Sorry, I'm not sure I understand what you want to know about making a phone call," Yuming answered.

The two women stood looking at each other as if there was a stand-off. Kellie hadn't understood everything Yuming had said, although she was certain that her Cantonese was fine. Yuming had understood some but not all that Kellie had said.

Kellie repeated her question with hand gestures and then motioned for Yuming to follow her back to the room. With Yuming standing next to her, Kellie picked up the handset. "Hong Kong," she said, then pretended to press numbers on the phone and shrugged.

"No, no," Yuming said in Chinese. She pointed to the phone, saying, "Office only."

"Thank you," Kellie said. She guessed that Yuming must have come to work here from a different province some distance away, and they had spoken different dialects. That could cause some problem understanding each other. Kellie also reminded herself that she wasn't a native speaker, and that might have contributed to the difficulty communicating.

Yuming pointed to herself and hand-gestured that she was leaving. "Work."

Kellie smiled. "Thank you," she said again as Yuming left. She closed the door, and now that she was alone, she locked the door as it gave her some measure of control. As she sat down, she realized she didn't know where she was in China, and she had no way of contacting Aaron. While she was still in the clothes she had worn to the meeting the day before, other than feeling a bit groggy, she had no aches or pains. She started to explore her living accommodations. Kellie was relieved to find a modern bathroom with a shower.

A long shower cleared the mental fog Kellie felt when she first opened her eyes and was getting out of the car. The May sun on the windows raised the temperature in the room, and she dabbed sweat from her face and neck. Looking around, she realized air conditioning did not come with the room. She combed her long black hair and let it air dry. She found a pair of jeans and a sky-blue-colored blouse to put on but realized she had no change of shoes. Thankfully, she had opted for something comfortable when she went to the meeting.

Showered and dressed, she sat on a straight-back wooden chair. There were no creature comforts in this place. Her initial impression of the place being like a prison returned to her. She felt a wave of panic through her body. She closed her eyes, trying to redirect her fear and her negative thoughts. She told herself, *Don't dwell or waste mental energy on something you can't control. Whatever Aaron was doing was completely out of her control.*

Liwei bringing her across the border was also no longer something she could control. Time to deal with what was coming next. She had been sitting for a couple of minutes in silence. She put her hand to her forehead and closed her eyes, trying to gather her thoughts. One thing was certain, sitting alone in this room was not going to help her.

After calling the office, Kellie went outside and stood in the shade cast by the building, waiting to meet Liwei. He walked from the office building just up the street and entered through the wide vehicle entrance.

"Feeling better?"

"I couldn't feel worse," Kellie said tersely.

Liwei knew she was still angry. He understood his questionable tactics were rarely received well by those on the receiving end, but he believed they generally got him what he wanted.

"You need to understand there are reasons for the questions I was asking yesterday at the meeting," Liwei began. He wanted to justify his pressing questions from the day before. "Let me show you around. Oh, let's speak English while we are inside these buildings," Liwei suggested.

One end of each building had large doors big enough for a truck. Inside, there were rows of workspaces along with a room to line up pallets ready to ship out. Kellie saw dozens of workers assembling parts. It was a human assembly line without any mechanization. At the end of the building where she was standing, the assembled products were put in individual boxes, then stacked into a larger box to be closed, taped, and labeled.

"Residential smoke detectors and carbon monoxide detectors are assembled and boxed in here," Liwei explained.

Kellie walked over to several pallets that were each about six feet high and wrapped and ready to be trucked. She looked at the labels. "These are going to Kenya?"

"They'll go through the port in Mombasa and be distributed in the region, yes," Liwei answered.

She kept walking and looking and reading the labels. "Canada? Why not Mexico?"

"We send products to both Canada and Mexico. This just happens to be Canada."

"I don't see anything here headed to the United States."

"That's why we need to talk. I want you to see things before we have our conversation. If you remember some of the discussion at yesterday's meeting, you might remember that it was explained that we have facilitators in various parts of the world. Sometimes, it's easier to have them in places where there are fewer obstacles to getting things into the country."

"You're saying that the United States is more of a challenge," Kellie suggested.

"It depends on the product. For some of our products, places like Canada and Mexico are much easier to enter, and then the goods can be transshipped to the US," Liwei added.

Liwei walked out the door of the building, and Kellie reluctantly followed as Liwei continued with his tour of the facilities. In one of the buildings, workers were assembling small fire extinguishers designed for vehicle and residential use. In another building, one end contained large bins of zippers, handles, shoulder straps, and buckles to be assembled to make handbags and book bags of various sizes. Kellie noticed that at the end of the assembly process in each of the buildings, there were bins with different brand names that were either placed on the assembled product or boxed separately so they could be affixed to the final product after arriving in the country where they would be sold.

The more she saw, the more she understood why Liwei had asked the questions he had been pressing at the meeting. Now, her curiosity was growing, and her fear was subsiding. What about the others who were part of ChiTran? What other goods were they making, and where were they shipping things to?

Although she wanted to get back to Hong Kong, she wondered whether it was better to try and find out more about Liwei and the operations of others in ChiTran or try to get out as fast as possible.

"What about testing things like the extinguishers and smoke detectors?" Kellie queried.

"That's done elsewhere. Samples are taken regularly from batches of product," Liwei answered.

Kellie wasn't convinced about the testing but nodded rather than prompt an argument. She immediately realized the questions Liwei had peppered her with at the meeting wouldn't have been that important if Liwei's operations were on the up and up. Given her current predicament, however, she decided it was safer not to press the issue.

The tour of the facility had taken longer than she had expected. She needed time to think and formulate a plan. She yawned and feigned drowsiness. "Would it be possible for me to rest for a little while?" she asked as she yawned again.

"Of course," Liwei replied. "I'll arrange for a late lunch to be brought to my office after you rest. It'll be more comfortable there. And when we talk later, I'd like to revisit your thoughts on how to expand, what goods should be made, and where things should be exported to so we can increase our revenues. After all, I was under the impression that part of the reason for your trip to Hong Kong was to help us with these matters," Liwei said.

Back to that again, Kellie thought. "Let me go back to my room, get a little rest, and put some of my thoughts together. We can discuss it more this afternoon." She started walking toward her room with Liwei beside her.

"Just let me know when you are ready. I'll have someone walk you to my office," Liwei said as he turned and headed toward the open gate and his office.

* * * * *

As she walked back to her room, Kellie wondered what would happen if she just waited until Liwei was in his office building and she walked out. While Liwei was walking up to the door of his office building, she took a few steps in the direction of the entrance. It had no gate. She stopped. She couldn't be rash, and just walking out left too many obstacles to overcome. She didn't know where she was, she had no money, and she couldn't name anyone she knew. Most importantly, she had no documents. She turned slowly and went back to her small room.

Once alone again, Kellie realized she needed a plan if she wanted to control this situation in any way. Kellie spent her time alone writing herself notes for the afternoon. She needed a plan to appear helpful, but not too helpful. If her suspicions were true that Liwei didn't really have proper testing of some of his products, she could be putting herself at risk, helping Liwei make and export things that might seriously injure or kill people. However, if she didn't appear to be helpful at all, could she be sure that Liwei would return her to Hong Kong unharmed? After all, how would anyone know that Liwei kidnapped her and brought her to Shenzhen? No, the only course of action was to at least appear to be helpful because, above all, she needed to buy time. Only time would allow others to rescue her or allow her to come up with a plan to rescue herself.

Needing a plan and trying to create a plan helped Kellie calm herself.

* * * * *

When she was escorted to Liwei's office for lunch, she was surprised by the amount of food he had ordered.

"Come, let's sit and relax while we eat and work," Liwei suggested.

The aromas of the various dishes filled Liwei's spacious office. Kellie realized how hungry she was. She hadn't eaten since lunchtime the previous day, and even then, she had just nibbled on her food.

As she entered, she surveyed the room. It was surprisingly large and well-arranged. On one side, there was a large executive desk with a high-back leather chair for him and two large leather chairs facing the desk for guests. The opposite side of the room had a large lengthy sofa, a long glass coffee table with leather chairs flanking it, and two other leather chairs facing the sofa. The office could comfortably host a meeting of ten people. Liwei had several Monet water lily reproductions framed and hanging on the walls. One side of the office was nothing but windows. Various plates of food covered the surface of the coffee table.

"Is someone joining us?" Kellie asked.

"No. I apologize. I realized that I dragged you through the facility without anything to eat this morning," Liwei said, returning to speaking in Chinese. "I assumed you might be hungry, so I had my staff bring in a variety of dishes."

They had lunch without much conversation. Kellie was reluctant to ask Liwei questions about family or anything personal, and she didn't want to initiate their business conversation while having lunch.

Although she hadn't intended to eat so much, she suddenly realized she had finished two plates of food. Perhaps it was just as well. Who knew when she would get another meal like this? She decided it was time to start. "I've been thinking that it might be good to share my thoughts with you and others from your staff. Perhaps someone can take down some of the things I say. Then you would have something to consider with your people. During yesterday's meeting, it was very difficult at times to listen and speak in Chinese and think in English. I think I can explain in Chinese, but having someone else do any writing would make things more efficient." She was pleased to see Liwei listening and nodding in agreement.

"I'll call in my plant manager to sit in with us, and my secretary can take the notes." Liwei pulled out his cell phone and made a quick call. To avoid an awkward silence while they waited, Kellie asked Liwei about the Monet prints he had chosen for his office.

"Someone had a catalog of pictures to choose from for the office, and I saw these. The salesman explained what they were. They appealed to me. After seeing these pictures, I started to read about him and when he painted some of these pictures. It's very interesting. I hope I can visit this place, Giverny, someday."

Tapping on the door stopped Liwei's explanation. Liwei's secretary and the plant manager came into the office. It gave Kellie a chance to get up and position herself in a chair facing the sofa rather than continuing to sit on the sofa. The secretary and plant manager sat down on the sofa.

Liwei sat in the chair next to her, facing his two employees. "Ms. Liang walked through our facilities today, and she's going to share some thoughts about our operations and product exports," Liwei explained in Chinese. He looked at Kellie and nodded to signal her.

"Your operations here are very impressive. The export strategy is commendable. The products you are exporting are interesting. Nothing I saw today was labeled for destinations in the United States. I am worried that if your home safety products are exported to the US and Canada, you will put your import facilitators at some risk," Kellie began. She adopted the use of the same word as Mr. Qian used the day before. She watched Liwei's secretary jot down a few notes. The operations manager was sitting back relaxed, his one arm stretched out on the back of the sofa and legs crossed.

"Are any of the smoke detectors, extinguishers, or things like that exported to the US?" she asked.

"Not directly," Liwei answered. "The items you mentioned are sent to Mexico and Canada, but we're paid for the items. If our facilitators successfully import them, then we let them decide whether to further export them. And if so, they take care of any onward journey."

"Does that mean they are sent to the US?" Kellie pressed.

"It's possible," Liwei said.

"Have you had any problems?"

Liwei looked at his manager before answering. "We did hear of a recent shipment that was seized by American customs."

"Do you know what happened? Why?"

Kellie suspected that her earlier instincts about testing were correct.

"Perhaps we or our facilitators were not as familiar with American standards. We may need to ship what we have to other places," Liwei conceded.

"You must reconsider some of these exports if they might endanger people and you are not familiar or confident about standards," Kellie warned.

"Can we continue to ship the leather goods as usual?" the manager asked, leaning forward with arms folded and talking directly to Liwei as if Kellie wasn't part of the conversation.

"What do you think?" Liwei inquired, turning to her.

"I saw the buckles and labels of famous brands ready to be used. What do you do with them?"

Liwei paused and looked to his manager for a moment before answering. "We have orders for various products that will have these brand names on them. People like the names or designs. We're here to provide what they want. That's how this works. It's business."

"Then try to avoid direct shipments to the US. If they're found by customs inspectors, they'll add your name or the name of your facilitator to a list, and your shipments will be checked more often," Kellie warned.

"We can't stop exporting to the United States. Besides, we make sure to get our payments and let the importers on the other end deal with these issues."

"I understand that you're getting paid right now, but if you send too many shipments that end up detected and prevented from entering the market, you'll eventually lose your orders. At some point, your facilitators in other countries will decide that they're taking all the risk and they're losing money," Kellie explained.

"Do you have any suggestions?"

Kellie knew she was in a bind. Liwei wasn't about to just walk away from profits there for the taking. She needed to say something he wanted to hear. "If you're committed to making the home safety products like those detectors and extinguishers, and don't know if they meet American safety standards, limit them to your Africa and South American markets, but keep them out of the US and from your facilitators in Mexico and Canada so that they aren't tempted to forward them into the US."

Kellie was troubled that she was putting people in other parts of the world at risk, but what else could she do? First, if she tried to shut it all down, it would put Liwei out of business, so that wouldn't work. Second, if she didn't word things carefully, Liwei would construe her comments as accusing him of lying about the testing. That would also be counterproductive.

Liwei and his manager said nothing for several seconds. They looked at each other as they avoided looking at Kellie. Then, Liwei turned slightly in his chair toward her. "We'll fulfill the orders we have, then stop sending the products you've mentioned to North America, but we'll follow your suggestion. What about leather goods and other things like that?"

Kellie thought for a moment and remembered a remark Aaron had made a few months earlier. "You can do as you are doing now, or you could reduce your risks by making a minor change to your operation." Kellie paused to look at her three-person audience as they waited for her to continue. "You already have labels, buckles, and other things that have the brand names you plan to put on your products. Don't put them on the products before you export them. Send the labels, buckles, and other items with the brand names separately."

"What? Why? Our operation here is set up to ship everything together," Liwei said.

"Fine, do what you've been doing for your African and South American markets, but the US is different. The Americans are trained to stop certain things that other countries don't," she explained.

Liwei nodded, looking convinced by Kellie's suggestions and explanations. "This has been very helpful, but it'll take time to redirect because we have orders, commitments."

Kellie took a deep breath. If Liwei followed her suggestions, the only thing she accomplished was to save some Americans from untested detectors and extinguishers, but now all those things would go elsewhere. How many other people had she just put in danger? She wasn't feeling good about what she had done.

"This is a good start. My manager can begin making some adjustments to our packaging and shipping arrangements. We might be able to show you what we do in a day or so, and you can give us your input," Liwei said.

Kellie was surprised by Liwei's satisfaction with the exchange. With Liwei's positive reaction, she recommended that they stop for the day as she feigned continuing fatigue from what had been put into her system the night before.

Back in her room, Kellie opened the windows and hoped for a breeze to keep her dry. She went through a mental checklist. So far, Liwei had done nothing to physically harm her. His questions all dealt with his business. He was into some suspicious products. Somehow, it seemed to her that he wanted to appear like he was playing the game, but in reality, he was going to take risks.

She didn't feel restricted in her movements within the grounds, but she hadn't tested that theory. She knew enough about the operation to feel guilty about helping Liwei. Until she could figure out how to get back to

Hong Kong and so long as she was physically safe, she could keep her eyes open and observe Liwei's operations. Later, she could pass the information on to someone who could do something about it. Who would that be? Aaron? Roger? Her boss?

Kellie needed a phone. She needed to let someone know where she was. Otherwise, how would she ever get back to Hong Kong?

Chapter 8

Suspicions

Hong Kong (Friday, May 15)

Aaron was running on a treadmill. His shirt was sweat-soaked. He had gotten to the hotel gym at six in the morning, trying to work off the stress building after finding Liwei's house but not finding Kellie. After meeting with Cheng in the bar, he had hopped into a cab back to the hotel. He had tossed and turned for about four hours and finally gave up trying to sleep. He and Roger were set to meet with Meilin and her father this morning. By eight, Aaron was dressed and in the hotel lobby with the video camera on the table and an espresso.

When choosing a table, Aaron thought about Roger and chose a table on the fringes of the large area. It allowed Roger to have the wide view he liked so he could conduct his own surveillance.

"Don't see Chuck anywhere," Roger said as he sat down.

"He might still be asleep. You had him up late last night," Aaron quipped.

"I'm sure Meilin gave her father a detailed report of what happened. She's a real spark plug. She surprised me when she stepped in and jabbed that guy last night," Roger said, laughing. "I didn't see that coming at all. I guess I should've kept a closer eye on her after one of the exchanges when she didn't translate anything."

Aaron caught the eye of a waiter and lifted his cup, signaling he wanted another, and gestured for him to bring two.

"You're going to be buzzing this morning if you keep up this pace," Roger said.

"One's for you."

Aaron looked toward the hotel entrance and saw Guang, who slowed as he stepped into the lobby lounge and searched the room.

"He's alone. I wonder why Meilin isn't joining us," Aaron said.

Guang had a gray suit and white shirt but no necktie. "Good morning. Sorry, Meilin is running behind schedule. She said she will join us shortly. She told me what happened at Liwei's house." Guang eyed the camera on the table as he lowered himself into a chair. "Can I see the video?"

Roger and Guang switched places at the table so that the small video screen couldn't be seen by anyone other than Aaron and Guang. Aaron plugged in the earpiece so Guang could hear the audio. Although he knew what to expect, Guang watched intently. He snapped back in his chair the moment he saw Meilin's arm and hand unexpectedly stab at Shing Fang's neck. Guang leaned back in, saying, "She didn't tell me she did that."

After watching the video, Guang rubbed his chin in thought. "We need to keep this matter limited to just a few people."

"How limited?" Roger asked.

"We are only a few people who know. We need to make sure Liwei understands that Kaili must not be harmed and returned to Hong Kong. Getting more people involved doesn't help us achieve these objectives, so I believe we should not involve any more people," Guang explained.

Aaron and Roger looked at each other across the table.

"Mr. Lai, you have to be realistic. Shing Fang, who is in the video, was a driver for Mr. Qian yesterday. So I think it is safe to assume Mr. Qian knows what's going on. Also, it wasn't easy to conduct our search last night. We didn't know what would happen, so another American friend and my driver assisted us. Then, after what we heard from Shing, we met late last night with a Hong Kong Customs officer. He saw the video. I've already put my job on the line. So you need to understand, if we need to persuade Hong Kong Customs to start messing with this guy, Liwei, and his shipments, that's what I'll do," Roger said.

"No, no. That shouldn't be necessary. We should be able to take care of this situation without getting Hong Kong Customs or anyone else involved," Guang insisted. "There are other ways to convince Liwei that what he's done is unacceptable, and he must correct his behavior immediately."

"I know Mr. Qian as well," Guang continued. "Together, this will be taken care of, but please give me a day or two."

"Are you out of your mind!" Aaron blurted out, attracting the attention of people at the tables near them. Aaron, glaring at Guang, felt a firm grip take hold of his forearm and looked at Roger with fiery eyes.

"From what you're saying, am I right to think that Liwei is part of ChiTran?" Roger asked and continued without letting Guang answer. "What, exactly, is Liwei's company in China?"

Guang didn't want to divulge that information but didn't believe he could withhold it and have Roger trust him. "It's called ChiTran Guangdong Specialties Company."

The palms of Roger's hands slapped the table louder than he intended. Guang wasn't the only person who snapped back into his chair as a few others at nearby tables instantly craned their necks toward the three men.

Roger pushed himself out of his chair. "Okay, two days, but I need to make a couple of calls to put the brakes on a couple of things," he said and walked away to make the calls privately.

Once he was on the other side of the room, Roger dialed Ray.

"Have you met with your delegation yet?" Roger asked.

"I'm on the way now to meet them. Don't worry, your matter is on my agenda."

"Don't say anything now. Meilin's father assures us that he can deal with this."

"You'd better be sure about this. They're only here today and tomorrow to meet with their Hong Kong counterparts. They fly back to the US on Sunday. We can take advantage of them now while they're here. Once they're gone, it's hard to make the same impression about urgency," Ray warned.

"Let it go. Between the two of us, if necessary, we'll be able to bring in the heavy weights," Roger said.

"Before you hang up, what's the plan to check on our guy at the house?" Ray inquired.

"Glad you asked. Can we come by later and raid the toolbox? JJ can drive me and Aaron back to do that," Roger answered.

"Check in later, say, after six." Ray ended the call.

Roger pressed the numbers for his second call. He heard the phone ring at least seven times before it was answered in Chinese. "Chuck, good morning," Roger said slowly. "Have you told anyone about last night?"

"No. I'm at work, but I haven't had a chance to tell anyone yet."

"Don't tell anyone. If we need more help, I'll call, or we'll meet again. Understand?" Roger waited.

"Understand," Cheng said finally.

Roger hung up and went back to join Aaron and Guang. "I've reached out to various associates and asked them to do nothing for the time being.

But, Mr. Lai, I can call them again, and if I do, they will cause Liwei a great deal of trouble if he doesn't let Kellie return to Hong Kong very soon. Do we have an understanding?"

"Yes, of course," Guang answered.

Guang began to stand when Aaron stopped him. "What happened to Meilin?" Aaron demanded.

"I really don't know. She knew we were meeting and said she would be joining us. I'll call Roger's phone when I get back to the room and let you know why she didn't join us," Guang offered.

Aaron and Roger stayed at the table, watching Guang walk toward the hotel exit.

"I called Ray and Chuck and told them to keep a lid on things for the moment. I understand you want her back now, but I believe this is the better course. Believe me, if we don't see progress, we can put things back in motion," Roger said.

Guang walked through the growing crowds in the mall to get to the Conrad. He knew who Roger was. Rong and Shu wouldn't have brought Roger on board to work for them without running it by him. Guang had stayed behind the scenes when the Taiwan government was in constant talks with the Americans. The Americans threatened Taiwan exports to the US because of illicit goods that his and other Taiwan companies were shipping to the US. The money kept flowing into his account despite the threats because while the Americans made threats, they never did much about the problem. That's the way it was with the Americans—lots of talk but very little action. They had brought Roger in just for convenience's sake. He confirmed their own suspicions that there wouldn't be any action by the Americans to stop the flow of illicit products. They would complain, and there would be endless meetings where government officials from both sides would sit around and talk. All the while, he and his colleagues would be making money.

Guang's casual pace through the mall belied his anxiety. It did, however, allow him to think about his next steps. He needed to talk to either Rong or Shu as soon as possible so that they could find out what Liwei was up to and what he had learned from Kaili.

When he entered his suite, it was unusually quiet. He stood a few steps inside his suite and listened, but he didn't hear Meilin. Instead, it was dead quiet. Guang walked into the bedroom and noticed that the room had already been serviced by the hotel staff. In the bathroom, he noticed his toiletries had been straightened on the counter, but something was missing. That's when it hit him. He didn't see any of Meilin's belongings anywhere. He walked back to the sitting room toward the desk facing the window and saw the handwritten note.

"Father, I've decided to take the train back to the mainland. Perhaps I can be of better service to you and our cause there than by staying here. You know how to reach me. Meilin."

Guang wondered what her instincts were telling her. He had to admit that her instincts were usually good. Hopefully, that would be the case this time because so much depended on handling this situation skillfully.

* * * * *

Yuming was up and dressed in the same clothes as she had worn the day before. She walked toward the office up the street. She saw Tengfei wiping down Liwei's car, something he did every morning. Knowing that Tengfei was one of Liwei's fix-it people, she reported on Kellie. "She asked a couple of workers for a phone. No one let her use their phones. She asked for someone to walk off the property with her. I warned her to make sure she took her papers with her, as she might be asked for them. I'm not sure why, but that seemed to change her mind," Yuming reported.

"I'll tell Mr. Hsieh," Tengfei said. He was in no hurry to go into the building and inform his boss. He spent the next twenty minutes wiping down the car.

Liwei sat at his desk. After the previous day's meeting with Kellie, he looked over the orders in the pipeline to be filled and the time it might take to make the adjustments that Kellie suggested. And after hearing Yuming's report about the attempts at finding a phone, he knew that he had to let Kellie make her call soon.

He took a break from looking at his spreadsheet and pressed the redial on his cell phone and waited. Shing Fang didn't answer. It was midmorning. This was his third attempt to reach him.

"Tengfei!" Liwei shouted from his office, assuming that Tengfei was a couple of doors down in a pantry room, sitting and sipping tea.

After wiping down the car and giving Liwei the update about Kellie's failed efforts at finding a phone, Tengfei sat leisurely in the pantry.

"Have you heard from Shing Fang? Has he called you?" Liwei asked when Tengfei appeared at the office's doorway.

Tengfei simply shook his head in the negative. "Find the company jeep and go back to the house and see if he's there. I don't understand why he's not answering his mobile. I'll call Mr. Qian and Ms. Tai to see if he's doing something for one of them," Liwei said. "When you find him, I want to know why he has refused to answer my calls."

Tengfei turned and left.

* * * * *

Guang sat and waited for Rong and Shu in the large conference room where they had met two days earlier.

"Liwei is bringing attention to us, but in the wrong way," Guang began. "He took her to his home in Tai Po and sent a couple of his goons to Kaili's hotel room to get her things. While there, they had an unfriendly encounter with her boyfriend. If that wasn't enough, he took Kaili across the border. As a result of his actions, the wrong kind of people are noticing our operations, and if we don't fix this, others will notice them. Kaili's boyfriend, Aaron Foster, has already made some calls. He's also very good friends with the last American customs attaché, Roger Steeg, who is now involved. As you know, Mr. Steeg is on our payroll. I'm not sure if Mr. Steeg's loyalties lie with us or Mr. Foster."

"I'll take care of Mr. Steeg," Rong interrupted. "I met with him yesterday to discuss a shipment seized in the US. He was not pleased to learn about some of the things our colleagues are sending to the US. By the way, was Shing Fang one of the men Liwei sent to the hotel?"

"I have no idea who Liwei sent to get Kaili's things. Why?"

"Shing Fang picked me up at the hotel and drove me here yesterday when I met with Steeg, and I noticed what seemed to be some bruising on one side of his face. I didn't ask him about it. He's young, so I thought he might have gotten into a tussle with someone at a bar or something," Rong explained.

"Do we know anything more about Kaili?" Shu asked.

"Nothing. We should try to find out how he was able to gain Kaili's cooperation to allow him to take her across the border or if he did something to her. I doubt she went voluntarily," Guang said.

"She's an American citizen, so how did he get her across the border?" Shu asked.

"Liwei was able to provide the proper papers at the border," Guang said matter-of-factly.

"I'm concerned about Liwei. He's the one shipping some of these things that are catching the Americans' attention," Rong said.

"He's not the only one. There are hundreds of companies doing the same thing," Shu added. "That includes several in our network."

"Right now, the immediate concern is that to Mr. Steeg and Mr. Foster, it appears that Kaili has been kidnapped. She hasn't called to say what's happened. Mr. Foster said he is sure something is wrong because she would never fail to call him if she willingly made a change of plans. As we know, Mr. Steeg has connections. He could try to use them to interfere," Guang warned. "I met with them this morning, and I believe I've convinced Mr. Steeg to let me handle this for a day or two. Unfortunately, I have no idea about Mr. Foster and whether Mr. Steeg can keep him from doing something."

"Kaili's boyfriend, Mr. Foster, do we know anything about him?" Rong asked.

"No, but he seems to be a very close friend of Mr. Steeg," Guang answered.

"If this young man has been able to enlist the help of Mr. Steeg, there is more to this friendship than we know," Shu added.

Guang debated whether to tell Rong and Shu about the video he saw and Meilin's involvement in the rescue effort to get Kaili. He decided it was better for Meilin and him not to say anything about that for now. "May I suggest that Rong will stay in contact with Mr. Steeg and try to keep him out of the Kaili situation? Shu, perhaps you could contact Liwei and express your concern for Kaili's safety. You might add that he may be putting both the network and his position within the network at risk if he does not resolve this situation quickly," Guang suggested.

"My experience with the Americans and what they've proven to us in recent years is that they do not act quickly on the threats they make. Even if they catch a few shipments, most of our products will get by them. It'll be months or years before we feel the effects of their enforcement. So, if we can resolve this situation, we can continue to enjoy the profits from our labors," Guang added.

Guang's two listeners shook their heads in agreement as he made his last point. These three elders of ChiTran knew that they had taken steps to secure the comforts of old age. They didn't need one of their ambitious young operations managers doing stupid things that might cause undue attention on them from Beijing, Taipei, or Washington, DC.

* * * * *

The dark clouds were building for the seasonal late afternoon showers when Tengfei drove up the driveway. He parked behind the vehicle he and Shing Fang had used when they went to the Marriott.

Shing Fang heard an engine sound. He had the urge to call out but didn't.

Tengfei opened the rear door leading to the kitchen and stepped inside. He winced and covered his nose and mouth with his hand. He felt like he'd been hit with something drenched in urine. "Shing!" he shouted without inhaling.

"Untie me!"

Tengfei left the door open, pushed open a window, and put a handkerchief to his nose and mouth before rushing over to Shing. Tengfei pulled his Swiss Army knife from his pocket and started cutting at ropes and zip ties to free Shing. As he crouched down to untie Shing's ankles from the legs of the chairs, he saw the dried blood on Shing's face and shirt. "What happened? Who did this? How long have you been tied up?"

Ignoring Tengfei's questions, Shing jumped out of the chair and ran straight to the bathroom. His first thought was to get out of his urine-soaked pants, shower, and put on clean clothes. He left Tengfei squatting in the kitchen by the chair where he'd just cut the last piece of rope that had bound Shing to the chair.

Tengfei heard the water start running in an upstairs bathroom. He found a bucket and mop to clean up the kitchen floor. When he finished, he went upstairs, finding Shing putting on a pair of jeans and rummaging through a drawer for a shirt.

"You've got a cut and a large bump on your forehead. Do you need to see a doctor?"

"I'm all right. It's very sore, but I don't need anything."

"We have to call Mr. Hsieh," Tengfei said, sitting on the bed in Shing's room and holding his cell phone. "When did this happen?"

Shing paused, looking down at the floor to think about the time of the intrusion. "Last night. Ten, eleven."

"You were tied to that chair for eighteen to twenty hours," Tengfei said, seeing Shing nod in agreement. Tengfei pressed the buttons to call Liwei.

"It's Tengfei. I'm at the house. Shing couldn't answer the phone because he's been tied to a chair since last night. He has a large cut and a bad lump on his forehead, but he says he's fine."

"Put him on the phone," ordered Liwei. Liwei heard the hand-over. "Shing, tell me what happened. Do you know who did this?"

"No. I just know there were three men and a woman. They all had their faces covered. Only the woman spoke in Chinese. She was small. I mean she was tiny, very thin, not tall."

"Were they there to rob the house? Was it a burglary? What?"

"They asked questions about the woman we drove to the house. That was all they were interested in," Shing explained.

"You can't describe any of the men, nothing?"

"Nothing. They were dressed all in black and had their faces covered. One did have a video camera and recorded while they asked me questions."

"What did you tell them when they asked about Kaili's whereabouts?"

"I said you had taken her to the mainland."

"Lock up the house and come back here immediately," Liwei instructed, then disconnected the call.

Liwei got up and stood at the window in his office. He knew that Guang had seen Kaili leave with him. The surprise was finding someone in her hotel room, but how would her boyfriend know about his house? The only link was between Guang and the boyfriend. Liwei concentrated on that possible connection. Ahh, Meilin. It was easy to overlook her. She was always quiet at meetings. She never or rarely spoke. She stayed in the background, fading into the wall or was like a piece of furniture that is put in a corner and easy to overlook, forgotten. She was at the house once, but that was at least fifteen years earlier. Still, Shing's description of a tiny woman fit Meilin.

Liwei had miscalculated. It was one thing for Tengfei and Shing to run into the unexpected boyfriend, but hearing of Shing's ordeal meant there was more to Kaili than met the eye. What Shing described made Liwei suspicious of Kaili's connections. If a team was already searching for her last night and if Meilin was involved, he needed to get ahead of this with ChiTran because Guang would try to use this to his advantage.

He made sure to lock the door to his office, not that anyone just walked in on him when the door was closed. Liwei speed-dialed Mr. Qian.

"Mr. Qian, how are you today?"

"I could be better," the older man answered. "I'm aware of your actions. I'm sure you know what I'm talking about. You need to put an end to this type of careless behavior."

"I need to understand a few things about Ms. Liang's involvement with ChiTran," Liwei said, ignoring Rong's warnings.

"How did she become a source of information to us? Who made the introduction? Did you or Ms. Tai check her background? I'm surprised she was thrust upon us at the meeting with so little consideration of who she is," Liwei pressed.

"How she came to us has nothing to do with your careless actions. But we became aware of her through a very trusted person. As you know, Guang is part of the founding group of ChiTran. He knows her, trusts her."

"But what is Guang's connection to Ms. Liang?" Liwei's questions were a direct challenge to the ChiTran management group.

"Guang has never done anything to jeopardize our success," Rong insisted. "No one questioned me or Ms. Tai when we recommended that we bring you and your company into ChiTran."

"It's not the same. The difference is that I'm Chinese and this is a Chinese company. Ms. Liang is an American no matter how useful her advice may be or how well she may speak Chinese or how she looks," Liwei rebutted.

"Her presence at the meeting didn't create the problem. Instead, it was you, taking her from the meeting, that caused the problem. You need to take care of our problem in a way that doesn't make things worse. Remember, this is no longer just your problem. The next time we speak, I want good news," Rong replied and abruptly ended the call.

Liwei held the phone to his ear for a few seconds longer, then realized that Rong had hung up on him. Holding the phone, he let his arm drop to his side. He wasn't going to be in any hurry to call Rong again. He'd give the old man an update about Kaili when he decided it was time.

With the phone still in his hand, it reminded him that he had to let Kaili make a call before much more time passed. He asked his secretary to have Kaili come to his office to make the call to Hong Kong.

Liwei stayed at his desk while he waited for Kaili to walk up to the office building.

"I know you want to call your companion. I've written down the hotel phone number for you. Please, feel free to use the phone there by the sofa," Liwei offered.

When Liwei left his office, Kellie called the Marriott. Once the hotel operator dialed the room, the phone was answered after one ring.

"Aaron, it's me."

"Where are you? How are you? What's happening? When will you be back?"

"Slow down. Give me a minute to answer," Kellie interrupted. "I'm fine. I'm at one of Liwei's production facilities somewhere in the Shenzhen area. I can't explain how to get here because I was drugged when they brought me here, but since arriving, they have treated me well. I'm not sure why he thinks I know this, but he's been cross-examining me about how to export some dodgy stuff into the US. I've already seen them packing up smoke and carbon monoxide detectors and fire extinguishers that he claims they're testing, but I'm not sure that's true. I've been trying to subtly persuade him not to ship this stuff because he's putting people's lives in danger with his stuff. Given that he appears to be motivated solely by profits, I'm not sure I've been convincing."

"We've been looking for you since you disappeared. We were lucky to have someone lead us to Liwei's house in Tai Po, where he originally took you. But you were gone already. One of Liwei's minions was at the house, and he told us you were in the mainland. Roger's been very helpful in trying to find you. When are you coming back? Now that you've answered his questions, are you free to leave?"

"I assume so, but I don't know. Liwei has my passport, and I have no way of knowing where he's got it."

"He must also have other documents that got you across the border. Otherwise, how else did you get into China?"

Kellie suddenly remembered that she was given the Mainland Travel Permit. "You're right. He has that, too." Kellie paused to think before continuing. Liwei might be listening. "Until I get out of here, I'll keep my eyes open for you, if you know what I mean. We can discuss things once I'm back."

"I don't want you doing anything that might endanger you. He was willing to drug you, break into our hotel room, and take you across the border. Don't take any chances. Remember, we don't know how dangerous he might be." Aaron paused before continuing. "Find a way to get your travel documents or for him to let you return," Aaron said firmly.

"Just know that I'm safe and fine. Hopefully, I'll be back with you very soon, or he will let me call again soon. I should go now." Kellie hung up.

"Damn it!" Aaron slammed the receiver down. He picked up the phone, raised it, but put it back on the desk. His wits returned, and he knew that throwing the phone across the room wouldn't solve his problem.

After hanging up, Kellie got up and walked out of Liwei's office. She saw him sitting in a chair in the front office waiting area positioned to the side of his secretary's desk. Her stomach tensed when she saw a phone on a small side table by his chair. Had he listened in on her conversation?

After eyeing the phone next to Liwei, there was only a moment of eye contact. She marched out of the building and back to her dormitory room. She was angry at herself for not being careful. She'd just have to wait and see if there was any change in the way she was treated to indicate whether Liwei or the secretary had listened in on the call.

The trees along the perimeter fencing cast longer shadows during the late afternoon. Kellie saw some of the young women workers, finished for the day, sitting and standing around the benches. They all looked like they should still be in high school, young, laughing, and playing around like school kids. She saw a couple of coolers on the ground. Farther away, she saw a similar group of young men. She was surprised that they weren't mingling.

Kellie had just gotten back in her room, sifting through some work notes, when someone knocked on her door.

"You want to come?"

"What?" Kellie asked. She was surprised by Yuming's question. "Come where?"

Yuming pointed toward the bench and the young women.

It would be rude to refuse, she thought. "Yes, thank you."

Yuming wandered toward the five other young women already at the bench. Yuming waved Kellie over with a big smile. She bent down and said something to two of the young women, and they scooted over to make room for Kellie on the bench. Yuming reached in to get a bottle of beer and handed it to Kellie once she was sitting.

Kellie was the center of attention. They were curious about her background because she spoke Chinese, but they knew she wasn't one of them. She wasn't fond of beer and sipped slowly while everyone else emptied theirs.

"We don't work tomorrow," Yuming said. "We have one Saturday free each month. Tomorrow, we don't work," Yuming added, justifying their beer consumption.

As the sun was setting, Yuming led her little group on a short walk to a local restaurant. Kellie had drunk her couple of beers while the others were a few ahead of her. They were loud and playful as they wandered to the Chinese eatery. Half a dozen simple red lanterns hung along the front of the restaurant. An old man and woman greeted Yuming and her work colleagues as familiar guests. The old man eyed Kellie, whose clothes and appearance were distinct from the others.

Yuming chose a round table in the corner and gestured for Kellie to sit with her back to the corner. Yuming sat next to Kellie, and everyone else sat around the table. Plates of food came out as if the group had been expected—pork, chicken dishes with sauces, different vegetables in sauce, and fish. Kellie saw some things she recognized and decided not to inquire if she didn't. Everything was being shared. Beers appeared at the table.

Earlier, the young women had talked about the different places they had come from and their families. Kellie listened to them explain why they had come to Shenzhen or why they had left school and what their hopes were.

"Do you have a boyfriend?" one of the young women asked.

"Yes," Kellie answered simply.

"What does he do?" another asked.

"He's a lawyer," Kellie said, keeping things simple.

"I read something that all American lawyers are rich. Is your boyfriend a rich American lawyer?" Yuming asked.

"No, he's a government lawyer. They aren't rich." Kellie regretted what she said as soon as she was finished answering.

"People who work in the government aren't rich, but they have some security," Kellie heard someone say, though now she needed to be careful.

"You're right," Kellie agreed.

"Do you live with your boyfriend? Did he travel with you?" Yuming asked.

"Yes. We've been together for a couple of years, but I've known him for several years," Kellie answered.

"Is his government work interesting, or is it boring legal work?"

Kellie had looked down at her plate and didn't know who had asked the question, but it didn't matter. She wasn't just feeling cornered with the questions, but she was physically cornered with no way to leave the table without causing two or three people to move. It hit her that she had no local currency and couldn't make any excuses to leave. She was dependent on Yuming and the others for dinner and drinks. As the questions kept coming with an air of politeness, she convinced herself that the whole evening had been a setup. Liwei was using Yuming and her small group to interrogate her under the guise of a friendly evening of food and drinks.

The circumstances of the dinner convinced Kellie that she knew the answer to the question of whether Liwei had listened in on her call with Aaron.

* * * * *

Aaron paced in his hotel room, occasionally peering out the window. Outside, the day was sunny and humid and just another ordinary day in Hong Kong. After the brief call from Kellie, he found nothing to be happy about being stuck in the room with no way of bringing Kellie back. All he wanted was for her to come back and for them to fly home. At least she was safe, and for now, all he could do was wait for her to return.

If he was going to stay sane while he waited, he needed to do something, but what? Suddenly, he had a thought. He picked up the phone and dialed Roger's number.

"You know that late-night call you got about a seizure when I stayed at your flat? Then at your meeting the next morning, you discussed a seizure? Well, I think we may know the source," Aaron said as he gripped the phone's receiver.

"How would you know?" Roger was curious.

"Kellie called. She said she's fine for now. This Liwei guy took her through his facility in China. He has some crazy idea that she knows how to get things by customs. Because of that mistaken belief, he showed her some of his operations, and she saw them packing up smoke and carbon monoxide detectors and fire extinguishers."

"Maybe with that bit of info, we can rile things up. I'll try to get Ray back into this. I'll give you a call if I can set things up." As he hung up the phone, Roger thought this wasn't the way his post-retirement job was supposed to be going. He couldn't just jettison his old loyalties for his new employer, especially if they were playing on the wrong side of the rules. Giving it thought, he wondered if he should dangle an incentive in front of Cheng and enlist his help. But before he contacted Cheng, he needed to talk to Ray.

"Ray, it's Roger. Aaron heard from our missing person. While she was taken across the border without her consent, she's fine for now. She relayed info to Aaron that you might want to pass on." Roger told Ray about the dodgy products, then added the details he knew from his meeting with Mr. Qian. "Can you get HQ to authorize Aaron's stay here as official business for a few days?"

"Will definitely pass on the info about the goods. I'll make sure they understand the injury potential. I'll also ask about Aaron being here officially. Given the personal nature of some of this, I'd prefer not to use my staff if we can help it. Besides, they're fully occupied right now, so having an extra body would be helpful. They may need a little convincing, but with some of the details Aaron has given us, I shouldn't have a problem. I'll explain that we have a situation, and Aaron being here gives us the staffing needed to deal with it. But given the time difference and the fact that it's a weekend, I might not know officially for a couple of days. Remember, we'll need to endure the bureaucracy to get approval since Aaron isn't an investigator."

"Should we rope in Hong Kong Customs? I could call our friend who saw the video."

"We can give it a try, but don't get your hopes up," Ray said flatly.

"No harm in trying, right?"

"Agreed," Ray said. The call with Roger ended, and Ray stared at a world map. To Ray, it didn't seem like it was sufficient to share the info with his colleagues back in Washington. He thought more could be done. He sifted through a pile of binders on a bookcase in his office. When he saw the World Customs Organization's insignia on the cover, he went to the page with the contact details of the organization's regional liaison officers in case he needed to bring some additional human resources into play.

An hour after the call with Ray, Roger sat waiting for Cheng in the bar where they'd last met. He sat in the same booth they had occupied a couple of nights earlier. As he waited, the only other person in the bar was the older woman who managed it. It was too early in the day for the working girls. Roger rotated the sweating glass of beer sitting on the table. The glass was near full. He had taken a couple of sips and didn't plan on finishing it.

When he saw Cheng enter, Roger dried his fingers. He watched Cheng nod to the woman behind the bar and walk straight back to the booth.

"You don't go to the hotel anymore?" Cheng asked as he slid into the booth.

"For this conversation, it's better to find a place where we're not going to be overheard and here, I can see everyone," Roger explained. "You've been following me and keeping tabs on me for a while. But wouldn't you like to give your superiors something useful rather than just who I meet with in public? Wouldn't your bosses prefer information they can act on?"

"But they are interested in the people you've met, especially Mr. Lai. He has interesting connections with people in trade."

"Forget about him for a minute. What if Hong Kong Customs could stop some suspicious products crossing the border or being shipped through your container terminal?" Roger asked.

"I'm sure you know we have very strict rules about that. We don't open containers from China that are here solely to be put on ships going to other countries. If the container is sealed in China, we don't look into the contents."

"Even if the contents are found to be dangerous," Roger pressed.

"It's a delicate situation. If we become an obstacle to China's exports, China could create problems for Hong Kong."

"What if we could narrow the search so that you know specifically whose goods to look at and what we're looking for?" Roger queried. "Doesn't it matter if you might be saving lives?"

"It wouldn't be Chinese lives being saved," Cheng answered with no concern in his voice.

Roger took a gulp of his beer in frustration. "Are you sure your bosses wouldn't want the information or wouldn't do anything to interfere with the kind of shipment I'm describing?"

"Maybe, but it isn't our practice to open containers in transit from China if they're being exported. Those containers have nothing to do with Hong Kong except that they are leaving our container terminal. If you say that these containers have explosives or weapons, then we might look, but we would need very good information. If that's what you're talking about, it'll be easier to convince my bosses, but otherwise, it'll be difficult, if not impossible."

Roger glared at Cheng but knew that he didn't make the rules. He pursed his lips, and his grip on his beer tightened. His frustration and anger were growing. "Who would we have to convince?"

"I'm not sure. Maybe as high as the commissioner," Cheng answered.

Roger knew that he wouldn't be able to reach that high in his current position. In his old job, he would've picked up the phone and made a call or arranged a face-to-face. The question was whether Ray could do what he couldn't. Roger understood that the bottom-up approach through Cheng would take too long. More importantly, Cheng didn't have the influence and wasn't inclined to leap-frog levels of his superiors to get to anyone close to the commissioner.

"Okay. I understand. I'll work on another way," Roger said. "Before you go, did you say anything to anyone about the video?"

"No. I honored your request," Cheng responded. He knew there wasn't much he or anyone else might be able to do even if he had informed his bosses about someone being taken across the border. There was no proof of a crime. The only crime that might have been committed was the one committed by the people who tied up Shing Fang.

"Am I still being watched?" Roger asked as Cheng got up to leave.

"We're still interested because of the people you know and meet."

"Would it help if these products I'm talking about are coming from the people I know or the people they know?"

"That would definitely help," Cheng said before leaving.

Watching Cheng exit, Roger picked up the glass of beer. While he hadn't intended to drink it, he gulped down what was left in frustration. He slid a couple of paper napkins toward him and started writing. He created a bullet point list to discuss with Ray. He needed to be focused, and Ray would need it if he was going to try and get to the commissioner. Roger knew he needed this to get done now, today. He pulled out his phone and dialed Ray's number again.

International drug trafficking, organized crime, and the added task of putting aside time to meet and brief a few people from Washington had Ray dealing with a lot of moving parts on his daily schedule. The last thing he needed was Roger insisting that he get to Hong Kong's Customs commissioner.

"Don't call. Go there and demand five minutes of his time," Roger was saying over the phone. "I've laid it out for you. We have a legitimate concern that these guys are letting goods through that could have lethal consequences. Scare him if you have to but get him to agree to screen shipments you designate coming into the Hong Kong territory. I've given you info to pass on so they can zero in on the target."

"You know that I can't guarantee anything other than I'll insist on seeing him," Ray answered. "It's getting late in the day, but I'll try to leverage this. I also have the head of the delegation that's here to back me up on this, if necessary."

"However and whatever you can do, do it," Roger insisted.

* * * * *

JJ drove past Liwei's house and pulled over a couple of hundred yards past the house. There was a faint light through one of the windows.

"Didn't we leave a light on in the kitchen?" Roger asked.

"We did," answered Aaron.

Roger turned in his seat. "We'll approach with the assumption there's someone in there. Same as last night, except I'll go to the back and try to enter, and you and JJ will stay at the front," Roger said.

Roger had stopped and picked through Ray's toolkit earlier while Ray worked on meeting with Hong Kong's Customs commissioner. Everything he hoped they would need was in the back seat.

"I'll let you be our firepower if it's needed," Aaron said as they picked from the gear that Roger had placed on the back seat. "It's been too long since I handled a gun."

Roger shrugged. "No problem."

JJ had no experience with a firearm of any type. Roger made sure that the one Glock left in the car was covered and on the floor behind the driver's seat.

"We don't cover our faces until we're at the driveway," Roger instructed.

They walked in a single file with Roger leading. As they stepped off the road and onto the driveway, the balaclavas were pulled on. Roger walked toward the back of the house as Ray had done the night before. He peeked into the windows on the side of the house. The light didn't help him. The sheer curtains were enough to prevent him from seeing anything clearly.

Reaching the back of the house, the same vehicle they saw the night before was still parked. Roger gripped the doorknob. Unlike Ray's luck, it was locked. He remembered leaving Shing Fang in the lit kitchen and realized that it was the kitchen light that was casting shadows. Roger put the small flashlight he had between his teeth while he found what he needed to pick the lock and went to work. Every sound he made as he worked the lock seemed to be too loud.

Finally, he felt the lock give, and he turned the doorknob. He opened the door a few inches and leaned into the opening. He put his small flashlight away. His nose told him Shing Fang had been found. No one could stay tied up for twenty-four hours and hold the bladder. He should've smelled urine or worse if Shing Fang was still a prisoner to the chair.

He stepped into the house and pushed the door closed. He stopped to listen and heard nothing. Roger crept toward the kitchen, looking around the door frame and into the fully lit kitchen. He saw the empty chair. There was no reason to let Aaron or JJ into the house. He checked all the rooms on the ground floor, then made sure no one was upstairs. Knowing the house was empty, Roger exited through the back door.

"Someone came for him, and they cleaned up," Roger said as he found JJ and Aaron at the back of the house when he came out. "Not sure there's anything more we can do here," Roger concluded.

They removed their balaclavas and walked back to the car.

"Aaron, we're at a dead end, or I think I am," Roger said from the front seat. "There isn't anything more Ray or I can do."

"I understand. I'm worried about Kellie. Just because he hasn't harmed her doesn't mean he won't."

"I agree," said Roger. "We're on their turf, and if we do something stupid, there's no cavalry to come and pull our asses out of the fire. I've asked Ray for as much help as I can expect."

"Understood. I'm running out of time," said Aaron.

* * * * *

Sleep came fast and easy when Kellie got back to her room. The few beers she shared with the young women helped. As she rolled over, she heard the gunning of idling engines. Truck engines. She remembered the girls had said they didn't have to work in the morning, but she was sure someone was constantly pressing the gas pedal as the truck idled.

Kellie reached over and felt around for her watch. The sliver of light coming through the window didn't help her see the time. She sat up and turned on the lamp and saw that it was still the dead of night, 3:30. She wondered if anyone else was bothered by the noise. She dressed and walked out of the apartment and into the open dormitory area. She heard nothing but sounds of deep breathing.

Kellie walked out the door and toward the sound of the engines. She saw that a couple of the buildings were lit up. Work crews of men and women were loading one truck, and another truck was parked, waiting to be loaded. She stood and watched for a few minutes before wandering away in the opposite direction from her dormitory building.

There was a glow of light in the night sky toward the far corner of Liwei's complex, calling Kellie to check it out. As she approached, she detected a slight odor in the air that wasn't familiar. The sounds of different machines were obvious as she approached. The building had a wide center door that was closed and a window on each side of the door midway between the door and the corner of the building. She walked toward one of the windows to get a look inside.

"No! No!" a male voice said in Chinese from the corner of the building, and a young man came running at her. A second young man came from the other corner of the building. She stopped and stood still, not knowing if they'd grab her if she continued moving.

"Go!" the young man said.

"Sorry," Kellie said. "The truck engines woke me up." She stood there for a moment and then turned to walk back to her room. She glanced back over her shoulder and noticed the two young men were watching her.

Kellie hadn't seen any security guards during the day but realized she hadn't been looking for them while being shown around by Liwei. She guessed that things were different in the middle of the night. Of one thing she was certain, Liwei would hear about this in the morning.

Chapter 9

Hurdles

Hong Kong (Saturday, May 16)

Liwei walked past the dormitory building, where he assumed Kellie was still sleeping. He climbed up into the passenger seat of the truck cab that was still being loaded. This wasn't what he had planned for a Saturday morning. The orange, blue, and green hues glowing on the horizon hinted at sunrise. Normally, he'd still be asleep, not sitting in a truck.

He wore jeans, a khaki-colored long-sleeved cotton shirt, and a lightweight jacket that he knew he wouldn't need in a few hours. The first truck was loaded and waiting just outside the entrance. Something was gnawing at Liwei, causing him to worry about this particular shipment. He had nothing specific to point to, but the past forty-eight hours reminded him that things could go wrong without warning. He glanced into the passenger side mirror and saw a clipboard with documents being handed to a driver he didn't know.

Tengfei waited in a dented old Jeep parked on the street outside the complex. He would follow behind both trucks and give Liwei a ride back. Liwei wanted to be sure the containers on these trucks made it to Hong Kong's container terminal for their onward journey. This early in the morning, Liwei hoped for an uneventful drive to the border. But the increased traffic congestion that accompanied Shenzhen's economic growth was creating new choke points around the city and the border. As a result, the drive had become less predictable.

It took forty-five minutes to arrive on the China side of the border and hand over the documents for Chinese Customs officials to take a quick look. Liwei watched in the mirrors as the customs officers took a stroll around the truck before handing the documents back to the driver.

They rode across the Sham Chun River. Liwei knew that the easy part was behind them.

The Hong Kong Customs checkpoint was straight ahead. Liwei looked in the side mirror and saw Tengfei moving slowly behind the second truck. Tengfei wouldn't have any problems. Liwei's driver got the truck to lurch forward in the procession of vehicles until a customs officer motioned him to stop.

The driver handed over the documents to the uniformed Hong Kong Customs officer. Liwei looked over and could barely see the officer's face because of the height of the truck cab. This officer took his time reviewing the documents.

Liwei tilted his head back against the back of the seat when he saw the customs officer turn and walk into the customs office.

"Did he say anything?" Liwei asked the driver. The driver looked at Liwei, shrugged, and nodded no.

At that moment, Liwei had no reason to believe Hong Kong Customs would be a problem. He didn't know about Ray's last-minute meeting with the Hong Kong Customs commissioner. Ray's meeting didn't get him much. The commissioner refused outright to open and check any cargo even if his officers could identify the company and truck that had the questionable cargo. But the commissioner was willing to issue an immediate instruction for all his officers to be looking for cargo originating from Liwei's ChiTran Guangdong Specialties Company and send the information about its routing and description to the commissioner's office. The commissioner agreed to share the information with Ray, but that was all he would do. Hong Kong Customs would not interfere with the export of the shipment.

The customs officer followed the instructions and had one of his colleagues make copies of the documents describing the goods and their routing and destination.

Liwei checked his watch, wondering what was going on and why the delay. "Does this happen often?"

"No. This is the first time I've had customs take documents inside to check," the driver answered.

Liwei looked past the driver and focused on the door the customs officer had gone through, though he couldn't see anything inside. When the door opened again, Liwei leaned slightly forward, trying to read the customs officer's expression as he walked toward the truck. The customs officer reached up and handed the paperwork back to the driver, giving the driver a saluting gesture. Liwei felt his shoulders relax, his body slumping a bit into the seat.

The driver put the truck in gear and drove slowly, while the second truck experienced the same delay. With both trucks resuming their drive, they went a few miles before Liwei saw Tengfei waiting for them. After passing through Hong Kong Immigration, Tengfei had pulled over and waited for the trucks.

The three vehicles made their way to the Hong Kong container terminal without any more delays. When the two trucks arrived at the container terminal in Kowloon, Liwei decided not to wait around for the containers to be taken off the trucks. He joined Tengfei for the ride back to Shenzhen across the border.

* * * * *

Kellie sat at the desk in her room and reached out, using her pen to pull the thin curtain open so she could see out the open window. The voices were carrying a good distance in the morning breeze. Beyond the facility entrance and in front of the building where Liwei's office was located, she could see a small cluster of people. There were at least four, maybe five, people standing at the base of the few steps leading up to the office building entrance.

Kellie stood up as if that would help her see who was engaged in the animated conversation. A woman and two men were dressed in black pants and sky-blue shirts. The woman was obscured by a man. They were talking to Yuming and the manager that Liwei had included in her meetings.

Curious, Kellie walked out of the dormitory building. She could hear the voices but couldn't follow the words being exchanged. The words seemed rushed, and the tone harsh. It sounded more like an argument between the woman she couldn't see and Liwei's two employees. When Kellie was beyond the facility entrance and walking up the street toward the five people engaged in whatever disagreement was occurring, she had caught the attention of someone, and then all looked her way.

The woman who had been obscured by one of the men took a half step forward and turned. She looked familiar. Kellie recognized her but had trouble recalling where exactly she had seen her.

"Ms. Liang? I hope you remember me from the meeting in Hong Kong a few days ago. I'm sorry we didn't formally meet," Meilin said, taking another step toward Kellie, who continued her approach.

"I'm sorry I couldn't see you," Kellie said, hiding the fact that she really didn't remember this woman who hadn't spoken to her during the meeting. She remembered the woman being fully embraced by the chair and seeming so small. Now, Kellie saw that she was petite, though perhaps a few inches taller than she had originally thought. Kellie still towered over her.

"I'm Moy Meilin, Mr. Lai's daughter," she explained in Chinese. "I would be happy to take you back to Hong Kong if you wish to return."

"Mr. Hsieh isn't here. You can't just take her away," Liwei's manager objected. He reached down and pulled his cell phone out of its carrying case.

The young man next to Meilin grabbed the manager's wrist and stopped him from making the call. The manager let his arm go limp and let the man take his phone. The second man with Meilin stepped toward Yuming and put out his palm in a gesture to prompt Yuming to surrender a phone if she had one. Yuming looked into the man's empty palm and folded her arms. She was immediately frisked. She had no phone.

Meilin stood, smiling at Liwei's two employees, enjoying the moment. Her two young men were well trained in martial arts. She required it of anyone she hired as part of her protective detail. Her own training started years ago, and she still took classes. She realized that it was a necessity for someone of her diminutive size. She could have done what the two young men did so instinctively. She was proud of how their motions were smooth, quick, and effective.

"It's up to Ms. Liang. If she wants to return, she should be allowed. It isn't a decision for Mr. Hsieh or you," Meilin said as she let her eyes roam from Kellie to Liwei's two employees. Meilin looked at Liwei's manager and said, "Your phone will be returned before we leave."

Kellie watched as the tension escalated between Meilin and Liwei's two employees. "Of course, I'd like to go back to Hong Kong, but I can't. Mr. Hsieh has the documents I need to cross the border."

"What do you mean?" Meilin asked as she turned to the manager and Yuming. "Are you able to find Ms. Liang's documents and provide them to her? They are her property, not Mr. Hsieh's." Meilin was met with shrugs and silence.

"I don't know if I should leave without the documents in my possession. Even though Mr. Hsieh brought me here without my permission, everyone has treated me well since I arrived," Kellie said.

"Are you certain your treatment will continue to be fine?"

Kellie had to admit that she couldn't be sure of anything if she stayed. But she didn't know this woman, although knowing that she was Guang's daughter made her feel a little more confident that she'd be safe.

"Would you prefer better accommodations while I work on getting your documents from Mr. Hsieh?"

Kellie wanted to scream, "Yes!" but she resisted her initial urge. "If better accommodations could be found, I'd appreciate it, but I never planned to be in China, so I have limited funds."

"Don't worry about any of that. Whatever you need while you are in China, I'll take care of it," Meilin reassured. "If you want to leave, please collect your things as quickly as you can."

Kellie looked over at Yuming and the manager, who were listening, watching, and glaring at her. They made no attempt to stop her.

Kellie turned and walked briskly back to her room.

"You'll need to let Mr. Hsieh know who came and took Ms. Liang away. Here's my business card. It'll make things clear to Mr. Hsieh," Meilin said as she gave Yuming and the manager each a business card.

In just a few minutes, Kellie returned with her belongings. Since she didn't have much, it didn't take long to gather her possessions.

Meilin and Kellie slid into the backseat of a large black Toyota sedan. One of Meilin's young men put Kellie's bags in the trunk, and the other returned the cell phone to the manager.

"Liwei will know what's happened before we're a mile away," Meilin said.

"Where are we going?"

"There are some new modern hotels in Guangzhou, don't worry," Meilin answered.

"Once we're there, I'll need to make some calls. Will that be all right?"

"Do what you need to do. I'll take care of things," Meilin said again.

Kellie settled into the corner of the back seat, not knowing how long they would be on the road. Meilin's confident and assured nature struck her as completely different from a few days ago. She had interpreted the silent, small woman as just a quiet servant for Guang, but she was projecting a different personality this morning. Kellie noticed that Meilin, the driver, and the other young man were dressed alike, as if they were wearing uniforms.

"How does your father run a business in China? I thought he was living in Taiwan."

"I manage his China operations. We talk regularly, but I make the day-to-day business decisions here," Meilin explained.

"Liwei gave me a tour of his facilities yesterday. He's producing a lot of different things at his facility. Then, last night, there was a lot of activity with trucks and noise from some of the buildings that awakened me. When I went outside and walked around, I was stopped by some security guards."

"Chinese companies are producing many different things for export. We need hard currency, and we must keep people coming from rural areas employed. When we contribute to economic growth, the government stays off our back because we're doing our part," Meilin explained. "If we employ people, produce goods, and generate revenues, everyone stays happy, and the government sometimes looks the other way even when we bend the rules or break them so long as we don't cause too many political headaches," Meilin added.

Kellie wondered what Meilin's facilities produced but decided not to ask. At the moment, she was in no position to let the conversation stray into areas that might antagonize the person who was helping her.

The trip from Shenzhen to Guangzhou was a time-consuming drive through a lot of congested areas. Kellie knew that the distance was about sixty-five miles. The drive seemed to be taking longer than she expected. She glanced at the time. It was almost noon, and she realized they had already been in the car for more than a couple of hours. As they reached the outskirts of Guangzhou, the city was a maze of streets, high rises, and new and old buildings. She had no idea where she was, although she occasionally saw a river as the driver navigated the city traffic.

"We'll be at the hotel in a couple of minutes. Do you have any identification with you?" Meilin asked.

"The only thing I have is my American driver's license. I guess Liwei didn't think that was valuable enough to take."

"All right, I'll speak to the hotel manager. While they normally want to see a passport for any foreign guests, I'm sure we can reach some understanding."

Kellie watched the streets straight ahead, knowing she was nearing the hotel. The White Swan Hotel was on the riverfront. It was inconspicuous among the other buildings by the river. "We're here," Meilin said as she gestured for Kellie to get out and enter the hotel when the car stopped.

"Don't worry about your belongings," Meilin said. She walked in and went straight to the check-in desk, asking for the manager. When the manager appeared, Meilin hid her surprise as he was younger than she expected, taller than the average Chinese man, and had a thick mustache. Meilin gestured for him to meet her at the end of the counter, away from his colleagues.

Kellie stopped and waited a few feet behind Meilin. From where she stood, she could listen to the exchange between Meilin and the manager.

"Ms. Moy, all foreign guests need to present their passports. It's a government requirement, as you know," the manager on duty was saying.

"I understand, but her documents have been misplaced since coming to China, and we're hoping to locate them very soon. She's in the country, so she did have them when she arrived, but she has either lost them or something else has happened since her entry. For now, please put the room in my name. I will pay for the room and any expenses Ms. Liang may incur while she is here," Meilin explained.

"How long will she need the room?"

Meilin wasn't at all sure. "Let's say five days for now. It may be shorter or longer."

The hotel manager looked away from Meilin for just a moment toward Kellie. "I'll want copies of your documents for the registry."

The long drive and Kellie's circumstances gave Meilin time to think and prepare for different contingencies. During the ride, Meilin had turned slightly away from Kellie to obscure Kellie's view of anything she might be doing with the contents of her purse.

Meilin reached into her purse and felt the folded envelope. She held it in front of her for the manager to take as she stood facing away from the hotel clerks at the front desk. "If there is anything that needs to be taken care of, I hope you'll call me. I appreciate you meeting my requests."

The manager smiled, nodded, took the envelope, and placed it in his inside suit pocket. "I'm sure everything will be fine."

"I've given you a number so that you can contact me directly if necessary," Meilin replied.

"If you could fill out the forms, we'll make sure your colleague is settled," the manager indicated.

Kellie watched the whole exchange and wondered how indebted she was going to be to Meilin and her father.

After Meilin filled out all the necessary check-in documents, she turned and took Kellie by the elbow and away from anyone who could overhear her. She handed Kellie the folder with the room key. "Here's a thousand yuan. That should be enough for a few days. I know you'll make your calls to Hong Kong. For now, just let them know you are safe in Guangzhou. To keep anyone from trying to rescue you and cause a problem, it will be better if you don't mention the name of the hotel. I'll deal with Liwei and try to get your documents. Once I have them, we can quietly go back to Hong Kong. I've arranged for you to have the room for five days. If we need it longer, we'll deal with that in a few days. Feel free to explore unobtrusively near the hotel. But stay close by, and whatever you do, don't call attention to yourself."

"Thank you" was all Kellie could come up with as she knew she was dependent upon Meilin for now.

"I'll call later," Meilin said before walking out.

Kellie stood there watching Meilin leave. Her bags were on the floor next to her. She hadn't noticed anyone putting them there.

* * * * *

"Took her away? Away, where!" Liwei was shouting at his manager and Yuming, both standing in his office and both looking down at the floor to avoid his steely glare.

"Why didn't you call me while she was here!"

"They took my phone," the manager answered sheepishly.

"Did you try to stop her from leaving?"

"No, there were two young men who accompanied Ms. Moy. When I did try to call, one of them grabbed my wrist and took the phone," the manager explained.

Liwei paced behind his desk with hands on hips. As he paced, he glimpsed at the business card that Meilin had left behind. He didn't need to study it. As he paced, he remembered Shing saying that a woman was there the night he was tied up. Meilin fit Shing's description. Now, with Meilin showing up here, he was sure she was the woman.

"Go! Out!" Liwei watched his two employees turn and rush out of his office. There was no point in shouting at them. They didn't know anything more than they had already said. He needed to think about his next step. Should he just offer up Kellie's documents and let all this go, or was there anything Meilin had that he could require in exchange for the documents?

* * * * *

"Roger, I got a heads-up from customs. Two trucks were identified as coming from our targets early this morning. By now, they should've arrived at the container terminal. I'll send over the info I received," Ray advised.

"Great, once I receive it, I'll get Aaron to come along. Maybe between the two of us and Aaron flashing his customs identification, we can access the containers. I'll have JJ be our interpreter in case we need one. Just out of curiosity, that delegation you're working with, when do they fly out?"

"Tomorrow morning. I can still loop them in this evening at their hotel if you come up with anything really interesting," Ray answered.

"Thanks. If we uncover anything we can act on right away, I'll let you know." Roger ended the call with Ray and pressed the numbers for the Marriott Hotel.

"Hope you're up for a trip to the container terminal. Bring your official ID. JJ and I are on the way to pick you up," Roger said without providing any other information or giving Aaron time to say anything.

Aaron was down in the hotel lobby and waiting for Roger and JJ within ten minutes of Roger's call. He was eager to be doing something, anything, other than sitting in the hotel room wondering about Kellie. He double-checked his pockets, making sure he had his official customs identification. When he saw JJ pulling up, he went out and waited for him to come to a stop.

"Ray came through for us," Roger said as Aaron lowered himself into the backseat. Roger turned in the passenger seat and gave Aaron copies of the documents that Ray had faxed over.

"The other day, you said you generally don't go into the terminal. Will we have any problems?" Aaron asked.

Roger looked out the windshield, rubbing his chin. "JJ, find a place to pull over for a few minutes." JJ had already exited the Marriott driveway but got turned around. He pulled back up and stopped near the hotel's main entrance.

Roger pulled out his cell phone and punched in the numbers. "Chuck, this is your favorite American calling. How are you today?" Roger turned in his seat and gave Aaron a wink.

It took a few seconds for Cheng to mentally transition to his caller. "Yes, hello."

"I'm sorry to be disturbing you today, but I need to ask if you can meet me right away." Roger waited and hoped he'd get the answer he wanted.

"Right away, now?"

"It's very important."

"Where?"

"I'm headed to the container terminal. Number five."

"It will take me an hour to get there," Cheng answered. Cheng never had any reason to go to the container terminals. His initial reaction was to say he couldn't meet. But if he could find out what Roger was up to and report back, it might be an opportunity for him. His surveillance duties had been cut back after what he told his superiors about Roger's meetings at the hotel. As Roger asked, Cheng hadn't mentioned the video he'd seen to his superiors. The only thing he knew was that there was interest in the companies that Roger was working with, and Roger's public meeting with Guang had surprised his bosses.

Having gotten Cheng to agree to meet at the container terminal, JJ drove Aaron and Roger to the container terminal. A highway created a perimeter around the container port. The roadway provided a broad concrete barrier between the thousands of containers and the surrounding commercial area. The cranes used to move the containers reached over ten stories high along the water's edge and were visible all around the port and adjacent neighborhoods.

When JJ found a place to park at the north end of the container port where terminal five was located, Roger got out and opened the trunk of the car. Aaron, curious, went to see what he was getting.

Roger grabbed a duffel bag and slung it over his shoulder.

"You didn't bring any weapons, did you?"

Roger laughed. "I haven't gone that far off the mental reservation . . . yet. I just thought it didn't hurt to bring a few tools like bolt or chain cutters, flashlights, and a few other things just in case we need to create our own access to a container and its contents." Roger waved for JJ to come along as the three headed into a building where they would wait for Cheng.

Cheng Gao walked into the terminal building seventy-five minutes after the call from Roger. He saw Roger, Aaron, and JJ standing a few feet from the door he entered. "It took longer because I made a wrong turn, sorry," Cheng offered.

"It's fine," Roger said, handing Cheng copies of the documents that customs had provided to Ray. "If you can show that guy these documents"—Roger pointed in the direction of the only other person they could see inside the building—"and ask him to show us where these two containers are, we'd like to take a look in them."

Cheng looked at the paperwork. "Open them? I can't make them do that."

"I know you can't, but if you show them your customs identification and say you are working with this US Customs official," Roger said, nodding at Aaron, "he might think he should cooperate and do as you ask."

As Cheng walked away with the documents, Aaron, Roger, and JJ watched and waited.

Cheng Gao waved to a middle-aged, well-tanned man to come to him. Cheng held out his Hong Kong Customs identification, giving the man time to look at it. "We need to see two containers that arrived this morning." Cheng guessed that this guy had worked at the terminal long enough that he wasn't someone who could be bluffed. "I'm with a US Customs officer," Cheng added, looking over toward Aaron and Roger.

"Wait," the man said and went to a desk with multiple stacks of papers. Whatever he was looking for, he found it within seconds as he pulled a few sheets of paper from near the top of one of the piles and compared Cheng's documents with those on the desk.

With the man's back toward Cheng and the others, Cheng turned toward Roger and shrugged. They watched as the man went to a transmitter and spoke.

Cheng took a couple of steps toward Roger. "He's getting someone to take us to the container."

A younger man, sweaty, tanned and gloved, came in and took a clipboard handed to him and waved for Cheng and the others to follow. They walked among the stacks of containers for a couple of minutes when the young man pointed to the two containers that Cheng's documents identified. One container was stacked on top of the other.

Roger stepped up to the container on the ground to see what was securing the doors. The two lock rods on the container door were secured with metal cables on each lock rod that ran the vertical length of the door. He let the duffel bag down carefully and pulled out his bolt cutter.

"No! No!" the terminal worker rushed toward Roger to stop him from cutting the steel cable seals on the door.

Aaron stepped in and raised his hands to stop him from interrupting Roger. "Chuck, explain to him that we'll replace the security seals and give him the information he needs to make notes on his documents. We'll coordinate it on our side so that the new seal numbers are consistent."

Cheng was out of his comfort zone. He had never been to the container terminal, and he wasn't familiar with the procedures to secure containers.

Roger stood, wiping some sweat from his brow. "Chuck, I need you to tell him what Aaron just said."

"I'm not sure I can explain it," Cheng answered.

If he could have, Roger would've grabbed Cheng by both arms and shaken him silly, but he couldn't do that. Instead, he waved Cheng over to him, and they took a couple of steps away from Aaron and the container terminal employee, where Roger told Cheng what needed to be done.

Cheng moved toward the terminal employee and got him to understand what the Americans were going to do. Cheng's listener took a couple of steps away from the container. His muscular forearms were folded, and he took up a stance that indicated that he would keep a close eye on what the Americans do.

After cutting the cable seals, Roger and Aaron worked on opening one of the container doors. The locking rods were heavier than they had expected, never having done this before.

"I thought you said you worked out," Roger taunted as sweat beaded on his forehead and ran down his cheeks. The look on Aaron's face was as if he was trying to lift a two-hundred-pound barbell.

After ten minutes of struggling, they had one door open. The opened door exposed pallets of boxes stacked and wrapped with layers of clear plastic.

"Are you able to make out anything?" Roger asked.

"I think we have a lot of boxes that contain boxes," Aaron answered.

"JJ, hand me a knife," Roger said. Once he had the knife, Roger wasn't sure where he should cut the layers of wrapping so he could see the boxes.

"Let's just do this," Roger said. He cut the layers of plastic to create a flap that gave him access to one of the larger boxes. The print on the outer box indicated that there were 48 units inside the box. He pressed the knife through the outer cardboard, trying not to damage the contents.

"What are you trying to do?" Aaron asked.

"I want to see what the packaging looks like in this box without damaging or destroying anything." Roger cut the cardboard, creating a foot-square opening. "We got lucky!" He was looking at the back of the box, not the side.

"Aaron, hand me the camera in the duffel bag." Roger made sure he had the full image of the back and got in close so that he had a picture of all the text describing the combination smoke-carbon monoxide detector. "I think we're done. Let's tape this back together."

"According to the paperwork, there are other types of stuff in here, but if there's a problem with this item, there are probably problems with the other stuff," Roger speculated.

Roger put the cardboard cut-out back in its place and taped up the plastic flap he had created. He and Aaron shoved the door closed and worked to get the locking rods back into place.

"We have a problem, don't we? You cut the security cables," Aaron said.

Roger smiled and reached into the duffel bag. "Not to worry. I brought replacements. They're not exactly the same, but they'll do."

Turning toward Cheng, Roger motioned him to come over. "Chuck, get the documents and that clipboard. You can write down the numbers of these locks on these documents. Let's put a note on them that Hong Kong Customs and Excise, as well as US Customs, have checked the container. That should satisfy anybody who's curious about the changes in the security codes."

Roger walked over to the unhappy terminal worker and thanked him. That changed his expression from looking pissed off to being more indifferent to what Roger and Aaron had done.

"I want a copy of the papers," Cheng said before heading to his car.

"That's not a problem. You guys provided the copies," Roger explained.

"I mean, I want copies with the new security codes."

"Fine, that's not a problem. I'll get them faxed to you later."

"No, I'll have them make copies now before we leave," Cheng insisted.

"Chuck, don't you trust us?" Roger asked. For a few moments, Roger and Cheng stood looking at each other. "Fine." Roger handed Cheng the papers and watched him walk over to the middle-aged man staffing the office.

After leaving Cheng and the container terminal, JJ drove Roger and Aaron back to Roger's flat.

Aaron studied the pictures Roger had taken. "I'm going to go out on a limb and say that the certification markings and safety language are all a bunch of crap. Kellie saw the operations and said she was afraid that there was no way these things were being tested," Aaron commented as he stared at the images.

"I'll call Ray. He may have a way for us to find out quickly." Ray didn't answer his cell phone. Roger tried Ray's office. It rang several times before Ray answered. "Ray, we were able to peek into one of the containers. I took a few pictures. Aaron and I are convinced that this Liwei guy is shipping bogus or otherwise deficient stuff. But, since our hunch may not be good enough, is there any way to contact someone to confirm our suspicions?"

"Since you and Aaron have Liwei's company name and the images, I'll send you the info so you can get confirmation from an industry rep. Have Aaron make the call since he can say he's a US Customs guy calling," Ray suggested. "Also, get me copies or fax everything to me so I can alert our guys. We should be able to identify the shipments and have them redelivered back to us. I'm going to be in the office for a bit longer so if you get confirmation of your suspicions, let me know. I can bug my people to jump on it ASAP."

"Given the time in the US, should we wait a few hours?" Roger wondered.

"Would you wait? If companies want us to look out for them, their reps can be bothered anytime we need their help. Make the call," Ray answered.

Roger went to his so-called desk in the corner of his bedroom. His desk was a wooden TV tray with a laptop computer and a folding chair. "Even if Ray sends the info right away, it'll take a few minutes to get here," Roger explained as Aaron stood behind him and waited. "First, I need to verify I have an internet connection. It's not good or reliable in these older flats," Roger added. "Let's grab a beer and wait in the other room while we give Ray time."

Roger opened two bottles. "Rather than waste these few minutes, can you take the pictures and documents we got from the container and transmit them to Ray? There's a shop down at the corner where you can make copies and send stuff." Roger jotted down Ray's fax number and held it out for Aaron to take. "And make sure your coversheet reminds him to have these containers tracked when they arrive in the US. We might as well find out who is importing and distributing this stuff."

"You sound like you still work for us," Aaron said, smiling. "One thing's for sure—I thought this was going to be a vacation. I knew Kellie would have a few meetings, but other than that, I envisioned us wandering around Hong Kong and enjoying ourselves. Instead . . ."

Before he could continue his thought, Roger interrupted. "Don't fixate on that right now. You know she's safe, and we're on to this Liwei guy and his operations. Don't start feeling sorry for yourself. In the last few days, you've done things you never expected to do. Although it may not seem like it right now, it'll be a great education and experience. Despite what's happened, there are lots of positives," Roger said, trying to raise Aaron's spirits. "Let's do this."

Roger guzzled down half of his beer. "Hopefully, when you get back, I'll have the info Ray's sending."

Aaron took a short swig of his beer, then left the flat with everything he needed to send to Ray. Aaron easily found the little shop at the corner of the street where Roger's flat was located. He entered and raised both hands with papers in each. "Copies? Fax?"

The young man behind the counter understood and led Aaron to the machines. Aaron faxed the documents to Ray. Once he saw the confirmation of the fax transmission, Aaron headed out, putting down money on the counter when he was done, letting the clerk take the amount needed. Aaron pocketed what the clerk left.

Aaron jogged back to Roger's.

"Let's take a look and see if Ray's message has come through." Roger bent down over the laptop and checked for new messages.

Aaron, sweating from his little bit of exercise, ripped off a piece of a paper towel and jotted down the name and phone number. Aaron stared at the number. "Does Ray's note say where this guy is located? The area code looks like it may be in southern California."

Aaron and Roger went back out to the living room. Before calling, Aaron made sure he had the documents he needed. Aaron looked at his watch. He knew that if his phone rang at nearly one in the morning, someone was probably calling with bad news.

Roger handed Aaron the handset. "Use the landline phone."

Aaron made sure to add the US country code numbers to the phone number as he pressed the buttons. He looked down at the documents, listening to the phone ring. He wasn't surprised that it wasn't being answered right away.

"Hello," a sleepy woman's voice answered on the other end after about eight rings.

"Sorry to be calling so late, but would Noah Harding be there?" Aaron heard nothing for several seconds.

"It's Noah. Who's calling?"

"Sorry to bother you so late. I'm Aaron Foster with US Customs, and I'm calling from Hong Kong," Aaron said, hoping that the call from Hong

Kong would explain why he was calling at such an odd time. "I understand you work for Millennium Laboratories."

"Yeah, that's right. Give me a second so I can go to another room."

Aaron waited until Noah spoke.

"You're calling from Hong Kong? I know we said you guys could reach out anytime, but this is a bit extreme, isn't it?"

"I'm calling because we got a heads-up about a shipment that's about to be exported and wondered if you can help us."

"Let me try to make this very simple. Right now, we're just in the metro Shanghai area for any product certification. If you've found anything made outside of that area of China that has our certification markings on them, then what you've found isn't legitimate. Meaning, the goods haven't been tested to our standards, and any attempt to make consumers believe they have is fraud."

"That clears this up. We'll follow these two containers," Aaron said, ready to hang up.

"Wait, wait! Are you able to give me some info about the shipper, producer, anything?" Noah asked.

"Not at this moment, but I'll see what I can do," Aaron answered and hung up.

He looked up at Roger. "You said something about this ChiTran company. If Liwei is shipping this crap to us, what are the other ChiTran companies shipping to us? And if they're willing to take the risk of shipping this stuff to the US, what the hell are they sending to places that barely check anything?"

Hearing Aaron's questions, Roger turned and looked out his living room window. "Those are great questions, and I'm afraid I know the answers," he muttered.

"One other thing. Noah's answer means we can see what activity there's been during the past few weeks. We can try to track them down. Just to be clear, I mean both the products and the people involved," Aaron said. "Let's pass this on to Ray. He can get things stirring back in the States."

A short time later, Ray forwarded Aaron's transmitted information to his West Coast contacts at customs. The information would be there waiting in the facsimile machine tray very late Friday night or in the early hours of Saturday morning West Coast time. As the fax machine printed a confirmation page of a successful transmission, Ray sat down at his desk to make calls. The time of day or—in this case, night—was irrelevant to him. Weekends were for people with regular jobs. That wasn't for him and others like him.

* * * * *

Kellie adjusted the room temperature in her room so that the air-conditioning ran on high, then showered. As she sat down, she realized she finally felt refreshed. She sat on the bed to use the phone on the nightstand and dialed the number to reach Aaron. He didn't pick up. She left a voice message.

"Aaron, Mr. Lai's daughter, Meilin, showed up at Liwei's complex this morning while he was away. I still don't have my papers, but she brought me to Guangzhou. I'm in a hotel here. Will call again later." Kellie hung up and enjoyed the view of the riverfront. She was also thankful that the hotel's air-conditioning system was working well. This was a welcome change from the dormitory room she'd been in for the past couple of days.

She wanted to call her parents but fought off the urge to make the call. Her parents would wonder what could be wrong if the phone rang in the middle of the night. She'd wait until they'd be up for breakfast before calling. She also needed time to figure out what she would say about where she was and what had happened.

Kellie debated the idea of a walk outside, but even that seemed to be something she shouldn't do, not because she didn't have documents, but more because of the humidity she felt during the few minutes she was outside when she arrived at the hotel. Instead, she decided she'd go down and find a spot in the hotel for tea and snacks.

The lobby lounge had an expansive view of the river. Kellie found a spot by the window. Armed with a notepad from the room, she needed to take stock of what was going on and what she could do. Sipping her tea, she stared at a blank piece of paper, wondering how this trip had spiraled out of her control. Though she turned her gaze toward the river, she saw nothing but a series of pictures in her mind of people she'd met since arriving in Hong Kong. Nothing about meeting Guang conjured up any problems that hinted at what was to come.

She concentrated on the day of the long meeting. Neither the introduction to Tai Shu nor the exchanges she had with Ms. Tai and Mr. Qian during the meeting led to anything other than discussions. She had to admit that even Liwei's aggressive questions weren't threatening. But the one thing that bothered her more than anything was the fact that people in that meeting believed she had been funneling information to ChiTran. Kellie looked at the blank piece of paper and wrote one word: "Father."

She remembered that Guang had said something about how her father had shared her insights with him. What insights, she wondered.

When she had finally mentioned to her parents that she was going out with Aaron, they had been naturally curious, asking questions about Aaron. Over time, her father had asked her about Aaron's job, what he did, how long he'd worked at customs, and the usual questions parents asked. What she realized as she thought about it was that over a long period, she may have provided a lot more information to her father than she could imagine. Each time she visited her parents or spoke to her father over the phone, she must have given him tidbits of information about Aaron's work. She never imagined that all those little pieces were being fit together like pieces of a puzzle. But even if those tidbits were being collected, how could they be that valuable to anyone? Why would her father have any use for it, and for what purpose?

Kellie concentrated. Her parents didn't live in some grand mansion. Yes, it was a big house and more than enough for a couple who raised one child, but not extravagant. They didn't own a fancy, expensive vacation home on the beach. In any given year, they might take one expensive trip somewhere. Her parents did have expensive cars, but they usually kept their cars for ten to fifteen years, so even that didn't seem outlandish to her. Her mother didn't have much in the way of expensive jewelry or anything out of the ordinary that she could recall.

Her mental inventory of her parents was leading her to a blank page. She saw no obvious benefit to her parents from anything she had said about Aaron's work. As she sat and stared at a list of single-line notes that she jotted down, she wasn't reaching any profound conclusions about her parents. She glanced at her watch. The time still wasn't right to call her parents.

She needed to do something. She got up and took her writing pad back to the room, tossed it onto the bed, and headed out. As she passed the check-in counter, she found a map to take with her and was outside and on the street in minutes. She didn't care about sweating in the humid air. Being out in the crowd, she wanted to be lost in this busy, crowded, noisy growing city. She didn't care whether she understood anything anyone was saying. Shoulders and arms brushed by her. She was jostled as groups of people swirled around her. None of that mattered because all around her, people were leading normal lives, and she desperately needed something to feel normal.

* * * * *

Meilin's driver didn't take her home or to her office. Instead, her driver negotiated the congested streets and stopped at a government building that included an office of China Customs' district office.

"I'll call when I'm ready," she said to her driver as she scooted out of the back seat. She entered the building to find two uniformed officers inside. Both smiled and nodded, but they made no effort to stop her or ask her who she was there to see. Meilin was familiar to the Guangzhou District Customs office and several district officials, including the man in charge, whose office was her destination.

The old government building needed to be refurbished. The inadequate overhead lighting in the wide and high-ceilinged hallways made the hallways very dim. The elevators in the ten-story stone building worked, but most of the people who worked in the building took the stairs because they were slow and frequent breakdowns often left people stuck for hours. A booming Chinese economy didn't mean that everything was getting modernized at the same rate of speed. Too many government buildings needed to be improved or, in some cases, demolished due to age. More importantly, Meilin thought, some offices needed to be moved to newly constructed buildings that were more reliable and could support the energy needs for all the new technology used in the offices.

Meilin decided she wouldn't risk using the elevators and climbed the central stairway to the fourth-floor office. She ascended the stairs and nodded to several familiar faces on the way. When she reached the fourth floor and turned in the direction of the office where she was going, a tall young woman in a customs uniform walking toward her nodded yes as if to signal that the person she wanted to see was available.

Even walking through the doors of the customs building meant she was taking a risk. Every visit meant she was initiating something that could get out of control. But this, like every one of her visits, was an opportunity to demonstrate to the people who were at the Hong Kong meeting that she should not be overlooked or dismissed.

When Meilin reached the door, she leaned closer and listened for a moment. She knocked lightly twice while twisting the doorknob.

A cigarette dangled between Shan Zhou's lips, his eyes squinting from the rising smoke and looking down at a document. Raising his head at the sound of the knock, he saw the door opening and placed the cigarette onto an ashtray. A smile spread over his face when he saw Meilin seemingly squeeze through the slightly opened door to his large office. She headed toward the chair in front of his desk.

Shan Zhou shared his four-hundred-square-foot office with numerous filing cabinets and a conference table that comfortably accommodated six chairs. His desk was angled in a corner. Though he had a secretary in a small adjoining office, he liked the control his office afforded him. His version of control meant he wanted all important documents in his office, and if anyone needed them, they had to come to him or his secretary. When his secretary came in to retrieve documents, she informed him who was asking for the documents she was taking.

"Visting my office on a Saturday? This must be very important," Shan said, smiling and exposing his cigarette-stained teeth. He leaned forward with arms folded and elbows resting on the desk.

Meilin made it her job to get to know certain people when she got into the trading business. She immediately understood how important it was to get to know some of the government officials who controlled the border and exports across the border. Shan Zhou was someone who was bright, friendly, and passionate about his job. She saw in him a person who could apply the rules strictly but still understood that the practical elements of business sometimes required the rules to be bent. When she met him over a decade earlier, he was a supervisor in the field but had risen through the customs ranks. Equally important to Meilin, his superiors at the provincial level liked him, which made him even more valuable.

"I have a problem, and China has a problem. They're connected," Meilin began. She watched Shan sit back in his chair and light up another cigarette, not bothering to ask Meilin if it was okay to light up. It was his office.

He crossed his legs and inhaled deeply. "I'm listening."

"My problem is that I have an American here in the city who has no documents. Her passport and Mainland Travel Permit have been taken from her by one of my competitors. I need some leverage to persuade this person to return the documents." Meilin watched Shan. He waved a hand, both in a gesture to continue and move the cigarette smoke away from his face.

"She arrived in Hong Kong, where she attended a business meeting. Somehow, my competitor brought her across the border and took her documents away from her. I've arranged for her to stay at a hotel, but we need to get her back to Hong Kong before things get out of control. Partly, getting her back is my challenge, but it's also a problem for you or, should I say, for China. First, we can't have headlines about an American abducted. Second, she came to Hong Kong with her boyfriend, who works for US Customs. Third, my competitor who brought her here is exporting some questionable products to the US. He's putting us all in a bad light. Together, this could cause some tension," Meilin explained.

"This competitor, who is it and where?"

"It's ChiTran Guangdong Specialties Company in Shenzhen," Meilin answered.

"Meilin, isn't your operation also ChiTran?"

"Yes, mine and several other companies are part of the ChiTran network, but otherwise, we each operate independently."

Shan Zhou inhaled and blew out the smoke. "We do have a problem. I'm here in Guangzhou. I have counterparts who oversee things in Shenzhen. We all have our separate areas of jurisdiction."

"But you can relay information to your Shenzhen counterpart and ask them to investigate."

Shan Zhou uncrossed his legs and sat up at the desk. "First, I would need more specific information from your American guest. Second, we might have to involve the public security bureau if these activities might be illegal. To some extent, you understand, these are domestic activities. If there are illegal exports, then we could get involved, but that goes back to my first problem. I'd have to address this the right way through my counterpart. You realize I can't just violate the authority of my colleagues in Shenzhen."

"But if I could provide more specific information, is it possible to leverage the situation?"

"Yes, it's possible," Shan conceded.

"Then I'll get you that information and call you."

Shan Zhou rose from his chair, sensing that Meilin understood that there was nothing more to say about the matters she raised without the information he needed.

"Thank you for your time. It was good to see you," Meilin said, smiling as she extended a hand. "I hope to speak to you very soon," she said, then turned and walked out. A few minutes later, she was back in her car, calling the hotel to talk to Kellie. Meilin jabbed the buttons on her cell phone, disconnecting the call after letting it ring a dozen times. A big sigh escaped.

Meilin didn't want to waste time, which is what she'd be doing if she went to her office or home. "Back to the hotel," she instructed the driver.

At the hotel, Meilin got out and told the driver to park and wait in the lobby lounge. Inside, she searched for the manager she'd spoken to earlier. Bellmen, hotel guests, and others scurried around the reception area, and after several minutes, she decided on a different approach and walked up to the reception counter.

"I'm sorry to trouble you, but I went out and must've left my key in the room. Could I please have a new key?"

The young, uniformed woman was happy to help. "Room number, please."

Meilin didn't remember Kellie's room number. "I'm registered as Moy Meilin," she answered. She waited as the young woman typed on the keyboard, confirming her as a guest.

Meilin took the elevator up to the room, knocked and entered after waiting what she thought was an appropriate amount of time. She settled into a comfortable chair and wondered how long she would have to wait. With the warmth of the sun-filled room, Meilin got up and found something cold to drink from the room's small refrigerator. Kellie wasn't likely to complain, considering that Meilin was paying for the room and any other expenses on the room's tab.

Meilin had finished off a soda. Frustrated with the wait, she stood and pulled the thin sheer drapes to look out the window every few minutes as if she'd be able to spot Kellie. She marched back to the small refrigerator and pulled out the miniature bottle of rum. She poured it into a glass, then added the last can of cola into the glass.

She had taken just a couple of sips when she heard the door opening.

Kellie took a couple of steps into the room and stopped. As she was putting the room key into her pocket, her head snapped up, surprised to see Meilin sitting in the room. "How did you get in?" she asked.

"I told the front desk that I had forgotten my key."

Kellie nodded slowly, realizing that if anyone checked, the room was in Meilin's name. She walked over to the bed and sat at the end of it.

"To help you get your documents, you need to help me. I have good contacts at China Customs here in Guangzhou, and we might be able to use those connections to pressure Liwei. But I need information to provide to customs. The Guangzhou office won't take any action directly because Liwei's facility is in Shenzhen. If you have any information that would give customs a reason to go and inspect Liwei, we can pass the information on to my contact. That might convince Liwei that he should return your documents," Meilin explained.

"I don't have anything concrete. No pictures, nothing to give you other than what Liwei let me see. Is that enough proof?"

"Are you sure you have nothing else?" Meilin pressed.

Kellie thought for a moment, realizing that there might be something, but not something she had. She saw Meilin studying her.

"Let's make a phone call," Kellie suggested. She walked over to the desk to use the phone.

Unlike Meilin's earlier unsuccessful attempt to call Kellie, her call to Hong Kong found Aaron in his Marriott room. He had just showered and was drying off when the phone rang.

"Aaron, it's—"

"Kellie, I got your message. What's going on? Are you able to get back to Hong Kong? Are you all right?" Aaron cut her off at the sound of her voice, elated that she called again after missing the earlier call. He'd heard Kellie's message after he returned from the trip he and Roger made to the container terminal.

Kellie looked over her shoulder and saw a slight crinkle in Meilin's brow and an expression of some confusion. "Aaron, I'm here with Meilin, who got me to the hotel. I still don't have my documents. Meilin swooped in and got me here, and she's trying to come up with a way to get my documents. We need to ask you a few questions. I'm going to put you on the speaker so I can take notes, okay?"

"Meilin is with you now?"

"Yes, she's standing right behind me. Why?"

"Roger and I thought she was going to be meeting us when we met with her father. Now I know why she wasn't there," Aaron answered. "Of course, put me on the speaker."

"I'm sorry I left without saying anything," Meilin interjected. She nodded to Kellie to continue.

"Meilin says she needs some information that she can use to persuade China Customs to investigate Liwei and make him more likely to return my documents. Remember what I said I saw?"

"Yes, yes. I remember. And, based on what you told me, Roger and I have been busy. I do have something for you. I was at the Hong Kong container terminal earlier today. Roger and I were able to take some pictures that put Liwei's operations in the crosshairs. I'm convinced that we have a company that is exporting some mislabeled smoke and carbon monoxide detectors and other stuff," Aaron said.

"How much trouble will this be on your end?" Kellie asked.

"What do you mean? I'm not sure I understand."

"What happens to the people or these things in the US?" Kellie clarified.

"The items, if they are what I think they are, will be destroyed if we catch them, and the folks on our end who are bringing them in could be prosecuted. Jail and fines are real possibilities. What we found at the container terminal earlier today and putting that together with what you told me, we don't want to wait for something terrible to happen, like a house or building fire or poison-related deaths. We've already got things started to try and get these things identified if they are already in the States," Aaron explained.

While Aaron had been talking, Meilin had ripped a piece of paper from the small notepad on the desk and wrote something, pushing the paper in front of Kellie.

"Meilin wants to know if you could fax the pictures you took today to us here at the hotel."

"If it's going to get you out of this, of course. Just get me a number." After sending copies to Ray, Aaron had brought the pictures that Roger had taken with him to the hotel.

Meilin used the pen in her hand as a pointer to show Kellie that the hotel's fax number was printed at the bottom of the paper she'd pushed across. Kellie read off the number to Aaron.

"What are your next steps? Is there anything more I can do?" Aaron asked.

Kellie turned in the chair to look at Meilin.

Meilin leaned closer to the phone, speaking slowly and deliberately in English. "Your pictures will give us more options with customs and with Liwei."

"What kind of options?" Aaron was curious.

"We'll have to see the pictures and decide how to use them," Meilin added.

"I'll let you know how we decide to proceed," Kellie said.

"Do you have Roger's cell phone number?" Aaron asked. "It doesn't matter. You should have it in case you need to reach me and I'm not here at the hotel. If I'm not here, I'm likely with him." After giving Kellie the number, he had another question. "Can we set up a regular call schedule now that you're in a hotel?"

Before answering, she looked back at Meilin. "Yes. I'll give you an update tomorrow afternoon, about the same time," Kellie said, then hung up.

"Why does he call you Kellie?" Meilin asked.

"Because that's my American name," Kellie answered.

"How long should we wait until we check for the fax from him?" Meilin wondered.

"Knowing him, he's probably running down to send it already."

"We'll both go down to get it. We didn't tell him that it should be sent to me and this room number," Meilin said.

In the lobby, Kellie and Meilin were directed to the guest business center, where incoming faxes arrived. Kellie sat alone and checked the clock on the wall, tapping her feet, wondering why Aaron's fax hadn't arrived. Meilin had left her to go check on the driver she had left in the lobby a couple of hours earlier.

Meilin returned, saw Kellie, and knew the fax hadn't arrived. "Should we call him?"

"Let's give him another fifteen or twenty minutes. I guess he might not be the only person trying to send a fax. It's a big hotel." Hearing herself say that helped to ease her impatience.

Meilin skimmed through a magazine as she sat and waited with Kellie. When the young woman working in the business center came out from a back room and tried to pronounce Kellie's name, Meilin dropped the magazine on a glass table. Several stapled pages were handed to her. Meilin nodded to indicate that she was the recipient. She handed the document to Kellie.

"There are more pages here than I expected," Kellie said. After the cover page, Kellie noticed a full handwritten page. That explained the delay. Aaron described what the images were and added a short summary about the shipment he had learned of a couple of weeks earlier.

Back in the room, Meilin and Kellie studied the images Aaron had sent. The pictures were black-and-whites, and the fax transmission added a snowy fuzziness to them. But Aaron's page-long explanation and the short captions under each page of images helped to explain what was being shipped.

"What do you think?" Kellie asked.

As her eyes moved from page to page, Meilin's head moved up and down slowly. "I think I can use them," Meilin said barely above a whisper.

Meilin was conflicted. Should she arrange a meeting with Liwei and confront him directly with the images and demand Kellie's documents or take them to her customs friend and make this the beginning of a complete take-down of Liwei's operation? She thought she'd be able to have both goals met if she went back to Shan Zhou at customs, but that might mean Kellie would have to stay in Guangzhou a bit longer, assuming Shan Zhou could be convinced to do what she wanted him to do.

* * * * *

Aaron took the stack of papers he had just faxed to Kellie and Meilin and exited the hotel and ducked into a cab. With the help of one of the hotel bellmen, the cab driver said he knew where Aaron wanted to go. The ride took longer than if JJ had been driving, but once Aaron recognized the buildings and streets, he pointed to a corner where the driver could let him out. Once the cab pulled away, he got his bearings to make sure he went down the right street, using the copy center he had used as the point of reference.

By the time Aaron reached Roger's flat, the sweat was beading up on his forehead, and he could feel sweat running down his back. He knocked on the door and heard some shuffling.

"Surprised to see you so soon. Miss me?" Roger said. He was barefoot, and his shirt was unbuttoned and opened to a white T-shirt.

"Got an unexpected call from both Kellie and Meilin."

"Both?"

"Kellie had left a message while we were at the container terminal. Then she called again a little while ago. She's at some hotel in Guangzhou where Meilin took her. That Liwei guy still has her documents, so she's still stuck across the border."

"What hotel is she in?"

"The conversation got going, and I never asked," Aaron answered. "But I did get a fax number so I could send her a document."

"Counselor, you need to work on your questioning skills."

"You're right, but I got caught up with Kellie being safely away from Liwei. Meilin said she had a contact at Chinese Customs who might be able to help apply pressure from that side of the border. But she said she needed documentation to get her contact to help. I immediately thought of the photos we sent Ray earlier. When I mentioned those, they wanted me to fax them."

Roger was now sitting forward in the only chair he had in his living area. "This opens up some interesting avenues of approach. If Meilin thinks China Customs is approachable because of the photos, why not see what Ray and Chuck think about that idea? We might have gotten too preoccupied by our thoughts of getting the info back to our guys in the States. Maybe we have something that would motivate the locals to do something," Roger suggested.

"We need to interrupt Ray and Chuck's weekend again," Roger added.

"It seems to me that Chuck is too timid to do anything."

"We'll have to keep trying. He's been willing to meet with us, and he showed up at the container terminal. If we package this the right way, maybe we can nudge him over the hump to do more, take some initiative," Roger hoped.

"What's your idea?"

"Basically, it's Meilin's idea. We just massage the idea a bit. We've got Liwei's company name, and we have the images. We need to convince our boy Chuck to move this up the chain at Hong Kong Customs and have his bosses reach out to China Customs and put the clamps on Liwei's operation. China Customs needs to get the impression that if they don't do something, the US may have to take a closer look at every China-origin shipment that either has these types of goods described on the manifest or has a tariff classification number relating to these goods. You and Ray can emphasize those points. I can't. I'm a private citizen," Roger said, smiling.

Chapter 10

Unplanned

US (Friday, May 15)

Alvin Liang stood in the check-in line for his flight to Los Angeles. He carried his laptop in a computer bag that weighed down the right shoulder of his tall but wiry narrow-shouldered frame. A small carry-on roller had enough clothes for a couple of days, toiletries, and some document-filled folders. The right sleeve of his sports coat covered most of his right hand as he was adjusting the shoulder strap every minute or two.

He checked his watch every few minutes though he had plenty of time.

He closed his eyes and shook his head for a moment to rid his mind of the call with his wife earlier in the day. This was an unplanned trip. He made up a flimsy story that he had a last-minute request to consult with a business group that he had been working with for years. She had pressed for details. He had been deliberately vague. He told her he'd be home in three days, four at the most. His explanation for the trip left out the possibility that he might fly to Asia if the situation demanded it.

"ID," the check-in clerk asked when Mr. Liang got to the head of the line.

Alvin reached into his jacket pocket and put his passport on the counter along with his ticket.

"Are you traveling onward?"

"No, just to Los Angeles. Why?"

"Nothing. It's just that most people use a driver's license instead of a passport as ID for a domestic flight." The young woman checked the photo page and glanced up, then put the passport back on the counter. After a few keystrokes, she handed Mr. Liang his boarding pass with a smile and a nod.

As he walked toward security, he guessed that warming spring temperatures were encouraging people to get away for the weekends. Despite the wide airport corridors, the airport was crowded. He hadn't given any thought to what it might be like to travel on a Friday evening at the last minute.

Seeing the throngs of people, he was glad he could afford a first-class ticket. For some unexplained reason, things moved along a bit faster for passengers with a first-class ticket. He needed to get through security and make calls for hotel and car rental arrangements before taking off. It would be a bit late to do that when he arrived on the West Coast. If the airport crowd was an indicator, he wondered if he'd be able to secure his preferred car and hotel.

Alvin made it through the first-class security line quickly and entered the airline lounge. In the lounge, he called and made his rental car and hotel arrangements without any hiccups. He wanted to be able to have a little time to relax before the flight so that he might be able to steal some sleep time on the cross-country flight. Though the lounge bar had a limited liquor selection, it had Scotch and whiskey. He gave himself a generous pour of Scotch.

To others in the lounge, Alvin Liang looked like an older Asian man dozing in a chair with his head leaning against a wall. He wasn't dozing. His mind was thinking about the office he needed to visit, the staff he needed to talk to, and how to avoid problems for himself. His goal was to be home in a few days. If things didn't get resolved the "right" way, he didn't know when he'd see his wife. He hadn't prepared a backup plan. The one thing he knew was that the bank account contained sufficient funds for his wife to join him in Asia. But if she joined him, where would he tell her to go when he wasn't sure where he'd be flying to if he left the country?

By the time Alvin disembarked his flight in Los Angeles and wandered to the pick-up point for the rental car shuttle buses, he looked haggard as his white-and-gray whiskers were reflecting light. The light breeze outside was blowing his thinning hair, and despite a couple of hours of sleep on the flight, his eyelids were partially closed.

By ten-thirty, he was safely in the hotel and ready to slide under the covers. His body clock was still on East Coast time, where it was one-thirty in the morning. Aside from the panicked call he'd gotten that caused him to fly cross-country, he didn't know what he would learn in the morning when he went to Sunrise Imports. A series of customs notices warning that one particular company's products were suspected of failing US standards and needed to be returned to customs caused the manager at Sunrise Imports to make several calls. Usually, one company wouldn't be a problem. But, in this case, the problem involved Sunrise's biggest customer.

PART II

The Present

Chapter 11

Maneuvers

US West Coast (Saturday, May 16)

"He was shredding papers when we walked in," Jake Evans's driver said.

Jake walked into the office and went to the shredder, lifting the top of the machine. It wasn't a cross-cut shredder, but one that cut paper in narrow strips. With time and a lot of patience, Jake knew people back at the office could match up the paper strips if it became a necessity. He hoped the two people he found working at Sunrise Imports would tell him what he needed to know and avoid the need to piece the paper strips together.

"What's your name?" Jake asked.

"Desmond Lupo," the Sunrise manager said as he took a step backward and sat down behind a desk.

Jake noticed that the man was a bit tall, perhaps six feet, with some graying hair beginning to lighten the youthful thick black hair that had dominated his scalp. Lupo had the usual middle-aged waistline protruding a few inches. Jake thought that Lupo was wearing someone else's shirt. The polo-style shirt was too broad at the shoulders and hung long on his body. He thought to himself that all these middle-aged men needed to spend a little more time working on their physiques. It was seeing people like Lupo that motivated him to keep up his own workout routine even though there were many days he dreaded doing it.

"Isn't it an early Saturday morning for you?" Jake asked.

Lupo looked at Jake and the other two agents standing in the office. "Saturdays are good for clearing out old files and making space for new transaction documents. It's paperwork. Otherwise, it'll just keep piling."

Jake nodded in agreement. Moving toward the wall, he leaned against it and folded his arms. "What time did you get to the office?"

Lupo shrugged. "I'm not sure of the exact time, but maybe an hour or an hour and a half ago."

Jake's eyes stayed on Lupo, but his head tilted slightly toward the man behind the desk. "You want me to believe that you crawled out of bed at, what, five-thirty or six o'clock on a Saturday morning so you could clean out some files?"

"I can't make you believe anything," Lupo said softly.

Over Lupo's shoulder and on the top of a short bookcase, Jake noticed a framed eight-by-ten photograph. It was Lupo with a young man in uniform. It wasn't a military uniform.

"Anyone in your family work for customs?" Jake asked.

Lupo half turned in his chair, twisting his head to the photo behind him. "My son."

Jake nodded. He didn't like the thought forming in his head. "He works here in Los Angeles or Long Beach?"

"Yes," Lupo answered.

"Write down his full name, address, and phone number," Jake directed. He stared down at Lupo as the manager fidgeted with a pen and piece of paper and started writing.

When Lupo finished, he sat back in the chair, not offering the piece of paper to Evans.

Jake used his eyes to signal one of the other agents in the room to get the paper. "You know what to do with it," Jake said, and the agent with the piece of paper disappeared out of the office.

Jake was about to say something more when an agent who had been in one of the other offices entered and whispered in his ear. Jake followed him into the adjacent office.

A drawer in a metal file cabinet was pulled open as far as it would go.

"This is strange. If they are cleaning out old paperwork to make room for new, why am I seeing only one company's folder empty and all the others looking like they are overstuffed?"

Jake stepped toward the file cabinet and squatted down to take a better look into the third drawer down. He saw several empty expandable pocket folders. ChiTran was written on the empty folders. Other than the ChiTran name tab, there was nothing in the folders. Jake stood and walked back to Lupo's office, where Lupo sat quietly in his chair.

"Mr. Lupo, we're going to be continuing our conversation in our offices. Your assistant is also going to be coming with us. We're going to collect and take some things with us. Rest assured, we'll secure the facility. Please give me the keys," Evans said with the palm of his left hand up.

Lupo sat back and searched the right front pocket of his slacks, pulling out keys. He stood and dropped them into Evans's outstretched open palm. "Do I need a lawyer?" Lupo asked.

"Do you think you need one?" Jake responded. "If you want one, we'll let you make the call after we get to our offices. You sit tight here. We need to take care of a few things before we go."

* * * * *

Alvin Liang drove toward Sunrise Imports. Once he turned onto the street, he slowed to look for the address. The SUVs he saw ahead of him caught his eye. As he noted the building addresses counting down to his destination, he felt his pulse quicken slightly, and he felt warm. His left hand reached down and pressed the button to open the passenger side window for some fresh air to circulate in the car, but it didn't help.

He was only a couple of buildings away from Sunrise when he realized that the SUVs were parked in front of Sunrise and in its driveway. He drove past Sunrise and looked for a place to park. He drove about a hundred yards and turned into a parking area that would accommodate a dozen cars in front of an office building. It was on the opposite side of the street from Sunrise and provided an unobstructed view except for the increasing number of cars passing by. He chose a spot where his vision wouldn't be blocked by anyone else who might pull in and park. He hoped that it would remain deserted on a Saturday morning.

He opened his window rather than run the engine and the air conditioning. As he sat waiting to see any activity outside of Sunrise, his pulse calmed. He had no idea how long the SUVs had been parked, but forty minutes into his vigil, he saw two vested men with large trash bags putting them into the SUV in the driveway. After another ten-minute wait, he saw Desmond Lupo, the office manager, being escorted into the SUV parked at the curb. He also saw someone else being put into the SUV in the driveway, but he couldn't see who it was.

Alvin knew he couldn't call Sunrise and had no intention of going near the office. He started debating with himself about whom he should contact in China. Guang should've been the natural choice because he was family, but Guang didn't directly control any operations in China. Guang left that to his daughter, and Meilin didn't have any influence on any of the others who fed into the ChiTran operation.

He realized he needed to call Rong Qian or Shu Tai in China. Alvin concluded that he needed both on the other end of the line at the same time. He checked his watch and started calculating the time difference. It was late at night in China.

As he watched three SUVs leave Sunrise, he decided to get back to the hotel to make that call to China. Half an hour passed before Alvin was on his phone in his hotel room. He found his black leather-bound notepad with an address book insert. He had to put himself into his Chinese language frame of mind. Speaking and thinking in Chinese was much easier for him than for his daughter. His upbringing was in Chinese, and he had regular professional contacts that required him to converse in Chinese.

Rong's snoring was as loud as the ringing phone. That didn't prevent his wife from being roused by the phone despite her own deep sleep. She reached out instinctively and switched on a lamp. She propped herself on an elbow and reached across her husband and picked up the receiver. "Who?"

"Liang Zhixin," Alvin said, using his Chinese name.

In her semi-sleep state, the name meant nothing to her, but whoever was calling was important enough to her husband to have the home phone number. She grabbed her husband's shoulder and shook with fingers digging into his skin until his eyes opened. "For you." She put the receiver in Rong's hand.

Rong flipped the covers off with his free hand and sat up slowly, his feet dangling from the bed.

"It's Liang Zhixin. We have some problems we must discuss. Can you have Shu Tai join us to discuss?"

Still trying to chase the sleep away, Rong said nothing for a few seconds before answering. "Let me go to my other phone, and I'll be able to call Shu Tai." He gave the receiver to his wife, instructing her to hang up once he picked up the other phone.

Rong glanced at the time as he shuffled out of the bedroom. He picked up the receiver and let his wife know she should hang up. He fumbled with buttons on the phone. "I'm calling Shu," he said, not waiting to hear if Alvin was on the line.

Once Shu was on the line, Rong apologized for calling so late, then let Alvin take over the call.

"Customs raided my Los Angeles office this morning, and they took two of my staff with them when they left. I saw them taking bags full of things, probably computers and documents. Of course, this means we may have to make major adjustments in our China export operations, especially what we are importing into the United States," Alvin explained.

"We know which operation we need to adjust," Rong interjected. "What if we use a different US office to get things into the market? Will that keep the revenues flowing to us?"

"Possibly, but that's a short-term solution if customs did get documents. And, if Mr. Lupo, my manager, is questioned and provides all that he knows, we could lose everything," Alvin continued without saying everything running through his mind. He suspected that some of what he was dealing in could land him in jail. He didn't think his China-based friends appreciated the level of risk that he was taking.

"Liwei is a problem," Shu said. "What he's done in recent weeks and in the past few days must be attended to," she said. She assumed Alvin already knew about his daughter's situation, but if he didn't, she wasn't going to get into that on this call.

"We can't just stop all our US business. That's too much to abandon. Are we agreed on that?" Rong inquired.

"I have to consider the risks," Alvin answered. "What changes you make to the operations in China are important. We're under close scrutiny here. I agree that shutting down in the US is our last resort."

"Give us some time to make some adjustments," Shu added.

"I must warn you that we may not have much time. Depending on what information customs gets out of the two people they took away, there may be no time at all," Alvin warned. "Remember that our agreement, our compact, commits us to protect one another. We went into this endeavor with that as a core element for our success. I expect you to act accordingly."

"We understand the situation, but it won't get solved in the middle of the night when we are not thinking properly. Keep us informed, and we'll talk again very soon." Rong hung up.

Alvin moved the receiver from his ear and just stared at the phone. Rong had just hung up on him. He wasn't convinced that his Chinese colleagues appreciated his predicament. Now what? Even if Guang couldn't do much to fix the China problem, Alvin thought he needed to get Guang up to speed because he didn't feel confident that either Rong or Shu would act as fast as he needed them to act. Alvin referred to the handwritten notes from a few days ago and called the Conrad Hotel in Hong Kong. One more person was getting a very late-night call.

After explaining what happened at Sunrise Imports and describing the call with Rong and Shu, Alvin was encouraged by Guang's more sympathetic reaction. They were cousins, family, and business colleagues.

"I'll try to have a plan by morning, but I can't promise anything," Guang said. "There are sensitivities just as there are many different relationships that must be considered, and some need to be maintained if we're to protect ChiTran and our future."

Alvin Liang thought he understood what Guang was trying to communicate. He wished people would just come out and say what they meant instead of leaving so much to be interpreted, creating a lot of possibility for errors in understanding. He knew there were dozens of relationships that facilitated ChiTran's money-making ventures, but he wasn't sure which ones Guang was concerned about as Alvin thought about the business relationships he might need to sever.

After hanging up from the call with Guang, the question Alvin needed to answer was where he would be going next. Was he heading home or somewhere out of the country?

* * * * *

Agent Evans placed Lupo and his assistant, Jacqui Ramirez, in separate offices with a customs agent. They would have to wait. Jake was making notes to himself from the key points of Attaché Jackson's fax transmission from Hong Kong. He could already tell that ChiTran was central to this investigation, and he highlighted the information about products exported to the United States and the confirmation from Millennium Laboratories that any label on the goods indicating they met Millennium's testing standards was false. To Jake, that meant some of the products either might not or did not meet government and industry standards, putting people at risk.

Through the open door to his office, Jake waved one of his agents into his office. "We need to get someone on this and track down the most recent shipments and try to get them back. See what you can do." Jake handed the agent a slip of paper with handwritten notes.

Jake picked up the notepad that had his notes and a fresh pad. He walked a few doors down to the office where Jacqui Ramirez sat with a glass of water on the desk in front of her. Jake took the chair behind the desk to face her. The office was a regular office normally occupied by someone during the week. Nothing in the office suggested it was an interrogation room. It had no mirror on the wall, no camera, nothing. Jake wanted her to be at ease and give him the information he needed.

Ramirez sat slightly forward in her chair and was leaning forward. Her elbows rested on her thighs, and the fingers of her hands were intertwined. Jake noticed the tension around her mouth and eyes. With any rocking back and forth, she would be nearing panic mode. When Jake sat down, he realized that the person who normally sat in the chair was a bit shorter as it seemed to be set high, making him appear taller and bigger to Ramirez. Though not a big man, his broad shoulders might make him seem a bit more intimidating to Ramirez.

"What's your husband doing today?" It was an off-the-wall question, but seeing Ramirez's ring, he thought he'd start in a way that might be unexpected. He saw her brow crinkle.

"I don't know," Ramirez answered, shrugging her shoulders as she answered. "He was still sleeping when I left this morning."

"Did he know you'd be going to the office today?"

Ramirez turned her head slightly as if prodding Evans to ask the question again. He didn't. "I told him last night."

"When last night? What time?" Evans pressed.

Again, Ramirez shrugged. "I'm not sure about the time. I know it was after dinner."

"Ms. Ramirez, I want to understand this. Is it correct that Mr. Lupo didn't tell you to come to the office this morning before the end of the workday yesterday?"

"No, no. I know he called me after my family had dinner, but on Thursday night. I'm sure of that."

"A few hours after you'd left the office and been home," Evans said. She nodded in response. He noticed that she was sitting up straighter and further back in the chair, looking a bit more comfortable than just a few minutes earlier.

"How often does Mr. Lupo have you or someone else from the office come in on Saturday mornings to clear out old documents?" Jake wanted to know.

"We try to do this during the week if we have a few minutes here and there. I might have been asked to do this on a Saturday once or twice before, but he usually lets me know a few weeks in advance if I need to work on a Saturday."

"How long have you worked at Sunrise?"

"Four or five years," Ramirez answered.

"Would you say that his call Thursday evening was out of the ordinary?"

"Yes, very unusual."

"Did Mr. Lupo explain why he was making this late call and request for you to be in the office so early today?" Jake inquired.

"He didn't really explain except to tell me that he'd pay me extra if I could come in early. That's all."

For the moment, Jake was satisfied that she didn't know much more than she was telling.

"I'm going to have you wait here while we talk to Mr. Lupo. If you want something to drink or need to use the facilities, just let my agent sitting outside this office know," Jake said as he stood and walked out. Desmond Lupo awaited him.

Jake was in an open work area with several desks. The agents who had been with him earlier sat in pairs or threes, writing up a report of the morning's activity.

"Any news about the son?" Jake asked.

"We've located him and have three agents on the way to pay him a visit and bring him in for a little chat," one explained.

* * * * *

The agents parked on the curb and walked past a small office and an open iron gate. Inside the iron gate, the apartment building could've been mistaken for a motel building. There were two levels of apartment doors that opened to the outside. The apartment building surrounded a small swimming pool and sunbathing area in the center.

There were six sets of exterior stairs leading up to the second level, where the younger Lupo's apartment was located. The agents climbed the stairs and stopped at apartment 222. Using the heel of his fist, one of the agents drummed on the door hard enough for anyone inside to hear but not so hard that it would arouse the neighbors who might be sleeping in on a Saturday morning.

The younger Lupo lounged on the sofa in his boxer shorts with one leg outstretched on it. A large mug of coffee sat on the coffee table in front of him. His head jerked up from a magazine when he heard the low pounding on his door. He swung his leg around, standing up, wondering if he should throw on a pair of jeans.

"I'm coming. Give me a second!" he shouted out as he went and grabbed his jeans from the floor by his bed. He heard another series of knocks. "Damn it!"

Before opening the door to his impatient unexpected visitors, he peeked through the peephole. "Shit," he whispered to himself.

He opened the door, and his eyes went straight to the badges hanging on chains around the necks of the three agents at the door.

"Throw a shirt on. You're coming with us," one of the agents informed Lupo.

Lupo didn't say anything. He made an about-face and walked back into his bedroom with three agents following behind him. A few minutes later, he was in a car. The only good thing was that he wasn't handcuffed.

* * * * *

"When they get here with the son, sit on him till I'm ready. That might be a while. We'll see how Daddy performs first," Jake said.

Desmond Lupo, the manager, sat in an office identical to the one Ramirez occupied.

"Do I need a lawyer?" Lupo said before Jake could sit down.

"If you want a lawyer, feel free to use this phone," Jake said as he just pointed to the phone on the desk. "At the moment, you are not accused of anything. We're trying to understand some things, and you may be able to help us do that. If we reach a point where you feel that you need to call your lawyer, that's no problem as long as you understand that when you do that, I'll need to call the lawyers we work with, and we'll all be here a lot longer," Jake answered. Jake already understood that either way, they would be there for hours.

Lupo shook his head, affirming his understanding. He pushed himself back into the chair and crossed his legs. With his elbows on the arms of the chair, he steepled his hands as the fingertips of one hand touched those of the other. He tried to present a relaxed appearance as Jake settled into his chair, but Jake, an experienced interrogator, noticed Lupo's tension.

"Tell me about ChiTran," Jake started.

Lupo shrugged, his hands not moving. "It's a Chinese company. We clear shipments for them like we do for other clients."

"What kinds of products and how often?" Jake continued.

"A variety of consumer goods, household-related goods. We do multiple shipments for them a month."

"Why were you culling the ChiTran file and not others? Some of those folders for your other clients were pretty full."

"We needed more space for filing ChiTran documents because we've had an uptick in recent weeks with their transactions," Lupo answered.

"When did you decide you needed more filing space for ChiTran? And, before you answer this question, you need to be clear because we can look at a lot of things to determine your veracity, including phone records and questioning your son," Jake warned.

Lupo lowered his hands into his lap and uncrossed his legs. "Lately, a few shipments have been questionable."

"Questionable, how?" Jake pressed, wondering how Lupo would explain recent shipments.

"There was a concern that some of the items they shipped may have been sent without being tested." Lupo was being careful.

"You realize you're facilitating the importation of questionable goods and suddenly decide to rid your files of documents related to those items. It appears that you realized there was a problem. Did you call Ms. Ramirez Thursday night and get her into the office to shred documents this morning? Does that sum up the situation?"

Lupo shrugged but said nothing.

"What did your son tell you?"

"Nothing, really."

"What the hell does that mean? You realize he's going to be out of a job, and after we question him, he may be facing charges," Jake warned. "Either he said something or really said nothing. Which is it?"

Lupo's tight lips and slightly squinting eyes made him look like someone weighing his options before saying anything more. "My son worked for me before he started working for customs. He was familiar with the ChiTran name," Lupo offered.

Jake said nothing. He was waiting for Lupo to continue. There was silence for a very long fifteen seconds. Lupo squirmed in the chair, pressing into the back and repositioning his feet. He was visibly uncomfortable. He kept shifting in the chair, raising himself slightly, and tugged at the fabric on his legs as if there were folds under him that were uncomfortable. "My son became aware of recent redelivery notices and agreed to look into what the problem might be. A few days ago, he let me know there might be some other activity that might not be good for my business."

"You sitting here, that's not good for business," Jake said. "You're very wrong thinking that shredding those documents helped you. I've got people who can pull documents, and we'll find out how many shipments you processed, what was in those shipments, and where they went. When we get those redeliveries, we're going to get someone to examine them, and you may be looking at criminal prosecution."

Jake got up and took a step toward the door then stopped. "What's your son's name?"

"Damien."

Jake walked out, leaving Lupo sitting in the office, staring at the ceiling. Jake saw three of his agents standing around a young man sitting in a chair at the side of a desk. Nervous energy caused the young Lupo, Damien, to drum his fingers on the desk while his eyes seemed to keep moving from one agent to another, waiting for something to happen. Good, Jake thought. Damien should be nervous and scared. Jake gave the agents one nod, and he saw one of the agents tap the younger Lupo on the shoulder.

Jake found another vacant office and sat down. When Damien entered, Jake's eye movements were enough to command the young man to sit.

Jake settled comfortably into a high-backed upholstered desk chair. "Nice photo of you in your inspector uniform at your father's office," Jake started. "Too bad you won't be wearing that much longer," Jake said and saw Damien swallow.

Damien's hands gripped the arms of the chair, one knee pumping nervously up and down. His T-shirt, faded jeans, mussed black hair, and unshaven face gave him a disheveled look.

"I don't know—"

"Stop! You're in the shit up to your neck. Starting with this 'I don't know' bullshit will get you nowhere. It'll just take you deeper into it, and getting out of it will be almost impossible," Jake warned. Jake's eyes darted for a second to the agent leaning against the doorway and saw the look of enjoyment on the agent's face.

"I worked at my father's office for a year, maybe. It wasn't that long," Damien began.

"I'm not interested in your work history. Tell me about the shredded file," Jake prompted.

"I'm not sure—"

"You're beginning to piss me off big time," Jake interrupted. "Your father is sitting in another office. We've been to the office, and I've already spent some time with him in another office. I can put your ass into a more uncomfortable place. It's up to you. Right now, I'm exercising some professional courtesy questioning you here. I could've had my guys bring you in wearing cuffs," Jake said, even though he hadn't given any thought to having the younger Lupo cuffed.

"I got wind of some problems with ChiTran imports, and I know my father processes a lot of ChiTran shipments. It's a big client, and he's been dealing with them for a while," Damien admitted. "I let him know that there were several shipments being called back for re-examination. I'm not completely sure, but it appeared that some of the products might be hazardous or something. I thought he should know."

"You worked at Sunrise. What do you know about ChiTran?"

Damien gave a slight nod and hesitated, thinking about an answer. "ChiTran isn't one company. I think it's a group of Chinese companies that are part of ChiTran. It's like you have General Motors with different companies like Cadillac or Buick or Chevrolet, right?"

"Have you seen ChiTran import documents that have these different company names?" Jake followed up.

"I've seen a few different company names that included ChiTran."

Jake nodded and jotted down notes. "Why shred? Your father should know that it won't help him. We have the paper trail that leads back to him."

"I guess he panicked," Damien speculated. "Will the other office be shut down, too? I mean it'll put the family in a financial bind."

"What other office?" Jake asked.

Damien closed his eyes and sighed. "I thought you knew there's another Sunrise Imports office."

"Where?"

"San Francisco."

"Who's in charge of that office?" Jake inquired.

"Technically, my father manages both, but he can't be in two places at once, so he has a manager there. He flies up there regularly, and they have regular calls."

"Is your father the owner of Sunrise Imports?" Jake wondered.

"I guess. I've always assumed it, but he's never really said one way or the other, and I guess I never asked."

Jake sat back in the chair, appraising Damien. If something was missing, it was because he hadn't asked the elder Lupo all the right questions. The two looked at each other for a few silent moments before Jake pushed out of his chair.

"What happens to me now?" Damien asked.

Jake moved to the front of the desk, leaning back on it, and looked down at Damien. "You're done. You'll give notice effective immediately, and I'm going to make sure your personnel file includes a notation that you violated rules about confidentiality, as well as using your position and access to information to notify a private entity of impending action against them. I don't want there to be any chance that you might try to get a job with another agency. Just so you understand the gravity of what you've done, you knew the shipments might cause harm to consumers and, nevertheless, helped your father cover up that fact. Who knows if the US Attorney will decide if you should face any charges?"

Jake walked out of the office and went to one of his agents. "Detain the bastard. We can justify it for a few hours or even a day. What he did disgusts me." Jake needed a bit more time with the older Lupo.

Jake found Desmond Lupo appearing to be dozing in his chair, arms folded and chin resting on his chest. Lupo's head popped up before Jake got to his chair.

"Your son tells me that you have an office in San Francisco." Jake took a notepad and pen and placed them in front of Desmond. "Write down the name of your manager, the office address, and phone numbers to the office and your manager's home phone."

As Lupo started writing, Jake pressed on for information. "Who owns Sunrise Imports?"

"A corporation owns Sunrise."

"But there must be someone who you've dealt with, the face of the corporation that owns Sunrise. Who hired you, or who do you report to?"

"I've always dealt with the same person. His name's Alvin Liang."

"He's here, local?" Jake asked.

"No, he's back east. I don't see him much, and we don't talk much. I just send him regular reports about how Sunrise is doing."

"While you're writing down the info for your San Francisco office, you can add whatever you have about Alvin Liang," Jake instructed.

"I don't have any of that info about Mr. Liang with me."

"Then just add Liang's name to the list. We'll come back to the Liang info later. Just give me the info about San Francisco." Jake let Lupo finish writing. "The idea of shredding ChiTran-related documents—was it your idea or Liang's idea?"

"You need to understand, ChiTran was the first big client we had. Mr. Liang said early on that we were all going to do well as long as we took care of ChiTran."

"And you thought that what you were doing would be helpful to your client?" Jake asked. "So, Mr. Liang didn't have anything to do or say about the shredding?"

"No," Lupo said softly.

Jake went out into the work area and huddled with a few of his agents. He tasked one to contact agents in San Francisco and get things moving to get inside that office and do a search there. He tasked another to start looking into California and Delaware business registration records to find anything about Sunrise Imports and, once Lupo provided Liang's name, to do a business records search on his name.

* * * * *

Alvin Liang stood at the window of his hotel room, staring down into a parking lot. The hotel building was casting a long shadow over the lot and the cars below as if it was much later in the day than it was. He rubbed his face with both hands, trying to chase away the physical and mental fatigue that had crept over his body. His thoughts had raced in so many directions during the morning and early afternoon that he was tired from thinking about how to react to what he'd seen at Sunrise without any time to plan for the next steps he needed to take.

He walked over to the desk in his room and plopped down into the desk chair, then put his head in the palms of his hands and closed his eyes. He wanted to walk into a bank and withdraw a large sum of money, but he couldn't. He was in the wrong place to do that. The amount in his mind would only be allowed if he was at his bank, thousands of miles away. It was something he'd want to do. He couldn't call and tell his wife to do it. She'd want to know why, and he couldn't explain it to her, not now. He had kept her out of his business, as much her choosing as his.

Did he need to assume the worst after seeing Desmond Lupo being taken away? The only answer to that thought was, well, of course. That being the case, where should he go? Neither the San Francisco office nor home seemed to be the right answer.

Chapter 12

Disarray

Hong Kong (Saturday–Sunday, May 16–17), US (May 16)

A sliver of light cut through the room as the sun rose in the eastern sky. The drapes were pulled but not blocking out all light. Guang was still in bed but awake with the palm of a hand on his forehead. He tossed and turned most of the night. Sleep evaded his efforts as he could not calm the thoughts colliding in his head after the call from his cousin, Zhixin Liang, Kaili's father. His thoughts spun all night without any plan forming. The only thing he was sure about was he couldn't let any part of ChiTran collapse. There were too many people depending on the profits, especially him and Meilin, to allow any part of the operation to fold and thereby decrease revenues.

When he sat up and turned onto the side of the bed, he could feel his pajamas twisting and tugging on his body. He slid off the edge of the bed and tried to stand upright. Along with a lack of sleep, his lower back was preventing him from standing straight as he walked into the adjoining room. He felt his body acting its age. He squinted as he pulled open all the drapes and let the morning sun cast its light into the room. Meilin was on his mind. He needed to talk to her and find out what she was up to and keep her from doing anything rash.

It was a few minutes after six. He pressed the buttons for Meilin's home phone. An answering machine announced that he had reached the ChiTran Research and Manufacturing Group. Typical of Meilin, he thought. She was all business. His mouth opened to say something when she picked up and cut off the pre-recorded greeting.

"Hello?" The voice sounded cautious, answering at such an early hour.

"Meilin, we must talk."

She recognized her father's voice. "I agree. I'm sorry I haven't called, but a lot is happening."

"Then you should tell me," Guang said, hoping that her news might help him.

Meilin explained that she had gotten Kellie out of Liwei's facility without getting her documents and drove Kellie to a hotel in Guangzhou. "Kaili and I had an interesting call with her boyfriend, Aaron. He faxed us pictures of Liwei's shipment that he and Roger Steeg took at the container terminal. Liwei's shipment is full of goods that will jeopardize ChiTran. Aaron said that the Americans are on to what's going on because of shipments they identified weeks ago." Then she added, "I spoke to the Guangzhou Customs district director. I think we can use the photos and information about Liwei's other shipments and shut him down."

Guang ran his free hand through his uncombed hair. Nothing that Meilin said relieved him of his stress. "You can't just shut Liwei down. It's not your decision."

After a pause, Meilin responded. "It won't be my decision. I'm just giving Chinese Customs information, and it'll be their decision."

"Meilin, I'm asking you not to pursue the customs route until after this has been discussed with Rong and Shu. We must consider everything."

"I've already been in contact with customs. Not only will it look strange if I just stop my interaction with them, but it could negatively impact our operations. Right now, it is Liwei's actions that are jeopardizing ChiTran, and he's doing it because our top leadership is too afraid to do what's necessary," Meilin countered.

Guang knew there was truth in Meilin's statement, but she wasn't the one to decide. "We'll convene a special meeting with just a small number of people to resolve the problem. I promise that whatever we decide, it will limit Liwei's future influence and role in ChiTran. We need to handle this opportunity to give you an advantage."

Meilin found her father's request to hold off contacting customs distasteful, but she was reluctant to refuse his request outright. "I'm willing to compromise. I'll limit my customs approach for now, and I'll wait to hear what you, Rong, and Shu decide to do about Liwei. But if I don't think Liwei is disciplined sufficiently, I'm going to follow through with what I said I'd do."

"I promise we'll act," Guang said.

"You are more optimistic than I am. As one of the elders, you and the others must, like the rest of us, remember that you must act for the good of all of us," Meilin reminded her father and cut the connection after several seconds of silence. As she hung up, she smiled. Her father hadn't noticed her careful wording regarding customs. If she wasn't assured of an acceptable resolution, she wouldn't hesitate to go back to Shan Zhou with the documents she now had.

* * * * *

Ray, the customs attaché, stood with Aaron inside the Hong Kong Customs checkpoint just south of the river separating Hong Kong and China. Cheng Gao was several feet away, talking to a few of his Hong Kong Customs colleagues. No one in the huddle of Hong Kong Customs officers looked welcoming to their American visitors.

"They don't look happy," Aaron commented.

"I'm not exactly beaming myself. I don't do well on four hours of sleep. And that's all I got before we started this little trek," Ray said.

Aaron, Ray, and Cheng were out of bed well before the sun rose. The early morning activity was all thanks to Roger, who was likely in bed asleep. Roger's mind had gone into full-throttle strategy mode after Aaron had related his call with Kellie and Meilin. Roger's folder of contact names included Chinese Customs officials in Beijing with their work, home, mobile, and fax numbers, as well as addresses. He made full use of that list and those numbers late Saturday. To get what he wanted, he described the situation in detail and emphasized that he had photographs. He let them know that there was proof of previous shipments that might cause problems between Chinese and US Customs. To his contacts in Beijing, it didn't matter that Roger was no longer the customs attaché. They knew he still had influence, and that was enough for them to act on the information. Roger had built a strong bond of trust between himself and his Chinese and Hong Kong counterparts during his time as attaché. His reputation as a straight talker and doer meant his foreign colleagues put a lot of weight on what he said and the information he shared.

One of the many things Roger learned as an attaché was that sometimes officials at the provincial level needed a little nudge from Beijing, and sometimes they needed a strong shove. Roger didn't care how much or how little pressure was needed from Beijing as long as he got the desired outcome. It took several hours to get the dots connected between the customs offices in Beijing, Shenzhen, and Hong Kong, but by using Ray's office to transmit documents and make calls, it got done. Roger, no longer a government official, begged off from the trek to the border, leaving that to Aaron and Ray, who had government agency identification.

Cheng left the huddle of his colleagues and approached Ray and Aaron.

"Is there a problem?" Ray asked.

"We don't think so," Cheng said flatly. "We're waiting for the Shenzhen Customs district chief. Where's Roger?"

"He's not coming. He's not a government official anymore."

"But he arranged everything, right?"

"He arranged it, but your commissioner and the officials in Beijing are the ones who ordered this to happen," Ray explained.

Aaron let Ray take the lead and do the talking, given Ray's attaché position. Another quarter hour passed before Aaron and Ray saw Cheng and his colleagues exit the building and go to a black sedan slowing to a stop. One of Cheng's colleagues walked over and opened the passenger door. The man who exited kept a stern look. Though he had the usual black hair, the sides were cut so short that it seemed like the sides of his head were shaved. His black uniform had some rank insignia on the shoulders.

When Cheng approached the Shenzhen Customs district chief, he made a slight gesture of a salute but not a snappy military salute. Aaron and Ray waited inside the checkpoint building. After a brief conversation, Cheng, who was several inches taller than the stocky, broad-shouldered district chief, led the contingent into the building. The only person not part of the entering group was the district chief's driver.

Aaron and Ray stood facing the whole group. Cheng was half a step ahead of the district chief.

"The chief's English is very limited, so I'll make the introductions. He wants to see your US Customs identification. It's just a formality," Cheng explained.

As Ray and Aaron pulled out their identification, the district chief reached out to examine them one at a time. Whether the district chief could read what was on the identification cards wasn't important. He held each one for a minute or two as if considering whether they were authentic, although he was already under orders to take these two Americans across the border.

After Ray and Aaron had their IDs returned, the district chief turned to get back to his car, chattering with Cheng as they walked. Cheng broke off and went back to Ray and Aaron.

"Follow me," Cheng instructed. Cheng, Ray, and Aaron found a waiting official Hong Kong Customs vehicle in which they would follow the district chief. It took only a couple of minutes to get to the China side and Chinese Immigration. The Shenzhen district chief took only a few seconds to ensure that the car following him would be allowed across the border.

"We're being allowed across even without you having the proper documentation," Cheng said. "The condition is that we need to get back across within eight hours."

"Shouldn't be a problem," Ray said.

The two cars glided through the early Sunday morning traffic. Cheng's driver never let any of the few cars on the road squeeze in between the two cars. Aaron looked out one of the rear passenger windows, impressed by the modernity of the city. There was a mix of newly built skyscrapers, some old traditional wooden buildings, and aged block office buildings. Aaron glimpsed the sun between buildings and could see they were continuing to head north as the intense concentration of newer high-rises gave way to fewer new buildings.

It seemed that they were on the outskirts of Shenzhen when the cars slowed on a four-lane road that had warehouses and squat office buildings on both sides. The district chief's driver flipped on his turn signal even though there was no street to turn onto on either side of the road. The chief's driver made an abrupt U-turn and parked in front of a five-story building. Cheng's driver did the same. The customs district chief was already out of the car and standing by the car when Cheng's driver pulled up to a stop.

Cheng instructed his driver to wait in the car. Cheng, Aaron, and Ray got out, joined the chief, and started toward the building's entrance. Aaron handed Cheng a folder. Before they reached the doors, Liwei exited, flanked by Shing Fang and Tengfei Meng.

Aaron's stomach tensed, and his jaw clenched at the sight of the two young men on either side of Liwei. He knew he had fought off Shing Fang in the hotel and suspected the other man had been his partner. Aaron tilted his head and turned slightly toward Ray.

"You recognize someone?" Aaron whispered.

"Dimples," Ray said under his breath.

"He won't be able to recognize us from our visit to the house," Aaron added.

The two groups were getting too close to each other for Aaron to say anything more to Ray, but he was suspicious of the customs chief. How did Liwei know to be here waiting and greeting them on arrival on a Sunday morning? Liwei seemed to know exactly when they were arriving, being able to come outside before Aaron and his group ever stepped into the building. Did the customs chief call him on a cell phone? It looked that way to Aaron. Even if Liwei worked every day, it seemed strange that both of his young thugs, as Aaron saw them, were here with him on a Sunday morning.

Both groups stopped, standing about four feet from each other.

Liwei directed his smile toward the customs district chief, and the two men shook hands, making it appear to Ray and Aaron that the two men knew each other. Aaron and Ray were at a loss as Liwei and the customs district chief were speaking Chinese. Ray, standing next to Cheng, tugged on Cheng's sleeve and leaned toward Cheng for a translation.

"Always good to see you, Chief," Liwei said, never looking over at the three others with the chief. "You have an entourage with you today."

"Good to see you as well. I'm sorry that we are interrupting you this morning. We have something to show you, and we hope you might be able to explain some of your business activities," the district chief began. The chief turned his head toward Liwei's facility down the street. "Maybe there's somewhere there where we can discuss things?"

Aaron, Ray, and Cheng turned their gaze in the direction that the chief was looking and noticed the signage and fencing around the facility a short distance down the street. The Chinese signage meant nothing to Aaron and Ray.

"Who have you brought with you?" Liwei wanted to know, ignoring the chief's suggestion.

The customs district chief introduced Cheng Gao and let Cheng introduce Ray and Aaron. Liwei didn't smile. There was no obvious sign of anger. He was expressionless. He shook hands with his three strange guests politely with some firmness in his grip.

"There's enough space in my office. It'll be more comfortable," Liwei said and turned to lead everyone into the building. Shing Fang and Tengfei Meng trailed everyone into the building.

Although they didn't know it, Liwei's office had changed. The large leather chairs had been removed and replaced with simpler straight-back chairs. Liwei still had his high-backed leather chair at one end of the coffee table that was looking toward the windows. He positioned himself in front of it.

The customs district chief took a spot at the end of the sofa next to Liwei and appeared to be half Liwei's height, having sunk several inches into the soft leather cushions. Cheng sat in a chair on the other side of Liwei, facing the chief and Ray, and Aaron sat in one of the chairs to Cheng's left. No one sat at the far end of the coffee table. Shing Fang and Tengfei Meng did not join them in the office.

The district chief scooted to the edge of the sofa and leaned forward. He cleared his throat before speaking. "It has been brought to our attention that an American citizen crossed the border with you a few days ago and that you may have her documents," the chief started.

"She's not here," Liwei interjected.

With Liwei's abrupt response, the chief's eyes moved swiftly to each of the three men across the table. "She's not here? It was my impression that she was," the district chief said as he looked at Cheng Gao with anger in his eyes. "What about her documents? Are they here?" the Chief pressed.

Liwei knew he wouldn't be sitting and facing government officers of three governments unless they were absolutely sure he had the documents, so he wasn't stupid enough to deny it. Instead, he stood, walked to his desk, took keys from his trouser pocket, and unlocked one of the desk drawers. Liwei retrieved a letter-sized envelope and placed it on the coffee table in front of the chief.

The district chief lifted the envelope, letting the contents slide onto the table. Kellie Liang's US passport and her Mainland Travel Permit appeared on the table.

Ray reached out for the passport, but the chief raised his hand, stopping Ray from picking up the passport.

The chief examined the passport pages. "No visa," he said to Liwei and slid the passport across the table toward Ray.

"No, but there's her Mainland Travel Permit. I wonder how she got that," Liwei posed.

The chief examined the Mainland Travel Permit, then held out his hand to Ray, signaling that before Ray picked up the passport, he wanted to take another look at the passport. He opened both to the page with names and pressed both flat on the coffee table, noticing the discrepancy. Two different names but the same person in both photos.

Cheng Gao shifted in his chair. He looked across at the chief, then to Liwei. The three men looked at each other for a split second. Again, the chief reached out and picked up the Mainland Travel Permit. He examined it closely.

"Why are the names different?" the chief asked. Cheng Gao quickly translated the question.

"It's a common practice of many Chinese parents to give their American-born children an American name and a Chinese name," Aaron explained.

Whether the district chief was accepting the explanation or not, he nodded as if he did. He wasn't there to sort out this problem. His instruction was to get these documents back to the owner, whatever her name might be. But he was going to make sure everyone in the room understood and respected his position. He closed the documents and held them out for Ray.

Ray secured both in a buttoned shirt pocket.

"Do you know where she is?" the chief continued.

"I assume she's somewhere in Guangzhou. I believe the person who took her from here while I was away is in Guangzhou," Liwei offered.

"Thank you," the chief said. "Mr. Gao from Hong Kong Customs has something to share with you." He prompted Cheng with a nod.

Cheng removed photocopied pictures from the folder Aaron had given him and placed them on the table in front of Liwei. "These products were found in a container that came from here yesterday. All at the container terminal in Hong Kong. We know, and the chief is prepared to shut down your facility."

Liwei took a deep breath. He stood abruptly and took a couple of steps toward the office door, then called out to Tengfei. When Tengfei appeared at the office door, Liwei whispered something and returned to his chair.

When Liwei returned to his chair, he glared at Cheng. "The district chief cannot shut me down," Liwei insisted. "He has no jurisdiction here. The district chief knows he can't just enter a business operation outside of designated customs areas. He has no authority here." Still looking at Cheng, Liwei added, "If you want to look at my business operations or my goods, you need to do it the right way with the right people."

"Will you permit us to walk through your facility?" the district chief asked, trying to lower the level of hostility that Liwei was projecting.

"Absolutely not," Liwei answered. "Why should I allow Americans and Hong Kong Customs officers into my operations when I will not let you enter?" Liwei said as he stared at the chief. "I've given you what you came for, and now I believe our discussion is completed," Liwei added.

Not understanding the tense exchange, Aaron and Ray guessed that they were being invited to leave. They heard sirens increasing in volume outside and wondered what was going on out in the street. Tengfei appeared at the door, and Liwei stood up, pushing back the chair behind him, and took a step back. Liwei left enough space so that the chief could step by him, getting out from behind the table.

Liwei extended his left arm toward Tengfei and the door, a clear signal that his guests should leave.

The loud sirens had stopped. The district chief led his contingent out of the office and down to the lobby. When they exited the elevator on the ground floor, Aaron saw Dimples and four uniformed police officers. As they exited the glass doors, two public security bureau cars with lights flashing were parked out front.

Liwei rushed ahead and opened the door, holding it as everyone exited the building while two uniformed officers flanked the group on each side of the door. The uniformed police officers trailed behind. As the district chief reached his car, Liwei put his hand on the passenger side door.

"If you want to investigate my operations, you'll have to do it according to proper procedures," Liwei said. "Make sure that you have officers who have the jurisdiction and documents to conduct that investigation," Liwei added for Cheng's benefit and for the public security bureau officers.

The two cars that brought Liwei's guests filled with passengers. Pulling away from Liwei's office, Aaron turned in the seat to see Liwei standing and laughing with the police officers. He realized he might need to start a diagram of sorts to keep track of all the people and connections that had to be considered in the mess he and Kellie had fallen into. When he turned to look out the front, he saw that the district chief's car was no longer in sight.

"Where did he go?" Aaron asked.

"He did what he was ordered to do, and we're back on our own," Cheng answered.

"We still have to get these documents to Kellie so she can get back to Hong Kong," Aaron said.

"Where is she in Guangzhou?" Cheng asked.

"I didn't get the hotel information from her," Aaron answered. "Meilin, Guang's daughter, took her to Guangzhou."

Ray checked his watch and then his cell phone. No cell phone connection. "Chuck, does your phone have a signal?"

"Not here," Cheng answered. "We're far enough away from the border that I have nothing here."

"But we have time, and more importantly, we have Roger. Let's get back into the center of Shenzhen and locate a hotel or someplace where we can call Roger. He can then relay a message to Meilin, telling her where we are and the fact that we have Kellie's documents. Then we can see if Meilin can bring Kellie to us so we can drive her back to Hong Kong," Ray thought aloud.

* * * * *

As the driver headed toward the Shenzhen Customs District Office, the district chief pressed a button on his cell phone. Shan Zhou, his counterpart in Guangzhou, answered on the second ring. "You have a ChiTran company in your district, right?"

"ChiTran Research and Manufacturing Group, yes," Shan Zhou confirmed.

"You need to keep an eye on it. I just left one of ChiTran's operations in my district. Beijing ordered me to take American and Hong Kong Customs officials to meet with the owner of the operation here. There's solid proof that some exports are going to cause us problems. The Americans are aware of the manufacturer and exporter. They have procedures to track these shipments. We need to take some preventive steps. Otherwise, we need to make these companies aware of the risks involved in any questionable exports."

"I understand," Shan Zhou replied. As the call ended, he was also thinking about Meilin's unexpected visit to his office the previous afternoon. The more he thought about Meilin, the angrier he got. She was supposed to get back to him with information and evidence of what was going on in Shenzhen. If she decided to contact someone in Beijing and exert pressure that way, he found it unacceptable. She had made it sound like she would come to him, not use political connections that high up the ladder. Shan Zhou crushed out a lit cigarette. He stopped himself from flinging the ashtray. He didn't like being manipulated by anyone. He found his briefcase and the notepad with his list of contacts. Good, he had the hotel she had named on his list. He decided to show Meilin his displeasure in person.

Shan Zhou entered the lobby of the hotel. Thankfully, since it was Sunday, he wore civilian clothes, avoiding more attention than necessary. He spotted Meilin sitting with another woman in a far-off corner of the lobby lounge and headed toward their table. More than an hour since hearing from his counterpart, he was still fuming about what had happened. Seeing a third person, Shan Zhou felt that Meilin was tricking him into something. With each step, he saw that the woman with Meilin didn't seem to be Chinese. Now, his mind went to that bit of information that Americans had been with his counterpart earlier in the morning. He remembered Meilin saying something about an American being in the country without her documents.

Meilin spotted Shan Zhou, stood, and waved him over. She watched him making his way between tables and chairs. He hadn't nodded any acknowledgment of her or smiled at all as he made his way. "Something's wrong," Meilin said softly to Kellie, sitting at the table, all the while keeping her gaze toward Shan Zhou.

Before Meilin could extend a hand to Shan Zhou, he pulled out a chair and sat without greetings. After sitting, he was polite enough to say hello in Chinese to Kellie.

"You've been very busy since visiting my office yesterday," Shan started sarcastically without allowing Meilin to introduce Kellie.

Meilin's head cocked slightly, her eyes narrowing. "I'm not sure I understand," Meilin replied.

"I knew you were ambitious, but I didn't know that you would be so impatient as to contact Beijing rather than come back to me. Instead, I've learned that my counterpart in Shenzhen visited ChiTran Guangdong Specialties Company earlier this morning. He was accompanied by Hong Kong and American Customs officials by order of Beijing," Shan said.

Meilin leaned slightly over the table. "I never contacted Beijing. The only thing I did after our meeting was to ask for some evidence so that I could bring it to you as we discussed."

"Who had this information? Who did you contact?"

Before answering, the two women looked at each other for a moment.

Meilin started. "This is Liang Kaili. She's the one whose documents are missing. She's here until we can get them back and allow her to return to Hong Kong."

"Mr. Zhou, I—"

"Chief Zhou," Shan interrupted.

"Chief Zhou, I'm sorry," Kellie began in Chinese. "Ms. Moy said you wanted information or evidence of the operation in Shenzhen. I had been there and saw the operation." Kellie explained the call to Aaron, his trek to the container terminal, and the fax he had sent. She put a folder on the table and opened it up to the fax pages that Aaron had sent.

"These haven't been out of my possession, and I can assure you we haven't shown this to anyone," Kellie insisted.

"Then who?" Shan asked, still unhappy.

"I can only guess that if Hong Kong or US Customs officials accessed this at the Hong Kong container terminal, one of them contacted Beijing," Kellie speculated.

Shan Zhou said nothing as he mulled the explanation. It was believable, but he wasn't fully satisfied. "Be warned that your operations may also be looked at closely, especially anything you are exporting. All of ChiTran is now under suspicion. I hope you aren't abusing our working relationship, but if we find out that you are, there'll be serious consequences."

Meilin and the other two felt and heard her phone vibrating through her purse that was on the table. This was not a good time to take a call. She needed to reassure Shan Zhou that she wasn't trying to undercut or mislead him. She ignored the phone. It stopped but immediately started vibrating again.

"Maybe you should see who's calling," Shan suggested.

Meilin dug the phone out from the bottom of her purse and looked at the small screen. She knew the number. Her father was calling. Unconsciously, she closed her eyes and let out a sigh. Kellie and Shan saw Meilin's reaction. When the phone started vibrating in Meilin's hand a third time, Meilin got up and walked a few strides away from the table.

"What have you done?" Guang said before giving Meilin a chance to say anything.

"Nothing," Meilin insisted.

"Nothing? Then why is Liwei threatening everyone? He had a visit this morning from officers of Chinese, Hong Kong, and American Customs. They threatened to search his site, but he refused to allow them onto the grounds. Do you have any idea what you are doing?" Guang continued.

"I had nothing to do with that. I'll call you soon. I'm in a meeting with—" Meilin stopped herself before telling her father that she was with Shan Zhou. If she said that, he'd never believe she wasn't responsible for what happened earlier in the morning.

"I expect a call very soon, and I expect a full explanation from you after what I told you not to do," Guang said curtly and disconnected.

Meilin took her seat. She felt her red, hot cheeks and the perspiration on her forehead. She couldn't remember her father ever speaking to her that way. She focused on Shan Zhou, who was looking at her. Meilin knew she needed to allay Shan's suspicions. "I will let you know how this happened this morning when I have the details. And I'm sorry if I've placed you in a difficult situation."

Shan Zhou said nothing more. He stood, nodded to both women, turned, and left.

* * * * *

Rong paced in Guang's Conrad Hotel room. "Meilin has created a mess," he said to his small audience. Guang and Roger sat together on the sofa while Shu sat in a high-backed wing chair. "Liwei wants her removed from our leadership council." Looking at Guang, Rong added, "He wants you to find someone who will replace her."

Roger, unfortunately, didn't understand most of what was said in Chinese. He relied on Guang's sketchy and selective translating. Despite his Chinese language deficiency, he was able to stitch together the bits Guang was translating and guess what provoked the Sunday morning assembly.

"Meilin didn't cause this problem. Liwei initiated this when he took Kaili across the border without her consent," Guang explained, trying to calm his colleague. Despite his angry tone toward Meilin during his call to her, he also needed to protect her from an overreaction by Rong and Shu. "If I don't replace her, what is he threatening?"

"Liwei was wrong to take her across the border, I agree," Rong conceded, with Shu nodding in agreement. "But having customs go to his facility and taking Americans and Hong Kong Customs officers there, that was uncalled for. That crossed the line. Competition among our companies is expected, but this type of intrusion into the business is unacceptable."

"We need to have a day or two and work through this," Shu advised. "We shouldn't make any decisions with such pressure on us. We need to understand how this happened, then we'll adjust our strategic operations." Shu didn't speak much, but she was the one who usually spoke without allowing emotion to drive her decisions and advice.

"Liwei doesn't want to hear that we're taking time to think about this," Rong snapped back.

"Liwei is selfish. He should be more mature about how to work within the ChiTran system," Shu responded, looking up at Rong, still pacing slowly.

Roger, listening to Guang's occasional whispered English summary of the exchange, knew his time working for ChiTran was coming to an end. He wondered if that was days or hours. He raised his hand slightly, causing Rong to stop pacing. Roger looked at Rong. "Even if you ignore Liwei's taking Kaili across the border, you should remember our recent conversation about the increased number of ChiTran shipments coming from Liwei being seized. He's taking too many chances, and that means he's risking his and your businesses. I've said this before, and if you're going to ignore my warnings, then I don't know what I'm doing here."

Roger saw three sets of eyes now staring back at him.

"He's right," Shu said. "Mr. Steeg has been advising and warning us. It's also the same thing Ms. Liang said at our meeting." Shu bent down and pulled a pack of cigarettes out of her purse, tapping at one to light. Once lit, she sat back and inhaled deeply. As she exhaled, she had a calm expressionless look on her face. She looked like she knew exactly what needed to be done but said nothing more.

"What do we say to Liwei?" Rong asked no one in particular.

After a few seconds of silence, Guang spoke. "I suggest we convene a small meeting to have a frank exchange. Liwei, Meilin, and the three of us. We need to clear the air and make sure everyone understands what our business and financial priorities are and establish some rules that everyone must follow. We can't have unexpected customs visits like this happening to our operations, and we can't have US Customs stopping our shipments. We need Mr. Steeg to be there. Maybe he needs to tell us what could happen if we continue to be caught at the other end."

Roger waited for the English summary from Guang, realizing he might remain employed for a few more days. He thought he should also start considering an exit plan. If they found out how much he had done to cause China Customs to visit Liwei's office, he wasn't sure what might happen.

Roger stood abruptly, surprising the others in the room. He pulled his vibrating phone from his trouser pocket to answer. "Wait, give me a second." He walked toward the desk and looked out the wide window and the view of the harbor. He needed a little distance between him and the others.

"Are you good?" Ray asked.

"I'm in a meeting, but go ahead."

"We got Kellie's documents. We don't have a way to contact Meilin. We need someone to contact Meilin and tell her where we are. She can bring Kellie here, and we can bring her back," Ray explained. Ray gave Roger the name of the hotel where he, Aaron, and Cheng would be waiting for Meilin and Kellie.

"It'll be taken care of," Roger said and turned around to see three curious faces that appeared to be asking why he took the call. "Sorry for the interruption," he said, determined not to provide them with any details.

Shu kept her gaze on Roger and spoke in English. "Then it is decided that we have the meeting early this week." She tapped the ashes off the end of her cigarette and crushed it out in the ashtray. It was her way of saying they were done.

Rong followed Shu to the door. Roger fidgeted, patting his pockets as if something might have fallen out. He took a couple of steps toward the sofa and glanced over to see if Rong and Shu had exited the room. He started feeling around the edges of the sofa cushions.

"Did you lose something?" Guang asked.

"No. I wanted a minute with you before I leave." Roger told Guang that he needed to call Meilin and have her take Kellie to the hotel where Aaron and Ray were waiting for her. Guang didn't move. Guang stood looking at Roger as if his feet were glued to the floor. "You need to do this now," Roger insisted.

Roger watched Guang go into the bedroom and pick up the cell phone on the bedside table. Meilin's number was dialed with the press of a button. Roger left while Guang was on the phone.

Meilin was in the car heading to her office when her phone buzzed. She squeezed her eyes shut for a second when she saw that her father was calling again. She couldn't ignore him.

"Yes?"

"Are you with Kaili?" Guang asked.

"No, I left her a short time ago," Meilin said.

"The American Customs officers got her documents when they were with Liwei. They're waiting for her to bring her back to Hong Kong. You need to get back to her and meet with the Americans," Guang explained. "And I want to know how this thing happened with Liwei."

"I'll get Kaili to the Americans. About Liwei, I don't know how it happened. I had nothing to do with it," Meilin said. She waited for her father to say something, but as the line stayed silent, something came to her. "Kaili's friend, Aaron, and Roger Steeg went to the container terminal, and Aaron had pictures of what Liwei is shipping. Is it possible that they caused this to happen?"

"Mr. Steeg was in my room. He said nothing about this."

"But it's possible. He's very knowledgeable about these things, right?" Meilin suggested.

Guang thought Meilin's theory of what might have occurred was very possible. He wondered who posed the greater threat to ChiTran, Liwei or Roger Steeg, but he didn't say that to Meilin. "Yes," was all Guang said.

"I'll take care of Kaili. Where do we meet Aaron?" Meilin said as she had her driver turn around and head back toward the hotel. She called Kellie at the hotel and told her that they'd be going to Shenzhen.

At the hotel, Kellie stood in the lobby, waiting for Meilin when she entered. Meilin took care of the hotel bill, and they began the drive back to Shenzhen.

"It's been a strange few days," Kellie reflected as they rode.

Meilin shook her head in agreement. "Do you know Roger Steeg well?"

"Not at all. He's a friend of Aaron's. I just met him once when we arrived in Hong Kong. What little I know is what Aaron has told me, and that isn't much," Kellie added.

Meilin believed her and realized that she had probably spent more time with Roger. The night operation on Liwei's residence and hearing of Roger's trip to the container terminal started to create an image of a man who was still more of a law enforcement officer than a consultant to ChiTran. Meilin thought about the seed she planted with her father when she posed the possibility of Roger Steeg being behind the customs visit on Liwei. She was convinced that both men could be a threat to ChiTran's future.

It was only when the driver pulled up to a hotel that Kellie realized they had arrived at the meeting place. When the car rolled to a stop, Kellie opened the door to get out but noticed that Meilin had made no move to exit the car.

"Coming in?"

"No," Meilin said. "I've done what I needed to do."

Kellie reached out and put a hand on Meilin's hand. "Thank you." Kellie grabbed her bag that had been on the seat between them, then retrieved her carry-on bag from the trunk and went into the hotel.

Aaron, sitting with Ray and Cheng, was out of his chair and running to Kellie at the first sight of her. As they embraced, he whispered, "I was so scared for you." He grabbed her bag, and they walked over to Ray and Cheng. After quick introductions, the four of them were ready to begin the drive back to Hong Kong.

* * * * *

Alvin Liang stared at the Cathay Pacific plane ticket he had purchased late Saturday afternoon. He called and lied to his wife that his stay on the West Coast would be a couple of days longer than he had expected. He returned his rental car and rode the shuttle bus to the international terminal at Los Angeles International Airport. Everything looked good for an on-time departure of his flight later in the morning. It would get him into Hong Kong late Monday.

Jake Evans and his team of customs agents worked late on Saturday. He had let Jacqui Ramirez go home. He hoped the reports his team had written were strong enough to get legal action taken against both Lupo men. It was now out of his hands.

A call he received late in the evening had him up early on Sunday and back in the office with several of his team members.

"What do we know?" Jake asked.

An agent, sitting on the corner of a desk, summarized what his research had uncovered. "Sunrise Imports is a registered business in California, but not a surprise that it's incorporated in Delaware as Sunrise Trading Company, Inc. And surprise, it appears that the same Alvin Liang that Lupo mentioned is the incorporator. It looks like he and his wife are the sole board members of the corporation."

"Any info about where we can find Alvin Liang and his wife?"

"Yeah, Haverford, Pennsylvania. It's in the Philly area," one of the agents answered.

"Okay, get a hold of one of our guys in Philly and tell them it's a priority to get someone to contact Liang. Fill them in on what we have and why we need this to happen ASAP," Jake instructed. "Let's run Mr. Liang's name through some other databases. I can't imagine there are that many 'Alvin Liangs' from Haverford, Pennsylvania."

Jake's team accessed several highly restricted government databases and national law enforcement databases, hoping that something would pop up. There was nothing in the customs database and the same result with all the intelligence community databases. There was better luck in the Immigration and Naturalization Service system.

Jake and another agent stood looking over the shoulder of an agent sitting at a computer and searching through the immigration database.

"There really isn't much here. He's a naturalized citizen from Taiwan. He's been living here for decades. He's traveled back to Asia a few times, but not to mainland China," the agent said as he scrolled through the pages on the screen.

"Nobody thinks it's strange that we have a guy from Taiwan doing that much business with the mainland?" Jake wondered aloud.

"They're all in it for the money. It's no different from our companies doing all that business in China," one of the agents commented. "China is everybody's new gold mine, right?"

* * * * *

It was nearing Sunday noon, and the May sky was clear. A big black GMC SUV confiscated as part of a drug bust weeks earlier rolled along a neighborhood street lined with well-manicured lawns that fronted well-kept homes spaced modestly apart in Haverford. The dashboard thermometer indicated it was seventy-eight degrees out. Comfortable enough that Gil Thomas drove with his left arm resting on the open driver's side window and steered with his right hand. With the shade cast on most of the street, Gil's sunglasses rested on his head.

Agent Thomas was happy to get an easy tasking after several tense days on a weapons case. Luckily, the final chapter had gone well at a small airport the evening before, where he and a team of customs and FBI agents arrested several Americans delivering stolen American military arms to foreign buyers.

Gil had been instructed to take a couple of younger agents with him to interview Alvin Liang and his wife about Sunrise and ChiTran. Looking at the file as he listened to his boss, Gil decided that one of his young agents could read the file to him while they rode to their destination. They'd all find out what this was about together.

Agent Hanna Ames sat in the passenger seat and scanned the house numbers on both sides of the street. "It should be a few more doors down on your side," Ames announced as her eyes moved from one side of the street to the other. Agent Jimmy Iwata, who was in the back seat, rounded out the team.

"There it is." Ames pointed.

Gil steered the SUV into the center of the driveway. He stopped just a few feet short of the closed two-car garage door.

He liked being able to drive bigger vehicles so that he could easily swivel his long six-foot-four-inch body in and out of them. Agents Ames and Iwata weren't small except when standing and walking next to Gil, as he was seven or eight inches taller than his two younger agents. There was a tree on the tree lawn near the curb but no other source of shade in front of the two-story front-bricked house.

From the driveway, they walked single file to the front door. Once in front of the door, they stood side by side. All three had their badges on a chain hanging loosely around their necks. Gil stood in the center. Agent Iwata pressed the doorbell button. A clear glass storm door protected the door into the house, which had a peephole.

As they waited, Hanna looked around. The sun-drenched yard was well maintained, and the flowerpots on either side of the door looked to have been watered earlier in the morning. The sound on the other side of the door brought her attention back.

Elizabeth Liang pulled the door wide open in one swift motion, as one might do when expecting a specific person to be at the door. In a second or two, her eyes saw the badges and three strange faces looking back at her.

Gil noticed that her expressionless look as she pulled the door open gave way to some tightness in her jaw, and her nostrils flared just the slightest with a sudden deep inhale. Gil waited as she gripped the handle of the storm door and pushed it open toward her three strange visitors.

"Mrs. Liang? I'm Agent Gil Thomas with the US Customs Service, and these are two of my colleagues, Agents Hanna Ames and Jimmy Iwata. We were hoping we could speak to you and your husband." He gave her a few seconds to look at his federal identification before putting it back into a pocket.

Jimmy was the most surprised of the three when he saw Elizabeth Liang in the doorway. He expected to see an Asian woman, which Mrs. Liang wasn't. He thought he'd see someone who looked more like his Japanese mother. Mrs. Liang seemed taller than average. Given what he expected to see, the brown hair with a slightly reddish tint was another surprise.

Mrs. Liang still held the storm door open with her right arm but started to step back as Hanna held it open from the outside. As Mrs. Liang retreated another step, she motioned the three agents to follow.

"I'm sorry. The badges made me think you might be the police coming to give me bad news about Al, my husband," she said over her shoulder as she walked down the center hall that divided the house in half and led to a large eat-in kitchen area at the back of the house. "Coffee?" she asked.

She found three takers. "Sit wherever you want. It's just me around here." She moved behind a large granite kitchen island, getting coffee cups and prepping the coffee. Except for a few small kitchen appliances out on the counter, the kitchen was immaculate. Jimmy sat on a stool at the island while Hanna and Gil sat at a small breakfast table off to the side of the island tucked into space created by a bay window. The kitchen and eat-in breakfast area opened onto a large family room that was well furnished.

Gil caught Hanna looking around the room and gave her a nod, a sufficient signal for her to get her focus back on Mrs. Liang.

"Is Mr. Liang due back shortly?" Gil asked, picking up on the comment that she was by herself.

"Probably not for a few days," she answered. "Sugar, cream," she said and looked at her three guests.

"Not for me," Gil said, but Hanna and Jimmy wanted both.

"Is he out of town on a business trip?" Gil fished.

"In fact, he is. He left for California a couple of days ago and called yesterday to tell me he needed to stay a couple of days longer." Elizabeth missed the quick glances between the three agents. "I'm sorry. I'm kind of rambling this morning. You said you're with customs. What did you want to talk to us about?"

"Do you and your husband have an importing business called Sunrise Trading Company?" Gil started.

"My husband has it. I'm just a name on the document. I don't really have anything to do with it."

"Would you know if there are two offices in California?"

Elizabeth poured the coffees and took them to the three agents. Before answering, she perched herself on an island stool at the opposite end from where Jimmy sat.

"I do know that my husband set up offices for the company in Los Angeles and San Francisco. I don't get involved in the actual business or have anything to do with personnel. So, do I know they exist? Of course. Do I know about the different offices? Yes, but I wouldn't know who his managers are or exactly what goes on day to day," she clarified.

"Do you think the business makes money or that any money it makes benefits your lifestyle?" Gil asked.

Elizabeth tilted her head slightly as she looked at Gil, then the other two. "We have a modest home. We don't really want for anything. We do just fine with two university incomes. But Al might have something different to say. You'd have to talk to him."

"Do you know if Mr. Liang visited Sunrise Imports in Los Angeles within the last couple of days?"

"I can't say for certain. I'm pretty sure there was something going on there that caused him to fly out suddenly. He didn't explain. Yesterday, when he called, he just said he'd have to stay a couple of more days. I'm sorry, but is there something I should know that you're not telling me?" Elizabeth asked.

"As you probably know, customs can inspect anything and everything. We've noticed that shipments that Sunrise is processing contain goods with some very serious violations. Those violations could result in criminal liability," Gil answered. He wanted to let that sink in before adding, "Some of these products could cause serious injury or death. That's why we need to talk to your husband ASAP. Where is he staying? Do you have a way of getting a hold of him?"

"When he goes on these West Coast trips, they're so short that I don't even think about getting his travel details," she said.

"What if there was an emergency and you needed to contact him?" Hanna asked. "Doesn't he have a cell phone? Can you call him?"

Elizabeth popped off the stool. She left the three agents sitting as they heard her going up the steps. She returned with her phone and dialed Alvin Liang's cell phone number as her audience sat and listened. "Al, it's Liz. Please give me a call as soon as you can. It's important."

"He wasn't at all specific about what day he would come home," Gil pressed.

"No. He said very little other than he found things to be more complicated than he had expected when he got to the West Coast," she offered.

"Mrs. Liang, we really need to talk to your husband. To give you an idea about the seriousness of this matter, I will tell you that yesterday morning we had agents shut down both the LA and San Francisco offices.

We questioned the LA office manager, Mr. Lupo. Do you know him?" Gil asked.

"No. I don't recognize the name, and I'm sure I never met him."

"Your husband wasn't there when we took Mr. Lupo in for questioning," Gil added.

"What about locating Mr. Liang through his money trail?" Jimmy thought out loud.

"What money trail?" Elizabeth asked.

"If he uses a credit card for a hotel room or a rental car or plane ticket, there'll be some way to find out what hotel is charging him," Jimmy added.

"Should I call the credit card company?" Elizabeth asked.

"If you don't mind," Hanna answered.

Again, Elizabeth popped up and left the kitchen. "What do you think?" Gil asked his two young agents.

"Hard to say," Hanna said. "Isn't she a university professor or something? She isn't stupid, but she doesn't know much about her husband's business. Something doesn't seem right."

"But she's being cooperative so far," Jimmy said.

"Let's play this out," Gil suggested.

Once back in the kitchen, Elizabeth got out the credit card she thought her husband would use and called the customer service number, read out the card number as directed, and waited for a customer service representative. After asking for the most recent charges, Elizabeth asked for the representative to repeat and held the phone out. Jimmy took it and held the phone to his ear, then returned the phone to Elizabeth.

"There are no hotel, car, or plane expenses on that credit card. What about other cards he could've used?" Hanna asked.

"Hold on," Elizabeth said as she left them again. This time, there were no footsteps on the stairs.

"Find out where she went," Gil said as he prompted Hanna.

Hanna walked back toward the front door and saw Elizabeth in an office just to the left of the front door. "Can I help you look?" Hanna offered.

"No, thanks. Al is very good about filing and keeping things in order. It'll either be where it should be or not here."

Hanna watched the older woman working her way from front to back of the second drawer in a four-drawer file cabinet. About halfway through, Mrs. Liang pulled a thin labeled folder, dropped it on the desk, and opened it. Finding the piece of paper she needed, she picked it up and walked past Hanna toward the kitchen.

With the paper in front of her, she was on the phone again, asking to speak to another customer service representative. This time, she put the phone on speaker to let her visitors listen to the call. After providing all the details, they listened together to the list of recent transactions. The first transaction was the plane ticket to Los Angeles, then the rental car, followed by another plane ticket.

"Excuse me," Elizabeth was saying into the phone. "Another plane ticket was charged? When?"

"Yes, ma'am," the representative confirmed. "A ticket was purchased yesterday. It was a charged purchase from Cathay Pacific."

"What flight and when is it?" Elizabeth asked.

"That I don't know," the representative answered. "I only have information about the date and amount of the charge, nothing about the flight details."

Elizabeth disconnected and looked blankly at her guests.

"Mrs. Liang, do you have a computer we can use?" Gil asked.

Without a word, Mrs. Liang got up, and Jimmy followed her. She took him into the office where she'd been searching through the file cabinet earlier. "There's the computer. Do what you have to do," she said and left him alone and went back to the kitchen.

Gil and Hanna were looking through the folder that they had brought. "Hanna, call the office. We need a number to give our LA guys a heads-up if Al Liang is taking off on us," Gil was saying as he watched Elizabeth slide onto the stool at the island.

"Mrs. Liang, did your husband take a lot of luggage with him when he flew to the West Coast?"

"No. He only took an overnight bag with a few changes of clothes. Like I said, he wasn't expecting to be gone for more than a couple of days."

"Can you think of anything that would cause him to fly out of the country?" Gil asked.

"Nothing I'm aware of. But as I've already said, if it's anything to do with Sunrise, he wouldn't bother me with it. However, I would expect he would tell me if he was traveling internationally," she answered.

Jimmy appeared at the doorway to the kitchen. "There's a Cathay Pacific flight to Hong Kong. It'll take off soon from LA."

"I've got the number to alert our LA team," Hanna added.

"Give me the number, and I'll make the call," Gil said as Hanna put a piece of paper into his hand. "I'll be back in a few minutes." Gil went out to the SUV and called Jake Evans in LA, giving Jake a flight number and wishing him luck to get to Alvin Liang in time.

Gil went back into the house and was concerned about one thing. Mrs. Liang had been cooperative and helpful, but he needed one more thing. "Can you check on your husband's passports? Are they gone?"

Again, Elizabeth left the kitchen and headed upstairs to the master bedroom. Hanna followed and stopped in the doorway as she watched Elizabeth going into a closet, disappearing then reappearing with a locked metal case. Elizabeth opened the locked box with a key on her key ring.

"They're both gone," Elizabeth said.

"What do you mean both?" Hanna asked.

"He has an American passport, but he also has a Republic of China passport in his Chinese name."

"Which is what?" Hanna wanted to know. She had Mrs. Liang spell Mr. Liang's Chinese name.

"And his American passport is in the name of Alvin?" Hanna asked, and Elizabeth's nod confirmed it.

After replacing the lockbox, Hanna followed Elizabeth back to the kitchen.

"Do you have a passport?" Gil asked.

"Of course."

"May I see it?" Gil asked.

For a moment, Elizabeth stood motionless in the kitchen. Her compliant attitude was changing.

"Why didn't you have her"—Elizabeth looked over at Hanna—"ask me while I was upstairs?"

The atmosphere among them had changed. The thought of Alvin Liang flying off to Asia without a word bothered everyone in the room, but for different reasons.

Elizabeth went slowly up the stairs again to retrieve her passport from the metal lockbox and took it down to the agents. While Elizabeth was upstairs, Jimmy used his phone to take a photo of a picture of Alvin Liang that he noticed on a table in the living room. "Great idea. We may not need it, but good to have," Gil said.

Back in the kitchen, Elizabeth opened her passport and showed the photo page to Hanna. When Hanna reached to take it, Elizabeth shook her head no. "You can copy the information, but I'll hold on to it."

"Thank you for that," Gil said. "We'll leave you now. We appreciate your help." Gil led the way out.

"Can I expect a call about what's going on, what you're investigating?" Elizabeth asked after all three were out the door and walking to the SUV.

"It depends," Gil said as he entered the vehicle and closed the door.

"On what?"

"Whether we're in time to get him off the flight to Hong Kong," Gil said through the open driver's side window. He reached over and started the ignition.

* * * * *

A three-man team of agents was in a stop-and-go race to get to the gate of a Cathay Pacific flight to Hong Kong. They sprinted a few strides, then slowed to a walk because of families and groups of travelers in their way. They'd run then stop to cut through a long line of embarking passengers at gates between them and their destination gate. They knew when they got the call that the odds of making it were slim and none. Unless there was a mechanical or luggage delay, this was a lost race from the start.

When Jake Evans got the call and information about Alvin Liang's travel plans, the first thing he did was alert a team of agents at the airport. There was always a team working there. He was hoping for the best. He had no real grounds to cause the flight to be delayed. He didn't have enough to obtain authorization for that.

Each of the agents racing to get to the Cathay Pacific flight gate checked his watch, convinced that there was no way they would ever get Alvin Liang. The call they got was already after the final boarding call had been made. By the time they finally arrived at the gate, the ticket agents and everyone who processed boarding had left the area. The hundreds of passengers who had filled the area thirty minutes earlier were all gone. The three agents stood together, looking out a window, and saw a large Boeing 747 Cathay Pacific plane lumbering down the runway.

When Jake got the message that the airport team wasn't in time, he wasn't surprised. From the minute he got the call from Agent Thomas in Pennsylvania, he knew it was a long shot to get there in time to pull Alvin Liang off that flight. His dejection lasted only an instant. Alvin Liang was going to be stuck on a plane for well over fourteen hours. Jake understood they had an advantage. They knew Alvin Liang could be traveling under either his American or Chinese name. There was also plenty of time to send the names, the flight number, and the arrival time to Hong Kong so that Ray Jackson, the attaché, could arrange some type of greeting. Part of this case was going right back to where everything had started.

* * * * *

Tengfei Meng drove the jeep as Shing Fang sat in the passenger seat. They had studied the map with Liwei of Meilin's facility. The three men had clustered around the most recent road map they could find, which was not easy with the fast-changing areas in Guangdong Province and in Guangzhou city. After studying the map, they wrote down detailed directions to the address they had. Liwei, like other ChiTran executives, had addresses and contact details of the other ChiTran people of any note. The information included the location of the primary facilities of each of the ChiTran member companies.

"You must be very careful," Liwei said before they left. "Check the area before it is completely dark, but get this done as soon after it's dark as possible and then come back. Remember, you must make sure that no one gets hurt," Liwei insisted.

Liwei hoped that Tengfei and Shing could pull this off without a hitch. He didn't blame the two young men for what happened in Kellie's hotel room. And what happened to Shing at the house was just bad luck, Liwei thought.

Predicting sunset and the time it would take for darkness to envelop the landscape was increasingly more difficult these days. The air was thick with industrial smog, which made it darker sooner than any official forecast might predict. Tengfei pressed the gas pedal, accelerating as traffic was light by Guangzhou standards. He needed to get to the western edge of the city as quickly as possible, as light was fading faster than anticipated.

A roughly two-hour drive and the detailed directions had the two men driving by Meilin's factory. They spent several minutes driving around the perimeter of the facility. There was a large main gate for entry and exit. By the main gate stood a small sentry enclosure with someone inside who would have to physically allow any vehicle onto the premises. Otherwise, there was no view into the facility from the road at any part of the perimeter. This limited their options if they wanted to get away quickly.

Tengfei, once back on the road that fronted the factory, drove a short distance away, turned around, and drove back toward the facility but parked on the side of the road fifty feet from the corner of the facility. The two sat and said nothing as each was focused on the front of the facility that was fenced.

"They have security cameras," Tengfei said, pointing to the top of each corner where there were two cameras at each corner pointing in two directions. One pointed to the front, and the other was aimed along the walled sides of the facility.

"The road isn't straight all the way. It's straight and wider in front of the factory, probably to make it easier for the trucks, but the road curves toward the corners of the place. The road is closer to the corners," Shing noticed.

"We need to be careful. Liwei doesn't want anyone hurt," Tengfei said.

"I know. You drive me to the other side, and I'll prepare to ignite over there. I'll wait till you've driven back across. Then I'll ignite and throw mine while you prepare yours. That way, the guard will come toward mine, and he won't be injured. Once you've thrown yours, you'll drive over, I'll jump in, and we're on our way back," Shing explained.

Tengfei looked around. This was not a residential area, and there was nothing around except Meilin's facility. They waited. Shing crawled into the back of the jeep to prepare his part of the plan. He put on gloves, then got one rag and dripped some gasoline onto it, and stuffed it into a bottle that was already filled with fuel. He got a jar and filled it with more fuel, then put a lighter and matches in his pocket. As he crawled back into the passenger seat, Shing put the bigger jar of fuel between his legs on the seat and his ready-to-go Molotov on the floor between the seat and door.

They sat and waited another twenty minutes before Tengfei started the engine and drove. He drove a quarter mile beyond the facility, then stopped for Shing to get out and make his way back toward the factory on foot. Tengfei waited a full minute before driving back and hoped the sentry wasn't paying attention to his back and forth.

Tengfei had the jeep turned around and facing in Shing's direction so that he could get back into the jeep, start it, and get Shing for a quick getaway. Tengfei grabbed a jar of fuel and quietly made his way to the corner of the facility. Like Shing, he had gloves. He didn't think the cameras would be able to do their intended work in the dark. Tengfei opened the jar and tried to spread the fuel over several yards along the front of the fence.

He placed the jar behind him once it was empty. Just then, he saw the flames from Shing's Molotov cocktail. As the guard ran out toward the flames, Tengfei lit a match and threw it in the direction of the groundcover he'd just doused with the fuel. The short grass and weeds leaped into a flame instantly, and Tengfei grabbed the jar and ran for the jeep. He'd left the keys in the ignition to save time. He had the vehicle moving toward Shing in seconds.

Shing, instead of running toward the jeep, ran toward the sentry gate, stopped, and threw something that Tengfei didn't see.

Tengfei was looking over his shoulder in the idling jeep when he covered his eyes at the flash inside the facility.

Shing ran and jumped into the passenger seat. "Go, go!"

Tengfei's foot pressed the gas pedal to the floor, and the wheels screeched on the pavement. At first, the jeep jerked, thrusting both forward. Then when the tires grabbed the pavement, they were pressed back into their seats.

"What did you do?" Tengfei asked.

"A little surprise for them."

"If someone is hurt back there, we're going to be in trouble," Tengfei warned.

"Don't worry, I threw it into an open space," Shing said confidently. "I wanted to be sure they're too busy to come after us."

The scorched ground a few yards inside Meilin's facility was the only thing for Meilin Moy to see when she arrived a few hours after Tengfei and Shing had created the fuel-fed brush fires. No one had called to give her the news immediately after it happened because no damage had been done, but the change-over in shift to the daytime sentry and the overnight report made the new sentry coming on duty uncomfortable. He called Meilin's office inside the compound and reported it, adding that no damage or injury had been caused.

Word got to Meilin, and she was at the facility within an hour of the sentry's report. Everyone from senior staff members to the lowliest on the premises knew Meilin. A few of her immediate staff had worked for her for well over a decade. Among her employees, she had their respect for building up the business and keeping things going and maintaining a humane workplace, unlike many that her employees had read about and heard about from others.

After arriving, Meilin got out of the car and walked over to the security chief standing by the entry. He showed her the scorched ground. There wasn't much to see other than the discolored grass and some of the pebbled driveway.

"Did the security cameras get any clear images?" she asked.

"Too dark. They were aware of the cameras and were careful," her security chief answered. "We have a jeep on camera going back and forth a few times."

Meilin looked up at her security chief. "A jeep vehicle? Anything else to identify it, like color?"

The security chief shook his head in the negative.

"It's okay. I think I know who is responsible for this," Meilin said as she marched toward the building where her office was located.

Meilin looked at the clock in the office building's reception area. It was 6:40 a.m. A few minutes ago, the rainbow-like colors were welcoming the new day before the sun appeared over the morning horizon. The time didn't matter to Meilin.

Meilin called Liwei's office in Guangzhou. After several rings, she was instructed to leave a message. "Liwei, you know who this is. You are too impulsive, and it will be your ruin. Your impulsivity has spread to those who work for you. You're lucky they didn't cause injury. One last thing, I had nothing to do with the visit you had from the customs officers, but I will be part of your downfall." Meilin hung up.

Meilin could be impulsive, but she didn't run a successful business by operating that way. She usually caught herself before acting hastily and stepped back to think things through strategically. Things were on a collision course with Liwei. She needed to be strategic now, and it might not allow for any consulting with her father or others in ChiTran.

Chapter 13

Calculating

Hong Kong (Sunday–Monday, May 17–18)

"You can either be part of the solution, or we'll make it more difficult for every shipment arriving from Hong Kong," Ray said, challenging one of Hong Kong's assistant customs commissioners on the phone. "I know you can zero in on the problem exporter and containers if you want to, and the only question is whether you want to or not."

Ray's left hand was pumping, squeezing a stress ball. He was getting angrier by the minute as he listened to this assistant commissioner make excuses. It was clear the assistant commissioner didn't want to upset his mainland counterparts and didn't want to disrupt anything, leaving Hong Kong's container ports for foreign markets. For some reason, this official seemed more interested in maintaining Hong Kong's status as one of the busiest container terminals in the world over the possibility that the contraband they might protect from detection might kill people.

"One of your own officers was with me when we got the information about all the contraband exports from one source," Ray was saying. "I'm going to get a list of every ChiTran-related operation in China, and whether they export through Hong Kong or the mainland, we'll make sure to slow or stop every one of those shipments. And if I don't start hearing and getting cooperation, that information is going to be shared with our counterparts in Europe and through Brussels. I don't make empty threats." Ray slammed the receiver into the cradle, furious at his so-called friends at Hong Kong Customs. He wasn't sure if he could make those threats real in every part of the world, but he was sure that he could create problems for ChiTran in the US.

The time in the car with Kellie had been useful to Ray and Cheng. She repeated some of the information she had already given Aaron over the phone. She detailed the products she had seen at Liwei's facility, including the random parts used to assemble and the lack of any testing equipment at his facility for all the home safety products. Ray and Cheng found the explanation of her nighttime wanderings and what happened with the guards interesting. Cheng suspected there might be an illegal cigarette production line or two operating there. Contraband cigarette exports were a gold mine to companies. Companies understood that making those cigarettes was akin to printing money.

Ray was operating on only a few hours of sleep after getting up well before dawn in the morning to get across the border. The uncooperative exchange with his Hong Kong Customs counterparts had his adrenaline going, and his mind was racing. The problem was that his fingers on a keyboard were not anywhere near as fast as his mind's activity. He was typing up ways to have his US Customs colleagues place alerts in the national electronic system to identify any shipments from ChiTran and its component companies. He wrote up descriptions, names, and product information, and they could choose to confiscate them on the spot when they arrived at a port or trace them to those who were responsible for distributing the contraband around the country. That was a call for the locals to make.

* * * * *

The first thing Kellie did when she and Aaron returned to the Marriott was to take a long shower. She wrapped herself in the hotel-provided bathrobe, dabbed the excess water from her hair, and plopped down in a chair by the window overlooking Hong Kong harbor. She was exhausted.

"On the one hand, this has been an unforgettable week, and on the other, I'd like to forget it in so many ways," Aaron said as he sat on the bed. "Nothing has gone the way we had planned. I think we should arrange our flights home and just get out of here. We can always come back at some point and do those things we wanted."

"I agree," Kellie said in a low, tired voice. "This past week has felt like a month or two. It's like someone dropped us into a tornado, spinning our lives around too fast to figure out what's going on. Now, it's like the tornado spit us out and things are slowing down and going back to normal. I don't want to think about any of that right now. Instead, what I'd like to do this evening is for us to have a normal quiet dinner, just the two of us. We can deal with all that other tomorrow. The only other thing I feel like

I need to do is make a quick call to Meilin's father. I'm assuming he may still be over at the Conrad Hotel."

It took only a minute to get Guang on the phone. "I wanted to let you know I'm back in Hong Kong. Meilin was so helpful and wonderful. I'm tired but didn't want to let the day end before I contacted you," Kellie said in English.

"I'm very happy you called and glad that Meilin was able to help," Guang said as he debated what to say about Kellie's father. He decided to say nothing.

After the brief call with Guang, Kellie let the harbor view below relax her. Aaron had stood behind her, massaging her shoulders off and on for a while before Kellie was ready to put something on to go out for dinner.

Neither talked much during dinner. Kellie felt talked out after going over everything that had happened during the past several days during the ride back to Hong Kong. Aaron decided not to ask any more questions and let Kellie decide when or if she wanted to talk. During breaks between dishes, they reached out to hold hands. Aaron, too, had little to say as most of his time had been spent trying to get Kellie back. He didn't want to talk about that and place more burden on her. Now that they were together, there seemed to be little to say for the moment.

They drank glasses of white wine with their dinner of salad and different fish dishes. After finishing their food, they lingered over the wine. When the last drops of the bottle were poured and nothing was left in their glasses, they returned to the room. A physical relief and exhaustion filled their bodies. They fell asleep while cuddling.

The jarring sound of the phone ringing shocked their bodies into motion. Aaron's left arm was caught under Kellie's head and pillow as he rolled away from her. Kellie unconsciously kicked out toward the edge of the bed, then sat up in the dark as the phone kept ringing. Aaron freed his arm and rolled toward the phone on his side of the bed, grabbing it in the dark.

He cleared his throat. "Hello?"

"Aaron, this is Elizabeth Liang. I need to talk to Kellie."

The fog of sleep delayed Aaron's response. "For you, your mother," Aaron said. He reached out and turned on the bedside lamp, giving Kellie light to make her way around to his side of the bed.

As he stood up to let Kellie sit by the phone, he glanced at the time: 12:40 a.m. They had been sleeping for a couple of hours. Aaron went over to the chair by the desk and sat.

"What do you mean Dad is probably going to be here?"

Aaron straightened up in the chair. Kellie's question to her mother had his attention.

"When? Aren't you sure?" Kellie asked. "Why were you questioned about his business?" she was saying after a long pause, listening to her mother.

"What's going on? I was stuck in China for a few days without my passport until Aaron and his customs colleague got me back to Hong Kong," Kellie told her mother. She listened again for several minutes and hung up.

"What the hell was that all about?" Aaron posed to Kellie.

"I'm not sure. But we'll have to put our departure on hold for at least a couple of days," she said. "My mother seemed surprised that I'd been in China. It appears my father never said anything to her about that."

"What was that about your father?"

"My mother had a visit from three customs agents. They wanted to know about my father, and because of some of the questions, she found out that his passport was missing. The agents were able to find out that my father had a ticket and is flying to Hong Kong. According to them, they think he'll be on a flight arriving on Monday." Kellie twisted around to look at the clock. "Technically, I guess that means later today."

"Oh shit."

"What?" Kellie said.

"I don't like what's going through my mind at this very moment, but if your mother had a visit from some customs agents, I'm worried that what happened to you is somehow being connected to your father. But why would there be any link?" Aaron paused before starting again. "Your mother said 'agents.' I hope she's using the right terms to describe who visited because there are agents, there are inspectors, and people we might generically call officers. If she's positive that these people were agents, then there's bound to be a reason. Agents investigate criminal activity."

"I just don't know," Kellie answered. "I'm not sure I'm going to be able to go back to sleep. Are you okay with ordering up a pot of coffee?"

"Well, if that will help you to start connecting some of these dots, let's do it," Aaron answered.

* * * * *

Ray looked at the clock on the wall and realized he'd been up for nearly twenty hours. This had been a long day, and it was getting longer by the minute. His thirty-minute dinner break was too short, but it got him out of the office for some tasty Chinese street food and a short mental break. He heard the fax machine come to life, spitting out two pages. He toyed with the idea of leaving it for the morning, but then he looked at the cover sheet and knew he couldn't leave it.

Jake Evans had written on the cover sheet in large handwritten print: "ChiTran" and "Sunrise Imports." That was enough for Ray to put aside any thought of calling it a day. The day, which had started long before dawn, had already stretched into evening and was now going to continue into the night.

On the ride back to Hong Kong from Shenzhen, Ray heard Kellie Liang's woeful tale about being taken to and held at Liwei's place before Meilin rescued her. Now, reading Jake Evans's typed page-long summary of what his team and the team in Philly had learned made Ray wonder about everything. Was the last name Liang just a coincidence? What was Meilin's role in all of this? And did Aaron know more than he had said? The only problem with Ray's suspicions was Aaron and Meilin's efforts to find Kellie, including the trip to Liwei's house. Ray also questioned what, if anything, Roger knew about the things going on with Aaron and Kellie.

There were several alternatives open to Ray, but Cheng Gao was central to them. Over the past forty-eight hours, Cheng had helped Roger access Liwei's container at the Hong Kong container terminal. Cheng had also been with him earlier when they went to Liwei's in China and had assisted in getting Kellie back to Hong Kong. Ray realized he needed Cheng to help find more pieces to this weird puzzle that seemed to have a growing number of missing pieces.

The next twenty-four to forty-eight hours were crucial in Ray's mind. He knew he was going to have to enlist Cheng's help. Now that he had the information about Alvin Liang, he had to make arrangements. He would have to make himself scarce on Monday or show off his limited diplomatic skills with Roger, Aaron, and Kellie if they tried to contact him. It would be easier if he could avoid meeting with them.

* * * * *

Cheng Gao pushed himself to keep working. An unexpected call and fax from Attaché Ray Jackson convinced him to keep pressing on with the ChiTran situation. Having no wife and kids gave him the freedom to spend as much or as little time as he wanted with either work or other things. Work had consumed him the past few days.

The surveillance detail he had conducted on Roger Steeg was turning into opportunity after opportunity. But he was also taking some big risks by failing to tell his bosses all the things he was doing. He said nothing about the odd-hour meetings with Roger, the trip to the container terminal, or using his customs position to get Roger and Aaron a peek into Liwei's container. He was calculating when to give his bosses information and when to withhold it. Hopefully, his calculations were correct.

He parlayed information from Roger Steeg into assignments that might not otherwise be available to someone at his level under normal circumstances. The operation to go across the border was one of those benefits. Now, having been at Liwei's and in control of the folder with documents detailing Liwei's export shipments, he had access to information to make himself an important cog in any operation that involved ChiTran.

After hearing about Kellie Liang's ordeal and the information she had about Liwei's manufacturing and export operations, Cheng wrote a detailed memo. The fax from Ray and Ray's follow-up call about the expected arrival of Alvin Liang in Hong Kong kept Cheng at the office far later than his colleagues. Cheng sent his detailed memo to the Hong Kong Customs assistant commissioner in charge of intelligence and a copy to the assistant commissioner in charge of ports. He wanted both to know that he was deeply involved in the ChiTran case and hoped that any decision to investigate ChiTran would include him.

Someone tapped Cheng on the shoulder. When he forced his eyes open, he saw the morning sunlight streaming in through the windows. Cheng turned in the chair to see the colleague who woke him.

"What time is it?" Cheng asked as his eyes tried to find the clock on the wall. It was just after seven. He pushed himself out of his desk chair and went to the men's lavatory. As he splashed cold water on his face, he noticed that his right cheek was a deep red color, probably from having slept on it at his desk. He stepped back from the counter of sinks and looked in the mirror. He tucked his shirt in, trying to smooth out some of the creases and stepped toward the sink, using a little water on a comb to put his hair back in place.

He stopped at the pantry and poured black coffee into a cup. He stirred creamer into it.

A colleague stopped at the pantry doorway, saying, "Boss wants to see you."

Cheng nodded and headed toward a corner of the floor and knocked on the office door before letting himself into the office.

"You've been busy," Cheng's supervisor said. "I didn't know about those memos you sent out last night until I got a note this morning with a copy of the memo attached."

"I'm sorry, I should've made sure you had a copy of them," Cheng said. "It was late, and I was tired."

"You're going to be busy today, and it may be a long day. Coordinate with anyone you need to deal with. And remember that I'm your supervisor, and I want to know what's going on. I guess you should keep our US Customs friend in the loop." The supervisor held out a copy of the memo and note from their higher-ups for Cheng to take.

"Thank you. I'll keep the attaché informed," Cheng answered. Cheng walked slowly back to his desk and read the note written on the memo he had written. "Action: Prevent any/all ChiTran exports of known contraband. Detain Liang at arrival."

The note filled Cheng with a sense of accomplishment, having convinced at least one assistant commissioner to put a stop to exporting the two containers at the terminal. Cheng flipped through a short stack of papers on his desk and found the copies made for him at the container terminal. It took a few calls and forty minutes of his time before Cheng contacted the customs inspectors at the container terminal to stop Liwei's containers from being loaded on any outbound ship and arranged to send a notice to ChiTran Guangdong Specialties Company informing the company that the contents of the two containers would be prevented from export.

Having completed the most pressing tasks, Cheng dialed another number and cupped his right hand around the handset's speaker. "Mr. Steeg?"

Roger heard the accented English, but the sound seemed muffled and unclear. "Who is this?"

"Cheng Gao calling."

"Ahh, Chuck. Can you speak up? I can barely hear you."

"It's sensitive, and there are some people near me," Cheng explained.

"Okay, go on. I'll concentrate harder."

"I've just called our customs officers at the container terminal to prevent shipment of the containers you looked into, and we'll send Mr. Liwei a note that his goods are contraband and can't be shipped."

"That's great," Roger said. "Have you informed Ray Jackson?"

"Not yet. I thought you'd like to know."

"Chuck, this is great."

"I must go. I have some other things I must do."

"Of course," Roger said as he ended the call. Roger smiled. It was always good to recruit someone who would do things for you and had enough spunk in them to make things happen. He had misjudged Chuck.

* * * * *

JJ drove Roger to the ChiTran offices in Kowloon. While Roger enjoyed the money ChiTran was paying him, the more he learned about some of ChiTran's business dealings, the less he cared how long he was on its payroll. He might be an opportunist, but he didn't want people's lives on his conscience.

Roger made his way up in the elevator. An earlier call confirmed that Rong and Shu were there.

Pleasantries between the three were unnecessary.

"There are containers at the terminal that won't be going anywhere," Roger stated flatly. He sat facing Rong and Shu. The two Chinese sat at a conference table with large windows only a few feet behind them, forcing Roger to squint slightly as he saw more of a silhouette of the two while looking into the morning brightness behind them. "As we've discussed before, we know that some of your companies, especially Mr. Liwei, are making and trading in a variety of contraband goods. It's costing you, and it's costing you not just in dollars but in ChiTran's reputation as a reliable company."

"Mr. Steeg, we appreciate your concern," Shu began. Her English was slow, but each word or phrase was measured. "I think there's a phrase Americans use, something like having bigger fish to fry, yes?"

Roger listened and nodded.

"One container, five containers, maybe more will be stopped somewhere in the world. And, yes, we will lose some income. But we look at the bigger picture, the obligations we have to each other and to China. Many of these things you are not aware of, and you don't need to be aware of as long as you are able to keep us informed about what your former colleagues may be doing or may do in the future. We'll decide how to alter our operations, but that can take time. Although it is unfortunate, we'll sacrifice a few containers as we make the changes. I hope you understand," Shu explained.

To Roger's ear, Shu had said a lot without saying anything he could understand. If there were hidden meanings in her words, he felt inadequate in trying to decipher the message.

"As we discussed, we will meet and take care of things," Rong said, speaking for the first time. "After some decisions have been made about Mr. Liwei, we will want you to explain to us how and why your successor and any other American officials were at Mr. Liwei's factory. Your insights into this will educate us in our future business activities," Rong added.

"We were surprised to hear about US Customs officials making an unscheduled visit to a Chinese company in China. That seems to be an extraordinary thing to happen in China, especially when very detailed business documents are available and shown as proof of shipment. As such, it would seem some people went to extreme measures to make such a meeting happen," Rong said.

Roger wondered if the old man and woman sitting on the other side of the table knew about his visit to the container terminal, and if they did, how did they know, and who would've informed them? In that instant, he wondered what Shu meant about their obligations to China. She made a clear distinction between their obligations to their businesses and to China, the country. Had he let his guard down? Roger didn't think so. His gut said maybe he was being too paranoid. He realized there were layers of conduct he either wasn't aware of or didn't understand.

As Roger thought about these things, a long pause in the conversation occurred.

"Do not worry yourself over the containers, Mr. Steeg. We'll survive these slight obstacles. This will not affect the situation with you," Shu said as a way of ending the short meeting.

Rong pressed a button on the phone in front of him on the conference table. The three sat, saying nothing for a few moments before a young woman appeared at the door. Rong and Shu rose from their chairs but made no move otherwise. Roger turned to see the young woman and made his leave from the conference room.

Shu waited until she was sure Roger was down the hall from the conference room. "Something is wrong. Mr. Steeg made a mistake today.

How did he know about the containers being held before Liwei?" Shu said, more a statement than a question.

"A good point. In the usual course, Liwei would've been contacted by customs and called. He would've asked us to fix the situation with our local customs connections, or it would not have happened in the first place," Rong said. "Liwei may have a point about us having a problem with information. We need to remind ourselves that Mr. Steeg has good connections, too."

"Yes, he does. But his connections are also in positions to cause us problems. Our connections are to help us get out of those situations," Shu noted. "We have to be sure that our contacts can reverse or veto the decisions of Mr. Steeg's contacts."

* * * * *

The two Liwei containers at the container terminal in Hong Kong were being loaded onto trucks. They were headed to customs-controlled warehouses for a full inspection. The Hong Kong Customs senior inspector at the terminal tasked with preventing their export had his team working with the terminal operators to identify and move them. He was taking no chances that the containers might get loaded onto a ship.

The senior inspector was hoping that the containers would be at the warehouse by midday. Someone would fax Liwei's office as well as call and give him a verbal notice that his suspected contraband goods were likely to be destroyed if the customs team of inspectors confirmed the information they had received from Cheng Gao.

The senior inspector, hoping to give his team a little pat on the back, contacted the customs public affairs office in case they were interested in being at the warehouse when the contraband was inspected. A little publicity about the good work of customs never hurt and would be good for morale. He was aware that the commissioner liked having these discoveries of contraband highlighted. These inspections and detections of contraband never hurt the agency when customs argued that it needed more funds for staffing to inspect cargo and keep Hong Kong free of contraband.

Good publicity about finding and destroying contraband was something even the folks on the mainland wouldn't object to, as there had to be appearances of doing what was right.

* * * * *

"Ray, we've got some good news," Roger said.

"What would that be?" Ray didn't know what Roger was talking about.

"Those pictures we took Saturday of Liwei's shipment. Those containers aren't going anywhere. Our Hong Kong friends decided to snag the shipment. Chuck called and gave me the news."

Ray inhaled deeply and felt his cheeks getting warm. He wasn't happy. "I wasn't aware of that decision" was all Ray could say. His less-than-collegial call to the Hong Kong Customs assistant commissioner is what really did the trick. Nevertheless, he was bothered by the fact that Cheng had called Roger with the news.

"Maybe we need Millennium Labs to get more involved on both ends to squeeze these guys in China to do more," Roger offered.

"I've got a few other things on my plate at the moment," Ray responded. He wanted to get off the phone.

"Okay then, I'll talk to you later." Roger signed off.

"Shit!" Ray wasn't happy. As soon as the call ended, he was quick to dial up Cheng. It was good Cheng wasn't within arm's length of Ray at that moment. Ray wanted to physically shake the young man.

"What are you doing? Do you know what you're doing?" Ray said as soon as he heard the call being picked up on the other end, not hiding his anger.

"Hello, who is this?" Cheng asked.

"Ray Jackson. Why did you call Roger before calling me about the two containers? Roger is not customs anymore. You need to work with and through me right now. Do you understand?"

It was a weak sounding yes from Cheng.

"You need to treat anyone not part of Hong Kong or US Customs as being outside of our need-to-know circle. Do you understand?" Ray said tersely.

Cheng was still recovering from Ray's verbal take-down. "Yes, I understand," he said more confidently.

"One more thing. Even though Aaron Foster is part of customs, we must be careful. Some of his girlfriend's connections are questionable. You go through me, and I'll decide what Roger and Aaron need to know," Ray emphasized.

"Okay," Cheng said. "I've also coordinated for our airport monitoring later today. Do you plan to be there?"

"What's the expected arrival time?"

"The Cathay flight arrives at about six, but by the time he disembarks, walks to baggage, and gets to immigration, it'll probably be another thirty minutes," Cheng explained.

"I'll plan to be there just before the scheduled arrival time. When I get to the airport, I'll call you on your cell phone."

"I'll make sure everyone knows you're coming," Cheng said.

"Hopefully, all goes well the rest of the day, and we don't need to discuss anything. I'll see you at the airport." Ray was calmed down again. Sometimes, the younger guys needed to be reminded of their place, and Ray, though not part of Hong Kong Customs, wanted to impress on Cheng who was senior as they continued down this path of working together.

* * * * *

Rong and Shu didn't say much as they were being driven to the Tai Po area of the New Territories. Liwei wished he could have arranged to have the house aired out and ready to welcome them.

Tengfei Meng and Shing Fang entered the house first, leaving Liwei in the sedan parked in the driveway. No one had been to the house since Tengfei had freed Shing several days earlier. They opened windows and started fans to get fresh air into the house. Liwei gave them time to start airing it out before leaving the comfort of the air-conditioned sedan. He wasn't sure why a face-to-face meeting with the two elders was necessary.

Liwei was walking through the front sitting room and heard the approaching engine. He bent slightly to look out the window and confirm what he'd heard.

"Get tea ready," Liwei said, assuming that either Tengfei or Shing had heard him. Liwei went, opened the door, and waited for his two guests to appear.

Shu and Rong nodded as they walked through the door and passed Liwei, saying nothing.

"It's still lunchtime, and I know you missed lunch to be here. I can arrange something to be brought in," Liwei offered.

"No, thank you," Shu responded. She was still settling into a chair and pushing herself back. Once comfortable, she crossed her ankles as her feet didn't reach the floor.

Rong was in a chair several feet away from Shu. Liwei was left to sit on the sofa.

"You've put us in some difficult situations," Shu started. "The Kaili Liang thing was stupid and arrogant. We don't understand what you thought you would gain from that."

Shu saw that Liwei wanted to say something. She simply raised a hand with her palm toward him in a "stop" signal, something one would do with a dog. "Do you know that your containers were accessed here in Hong Kong? Do you know what they suspect? Those containers are now in customs' custody, along with everything that is in them. This could cause problems for all of ChiTran."

"We know you've been shipping a lot of contraband," Rong added. "The Americans also know what you've been doing. We're getting a lot of pressure to do something."

"My bottom line is still very good for all of us," Liwei said smugly. "You know that the Americans are a small part of the overall activity and revenue source."

"We agree," Shu conceded. "That's why you'll remain part of ChiTran. You are going to make some immediate changes, but in general, we have no intention of making big changes to your operations. However, there must be some minor adjustments immediately."

Liwei's eyes went back and forth to his visitors.

"You will do what you have to do with the provincial authorities in Guangdong Province and rename your company. After that is complete, you will export only from Shenzhen or Guangzhou ports. You will not use Hong Kong's container terminals," Shu instructed. "When you meet with and speak to the Guangdong provincial authorities, we want you to emphasize the point that you'll help them become a more active and dominant port that will become one of the most financially important hubs for China and divert container traffic from Hong Kong. You'll emphasize to them and any other provincial official that part of the long-term plan is to expand and employ more people, but you don't need to get into specifics."

"I can do that in a matter of days, but something must be done with Meilin and her father," Liwei insisted.

"That is not your call. Nevertheless, there will be a joint meeting with you, them, and us in a day or two. We'll have this sorted out," Rong said. "But things can't be settled if you continue to act in a way that provokes others to act against you. Do you understand?" Rong asked pointedly.

"I'll agree to meet, but I want Meilin to admit that she caused China, Hong Kong, and American Customs officials to come to my office. That is unacceptable, and she must be put in her place for causing that. I must insist on this. We're in this situation because she is giving out our business information and no one is keeping her in line," Liwei responded. His slight critique of his two elders wasn't missed by either of his guests.

"As we said, it'll all be discussed and taken care of," Shu insisted. "In the meantime, you attend to your business and only your business. I do not want to hear that you've been doing anything to antagonize or harm any other ChiTran business." Shu scooted out of the chair and onto her feet. She'd said what she came to say. She hoped the fact that they did this in person underscored to Liwei the importance of keeping his place within the organization. She hoped that by delivering the message this way, Liwei would understand that she and Rong expected their instructions to be followed without question.

At the door, Shu turned to Liwei. "No one is guaranteed a spot on ChiTran's executive counsel. I hope you'll conduct yourself in a way that shows us that you understand that."

ChiTran's two elders left Liwei's and headed back to Kowloon.

* * * * *

Ray was at a Hong Kong Customs warehouse, sweating in the stuffy facility, squeezing in this stop before his trip out to the airport. When Cheng learned of the location of Liwei's seized containers, he called Ray, and Ray decided it would be good to make an appearance at the warehouse. Large floor fans only moved hot, humid air but did nothing to cool the warehouse. The warehouse was a big open area for trucks to back up to the loading docks and load and unload their contents.

Ray stood back and let the team of Hong Kong inspectors do their work. The back of the container was open, and the wall of boxes was removed one row at a time. The boxes were brought out to long tables set up so that the contents could be taken out and examined. A supervisory inspector acted like a traffic cop as he had his ten-person team open and place the contents on the table.

Two others in civilian clothes stood away from the team of inspectors. A woman had a large camera draped around her neck, and her male colleague stood by her with a notebook.

Ray walked over and handed the supervisory inspector a folder of several pages that instructed the team about what to look for on the inner packages. After Ray and the supervisory inspector discussed the documents, the Hong Kong Customs official relayed the information in Chinese to his team. One of the pages was a summary that Aaron had prepared after his phone call with Noah Harding of Millennium Labs and what Noah had said about Millennium's limited operations in China.

Standing several feet behind the teams working at the tables, Ray stood with the supervisory inspector. The inspectors were looking for anything on the inner boxes of the products that indicated a connection with Millennium Labs, be it a corporate logo or anything else mentioning Millennium.

Within the first few minutes, the inspectors going through the first two large boxes stopped and waved the supervisory inspector over to the table. After a brief exchange, he walked back toward Ray and waved the man and woman from public affairs to move in for their photos and a write-up about the contraband.

"The first ten items have the markings you said were fraudulent. We'll start doing random checks of the boxes in the container. Unless we see otherwise, it looks like there's no need to open every box and check every item," the supervisory inspector explained.

"That's great," Ray said. "When your team has finished the random check, I'd appreciate it if you could have someone contact me and confirm the results with some of the numbers about boxes or items you're seizing."

Ray was about to turn and leave when he noticed one of the line inspectors waving his arms, trying to get the supervisory inspector's attention. Ray wandered over to the young man who had been waving, listening to the chatter between the Hong Kong Customs officers.

"We might have more than just these safety items."

"What's got his attention?" Ray asked.

"The weights of a couple of the boxes are different. I've instructed them to open those and see what's inside," the supervisory inspector answered.

Ray checked his watch. He wanted to leave, but he wanted to know what else was in Liwei's shipment.

Once the boxes were cut open, several tightly wrapped clear plastic bags were dumped onto the table. They were filled with pills.

"We'll get them tested and let you know what we find," the supervisory inspector told Ray. The supervisory inspector grabbed the documentation for the shipment being inspected. "We have clear violations for smuggling these pills, and there are probably other violations once we know what these pills contain. I'll provide a detailed summary once everything is done."

"Thanks," Ray said and shook the supervisory inspector's hand before turning and leaving.

Ray was glad he squeezed the warehouse stop into his schedule. The discovery of those pills was a surprise. This was going to make his report to his colleagues in the United States even more interesting and arouse greater suspicion about the shipments that had arrived in recent weeks.

His focus was the airport, but as he was leaving, he realized that the confirmation of illegal products from ChiTran Guangdong Specialties Company meant he could share the information with Millennium Labs. He could advise them to get more active in China with Chinese authorities. Finally, so as not to encroach on the activities of his counterparts on the mainland, he would advise Millennium to liaise with the US Customs attaché in Beijing.

Chapter 14

Convergence

Hong Kong (Monday, May 18)

Kellie finally fell asleep for a few hours before sunrise after the call from her mother had made sleep impossible. She and Aaron spent time trying to piece things together, but her mother had told her little to nothing useful. Kellie withheld her suspicions about her father possibly using innocent information she might have said about Aaron's work. Kellie thought that there was already too much guesswork to try and connect the dots without adding that to the mix.

Aaron jotted down the bits that Kellie provided, but the gaps in the story didn't allow him to see anything concrete. The agents going to Kellie's mom bothered him the most. He knew that wouldn't happen without solid information linking Kellie's father to something. He called Ray but was told that Ray was out at a series of meetings away from the office all day. Aaron thought about calling Roger but realized Roger had no reason to know why agents would go to visit Kellie's parents a day ago.

Aaron went through a mental checklist, trying to identify someone he could call. He came up empty. Even if he had thought of someone, it was hours before he could justify contacting someone in the US, given the time difference and his lack of information. With nothing else to do, he turned his attention back to Kellie.

"When do we want to head to the airport?" he asked.

"According to Cathay, the flight isn't scheduled to arrive till late afternoon. We have plenty of time," Kellie answered.

* * * * *

Cheng Gao stood next to uniformed customs Officer Yin in one of the many back rooms of the airport located where passengers are never allowed. Yin's black hair seemed tinged with brown, and his facial features hinted at a European connection in his lineage. His narrow shoulders and average height meant that he would otherwise be lost in the crowd except for the uniform.

Immigration Officer Wong stood in front of the room with Cheng and Yin. The room had twenty chairs, but this briefing of immigration and customs officers had twice that number packed into the room.

Cheng wasn't used to speaking in front of large groups. He was nervous and decided to brief Yin and Wong, giving them information and general instructions. Then, Yin and Wong would speak to their group of officers.

Wong spoke first. "Each immigration booth already has the names this passenger might use. Our goal is to identify and pull him aside. We aren't sure if he'll present an American passport or one from Taiwan or the mainland. We also have two possible names the traveler is using. It could be Zhixin Liang or Alvin Liang. Once he presents his passport, take a moment to examine it and be sure. Just signal one of the customs officers to keep an eye on him while you come to me." Wong finished by making sure his officers had the airline and flight number. "That information is also in each immigration booth, but I want you to write it down."

Customs Officer Yin then addressed his customs officers. Some were in uniform, and others wore civilian clothes. "Those of you in uniform will be concentrated in the baggage area and in the area behind the immigration booths. I want you guys"—Yin pointed to his civilian-clad officers—"to be in the arrival gate area and corridors where the passengers will disembark at least fifteen minutes before arrival time. Try to identify Mr. Liang as he gets off the plane. I know the picture we have is blurry, but we might be able to spot him. If you do, follow him as he heads toward immigration. If you do get eyes on him before immigration, pair up so that one of you can stay on him while the other lets our immigration officer know which line he's in. Remember, do not approach him. We'll take care of that once he actually steps up to immigration and presents his passport."

"Any questions?" Yin asked. There were none. No one in the room was a stranger to this type of operation, as they'd all been through this many times. Cheng was the only rookie in the room.

The two teams of officers began emptying the room. There was still an hour before the flight was scheduled to land.

"Let's go to the room where we'll put Liang," Wong suggested to Cheng and Yin. Before they exited the room, a young immigration officer appeared in the doorway.

"Mr. Jackson is calling, says he's the US Customs attaché. He said he's supposed to meet Mr. Gao here."

"Bring him here," Wong instructed. "We'll wait here." The three men waited another quarter-hour before Ray Jackson appeared. Ray was physically bigger than his three Hong Kong hosts. Cheng made the introductions, but they wasted no time as immigration officer Wong led them to an area closer to the arrival hall and the immigration booths.

"We have several rooms where we question passengers. We'll use the one at the far end behind the immigration booth. It has an observation room next to it," Wong explained. The four men went into the room where Liang would be brought. It wasn't big. Upon entering, the walls to the left and right had large mirrors, but only the one on the left was a two-way mirror. One chair at the table faced the two-way mirror. Two chairs faced the regular mirror, and there were two other chairs in the corners on the left side of the room. Small, flat microphones were on the table but were controlled by anyone in the observation room. The room was well lit, allowing anyone in the observation room to have a good look at and view of the person being questioned.

Wong took them into the observation room. It was the same size as the room where Liang would be questioned. It had four chairs, a table with a recording machine, and a button on the wall by the two-way mirror that could be pressed if someone in the observation room wanted the attention of the officers in the interrogation room.

"How do you know if we're signaling you?" Ray asked.

"There are lights above the mirror that'll blink," Wong answered.

"Who's taking the lead in questioning Liang?" Ray inquired.

"We'll both be in there," Wong said, pointing to Yin. "Based on the information we have, both Officer Yin and I will pose the questions, but if there's something specific that we aren't asking, just signal us, and we'll stop, and we can consult with you," Wong explained.

"I'd appreciate it if you challenge him about what was found in the two containers that have been stopped and get him talking. I'm hoping that your questioning will scare him enough so that it causes him to implicate himself about what he, his business, or his contacts here have been doing. Seeing that you can tape the interview, I'd appreciate it if you would," Ray asked. His hosts nodded they would. "It sounds like we're ready for Mr.

Liang," Ray said. "One last thing. Are we agreed that Mr. Liang has not, as far as we know, broken any Hong Kong laws?"

"We're still gathering information, that's all," Yin said.

"Then, I'd like to come in at the end with a surprise for Mr. Liang before you're done," Ray said without explanation.

Yin looked at Cheng, who simply shrugged since he had no idea what Ray had planned.

Cheng glanced at the time, then at both Wong and Yin. Wong's immigration officers were already working in their booths as other flights arrived, and the lines were long at passport control.

"I'm going to make sure my people are getting themselves in place," Yin said as he left the group. The customs officers would be spread out over a longer distance between the gate area and immigration. Ray and Cheng were left in the observation room to wait.

The arrivals hall was always crowded. Hong Kong was a destination for millions, but it was a busy layover hub for people staying one night before continuing to other countries in Asia. Many Americans, Australians, and Canadians who were going to other destinations in Asia wanted the overnight stay in Hong Kong just to get off a plane after long, grueling hours on flights.

In another part of the airport, Kellie and Aaron entered the arrivals hall, checked the monitors, then wandered around for twenty minutes before they found two seats together.

"How are you feeling?" Aaron asked.

Kellie sat looking straight ahead, right leg crossed over her left and arms crossed. Her dangling leg and foot were in constant motion. "I'm a bit confused and frustrated because I don't know why he's coming or what he might be involved in that would cause this abrupt trip. He knows we're here, so why didn't he call one of us?" There was an undertone of anger in her voice.

"I have to believe that someone on this end must know he's coming. Any idea who that would be," Aaron posed.

Kellie's leg stopped moving. She turned her head slowly toward Aaron. "I can think of only one person. Guang Lai," she offered. "But he said nothing yesterday when I called after getting back to Hong Kong." Kellie turned her gaze away from Aaron. Her lips were pressed.

Aaron saw the tight jaw muscles and lips pressed tightly. From experience, he knew she was fuming. He said nothing. Knowing her as he did, Aaron got up and wandered around the arrivals hall. It was better to give Kellie some time to herself after she said aloud the one thing that was now consuming her thoughts.

Aaron's aimless walk around the arrivals hall benefited one other person. There were multiple entries into the arrivals hall, and Guang spotted Aaron meandering around from about fifty feet away. Aaron stood out from the locals. And Guang had spent just enough time meeting with Aaron to spot him. Guang wasted no time in turning around and exiting through the doors he'd just used. He got into the taxi line to go back to the hotel. There was only one reason why Aaron was at the airport. Somehow, Kaili knew her father was flying in. He didn't want to be there when they came face-to-face.

Aaron stopped walking and stood staring at a monitor to check flight status. Alvin Liang's flight was not listed as having landed, but it was within minutes of its scheduled arrival time. Aaron took the seat next to Kellie.

"It shouldn't be too long now," he said.

* * * * *

Alvin Liang's flight touched down within minutes of its scheduled arrival time. Sleep had come easily during the flight, but it was a fitful sleep. He didn't feel rested, although his watch indicated that he'd slept for seven hours. He thought about Elizabeth, what he saw at Sunrise, and whether his decision to board the plane at the last minute was the right thing to have done. Feeling the plane taxi to its gate, Alvin Liang hoped his cousin, Guang Lai, was ready to whisk him to the hotel so that he could call home.

Kai Tak Airport's limited area in Kowloon meant that it didn't take long to taxi to and stop at its designated gate. Disembarking a few hundred passengers would take time as those in economy class seats stood and needed to stretch their legs after a fifteen-hour flight. Alvin Liang wasn't quite so stiff, having a first-class seat that reclined and allowed him room to stretch and sleep.

Alvin stood, waiting for the plane's door to open to start disembarking passengers. Just before the door opened, a flight attendant announced their arrival and reminded everyone to look around to ensure no personal items were left on the plane and advised them to check the monitors for their checked luggage. Alvin Liang didn't worry about that. He had only his carry-on bag. He calculated that he'd be out of the airport and on the way to a hotel within an hour.

In the corridor, two plainclothes Hong Kong Customs officers stood at opposite sides of the corridor about ten feet apart with eyes on the disembarking passengers making their way from the jetway. Both had studied a fuzzy black-and-white picture of Zhixin Liang, or Alvin Liang, that had been provided by US Customs. They hoped the photo would allow them to identify and follow Liang. Knowing that Liang was flying first-class, they hoped he'd be off the plane sooner rather than later.

A dozen passengers entered the wide corridor before one of the customs officers spotted Liang. The one spotting Liang allowed Liang to get about ten steps down the corridor before starting to follow. The other customs officer pulled a radio off the back of his belt and described Liang's clothing so others could spot him in case he got lost in the crowd. It was simple. Liang wore a buttoned-down white dress shirt and black dress slacks. He carried a black leather overnight bag over his shoulder. Everyone had the same fuzzy photo. The second officer waited just to be sure no one else entered the corridor who resembled the photo.

Liang followed the signs to passport control. He adjusted the overnight bag from one hand to the other, not at all aware that there were now two plainclothes customs officers behind him at different intervals and he'd be passing a third.

Alvin saw the long passport control lines ahead. Since he didn't have a Hong Kong or mainland China passport, he had to get in the line for foreign passports. All the lines were long, so all he could do was hope the line moved quickly.

Two of the customs officers who had followed Liang took up positions between lines of passengers, staying behind Liang. A third customs officer went to the area behind the immigration booths where Yin and Wong stood, letting them know what line Liang was standing in so that the immigration officer who would be presented with Liang's passport could be alerted. Wong waited until Liang was the fifth passenger in line before he communicated the information to his immigration officer.

Zhixin Liang, or Alvin Liang, stepped forward and presented his Taiwan passport. The immigration officer casually flipped through the pages.

In Chinese, the immigration officer made a comment. "You haven't come to Hong Kong for a long time. Is this business or pleasure?"

"Pleasure. I'm spending a few days with family, who are here from Taiwan," Alvin said. "When was your last trip to Taiwan?"

Alvin leaned in to hear the question. "It has been several years."

"How long will you be staying in Hong Kong?"

Alvin closed his eyes for a moment. Then as if finally understanding the question, he answered, "I'm not sure. It could be a week or ten days visiting with my relatives."

"Where are you staying?"

Alvin wondered why all the questions. He just needed to have this immigration officer stamp the passport and let him in. Stay calm, he said to himself. "I'm meeting my family at the Marriott," Alvin answered, remembering that Kellie was staying there.

"You have a reservation at the Marriott?"

"Yes," Alvin said, trying to move things along and get his entry stamp.

"Excuse me, I'll be right back," the immigration officer said.

Alvin's gaze followed the immigration officer. Seeing the young officer talking to two older men who wore two different uniforms. Alvin lifted his head slightly, took in a deep breath, and exhaled through his mouth. At that moment, his overnight bag felt like it would bring him to his knees.

The immigration officer headed back, but he was being followed by one of the older men in uniform. Though he didn't see them, the two plainclothes customs officers who had been keeping their distance came up behind Alvin and stood on both sides next to him.

The immigration officer sat in his seat. Immigration Officer Wong held Alvin's passport and motioned with his hand for Alvin to come through the narrow passage.

"Sorry for the delay, but we'd like to ask you a few questions. Please, follow me," Wong instructed. Alvin fell in a few paces behind Wong. Walking through the narrow path bounded by metal barriers, he glanced over his shoulder, noticing two customs officers who had trailed him to the immigration line and were now immediately behind him.

Wong led Alvin into the windowless interior room. A little over a week earlier, Aaron had been in a room like this with Wong. Wong extended his left arm and used Alvin's passport in his left hand to point him toward the lone chair on one side of the center table.

Customs Officer Yin sat down once Alvin pulled the chair out and lowered himself onto it. Wong took the chair next to Yin and continued to hold Alvin's passport.

Wong opened the passport to the page with Alvin's photograph. He placed it on the table between him and Yin.

"Mr. Liang, I'm with Hong Kong Immigration. Mr. Yin"—Wong cocked his head toward Yin—"is a Hong Kong Customs officer. We need to understand the reason for your trip."

Alvin knew he needed to say something before he waited too long. The mess in Los Angeles came crashing to the front of his thoughts, but he fought off the mental images of Desmond Lupo being taken away.

"It's a mix of business and pleasure. My daughter is here on a mixed trip as well. I thought if I came over, we could do some fun things together but also take care of any work we each had to do."

"How long is your stay here?" Wong asked.

"I have no set time. It depends a little on my daughter's schedule."

"Is there a Mrs. Liang? Did she decide not to come?" Wong probed.

"Yes, I have a wife. It's a long flight, and she decided she could wait till our daughter was back in the States to see her. She'd be on her own when my daughter and I are working." Because he never thought he'd be in this situation, Alvin was winging it the best he could. He knew there was truth to Kellie's trip being a mix of work and pleasure, but beyond that, he had to be careful.

"You said your daughter is staying at the Marriott? If she's here for a mix of business and leisure, did she travel alone?" Wong asked.

"No. She's with her boyfriend," Alvin answered.

"What's his name?"

"Aaron Foster."

Wong tilted his head very slightly at the mention of the name. He took out a small notepad from his uniform breast pocket. "Aaron Foster," Wong repeated back to Alvin to confirm. He got a confirmation nod.

"I'll be right back," Wong said, rising and tapping Yin on the arm to follow. Wong led Yin into the observation room where Ray and Cheng were watching.

"Do either of you know Aaron Foster?"

Ray and Cheng nodded that they did.

"Is there a problem?" Ray wanted to know. "He's telling the truth about that part. Foster is his daughter's boyfriend. He is a customs lawyer back in the States and was instrumental in helping us get her back from across the border."

"I needed a moment when I heard the name," Wong started to explain. "I had your Foster in one of these rooms when he arrived. One of my officers thought somebody might have tampered with his passport, so it was brought to my attention. You're saying he's okay, and some of this is just coincidental?"

"I think some of this is just unfortunate. If there's more than just coincidence involved, we'll look at it on our end. But I can assure you he is a US Customs attorney," Ray said.

Wong and Yin headed back into the room. They had a few seconds between rooms to decide what was next. They re-entered the room and took their seats.

"If I called your daughter at the hotel, would she know you are coming?" Yin asked.

Alvin's pulse picked up a few beats. This was a question he had no idea how to answer. His wife didn't know where he was, so she was in no position to tell Kellie. "Of course, she knows. I wouldn't just travel here without informing her," Alvin heard himself say.

"And your business here, what is it exactly?" Yin probed.

"I'm involved with a company that owns an import-export business. It has managers with direct responsibilities for the day-to-day business activities. Lately, we've discovered some problems with some of the imported goods from China that ship through Hong Kong. I wanted to see how I might be able to help prevent these problems from occurring in the future."

"What's the name of your company?" Yin wanted to know.

"Sunrise Trading Company."

"How much does your company import from China?" Yin asked.

"I would guess almost all of our imports are from China," Alvin offered. "I don't know the exact value of those imports."

"Do you have any connection, any links to the companies that make the products you import?" Yin wanted to get to the core issue.

Alvin looked at both men across the table. He replayed the question in his mind and focused on the way Officer Yin had put it to him. "Sunrise Trading has no legal relationship with any Chinese manufacturing operation. We import Chinese-made goods."

Ray Jackson was now wishing he had Aaron there to hear the exchange. The way Alvin answered made Ray think Alvin was parsing his words carefully. Ray hit the button to send a signal to Yin and Wong, who looked at each other for a second before they got up to leave the room again.

"I'd appreciate it if you would allow me in there," Ray asked the two Hong Kong officers.

"Is there a problem?" Yin asked.

"It's not a problem, but I want to press him and follow up on your last question," Ray said.

Ray followed Yin and Wong and took up a place at the table. He took the initiative. "Mr. Liang, I'm the US Customs attaché in Hong Kong. You need to know that I'm going to record our conversation, and it's a criminal offense to lie to a US government official. Before you answer any more questions, let me inform you of a few things so that you don't get yourself into deeper trouble. Your Los Angeles manager provided us with your name. Customs agents also visited your wife, so we know that you never told her about your trip to Hong Kong. I also suspect that your daughter might not be aware of your trip. I spent considerable time with her yesterday, accompanying her back from the mainland. She never mentioned that she expected to be seeing you."

Ray saw sweat beading on Alvin's forehead. Forcing Alvin to confront a few troublesome facts was Ray's way to gauge how much Alvin was holding back, and now Ray was convinced that there was a lot Alvin knew but wasn't telling. Ray turned and looked at Yin and Wong. He signaled with his eyes, and the three men went back into the observation room and joined Cheng, who had watched alone.

"I'd like you to deny him entry and have him sent back to the US," Ray said.

"That could be a problem. We have no grounds to deny entry. There's nothing proving that he has committed a crime in Hong Kong or anywhere else," Wong responded.

"Can you give me twenty-four hours? I'll get you a formal request from us to deny entry and send him back as a person suspected of criminal trafficking of contraband and other illegal goods," Ray said.

Wong was staring at the floor. Alvin wasn't a fugitive, and no criminal record had been established. "I don't have the authority to meet your request," Wong said.

Ray's gaze went to Yin. "Your request will have to go to someone much higher than us. We can't make the decision to hold him," Yin said.

"I just told you what the grounds are," Ray insisted.

"No, they don't exist right now. We have to decide why we would detain him right now, and he has not done anything in Hong Kong, and you haven't proven that he's done something in the United States," Yin said.

"What did he indicate on his immigration form as his temporary address while he's here?" Ray asked. "Does he have a reservation at the hotel? If he doesn't, did he lie on the form? Is that sufficient grounds to hold him temporarily?"

Wong found Alvin's immigration form to see how it was filled out. "He wrote down the Marriott as his temporary address." Wong left the room to give the hotel a call and find out if Alvin Liang had a reservation. He was back in five minutes. "You just bought a little time. There's no reservation. It's a weak basis to hold him, but technically, I can."

* * * * *

The crowd of people in the arrivals hall never thinned. Kellie paced behind a wall of people standing shoulder to shoulder, waiting to greet friends or family. Her father's flight had landed almost three hours earlier. This was like déjà vu when she and Aaron arrived, and at this point, she couldn't think of any reason why he hadn't come through the doors like everyone else. The monitors no longer displayed her father's flight because of the other flights that had arrived after his.

Aaron sat, watching Kellie pace. Mentally, he was going through scenarios that might explain the delay. With each glance at his watch or the clock on the wall and time passing, he was convinced something was wrong. There was an on-time arrival, then disembarking the plane, immigration control, and baggage claim. Even if he had a question from immigration, as Aaron had experienced, far too much time had passed. Aaron wondered how Alvin had paid for the ticket and how soon before departure the purchase had been made. He realized that it would appear suspicious to purchase a ticket within twenty-four hours prior to a trans-Pacific flight without some emergency unless Alvin could explain.

Aaron imposed a deadline on himself that once it had been three hours since Alvin Liang's plane landed, he'd call Ray for help. More time passed, and Alvin didn't appear through the doors.

Kellie was tired of pacing and sat next to Aaron. "You're the government guy. Any ideas?" She sat, slumped in the seat next to Aaron.

"I was going to call Ray, the attaché, when we hit the three-hour mark. I doubt it makes any difference," Aaron said as he checked his watch. It was ten minutes shy of three hours since the flight landed. Aaron pulled out his cell phone and called Ray's office. It was already late in the day, and it was possible people had already headed home. When he got no answer, it occurred to him that Ray was putting in a regular day and probably left the office after the long weekend hours that included the trek across the border.

What next, he wondered. Kellie wanted—no, needed—him to come up with a solution. Aaron pulled out his wallet, flipping through every part of it that might hold a card, cash, or photograph. He didn't find what he was looking for in the wallet. He stood up and grabbed a handful of whatever was in his right front trouser pocket and knew that his government identification wasn't there. His left hand felt the stiff card-like item in his left front pocket. He pulled it out.

"Stay here. Let me see if this will get me anywhere," Aaron said, showing Kellie what he had in his hand.

She sat up straighter. "I'll be right here. Nowhere else to go."

Aaron didn't know where to go. This arrivals area had a few security people but no immigration or customs officers. The people Aaron needed to find were on the other side of that wall and door that had a sign in multiple languages indicating that entry was prohibited. After checking all the signage in English, he looked for an information desk and strode toward the nearest one.

"Can you help me find an immigration or customs officer?"

The information desk had lots of advertisements and posters on the counter and on its back wall for hotels, bus tours, private tours, and restaurants. A young woman who looked to be college-age was the only person working the desk. "You might have to go up to the departure level where people go through immigration and security," she suggested.

"Thanks." Walking away, Aaron felt stupid for not thinking of that himself. Before looking for an elevator or escalator to the departure level, he let Kellie know where he was going. "Stay here," he said. "It's probably even more crowded and crazier up there than here."

Kellie watched Aaron disappear into the crowd.

On the departure level, people moved in every direction, looking for their airline check-in counters. Dozens of lines were formed with luggage on the floor and on carts. Aaron knew he needed to get toward the far side of all the airline check-in counters. There was so much signage hanging down from the ceiling warning of the airport's impending closure and other signage that it was difficult to see anything indicating the immigration and security areas. Aaron waded through and between the crowds and saw what he was looking for. He wondered if he could convince any of the Hong Kong officers to give him a couple of minutes. It wouldn't be easy with thousands of outbound passengers to process through the immigration line.

Aaron found space along a wall and walked toward the immigration officers checking and stamping passports. No one was looking his way. They were busy with travelers standing in front of them. Aaron went as far as he could go before being stopped by a metal barrier about four feet high that filled the space between the wall and an immigration officer's booth.

The officer gave Aaron a glance but then returned his attention to the next person up. When he looked over at Aaron again, Aaron tried to gesture to him that he wanted to talk to him, but he ignored Aaron. An idea occurred to Aaron, and he pulled out his US Customs identification, holding it in his outstretched arm, waiting for the officer to look his way again. At the next chance he had, Aaron pointed to the identification, hoping that would make the officer curious enough to come over. It worked.

Aaron watched the young immigration officer put up a stop gesture after he finished with a traveler and exited his little booth.

"Do you have a problem?" the officer asked.

"I'm a US Customs official, and I need to speak to one of your colleagues," Aaron said as he let the young officer inspect his identification.

The young man turned, looking for someone. "I'll be right back." The young officer wandered away, disappearing behind all the immigration booths.

Aaron mentally rehearsed his story while he stood there waiting. After all, he needed a believable story to tell. But the story only needed to work well enough to get him on the other side of this barrier. If he could get on the other side, then he'd need another plausible reason for someone to help. He needed to make sure that every piece of the story he was going to tell could be stitched together.

Several minutes passed before the young officer appeared. He stepped back into his booth to resume his work and pointed toward Aaron.

Aaron saw a tall thin uniformed man approach. He seemed as young as the other officer but had more insignia on his shoulder epaulets.

"What can I do for you?"

"I'm with US Customs," Aaron held out his identification. "I was expecting to meet an American on a Cathay flight that arrived about three hours ago. We have not seen him in the arrivals hall, and I was hoping that someone might help me find out if he did arrive and where he might be," Aaron explained.

"Where did the flight originate?"

"Los Angeles."

"His name?"

"Alvin Liang."

"I'll have the officer let you through, and you can come with me."

Aaron walked through the narrow passage and joined the immigration officer, following him to an office. Aaron stood, arms folded, watching the immigration officer make a call, speaking Chinese, then turning to Aaron.

"What's the name of the passenger you were expecting?"

"Alvin Liang."

The immigration officer repeated the name into the phone. He waited with the phone pressed to his ear. Finally, he turned to Aaron. "The only passenger on the flight was a Zhixin Liang, no Alvin Liang."

Aaron had never heard the name Zhixin. But he knew that Kellie had a Chinese name, so it made sense that her father would, too. "That may be the same person, but I need to make a call and verify," Aaron said. Aaron pulled out a cell phone and called Kellie. She needed a few extra moments to think about her father's Chinese name. Like her, her father used his American first name, but she knew from past conversations that he had a Chinese name. The best she could do was to tell Aaron that what he had said sounded right but would never swear to it.

"We think that Zhixin Liang is Alvin Liang," Aaron finally told the immigration officer. He waited as the officer listened, saying next to nothing before hanging up.

"He's here, but he's been detained. My colleagues and a customs officer are with him."

"Detained? You mean Hong Kong Customs?"

"Yes. They didn't give me any details."

"Can you take me to where he's being detained? Can I see him?" Aaron pressed.

"I'll take you, but I don't know if you can see him."

Aaron followed the immigration officer down corridors and stairways in parts of the airport that travelers never see except for those who found themselves handcuffed, detained, or otherwise on the wrong side of the rules. A few minutes after walking through the back areas of the airport, Aaron found himself in a familiar area. He saw the immigration booths for the arriving passengers. As he continued to follow the immigration officer, he knew that Kellie wasn't too far away on the other side of the walls in the arrivals area.

Aaron slowed as the immigration officer, a few strides ahead, stopped to talk with a colleague and then continued down a hall behind the immigration booths. The booths stopped, but the hall continued. Aaron stood a few feet away from the officer when the officer stopped to tap on a door.

The door opened outward into the hall and blocked Aaron's view of the person his immigration escort was talking to. No one came out, and the door closed. The immigration officer looked back at Aaron, saying nothing.

When the door reopened, something was said to the immigration officer who had brought Aaron this far. He turned and walked away briskly. Aaron's head turned to follow the officer walking away. Aaron didn't see Attaché Jackson come out of the room until Jackson was practically standing on him. Ray leaned in close. They were about the same height.

"What the hell are you doing here?" Ray asked. He didn't say it loudly, but he made it clear he wasn't happy.

Aaron took a step back. "Kellie and I found out about her father flying in during the night, and we've been waiting for him."

"And how did you get here?" Ray asked.

"I used my customs identification."

Ray grabbed Aaron by the arm and led him into the room where he'd been observing Alvin Liang's questioning. Aaron saw Cheng sitting at a table.

"Take a look at your Mr. Liang. This is as close as you get," Ray said, his brusque tone not waning as he spoke to Aaron.

"Is he being arrested?"

"Not here, but it remains to be seen whether that happens when he gets back to the US," Ray said.

"What does that mean?" Aaron wondered.

"Your girlfriend's father has been linked to some of the recent seizures in the US, ChiTran and possibly the stuff Kellie saw at Liwei's facility. When we put him back on a plane and he lands in LA, he'll be detained and questioned there. I wouldn't be surprised if he is prosecuted," Ray explained.

"What do I tell Kellie?"

"Well, if you want to be honest with her, you tell her the truth. It's possible that her father's business dealings might be responsible for what happened to her these past few days. Or you come up with something else to tell her. Truth be told, I don't really care what you tell her. And by the way, if I find out that either one of you knew anything and didn't tell me, I'm going to make sure that things are very uncomfortable for you," Ray insisted.

"Ray, we didn't know and don't know anything about Mr. Liang's business. I promise you that I don't know anything about any of his business activities or connections. I thought he was a prof in Philly. I'll help you any way I can," Aaron said.

"Okay, now out of here. And the next time we talk, make sure I'm the one initiating the contact," Ray said.

Cheng, who had been listening to the exchange, walked over and opened the door for Aaron to exit the room.

Aaron retraced his steps down the hall until he reached the area where arriving passengers headed toward baggage claim and exited into the arrivals hall. He realized his efforts had taken the better part of an hour. Now, Aaron became just one of many going through the sliding doors into the vast arrivals hall. There, most would be greeted by friends and family. Others would be picked up by hotels for business or holiday. He wished that would have been Alvin Liang's story. Instead, he was going to break a piece of Kellie's heart when he explained the situation.

Aaron followed the path of the travelers until he was able to weave through the initial line of people that was about three deep. His eyes searched the people sitting in the available seating. He saw Kellie after wandering for several minutes. Her long legs were stretched out in front of her as she slumped in a chair with her head resting on the back of the seat and her hair dangling straight toward the floor.

He tapped her foot with his. She jerked her head up and brought her legs in, sitting up instantly.

Kellie stared at Aaron as he lowered himself into the seat next to her as if he was moving in slow motion. As she looked at him, he looked straight ahead, not letting his eyes meet hers.

"What's the matter?" she asked.

"He's here, but he won't be coming through those doors," Aaron said, stopping without any more explanation.

"Are you going to tell me what that means?"

"It means either Hong Kong Customs or Immigration won't allow him to enter Hong Kong. Instead, they'll put him on a plane back to the States," Aaron answered. "Some connections have been made between your father, seized goods in the US, ChiTran, and possibly some of the stuff you saw at Liwei's. The bigger problem your father has is that he may be detained or arrested when he lands in the US."

Kellie let her head drop into the palms of her hands. For a moment, she thought about how she idolized her father as a child and how he made her feel safe. Then she thought about the unexplained comments by Guang and the people in ChiTran and remembered her own thoughts while she was in the hotel in Guangzhou. Even then, some of her thoughts had made her suspect that something wasn't quite right with her father, but she wasn't able to pinpoint it and had been reluctant to believe it. Listening to Aaron, she had to consider the possibility that she was a victim of the chase for riches. But how could her own parents jeopardize her safety because of that chase?

Without a word, Kellie popped up and was out of her seat and heading for the door. She was ten feet ahead before Aaron was up and following.

"Where are we going?" Aaron asked.

"No reason to stay here. Back to the hotel." Just like the distance she'd just placed between herself and Aaron by marching toward the door, she was working hard to mentally place distance between herself and her parents. Walking toward an exit sign, she had tunnel vision, visions of creating space and distance between her and her father.

* * * * *

"We'll put Mr. Liang in an overnight detention facility," Wong said to Ray and Yin. "Assuming that I'll receive something from you, I'll get things started so Cathay can send him back to the States. They won't be happy, but it happens."

"Once I leave here, I'll get things going so we can put him on tomorrow's flight," Ray responded.

"Let's give him the bad news," Yin suggested.

"I'll leave that to the two of you, and I'll get back to my office and start on the paperwork. Hopefully, I'll have something for you in the next few hours. Just let me know how I can contact you once I get what you need," Ray said.

The three men exchanged phone and fax numbers. Cheng had become an observer to everything that had occurred. He realized that Ray had skirted, but not broken, the rules to get what he wanted. It was another part of his education, but he also needed to keep this in mind for future dealings with Ray.

Yin and Wong re-entered the room where Alvin Liang had been waiting. For a while, Alvin had his forehead on the table surface and his hands in his lap. He lifted his head at the sound of the doorknob twisting.

"Mr. Liang, we're going to arrange for you to go home. In the meantime, we'll have a place for you to sleep," Wong explained.

"But I'm meeting my daughter. I have business."

"No. You had no hotel reservation where you said you had arranged to stay while in Hong Kong. We checked. There's no hotel reservation. That means both the statement on your immigration form and your verbal statement to the immigration officer are untrue. Let's see about retrieving your luggage," Wong continued.

"What?"

"Your luggage. I'm sure they've taken it off the belt and set it aside," Yin said.

"No, I don't . . ."

"Don't what?" Yin asked.

"I don't have any checked luggage."

"You traveled here on business and pleasure for at least a week, and you have only that overnight bag?" Yin said, nodding toward the bag on the floor. Yin and Wong stared at Alvin, who sat saying nothing.

"I think the case for sending you home just got a little stronger," Yin said. *No one comes to Hong Kong for a week or more with just an overnight bag,* Yin thought. Alvin's story became less believable to Yin and Wong.

Ray had left his Hong Kong counterparts to finish the interview with Alvin Liang. Although he dreaded it, Ray expected he was facing another night with only catnaps in the office if he was going to be in constant contact with his Los Angeles colleagues. Between phone calls and waiting for faxed documents, they would require him to spend hours in the office. After negotiating traffic to get to the office, he realized that if he had any luck, he might have what he needed to send to Yin and Wong by midnight, allowing him to go home and get a few hours in his own bed. He added one more item to the checklist for his communications with Los Angeles. They also needed to get a hold of Noah Harding at Millennium Labs to obtain a statement that the ChiTran goods were contraband items. That would help lay the groundwork for a criminal case against Liang and Desmond Lupo.

* * * * *

On the way back to the hotel, Aaron and Kellie discussed the call Kellie would make to her mother. Now back, Aaron wondered how Kellie would handle it if she learned her mother knew everything all along.

"You know what you're going to say to your mother when you call?" Aaron asked.

"Generally, yes, but let's see what happens," Kellie said as she sat at the desk and stared at the phone.

"It doesn't dial itself."

"Just give me a minute."

"I'll step out. No need for me to be here. You can give me a summary afterward." Aaron checked his pockets to make sure he had the keycard to re-enter. Once he was sure he had it, he left the room.

Kellie checked the time before she picked up the receiver. There was a chance her mother was already up as it was now a reasonable early hour, not the middle of the night or pre-dawn. She took a deep breath and dialed. The phone rang several times.

"Hello," Elizabeth Liang said slowly, cautiously.

"It's me," Kellie answered.

"How are you? Have you seen your father?"

"I'm fine, but I won't be seeing him. I don't know what he's done. Let me correct myself. He's done something to get himself into enough trouble that I won't be seeing him in Hong Kong, and the next time I see him in the States, he might be behind bars. And to top it all off, whatever he has done may have something to do with why I was kidnapped and taken across the border into China." Kellie was met with silence on the other end.

"Mom, are you still there?"

"Yes," she answered, but barely above a whisper. "I didn't know that anything happened to you in Hong Kong. As you know, your father and I don't discuss his business. It has always been just his concern, not mine."

"Well, you need to know he's in deep. We tried to meet him at the airport. He's being sent right back to the States. Aaron suspects he'll be detained as soon as the plane's doors are opened, and the next thing might be an arrest," Kellie explained. She spent the next ten minutes giving her mother details of what happened in China, what she saw, and what her father's dealings might involve.

"Does Aaron believe your father's going to be arrested?" Elizabeth asked.

"He thinks there's a very good chance criminal charges might be filed against him. Dad needs a lawyer. There's a lot to lose."

"Can Aaron help us?"

"Help us? He's trying to figure out what's going on, how dad got into this situation. And remember, he works for customs. I don't think he'll be in a position to help us without getting himself in trouble. Did you not hear me tell you what happened? I was drugged, smuggled across the border, and held captive. How do you think I feel wondering if my own father had something to do with that?" Kellie's mix of frustration and anger was building.

Elizabeth didn't reply to that. "Maybe I'll fly to LA and see your father," she said.

"Maybe?" Kellie let out a sigh, knowing her mother could hear it. "I'm not going to tell you what to do. I'm still trying to sort all this out myself."

"When are you coming back?"

The question caught Kellie off guard. She hadn't thought about that since Aaron told her about her father's detention and denial of entry. "I'm not sure, several days, a week," she answered. She and Aaron would have to decide what they were going to do. Kellie had nothing more she wanted or needed to say. "I'll call you once we finalize our plans." Kellie heard her mother say something, then the sound of the disconnect. She dropped the phone receiver into its cradle and sat staring at the phone.

Kellie was in a trance-like state. Her eyes were staring at the desk, but she didn't see anything, and her thoughts were garbled. Nothing was clear. Her body jolted at the sound of the doorknob turning. She had lost the last fifteen minutes to nothingness. She couldn't remember thinking about anything after the call ended. She used the desk to help push herself up out of the chair, turning to see Aaron walking into the room.

"How was it?"

Kellie shrugged. "Hard to tell. Some of it seemed like nonsense, crazy talk."

Aaron's eyes narrowed slightly. "What does that mean? You and I need to understand what's been happening and if your parents are involved. We need to know because we need to be prepared for what we might be facing when we get back to the States."

"The only impression I got was that she says she doesn't know anything. My father might be a whole different story," Kellie offered. "She did ask me when we're back, and I told her several days to a week. I just wanted to say something that would give me, us, time."

"That begs the question of whether there's any reason to stay here."

Kellie walked to the bed, plopping down on the end of it. She was pensive, sucking in her left cheek and looking up at Aaron. "Yes. I want to meet Guang. I assume he's still at the hotel. He was informative and helpful when we first met. But when I run through everything that's happened in my mind, including today at the airport, I wonder if he's a big part of this." She didn't say some of the other things going on in her mind. Guang being a big part of what had been occurring meant he, too, chased the money as part of ChiTran. But exactly how did Meilin fit into all of this? After all, Meilin helped her get away from Liwei. Everything seemed to be connected somehow, but not entirely. Perhaps to stay rational, Kellie was finding ways to mentally differentiate Meilin's actions from Guang's and the conduct of Liwei. Even if everyone was part of ChiTran, they weren't all pursuing the same goals, she decided.

"I'm fine if that's what you want to do, but let's get all this done and get out of here." I think we'll be better off at home.

"Tomorrow, lunch," Kellie said abruptly.

"What about lunch?"

"I'll call over and see if he can meet me over lunch. It'll give me the morning to consider the things I want to talk to him about," Kellie said. The thought of arranging a meeting with Guang refocused her. She was up at the desk and calling the Conrad Hotel. Five minutes later, she'd finished her brief call to Guang, and a lunch meeting at the Marriott was arranged.

"We can use the morning to go back over the past week and what I need to try and find out from him," Kellie said. "Now, let's get dinner. I could use a glass of wine. I may need more than one."

Chapter 15

Regroup

Hong Kong (Monday–Tuesday, May 18–19)

Guang yearned for a cigarette. He hadn't smoked for over twenty years. He accepted Kellie's invitation to lunch, not because he wanted to but because he had no choice. How could he refuse? The only thing that caused him concern about meeting with Kellie had to do with her father. The Liwei situation was completely out of his control, and he had given Meilin complete freedom to help Kellie.

He needed to have a mental wall between various subjects that she might raise during lunch. Guang's thoughts of the meeting kept being interrupted by the mental images of Aaron at the airport earlier, realizing that he, as well as they, had been there to meet his cousin, Zhixin Liang. That's what was causing his anxiety and desire for a cigarette. He knew his cousin was coming because of a phone call from Zhixin, but how did Kellie and Aaron know? Did they get a similar call?

He got up and got himself a drink from the room's minibar, hoping that might calm his nerves. He settled into a comfortable chair in the sitting room. Guang realized that Kellie didn't say that her father was joining them for lunch. What did that mean? Kellie's call had surprised him, and he was off the phone so quickly that nothing about her father had occurred to him until afterward. He knew he'd have to wait till they met to get any information.

His thoughts turned to something else. Thinking about his conversations with Rong and Shu earlier in the day, Guang believed he could control conversations about Liwei and ChiTran and avoid creating problems for himself and ChiTran during his meeting with Kellie. The Rong and Shu call allowed the three of them to reach an agreement on a few things. Liwei and Meilin would be summoned to meet with them on Wednesday to discuss business. Rong, Shu, and Guang agreed, after setting new rules for going forward, Liwei and Meilin would be persuaded to join a social outing that evening to smooth things over. These young people needed to learn how to cooperate so ChiTran and its companies could focus on profits.

Guang needed his daughter to respect the ChiTran structure. The three elders agreed that Liwei was the problem. Meilin needed to be part of the solution. After all, she had entered Liwei's facility and taken Kellie. Liwei was using that against her with Rong and Shu, and Liwei was saying Meilin caused the customs officials to show up at his office. While he would try to protect her, even Guang had problems believing his daughter on this. He had a nagging thought that she was the reason for that visit. Whatever the reason, the visit created a rift within ChiTran that needed to be patched.

* * * * *

Alvin Liang wasn't used to roughing it in any way. After Yin and Wong had finished their interview, which was more like an interrogation, Alvin was placed in an overnight holding room in a secure part of the airport. The room had four cots, allowing Hong Kong immigration officers to put others in the room with Alvin. Alvin hoped that he wouldn't have to share with anyone else who was denied entry into Hong Kong.

He had access to a shower and lavatory and took advantage of the chance to shower and shave. Sleep came late and only in short spurts. This was as close to camping as Alvin wanted to get. The only thing Alvin was thankful for was that no one else had been put into the room with him during the night.

It was shortly after six in the morning when he first heard voices down the hall. Another hour passed before an immigration officer came for him.

"Make sure you have all your belongings and follow me," the officer instructed.

The immigration officer led Alvin through a maze of narrow hallways before walking out into the public areas of the airport. Somewhere along the way, a second immigration officer had joined them, following as if taking up the rear. The three men arrived at a Cathay Pacific departure gate. Alvin was being put on a flight back to Los Angeles. The lead immigration officer asked a check-in agent to get a manager to come out. There was a short discussion, and documents were shown and given to the Cathay representative.

Alvin sat in the departure gate area. "What happens when I arrive in the States?" Alvin asked the immigration officer still with him. The young officer didn't say anything in reply. He saw the young man shrug his shoulders. Alvin sat and waited.

"All set," the immigration officer said after he conferred with the airline representative. "My colleague here will make sure you board. At the other end, I'm not sure who'll meet you, but it'll be either an immigration officer or a customs officer."

As the last words were spoken, Alvin saw the immigration officer already turning to leave. Since landing in Hong Kong, he hadn't been given any chance to call Kellie or anyone else. He hoped that once he landed in Los Angeles, it would be like the last forty-eight hours hadn't happened. But they had happened, and he was going to have to explain a lot of things to a lot of people, including his wife and daughter. He knew he was in trouble, but how much was still a mystery to him.

* * * * *

"What are you going to do while I'm meeting with Guang?" Kellie was curious.

"Don't know. I'll find a way to occupy myself."

"Maybe you can contact your attaché guy, Ray?"

"I don't think so. He made it very clear yesterday that I should just take a back seat for now and do nothing. He wasn't happy to see me. He said if he wanted to see or talk to me, he'd reach out to me, and I should just keep a little distance from anything related to all of this now that he knows your father is involved," Aaron explained.

"What about Roger? Does he know what's going on?"

"Good idea. I haven't spoken to him for a couple of days, and he usually has his finger on the pulse of what's going on."

Kellie had decided that it would be better to talk to Guang over coffee or tea in the lobby, not knowing how the conversation might progress and whether one or both wanted to cut off the discussion. Kellie and Aaron left the room together but parted ways once in the lobby. As she scanned the lobby for a semi-secluded table for two, Aaron headed out of the hotel and walked to the Victoria Peak tram station to meet Roger.

Kellie found a table along the periphery of the hotel's lobby area and ordered a large pot of tea. The large glass wall was behind her. She had a broad view of the lobby area and entrance. She saw Guang appear a few minutes after the pot of tea arrived. He seemed to live in a gray suit, she thought. She waved. He walked toward her, twisting and turning between tables and chairs. This was the first time she'd seen Guang without a tie. This was his casual look, she concluded.

"Kaili, I'm so happy to see you," Guang said in Chinese as he pulled out the chair to sit. "You've had some difficult days. I hope you feel fine."

She took Guang's cue and spoke in Chinese. "I was never ill. I was drugged by Liwei so he could take me across the border. I've been fine since the drug wore off," she explained. Given all that had happened, she was direct. "Why does Liwei think I'm able to tell him how to ship his products to the States? And why does he think I would help him?"

Guang picked up his tea. Taking sips, he wasn't in any rush to respond. "Over the past few months, maybe longer, we've been receiving information about how to take full advantage of our business in the US."

Kellie waited for more, but Guang picked up his cup again and sipped tea. "Mr. Steeg, the former attaché, has been working for you for all that time. Is that where the information came from, or did you begin receiving the information before he began his work with ChiTran?" Kellie queried.

"Maybe before Mr. Steeg," Guang answered.

"Who was providing ChiTran with information before him? Who would be in a position to give you information before Mr. Steeg?" Kellie pressed.

Kellie's questions made Guang uncomfortable, and he felt a bead of sweat roll down his ear. He raised a hand to his ear, hoping to catch it before Kellie noticed.

"Your father has made some suggestions about how we might ship things to the US," Guang offered.

Kellie believed that there was only one way her father would know enough to provide any 'suggestions,' and that was from his seemingly innocent conversations with her concerning Aaron's work.

"How did he come across the kind of information that allowed him to make these suggestions?"

"I didn't ask him about that," Guang answered.

Kellie stared across the table, trying not to look angry but realizing it might be impossible not to signal her irritation.

"Did he know that I'd been taken across the border?"

"Of course. I called and let him know," Guang answered.

"So, you've spoken to him several times over the past few days about what was happening to me?"

"I would say two or three times."

Kellie plunged in with the question she needed to ask. "When did he say he was coming to Hong Kong?" Kellie asked.

Guang, sweating, picked up the teacup again. She had come alone, without his cousin. He was replaying the calls with his cousin. Had his cousin said he was flying to Hong Kong? Guang wasn't sure. Did that mean his cousin was in a hotel room above them? Was he in Hong Kong?

"I don't remember your father saying he was definitely coming," Guang opted to say. "He called because he was worried and wanted to know if you had returned."

Kellie was puzzled. Why would her father fly to Hong Kong and tell no one, not even her mother? It wasn't believable that her father bought a ticket and had no one at the airport to pick him up. She needed to change course.

"My mother didn't know he was coming. I didn't know he was coming, and you expect me to believe that you spoke to him two or three times and you didn't know? You must think you're talking to a silly, stupid girl," Kellie said sarcastically.

Guang looked out the window for a moment. No, the problem wasn't that Kellie was silly or stupid. His problem was that she was smart and could see every gap in his answers.

Kellie gave Guang a moment, then continued with what she knew was her interrogation of her father's cousin. "ChiTran, what's he got to do with that?"

"He owns an import-export business that ChiTran uses to export things to the US. His business is our exclusive agent to get things into the American market," Guang answered.

Kellie let those words play around in her head. "So, his business would process every ChiTran-related shipment, and it wouldn't matter if the products were to standards or not?"

"His business imported everything."

"How much did you or others at the meeting last week know about Liwei's business?" Kellie asked.

"We hope that our companies follow the rules. But no one goes and checks. ChiTran operates on an honor system. I don't go to Liwei's operations. No one does. If there are problems that are brought to our attention, then we will address them," Guang explained. He watched as Kellie, looking away, tapped her right forefinger on her chin as she thought about what he had said.

"We became aware of some of Liwei's irresponsible actions, and we'll meet with him tomorrow. He's already been instructed to change his business operations," Guang added.

"What do you mean?"

"Kaili, some of the more specific business practices of ChiTran do not really concern you, and officially, I cannot share the details. I hope you understand and accept that."

Kellie got the message. There was only so much he would share with her. There were too many gaps needing to be filled. But as they sat and continued to chat, Kellie knew Guang would not be filling in those gaps. She would need to fill in those gaps with her own conclusions.

Despite the remaining gaps, she now had confirmation that her parents were benefiting financially from whatever Liwei and other ChiTran companies were doing. Knowing this, she had to make some adult decisions about her relationship with her parents.

* * * * *

Aaron sat at Victoria Peak, waiting for Roger to show up. He was sitting on the same bench he had shared with Roger just a week earlier. From the bench, Aaron saw the top halves of the buildings reaching up into the sky from below and the hazy view of the Kowloon side. He wondered how clear the view would be if there wasn't the drift of the industrial pollutants from southern China.

"Pretending to be the Thinker," Roger said, interrupting Aaron's contemplative moment.

"Didn't see you."

"That was obvious," Roger said as he lowered himself onto the bench. "How's Kellie?"

"Hard to tell. Okay, I think. But I'll know more when I get back. She's meeting with Guang right now."

Roger nodded and stared out in the same direction that Aaron had been looking. "He and the rest of them are an interesting group of people. It's hard for us to understand, but you need to remind yourself that for most Chinese, all this money and potential wealth is still new to them. As a result, they'll do a lot of strange things to build up that wealth."

"You seem to understand it."

"Understand it? I doubt it. What they're doing is no different than what goes on in the West. It's just a different way to pursue the money tree. It's a matter of doing anything and everything until someone or something puts the brakes on it. For example, this Liwei thing that we came across, that's nothing. It won't stop him or anyone else. They don't care that a container or two gets stopped. There's so much more where that came from," Roger explained. "What we stop is a drop in the bucket compared to everything being made and shipped."

Aaron watched tourists walking around, stopping for pictures, some people posing. He waited as groups walked past. "Have you talked to Ray?" Aaron asked.

"Not the past couple of days. I think the last time we spoke was before the two of you went across the border to get Kellie. No, no, it was a very brief call to let him know that the stuff in those containers would be seized."

"Kellie's dad flew in yesterday, got himself detained by immigration here. Ray said they were sending him right back to the States."

"What?"

"Although I don't understand it all, he or his businesses are connected to this mess," Aaron said.

Roger leaned forward, elbows on his knees. "Well, no sympathy from me. I get it that he's Kellie's father, but if he's done something wrong, I have no problems with him having to pay the price for doing something stupid."

"Yeah, I agree. Kellie insists that she didn't know anything. Her mother claims she knew nothing as well. I'm hoping that's true."

"First, unless you find out otherwise, you should assume Kellie's telling you the truth. You love her and have no reason to believe she would lie to you. Second, if Ray had anything suggesting that Kellie had done something, you'd know. That's a guarantee," Roger insisted.

"What happens to Kellie's dad in a situation like this?"

"Well, there'll be a nice welcome party when that plane lands, and he'll probably be taken straight to some location for more questioning. Remember, by the time he lands in LA, Ray will have the time to organize and send any info obtained here to our guys back there. That means everything they found in searches, document reviews, his interview, and such. That will be in addition to whatever was previously assembled in the US that got the ball rolling. As a result, the agents back in the States will have a nice file on him. For what it's worth, my advice to you is to stay clear of this. I know it might make your relationship with Kellie a bit touchy, but getting involved won't help either of you."

Hearing Roger's unsolicited advice, Aaron had to agree that what Roger said made the most sense. Anything he might try to do with his customs colleagues would probably make things worse, not better, and doom his relationship with Kellie.

"What's your situation?" Aaron said, steering the conversation away from Kellie's father.

Roger stared out into the hazy sky. "Not sure. The past several days have made me wonder if I should stick around. I've come to realize the only reason these guys wanted me here was so they could pick my brain and then find ways to get around the rules. I justified it to myself by saying when China sent counterfeit tennis shoes, for example, everyone, including the consumer, knew what they were buying. But this week, I've learned that people like Liwei don't care if they send goods that put people in danger. I'm not good with that."

"I wouldn't be," Aaron agreed.

"I think that within the next week or two, I'll know my fate here and whether there's a way I can work with ChiTran that doesn't offend my conscience," Roger added.

"As long as I'm here, I need to keep my line of communication with Ray open and on good terms. While I have obligations to ChiTran, I won't let those obligations endanger Americans. That sounds stupid. Let me rephrase that. If it gets to the point that ChiTran, Liwei, or others put lives on the line anywhere, I'll find my own ways to stop it if I can," Roger added.

"Glad to hear it. Remember, they probably have backup plans in case they run into barriers," Aaron responded.

"I have no doubt about that. Enough about me. What's next for you? Do you and Kellie try to get that vacation you dreamed of, or do you head home?"

Aaron shrugged. "Not sure. I'll have a better idea of that when I get back to the hotel and hear how Kellie's conversation with Guang went. I think too many negative things have happened here for us to relax and enjoy Hong Kong. So, I'm hoping we leave in the next few days."

Neither spoke. Roger stood up. "I'd love to spend the afternoon here, but I have some things I need to get done. If Kellie has any earth-shattering revelations that you think I should know about, you know how to get a hold of me."

Aaron looked up, squinting at Roger. "Will do. I also want to thank you for everything you've done for me and Kellie over the last week. I couldn't have done it without you, and I realize your help came at a great cost to you."

"I was happy to help. That's what friends do."

Aaron watched as Roger walked back to the tram station. He sat for several more minutes before beginning his way back to the hotel.

* * * * *

The hotel room door slammed into the door stop and rebounded back toward Kellie. She stopped the door before it hit her as she stepped into the room. She cocked her right arm to throw her small purse but stopped herself from throwing it across the room. Instead, she tossed it onto the bed.

She rummaged through her luggage and found the workout clothes that she had never unpacked and a pair of sneakers. She threw it all into the hotel laundry bag and left, hoping that a little time in the gym would help. Her anger toward her father and Guang built up inside her after Guang left, and she walked to the elevator and rode it up. She needed an outlet. She didn't want to be in this foul mood when Aaron returned, and the gym was a good place to relieve some of what she was feeling.

Aaron stepped into the room, looking around with hands on hips. He didn't hear anything in the room, surprised that Kellie hadn't returned. Seeing Kellie's small purse on the bed brought relief. He wanted no more excitement, no more unexpected events. He moved around the room slowly in case there was a note for him on the bedside stands or the desk telling him where she might have gone. Nothing. He noticed that Kellie's luggage had been pulled out from under the bed.

Having nothing more planned for the day, he checked the minibar.

Aaron sat in the desk chair and used the bed as a footstool. Aaron was sipping his second rum and coke when he heard the door open. He removed his feet from the bed and sat up in the desk chair.

Kellie's hair was combed straight down her back and still wet. She dropped the laundry bag that contained her workout clothes on the floor and sat on the bed. "Is this a sign that your meeting with Roger didn't go well?" Kellie asked.

"No, just that I had nothing else on my calendar today, so I thought I'd relax. And you?"

"I felt like Guang gave me the runaround. A lot of words meaning next to nothing. Between not being able or not wanting to tell me things and at the same time saying that my father's import business handled all of ChiTran's imports into the States, I felt like my head was going to explode. When I got back, I grabbed some things, went to the gym, and then sat in the sauna for a while."

"Did it work?"

"Not really. My father used me. Well, more accurately, he used us." Kellie fell back onto the bed, then rolled onto her side to face Aaron. "All those people at that meeting last week expected me to say something to help them do some of their dirty business. Liwei just happened to take it to the extreme."

"Are you sure everyone's in that category?" Aaron questioned. "It seems to me that Guang's daughter did a lot to find you and get you away from Liwei. Without her, you'd probably still be across the border. She remembered Liwei's place in Tai Po, where he took you. Her hunch paid off and put us on the path to finding you."

Kellie was silent for a moment. "I'm conflicted about Meilin. True, she did a lot to help, but she also runs a ChiTran company. So, she might be taking advantage of this situation, you know, the information I was supposedly giving them. There's no doubt that I'm indebted to her." Kellie paused. "When she showed up at Liwei's, she really took charge. She wasn't going to take any prisoners the way she talked to his people. At first, I didn't know what was going on or who was there. She'd been like a non-existent person when we were at the meeting. But at Liwei's, she was like a different person."

"You should've seen her at the house where Liwei had taken you. We were questioning one of his goons. It was in Chinese, and when he didn't say the right thing, she stepped in and jabbed him in the throat. She was so quick that none of us could stop it from happening," Aaron recalled.

"I guess she's got some spirit in her. We've both seen it."

The phone rang. Aaron twisted in his chair, reaching out and grabbing the receiver from its cradle. "Hello?"

"Hello, Aaron. It's Ray. Consider this a courtesy call to let you know that Kellie's father left on a Cathay flight back to Los Angeles this morning. He'll be greeted in LA by a few of our agents. He's got a serious problem that's likely to get worse once Millennium Laboratories sees what's been imported. My guess is that the US Attorney's office will get involved, given the number of shipments, the value, and the type of products involved. It doesn't look good. Daddy Liang will need a good lawyer." Ray stopped to let the gravity of the situation sink in before continuing. "When are the two of you planning your return?"

"My guess is two or three days, not much more," Aaron answered, though he and Kellie hadn't set a specific day to leave.

"Okay. Consider yourself on vacation," Ray said. They both understood that they would keep their distance from each other.

"Thanks." Aaron knew the call was over. He put the receiver down and turned to Kellie. "Ray, giving us advance notice. Your father's likely to be prosecuted. Ray's convinced that there's enough evidence to go after him."

Kellie rolled onto her back and stared up at the ceiling. "I guess I should let my mother know. I'll give her the bad news in a few hours. Who knows, maybe my father has information he can trade to try and lessen the punishment."

"Don't get your hopes up. My guess is that any information would have to be very reliable and lead directly to stopping more goods or prosecuting other people higher up the food chain."

"What about me? I was at Liwei's. I can provide first-hand information," Kellie said.

Aaron didn't like that idea. "Anything you have to say about Liwei's operation only hurts your father. It confirms that Liwei's products are contraband, that your father's business facilitated their entry, and he put you at risk. So how does that help him? I think that the best course of action is to stay out of it unless you are forced into it."

Kellie pondered Aaron's advice. "You're probably right."

"Ray raised another issue. When are we going home? We need to decide."

Kellie rolled onto her stomach. "How's Friday? That way, we have the weekend to recover, and we can both be back in the office Monday morning."

"Sounds fine."

"How about a drink before I call my mother?"

Chapter 16

Conflation

Hong Kong (Wednesday–Thursday, May 20–21)

Roger didn't know why he'd been summoned to a meeting with Rong and Shu. The call in the evening to be at ChiTran's office the next morning seemed strange and was out of the blue. JJ drove him through the morning traffic to the ChiTran office, where he'd met with Rong a few days ago. He walked into the familiar lobby and took the elevator. He checked his watch. It wasn't quite eight. During the elevator ride, Roger convinced himself that a short five- or ten-minute meeting would be all it took for him to learn he was being let go, services no longer needed.

He was taken to the same conference room where he'd previously met with Shu and Rong. There were water glasses and coffee cups for each seat in the room. The room was set and ready for a meeting with more people in attendance. Roger was asked to sit on the far side of the room but near the head of the conference table. The young woman left, leaving the door open. Roger swiveled to look out the window, but the view was limited by all the buildings surrounding the squat building where ChiTran had its office. He swiveled back and stood when he saw Shu and Rong at the door. He started to rise, but Shu gestured for him to sit.

Shu and Rong took their usual two seats at the head of the long conference room table. As Shu settled into her chair, Rong poured water for her and himself.

"The past week has tested ChiTran and our relationship with you, Mr. Steeg," Shu started. Her voice was low and steady. "We want you to know that we'll be meeting with Liwei later this morning and with other ChiTran company officials. The Liwei situation will be taken care of today. He'll no longer use Hong Kong for his business," she announced.

Rong reached into his suit jacket pocket and placed an envelope on the table. Shu slid the envelope across the table to Roger. "We hope you are pleased with this as payment for the work you have done for us. I regret to say that I believe it is in our best interests if you are free to pursue other things. Your services will officially end on Friday, but we consider this relationship ended once this meeting is concluded," Rong said. "Hopefully, the payment will allow you to assist your driver, who we know was part of this arrangement."

Roger was tempted to look into the envelope but knew he'd have to wait till he was out of ChiTran's office.

"I'm sorry that this did not work out better. I've spent many years preventing bad things from happening. I was just trying to help you understand how shipping bad products could damage or bring down your organization," Roger said. "Before I go, I will give you a word of warning. The more contraband ChiTran ships out, the greater risk ChiTran takes that anything connected to ChiTran will get flagged, and ultimately, smaller quantities will make it to market. While it may not happen immediately, that means that your revenue and your profits will eventually decrease."

"We appreciate your concern. We believe that we'll be able to make the adjustments necessary to keep the business healthy and profitable," Shu responded.

Rong stood, and he led Shu and Roger out of the conference room. Once they reached the receptionist's desk and the door, Roger shook their hands, said goodbye, and left. In the elevator, he glanced into the envelope and flipped through the cash. He guessed there might be enough for JJ to take some time off while looking for another job. If the amount was supposed to be hush money, it would take a lot more than seventy-five or a hundred thousand Hong Kong dollars to buy Roger off. He was happy he'd be able to give JJ a healthy cut of the money, leaving enough for him to ponder what was next for him during this unexpected holiday.

* * * * *

A short time after Roger's departure, Guang, Shu, and Rong sat in the ChiTran conference room. There wasn't much time before Liwei and Meilin would arrive.

"We need to convince these two impetuous young people that the competition between them and their individual desires must be dampened in order to benefit ChiTran as a whole. As has been the case from the beginning, everyone benefits when ChiTran benefits," Guang started. "For that reason, I think it would be best if Shu started the meeting," Guang said as he looked back and forth between Shu and Rong.

"You can speak to Meilin more effectively, woman to woman," Guang said. He knew that she had managed to outthink and outsmart a lot of men. She had taken her father's small garment operation and turned it into a successful mass-production clothing operation that shipped its products to Southeast Asia, South America, and Africa. She had taken the money to expand in the Shenzhen area and realized she wanted to control more of the export operations. As her father aged, she took more responsibility for the production and logistics of the business.

Guang knew that Meilin respected Shu's success. Shu had made many friends in influential circles in Guangdong Province—but enemies as well. Those enemies understood that she was so firmly entrenched in the group of influential people that no one dared to cause her any serious problems.

Shu didn't need Guang to explain. She understood. She wasn't close to Meilin, but she wasn't seen as close to any of the ChiTran corporate leaders. She was careful to keep her distance so that she could make business decisions with the least amount of emotion. She cared about the success of the ChiTran group, not necessarily any one company or person. She shook her head, acknowledging she would speak to Meilin.

When Liwei's arrival was announced by the receptionist, Shu, Guang, and Rong ended their pre-conference discussions. Rong excused himself when Liwei entered the room.

Rong walked down the corridor, stopping for a moment to have a word with the receptionist, then went into a smaller office down the corridor. He sat behind a cleared desk. A minute later, Shing knocked lightly and stepped into the office and was motioned to sit.

"I'm concerned that your work for Liwei will lead you the wrong way," Rong said to the young man whose cheeks bore the scars of an abusive father.

Shing said nothing.

"The arrangement was that I would make sure you had a job, and I would keep you out of trouble. But you have not learned discipline, how to control your impulses. And having you work for Liwei has not helped you in that regard."

"You instructed me to work for Mr. Hsieh. I've tried to be loyal to both of you," Shing said.

"This may be my fault. I put you in a difficult situation," Rong conceded. "Perhaps it would be good for you to work elsewhere among the ChiTran group. I'll work on looking for you to have a different opportunity. Ms. Moy might give you a better opportunity to improve your skills."

Shing's complexion reddened at the mention of Meilin's name. He couldn't see how a change from Liwei to her could ever be an improvement. Shing closed his eyes for a few seconds, hoping to control his emotions and temper at the suggestion Rong was now expressing.

Rong saw the young man take a deep breath and close his eyes. "I'm aware of the recent difficulties. Those difficulties mean that Mr. Hsieh's operations will be changing and there may be less reason for you to work for him. You will have less to do for him. I'll take care of informing Liwei of these changes. I hope it'll keep you out of trouble. Just let things be as they have been for the next few days," Rong said. "That's all for now."

Shing rose, leaving Rong alone in the small office. Rong promised Shing's father that the young man would be taken care of with a decent job. That had been the only way to remove Shing from the clutches of a father who had been a soldier under Rong in the short China–Vietnam border war in 1979. Unfortunately, Shing's father returned with emotional problems and took his frustration out on Shing. Shing had worked hard, but Rong wanted to make sure Shing didn't go down the wrong path. The only way for Shing to develop self-discipline was to work for someone less impetuous and volatile than Liwei. Although Meilin could be impetuous, Rong knew she had more self-discipline than Liwei, and she demanded the same from her staff.

Rong headed back to the conference room, convinced that the change would benefit Shing and allow him to fulfill his promise to Shing's father. He rejoined the others as they waited for Meilin together.

"You stay with the car," Meilin said to her two-man detail. "I'll call when I'm ready for you." She exited the car. She glanced at the car's dashboard clock. Although it was only five minutes, she was deliberately late. This was the meeting her father said would be convened to sort out the Liwei mess. But she knew Liwei would try to turn the tables on her, so she needed to tread carefully.

Meilin entered the ChiTran office. She saw Shing and Tengfei sitting in the waiting area before she saw the receptionist. Both young men stared back at her as she stepped toward the young woman. Shing had now seen her a couple of times and was convinced that she was the one who had struck him when he was bound up at Liwei's house.

"Ms. Moy, everyone is in the conference room, please," the receptionist said as she got up to lead Meilin down the corridor.

Quiet conversations in the conference room between Guang, Rong, Shu, and Liwei stopped when Meilin entered the room. This was an all-Chinese meeting. ChiTran's brain trust and its two feuding company leaders were present. They needed to reach an agreement and move forward to finding ways to increase profits. There was an adjustment made at the head of the conference table. Guang joined Shu and Rong. Shu sat in the center. Liwei sat with his back to the long window side of the conference room, while Meilin took a seat on the opposite side facing Liwei.

"We need to overcome our individual differences and resolve these issues and work toward the benefit of our ChiTran group," Shu began.

Meilin took advantage of Shu's pause. "If I may, I am not directly competing with Guangdong Specialties Company." Meilin decided to refer to Liwei by using his company's name. "I must add that there are no business-related issues between Guangdong Specialties Company and ChiTran Research and Manufacturing Group. Any friction that might exist arises from the fact—and they are facts—that Mr. Hsieh Liwei took an American across the border against her will and then withheld her travel documents from her. He, not his company, prevented her from freely returning to Hong Kong. No one at the front of this room had any idea how to find her or where to look. Had it not been for me, no one could predict what would've happened to Ms. Liang. She is now back in Hong Kong without any real harm being done."

Four pairs of eyes were on Meilin as she finished. She took the opportunity to stare back at each person, including her father. If any one of them thought she would wilt under their stares, they were mistaken. Meilin tried to sit up taller, straightening her back and squaring her narrow shoulders.

"Meilin, Liwei is already under some new direction because of his recent actions, which have caused unnecessary repercussions on ChiTran," Guang said. "He will no longer use Hong Kong as a port for his goods. We've instructed him to export exclusively from mainland ports. Another action Liwei will take . . ."

"It's already been done," Liwei interrupted. "My papers have been filed with the Guangdong Provincial authorities for a new name of the company, and we will continue operating without interruption."

Liwei said nothing that would sound like he was admitting to smuggling Kellie across the border or exporting contraband or having Shing and Tengfei engage in childish mischief at Meilin's facility.

"Your two operations are the biggest among all the ChiTran facilities. We cannot afford for either of your activities to be slowed or interrupted. The others are growing, but it will take time for them to be at your levels," Shu explained, hoping to get Meilin and Liwei to see how important each was to the overall ChiTran group. "We do not need to engage in any petty conduct among ourselves," Shu added.

She continued. "We have an opportunity to expand and exploit markets other than North America. I hope both of you consider all the opportunities that we have. There's no reason to compete against each other, to place obstacles in the way of each other when there's so much open to us." Shu saw Liwei and Meilin seemingly agreeing with her as they subtly nodded as she spoke.

The three at the head of the room had already decided on an evening outing, and an arrangement had been made. "We want to re-enforce our collegial cooperation and common bonds toward our mutually agreed objective of a strong ChiTran group. We'll go to Macau for dinner and drinks and then return. We've chartered a hydrofoil for this evening," Rong said, speaking for the first time. "There's room for some guests if you'd like to invite people, perhaps two to four guests?"

Rong ended the meeting with details of the evening trip to Macau. Meilin did not linger in the conference room. She pushed herself out of her chair, shook Rong's hand because he sat closest to her, nodded toward Shu and her father, then exited. She left the four others just as she had found them when she arrived.

Liwei lingered and spoke with his three elders. He needed to convince them that they should have confidence in him. He wouldn't be bringing any guests along for the evening. He would use the evening as a chance to ingratiate himself with the three elders and make amends after what he had done the past week. When he left the conference room, everyone was all smiles.

Meilin's driver headed back to Hong Kong Island and the Conrad Hotel. She was not sharing a room with her father. When he had called about the meeting, he had told her about the plans for the social outing. He mentioned the idea of inviting guests to a company event. The idea of inviting guests intrigued her. It had only been a few days since Kellie had returned to Hong Kong. Was she still here? Meilin wondered if that would make the evening more interesting.

** * * * **

A midweek social event out of the main ferry terminal in Hong Kong wasn't the most convenient idea. The timing conflicted with the city's evening rush hour. At least leaving from the Conrad Hotel was a little better because the hotel was on Hong Kong Island. Shu and Rong made plans to avoid the evening rush and arranged to meet with Guang at the Conrad to make the trek to the ferry terminal less time-consuming.

The chartered hydrofoil was scheduled to leave the terminal at six-fifteen, before sunset. It would get the group to Macau in about an hour. An eight-person crew was ready to make the round trip for the ChiTran group. For the evening's charter, the eight-person crew didn't include four others who would serve hors d'oeuvres and drinks for the ChiTran passengers aboard.

ChiTran paid a handsome price for the small event, but the ChiTran brain trust needed to do something to overcome what had occurred during the past week. It was one thing to have business challenges, but the past week had exposed the enterprise to more personal frictions. The personal animosity between Liwei and Meilin couldn't be permitted to damage ChiTran, and rather than lay too heavy a hand on them, there was hope that the evening would smooth over the problem, even if temporarily.

Guang, Shu, and Rong were the first to arrive, and each needed help from four crew members to board the bobbing vessel. Despite the hydrofoil being tethered to the dock, it felt like it was bobbing six to eight feet.

"It'll be much better once we're underway," one of the crew members said. The three ChiTran elders gripped the handrails and the back of the seats to make their way to seats that faced each other like a booth with a table. The bouncing hydrofoil had them holding on to the table or the edges of their seats.

The hydrofoil's passenger seating area was open and spacious, but only a few locations had seats that faced each other. When at capacity, it would hold well over a hundred passengers. Because of the speeds, there was very limited space to be outside during any hydrofoil trip, and those spaces were narrow areas used primarily for boarding and disembarking.

Liwei boarded only a little easier but still needed the assistance of the four crew members. While he didn't have a guest, he brought Shing with him. Liwei found the other three and joined them. Shing sat a few seats away by a window, peering out into the harbor and focusing on smoother water. His stomach wasn't used to the hydrofoil's water dance.

It was a few minutes before the scheduled departure when the sounds of footsteps on the metal stairway up to the passenger seating area caught the attention of the earlier arrivals. Meilin reached the top, grasping at anything to maintain her balance. Behind her was a taller woman with mixed features and a Westerner.

Meilin gripped the backs of the seats as she made her way toward a seat but glanced around at the faces looking back in her direction. They were not looking at her. She saw what she wanted to see. The stares and failed attempts to avoid staring.

Kellie and Aaron were easily seen over Meilin's petite stature. Both tried to smile as they looked down to maintain their footing.

Aaron leaned forward toward Kellie. "What the hell is Dimples doing here?" He hoped the noise of the water and the hydrofoil's engine that was beginning to come to life prevented anyone else from hearing.

Kellie said nothing, still working to control her own surprise at seeing Liwei and hoping to get her own pulse under control. Kellie felt her cheeks heating up, knowing that they were visibly reddening. The combination of Liwei's presence and Meilin's manipulation of her and Aaron to attend the evening's event caused an inner rage to build. She knew an outburst would not help, so she tried to control her emotions. She was trapped on the hydrofoil. Her mind was telling her that she was a prisoner for the rest of the evening as everything was being controlled by someone other than her or Aaron.

Aaron tried to look at anyone other than Dimples, but he unconsciously kept glancing toward him, remembering him from the night at the hotel. His mind kept wondering what Dimples was doing there, and then he recognized Liwei and Guang, but not the other two older Chinese.

The hydrofoil was moving. The rocking and rolling motions of the vessel decreased, though the movement required a sturdy grip for anyone standing. When Meilin saw that the four sitting at the booth tried to stand, she motioned them to stay seated. She braced herself in an aisle to let Kellie and Aaron move closer. Aaron was the only person needing to be introduced.

Meilin ignored the laser-like looks she was receiving from her father, Shu and Rong. Liwei's surprised look of wide eyes and raised eyebrows at the first sight of Kellie and Aaron was now relaxed and replaced with a cynical smile.

Meilin and her two guests took the booth behind Guang and Liwei. It was an awkward arrangement as Kellie and Aaron faced Meilin while their backs were to Guang and Liwei. Shing didn't move from his seat by the window.

As the hydrofoil picked up speed, a young man who was part of the four-person service team came out and pulled open more tables and created a sitting area that accommodated eight people around one table. He gestured to them to move to the table once he finished.

Though everyone understood the gesture, no one seemed to be in any rush to move. Rong resigned himself to make the first move. As he had Shu pinned in the corner, she couldn't move till he did. Liwei looked the other way as if he hadn't seen anything. Because of Liwei, Guang couldn't get out of the booth. Rong muttered something as he used the table to push himself to his feet and moved cautiously to the other table. The hydrofoil's speed had picked up, and the main part of the vessel was above the water, so walking no longer posed a hazard.

It was a slow procession as everyone except Shing moved to the new table where Meilin, Kellie, and Aaron sat across the table from the other four. When drinks were ordered, Liwei was the only person who ordered any alcohol—Scotch, neat. He swirled his glass when it arrived, spending a lot of time looking at it as it swirled before taking sips. The other six had water or soft drinks.

Rong regretted that he had brought up the idea of guests as the seven sat looking at each other. The strain and tension were palpable. Aaron started to tap Kellie's thigh, but when she gave him a silent glance, he put his hand and arm back on the table.

Liwei interrupted everyone's private thoughts. He spoke in Chinese. "Mr. Foster, there are some opinions that ChiTran needs some correction. What would you say about how we can improve?"

Kellie translated. Aaron knew that Meilin and Guang spoke English well enough to understand anything he had to say. He wasn't sure about Liwei and had just met Shu and Rong. He debated whether he should say the first thing that came to him as an answer. He looked across the table at his audience. "Well, based solely on what I know and what I've seen, I don't think you, Mr. Hsieh, should have control of any company."

If looks could inflict bodily harm, Aaron would've been in trouble. Liwei glared at Aaron as he heard Kellie's voice translate. Liwei's eyes narrowed, and his jaw clenched.

Meilin let her head drop slightly, hiding a smile and satisfaction in hearing Aaron's statement.

"But, Mr. Foster, have you ever had a company or been in charge of a company's operations?" Shu jumped in before Liwei could say anything.

"No."

"Is it fair to say that you have never had the responsibility of a company's production and all its employees to consider on a day-to-day basis?"

"Yes," Aaron said.

Shu was trying to save face, not for herself, but for Liwei and ChiTran. "If you've never done some of these things, isn't your statement about Mr. Hsieh harsh?"

Aaron weighed his words. The older woman was thoughtful and careful. He needed to be careful as well. She was clearly at the table for a reason.

"My statement is not without some concrete evidence," Aaron started, giving Kellie time to translate and for him to think. "I know there are ChiTran shipments originating from Mr. Hsieh's company being examined in the United States, and there are containers here in Hong Kong that will not be shipped because of some of the things Mr. Hsieh is responsible for producing. Either he's incapable of producing and shipping goods that won't violate our rules and laws, or he's irresponsible and doesn't care. If it's the former, he shouldn't be in charge of production. If it's the latter, then he jeopardizes you and everyone else at this table."

Aaron wished he'd asked for something stronger than water to drink. He had been looking at the four people across from him as he spoke and listened to Kellie's translation. He turned and met Kellie's eyes for a few seconds.

"Perhaps when we arrive in Macau, Aaron and I should take our leave so you can enjoy your business dinner. We'll find our way back to Hong Kong," Kellie offered.

"We appreciate you offering to allow us to continue among ourselves," Guang said. "If this were normal circumstances, I would reject your offer to leave us, but I think that this evening, we'll accept your gracious offer."

After her father's response to Kellie, Meilin didn't think she could do or say anything to try and convince Kellie and Aaron to stay with her. They were more than halfway to Macau. Meilin said nothing of consequence during the ride to Macau. She sat stiffly, trying to make sure that she kept her posture up, not wanting anyone to think that Kellie and Aaron's departure when they reached Macau was a disappointment to her.

After the hydrofoil docked in Macau and everyone disembarked, Kellie and Aaron let Meilin know that they would find their way back to Hong Kong. They made sure that Meilin understood that they had a flight on Friday and wished her a good evening, though neither believed it would be an enjoyable outing.

With Kellie and Aaron's departure, the ChiTran group made their way to dinner. The dinner was different from the ride to Macau in one significant way. Everyone indulged in alcohol, a couple more than others. Liwei knew that Shu and Rong were acting as his buffer, protecting him from what Guang would probably do if he could make decisions on his own. Liwei dismissed Meilin as less important to ChiTran, even if her company was doing better than his. He saw her as smart but believed she was weak. Her decision to bring two foreign guests displayed her weakness.

The alcohol did nothing to improve the atmosphere of the evening. Meilin ate and sipped a couple of beers, but she didn't engage in any lengthy conversations with anyone. Although she understood the reason for the evening, she didn't speak with Liwei at all. She sat between her father and Shu at a round table for the five of them. Rong tried several times to lighten the mood, allowing the alcohol to help him loosen up, telling jokes or exaggerating his relationships with some key government officials in Beijing.

Two and a half hours into the dinner, no one at the table wanted any more food. Liwei had stayed with Scotch all evening, consuming several glasses, and was feeling their effects. He was no stranger to late nights and alcohol, although they usually occurred in a couple of select clubs he frequented in Shenzhen. At the clubs, he would've been with other businessmen and several young women, and there would've been music to keep people awake and feeling alive.

Rong waved Shing over to the table. Shing had been relegated to staying away from the main table, sitting off to a side table and alone. Rong whispered in Shing's ear. The young man turned and disappeared.

As everyone sipped tea, Guang knew the evening had been a complete waste of time. Although he had not objected to the evening, it was never going to do anything to improve the relationship, if there was one, between

Meilin and Liwei. The two had never gotten along. They simply tolerated each other and exercised politeness when others were around.

Shing walked back to the round table but simply stood where Rong could see him across the table and nodded. Whatever the task had been, it was completed.

Shing was at the door of the restaurant when the party of five reached it. He stepped toward the first of two taxis and opened the back door.

As Shu and Rong took steps toward the taxi, Shu turned. "We've arranged to stay in Macau tonight. We enjoyed your company, and we hope that in the morning, we can look forward to days of prosperity for each of us and ChiTran. I wish you a safe return to Hong Kong." Rong was already in the back seat of the taxi. Shu slid in and closed the door.

Shing waved his arm to prompt the second taxi to pull forward. Liwei walked around behind the taxi and got in. Guang and Meilin stood looking at each other for a moment. Meilin used her eyes and gave her father an almost imperceptible nod toward the open door. He got in and slid into the middle, understanding that she had no intention of being squeezed in the middle next to Liwei. Shing closed the door, then went around to get into the front passenger seat for the ride back to the hydrofoil terminal.

At the hydrofoil, the crew and service team were ready and waiting for the return trip. It was much smoother boarding in Macau than it had been in Hong Kong.

"Others," a crew member said to Guang as the four boarded.

"No, just us. The others are returning tomorrow," Guang answered.

The sound of the hydrofoil's engines gearing up for the run back to Hong Kong drowned out the seating area. Meilin sat a couple of seats away from her father, whose eyelids were heavy. She watched him drink more than his usual amount during the evening and guessed that within minutes he'd be dozing. With all the vacant space, she got up and nudged him down onto his side so he could sleep. She noticed that Shing had taken his seat again by the window, looking into the darkness that engulfed the hydrofoil as it moved away from shore. Other than the lights on Macau and a few dim lights from some islands, it was completely dark outside.

Liwei sat in a center row of seats near the front of the expansive and empty passenger area. With the hydrofoil at speed and skimming the water, Liwei fought off the alcohol-induced sluggishness. He wanted fresh air, but there wasn't much space outside, and signs on the doors warned of the danger of stepping outside when the hydrofoil was moving.

Meilin, watching Liwei, looked around. Shing appeared to be asleep with his head propped back into the space between the back of his seat and the window. Her father's breathing wasn't quite a snore, but he was breathing deeply. She saw no crew members. Her focus went back to Liwei, standing by one of the rear doors. She watched him. He ignored the signs. He stepped out using both hands to open the door.

There was a walkway that ran the exterior width of the hydrofoil. When Liwei stepped out, he was protected from the wind by the main passenger cabin and a metal railing that prevented him from falling unless he climbed the railing's metal bars that were about four and a half feet high.

Meilin rose and strode to the door that Liwei had exited. She took off her shoes for better balance before stepping out. She knew that the back end of the hydrofoil was lower than the front end, and she would be able to have a better feel for the vessel without her shoes. She saw Liwei turn toward the door when the light changed from the door being opened.

"What do you want?" Liwei shouted over the sound of the engine and the water churning behind them. "It's settled, Meilin. You're not the favored one except in your father's eyes. That is what you should've learned from this evening. And bringing foreigners to our event, that was such a foolish thing to do!"

"This isn't about this evening. You should know that I'll do whatever it takes to destroy you. Did you think I've forgotten how you assaulted me all those years ago? How do you think I remembered where your house is? Then your adolescent behavior toward Kaili. I wonder how many other childish episodes and victims there have been since then!" Meilin shouted back.

"It doesn't matter, just like you don't matter. You never mattered!" Liwei shouted, smiling and looking down at Meilin.

The hand struck Liwei in the throat with lightning speed. Unlike the superficial contact she made with Shing's neck that night at the house, Meilin made no effort to hold back when her hand struck Liwei in the neck.

Liwei's hands grabbed for his throat. Gasping, Liwei was off balance. He tried to reach out for the railing behind him with one hand. He started to fall forward into Meilin, but she redirected his body, moving slightly to her left in the narrow space between the railing and the wall of the passenger cabin, pushing Liwei with her right hand. He went sideways, losing his balance completely. His one foot landed on a lower step that was used to disembark the hydrofoil. His body weight caused him to fall; gravity worked against him as the left side of his body hit a lower railing.

Meilin never heard a splash when Liwei's body hit the railing and went over the side. Her eyes focused on the water and the blackness of a moonless night. While she hadn't planned what happened to Liwei, a sense of relief overcame her. She stepped back inside the passenger cabin, put on her shoes, and marched back to where her father remained asleep. She looked at her watch. She might've been outside for three to five minutes. It would be another twenty minutes before they were back in Hong Kong. She felt the quickened pulse in her chest. She closed her eyes, took a couple of deep breaths, and focused on calming herself.

Meilin slowly turned in her seat, facing forward. She folded her arms in front of her and allowed her head to rest on the back of the seat. She brought her breathing back to normal. Her thoughts turned to what she would do when it was time to disembark.

A few minutes before arriving at the Hong Kong terminal, a couple of crew members walked through the passenger cabin. They knew that the number of people returning was less than the number who had originally gone to Macau. "Wasn't there one more?" a crew member asked Meilin, the only person in the passenger cabin who was awake.

She shrugged. "Did you check the toilets?" That was enough for the crew member to walk away. Meilin roused her father from his sleep and got him sitting up. She looked around and saw that one of the crew members had gone over to Shing and shook his shoulder so that he'd be awake when the hydrofoil arrived at the terminal.

As the hydrofoil slowed and began a bit of a forward lurch toward its position before being tethered, Meilin stood. "Are you ready," she said to her father.

"Yes, I'm fine, thank you," Guang was still rubbing the sleep from his eyes. "Shall we share a taxi back to the hotel?"

"I need to make calls to my staff when I get back to the hotel. I'd prefer that we just leave separately," Meilin said, already stepping away and heading toward the exit stairs to disembark.

Guang said nothing as Meilin distanced herself from her father. He was unsteady as he stood, holding on to the seatbacks in front of him as the vessel's bobbing made balance almost impossible for him. A crew member noticed, rushed up to him and took his elbow and arm to help him down the aisle toward the steps. Guang was grateful for the assistance and for getting himself off the bobbing vessel and onto dry land.

As soon as Meilin was allowed to get off the hydrofoil, she darted down the walkway into the terminal and hailed a taxi. Given the late hour, it didn't take long for the taxi to navigate the streets and drop her off at the Conrad. She took a long shower. She wrapped herself in the hotel bathrobe and then sat by a window in darkness. The neon lights of Hong Kong provided a colorful backdrop as she thought about her moves for the next day.

When Shing was shaken awake, he had seen Meilin and Guang before they both disembarked. He asked the crew and catering team about Liwei, but no one was able to tell him anything specific about Liwei. One crew member thought Liwei might have gotten off the hydrofoil sometime between Meilin and Guang's departure, but no one was sure.

Shing went and checked the toilet. Not finding Liwei, he disembarked and wandered around the terminal in case Liwei was somewhere in the building. Then he went out to the street in case Liwei was looking for him there. Nothing. Shing lingered for an hour, then retrieved the car he had driven earlier in the evening. It was well past midnight. The only place he knew to go was the house in the Tai Po area. He figured he could be there in forty minutes without the daytime traffic. Shing concluded Liwei was probably at a club having fun. He'd check on his boss in the morning.

* * * * *

Meilin awoke on her own at six-thirty. She surprised herself that despite the Liwei incident, she slept soundly. No calls disturbed her. She had room service bring her breakfast and then called to check in on her facility. She decided it would be best if she followed her normal routine when in Hong Kong. She realized she wouldn't be at the top of the list to be contacted when someone raised the alarm that Liwei was "missing." In the back of her mind, a question stirred, how would ChiTran's brain trust deal with a production facility in Shenzhen that didn't have its owner?

Shing didn't sleep well at the house. Alone at the house, it was too quiet and too empty. He kept seeing the images of the hooded group that had him tied up. He believed that the tiny woman who had jabbed him in the neck that night was Meilin, but he couldn't prove it. After a restless night tossing in bed, he was up shortly after sunrise and made a few unsuccessful calls trying to locate Liwei. He held a cell phone in his hand, wanting to call Rong but hesitating only because of the hour.

By eight in the morning, Shing couldn't wait any longer. He punched in Rong's phone number. "Mr. Qian, I'm sorry if I woke you, but I haven't seen Mr. Hsieh since we boarded the hydrofoil last night," Shing started.

There was silence for what seemed a prolonged time before Rong spoke. "I'm not sure I understand. Explain."

Shing told him about the four people boarding, including Liwei.

"What happened during the return to Hong Kong?" Rong asked.

"I slept most of the way. I'm sorry. I don't know. I was shaken awake just before we arrived. Mr. Hsieh wasn't in the main passenger cabin, so I checked the toilets while others disembarked. When I didn't find him on the boat, I waited an hour in the terminal. He wasn't there, so I left. I called a few places this morning where I thought he might be, but no one has seen him. It's unusual that he hasn't called me by now."

"And you saw the others?" Rong queried.

"Yes. Mr. Lai and Ms. Moy. They got off, and I saw them get into separate taxis as I was getting off."

"Where are you now?" Rong asked.

"I'm at the house in Tai Po."

"Stay there," Rong instructed.

Rong spent thirty minutes making a series of calls, none taking more than a few minutes trying to track down Liwei. He knew Liwei's tendency to visit clubs late at night and wondered if Liwei had evaded Shing and the others deliberately. He didn't know which places Liwei might frequent in Hong Kong. His call with Guang was the longest, but Guang admitted that he fell asleep just after boarding and slept the whole way back. Based on what Guang and Shing had said, the only person who might have seen Liwei during the return was Meilin.

Rong called the hotel and was connected to Meilin's room.

"Meilin, I hope you enjoyed the evening," Rong began, knowing that she looked bored and sullen during most of the evening.

"Business events are always less than the happiest of events unless one is the beneficiary of a profitable return," Meilin said, trying to be just a little diplomatic.

"I am concerned because Shing was unable to find Liwei at the terminal and didn't see him anywhere last night. Liwei has not arrived at his factory. Did you see him after your return?"

Meilin focused on the last words. She answered truthfully that she had not seen Liwei after the return to Hong Kong.

"I'll call the ferry company and see if anyone on the crew saw anything," Rong said.

After the brief call, Meilin wondered if anyone had seen the two of them step out of the passenger compartment. She tried to remember if she had seen any of the crew or the catering team once they were away from the Macau terminal. She saw one of the catering team hand Liwei a cup of coffee. That was the only time she remembered seeing any crew or someone from the catering team. She stayed at the desk and opened her laptop and tried to get some work done.

Rong made a call to the ferry company he had contracted for the charter. The back and forth with the morning manager didn't get him anywhere. The crew's report was simple. It provided the number of passengers that went to Macau and the number returning. Rong insisted that the number returning was incorrect. The ferry manager insisted that it was.

"Did the crew check the passengers?" Rong pressed.

"It was a private charter. We leave you alone. It's a private event, and our people believe any private group won't want crew hovering over them. We don't want to interfere. In this situation, my crew members could see the few that boarded. According to the trip report, everything seemed quiet. They tended to the vessel itself and provided what was necessary, like specific boarding time, departure and arrival times, the amount of fuel consumed, and the basic information for the post-trip. If you have someone missing, we're not aware of anything happening during the return," the manager insisted.

Rong called and gave Shu an update. He was mildly surprised that she seemed nonchalant about the Liwei situation.

"It was good of Shing to report this to you, but we know Liwei can be impulsive. Perhaps he perceived last night as a personal victory and decided to celebrate. If we are in the same situation in twenty-four hours, we'll have to do something about his Shenzhen operation. Let's give it a day and let his people oversee its operations," Shu said.

Guang spent the day going over ChiTran business records and focused on information that Liwei had been providing. The numbers were good. Liwei's operations were bringing in nice profits, but the records didn't reflect the problems those shipments were going to pose going forward. He sat back in the chair. He allowed himself to think about how ChiTran would deal with the problem if Liwei wasn't at his desk in the morning. Someone would have to sit in Liwei's chair, even if temporarily. He pulled out more folders and examined the info from Meilin's operations, but he didn't look at them for more than a few minutes. He knew how things were going—very well. Guang knew that he could convince Shu to allow Meilin to take the helm temporarily. It might be more difficult to convince Rong. He wasn't worried. Shu was results-oriented, and she'd be able to convince Rong if that was needed.

Rong and Shu were back in Kowloon at ChiTran's office when Guang called them mid-afternoon.

"Has anyone heard from Liwei? Has he called or appeared anywhere?" Guang asked.

"No," Shu answered as she and Rong were on a speaker phone.

"In that case, we need to make some decisions to deal with the situation temporarily," Guang suggested. Hearing no response, Guang continued. "Meilin is a very capable executive. She has the abilities to run her operation as well as Liwei's until he shows up. I realize there might be some objections, but we need a plan. Her operations are more modern and more efficient. With her at the helm, even temporarily, she might be able to move Liwei's operations in that direction."

"What if Liwei shows up and finds her in Shenzhen? He could lose his temper. Things might get out of control between the two of them," Shu said.

"I'll make arrangements so that Meilin will be fine," Rong said but didn't explain.

"Meilin also has her own security people. If we agree, I'll make sure she knows to have protection in case Liwei shows up," Guang said.

"We need to contact Liwei's staff. They need to know what's going on and how we intend to keep things operating while he's absent. It'll reassure everyone there," Shu said.

"Should we summon Meilin to tell her this in person?" Guang suggested.

"Yes. Hopefully, we can meet in an hour. Rong will make calls to Shenzhen and secure the situation," Shu said.

Rong was back working the phones. He needed to explain the situation to Liwei's manager in Shenzhen. The call he didn't tell anyone about was to Shing, who was instructed to be at ChiTran.

Meilin joined her father for the taxi ride to Kowloon.

"What happened during the ride back?" Guang asked.

Meilin, staring out into the bay, turned her head toward her father. "How would I know? I dozed off after you fell asleep."

Guang stared straight ahead. He couldn't contradict his daughter. "We're going to make you the interim head of Liwei's operations. ChiTran needs someone there until he returns. That's what we're meeting to discuss."

Meilin turned her head back toward the water. She smiled to herself. Liwei wasn't going to be at his desk in the morning or ever again. She didn't initiate any conversation with her father as they rode to ChiTran.

Meilin felt her cheeks reddening as soon as she saw Shing sitting in the reception area of ChiTran's offices. She wondered what he was doing there. She had been convinced that he was sound asleep when she and Liwei stepped out of the cabin compartment. Could he have been watching? Did he see anything? He couldn't have. She wouldn't be given temporary oversight of Liwei's operations if Shing had seen anything and told Rong or Shu.

Meilin followed her father to the familiar conference room where Rong and Shu awaited them. Once they were all seated, Shu spoke. "We've decided that, for now, we'll have you in charge of Liwei's operations. His manager has been informed that this will be the arrangement. It's temporary. If Liwei doesn't reappear and the manager gives you any problems, replace him," Shu said flatly.

"I understand, and thank you for having such confidence in me," Meilin responded.

"Don't make any changes for now. If you see things that should be changed, be tactful in suggesting without doing anything," Rong added. "There is one other thing." Rong let the receptionist know to send Shing to the conference room.

Shing appeared in the doorway and stopped. No one asked him to take a seat.

"He'll be assigned to you," Rong said. "He is under my direct instruction that he's to do whatever you ask him to do. I'm sorry to say that Liwei allowed him to stray too much. Shing was given a position with Liwei under my direction, so I am partly to blame for his misconduct."

"If he's going to do any work for me, I insist on certain training. All my personal staff are required to have certain qualifications," Meilin countered. "If you are entrusting me with Liwei's operation, then you should trust my judgment regarding personnel."

Rong hadn't expected this. He understood it, but he was finding it difficult to accept.

"She's right to insist that her staff meet her requirements," Shu intervened.

"Shing should be in Shenzhen when I arrive there tomorrow, assuming that Liwei will not be there. I'll make my own arrangements," Meilin said. Meilin turned in her seat to face Shing. "You can go, but I expect that you'll be there when I arrive." She watched the young man give her a nod and walk away.

"I think we're finished for now," Shu said. Shu wanted the meeting to be quick, easy, and without any drama, and it was. She decided that the Shing matter would be taken care of within days after Liwei's whereabouts were resolved.

Guang said nothing as he rode down in the elevator with his daughter. He waited till they were back in a taxi to say anything. "This is the first step toward being at the head of the table."

"Whose place will I take when I get to the head of the table?" Meilin said, smiling into the window, seeing her father's reflection in the glass.

"It isn't always about replacing someone. It's about reaching the head table," Guang answered.

In her mind, Meilin wasn't satisfied with the idea of sharing the head table. She knew that it would take some time to be sitting there alone.

* * * * *

When they arrived back at the Conrad Hotel, Meilin left her father as each went to their respective rooms. She politely turned down her father's invitation for dinner. Her excuse was that she needed to get ready for the morning if she was going to oversee two different operations. It was an easy excuse to make and one her father easily accepted.

Meilin wanted to see Kellie, knowing that Kellie and Aaron would be leaving in the morning. She never made it to her room as she reversed course and walked through the connecting shopping mall to the Marriott.

The knock on the door interrupted Aaron and Kellie's packing. There were bags on each side of the bed. Neither one expected any visitors. They just looked at each other and shrugged. Aaron went around the bed past Kellie and looked through the peephole before opening the door.

"Meilin, this is a surprise," Aaron said, then stepped out of the way to allow her into the room.

"I'm sorry I didn't call before coming, but the way things went last evening and knowing you are leaving in the morning, I wanted to apologize for last evening and say goodbye in person."

"You've done so much for us. There's nothing for you to apologize about," Kellie said.

"If you hadn't thought about Liwei's house in Tai Po, this whole ordeal could have been much longer," Aaron said.

"I was lucky that I could remember the place and the area."

"It doesn't matter now. It's over, and I'm fine, thanks to you," Kellie said.

"I apologize for putting you in an uncomfortable situation last night," Meilin added.

"Nothing to worry about. We got back here and went out for a nice dinner," Kellie explained. "Actually, would you like to join us this evening for dinner?"

"Kind of you to ask, but some things have come up that I have to attend to, so I will decline dinner. But, Kaili, if you have a few minutes, could we have tea downstairs?" Meilin countered.

Kellie looked at Aaron, who gave her a go-ahead look.

The two women left the room and went down to the lobby. Meilin realized that when she'd met with Aaron and Roger or anyone recently, discussions were always at tables along the fringes of the lobby service area. She stayed to that tendency and looked for a table that provided some privacy in the midst of the large lobby lounge. They sat and ordered tea.

"I wanted to let you know that I'll be taking over Liwei's factory for a while. He never arrived at his place this morning, and no one has seen him since last night's dinner," Meilin said.

"He's just disappeared?"

"Liwei has some strange habits which have created problems for him in the past. Maybe he took things too far with someone this time," Meilin said, watching Kellie's reaction. "Anyway, I wanted you to know. If this becomes permanent, I will be a very busy person, but I'll try to correct problems at his factory."

"Of course. You're more than capable from what I've seen," Kellie complimented her.

"And you? What happens when you go back?"

"I'll be sitting at my desk on Monday. This wasn't a very successful trip. My boss may not be very happy that I didn't have all the meetings I had hoped. We didn't really broaden our connections in Hong Kong with my trip."

"Then, may I propose that we remain in contact?" Meilin reached into her small purse and slid her business card across the table. "All of my contact information is on the card. At least email me next week. I'd like to be sure that your trip to Hong Kong was not a disappointment in either work or personal ways. This may be strange to say, but the situation with Liwei might become a great benefit to both of us. I can make my enterprise and his, if I'm in control, grow, and it could work to our mutual benefit."

Kellie felt like she had a friend in Meilin. "I think it would be great to stay in contact with each other," Kellie agreed.

"I'm sorry for what you went through but very happy that we are good friends as you prepare to leave Hong Kong. And we should remember that we are family. Thank you for meeting me here. Now, unfortunately, I do need to go and prepare for a day of unknowns tomorrow," Meilin said, suggesting that she needed to leave.

Kellie walked with Meilin to the door that connected to the shopping mall. Kellie bent down and embraced Meilin. "Somehow, I think you'll do just fine. You have something special inside you. It's your spirit. Maybe I'll see you in Washington, DC."

Meilin smiled. "Yes. Let's plan on that. I have my opportunities here, and I'm sure you have them there. Hopefully, we can find a way to combine those opportunities for something special."

* * * * *

"Guess who I heard from today," Kellie said as she was opening the containers of Chinese takeout she picked up on the way home after work.

Aaron looked up from his computer in the corner of the small dining room in their apartment. "I give up. Who?"

"Meilin. She sent along an attachment from a local Hong Kong paper. A body was found in the waters between Hong Kong and Macau. Even though the body was in bad shape after being in the water for a couple of weeks, they identified it as Liwei Hsieh. So, I guess we know what happened to him."

Aaron had been looking at Kellie as she spoke, but hearing this, he turned his gaze back to his computer. He didn't say anything but wondered if they did know what had happened to Liwei.

"Do you have any idea where that leaves Meilin and that whole corporate business?" Aaron asked.

"In her email, she said that there'll be some final decisions made in days, but she's fairly confident that ChiTran will officially make her the permanent head of Liwei's operations."

"Sounds like Liwei's misfortune is Meilin's good fortune," Aaron said.

"Yes," Kellie agreed. She finished dishing out the food onto two plates. A smile spread across her face that Aaron couldn't see. Good fortune for Meilin might bring good fortunes to her as well. She hoped their paths would cross again, sooner rather than later.

Acknowledgment

This book, like all books, involves people other than the author. Knowing that a publisher would be there to consider this work relieved me of some of the concerns writers have in setting out on an endeavor to write a novel.

My first conversation with John Paul Owles, my publisher, in 2017 was about publishing a non-fiction book. That conversation was well over an hour long. In the years since that first conversation and having that book published, we have had many conversations. John Paul has been supportive and encouraging in my efforts to write short articles as well as book-length works. John Paul's constant encouragement and receptivity to my efforts contribute to my continuing efforts to write, and I am grateful for his ongoing support that makes this book possible.

Feedback is critical. While the story and the characters might be interesting to the author, the question is whether they are interesting to others. A special thank you goes to friends and professional colleagues. Mark Traphagen provided me with storyline issues to consider and possible edits based on his travels to Hong Kong and his familiarity with the dynamics of international trade. Chen Wang's valuable comments on the manuscript helped to gauge the accuracy and correctness of my writing about Chinese characters and the business environment in general. I thank them for their contributions.

My live-in editor and wife, Corina Trainer, provided the greatest amount of assistance in preparing the manuscript. This book would not be possible without her commitment to read, reread, edit, and challenge me about aspects of the storyline and characters. Her keen sense of what she expects as a reader and her sharp legal eye for detail contributed greatly to refining the story.

Books by Timothy Trainer

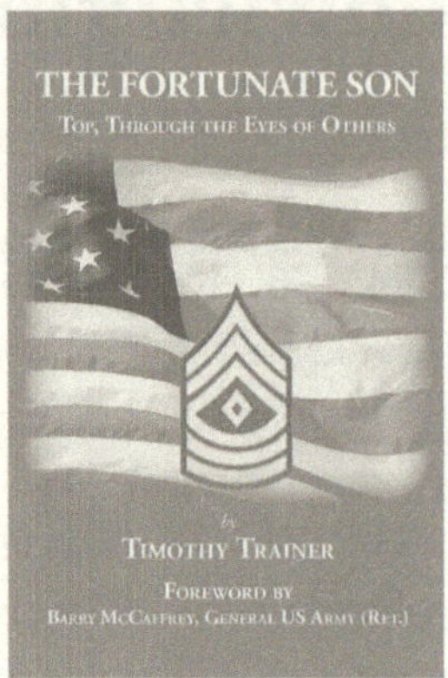

The Fortunate Son recounts the parallel lives of an army brat and a group of Vietnam veterans who intersect decades after the war. The veterans open up to me, the army brat, perhaps in a way they never have with their own families. Why? Through my father, Top, their First Sergeant, we have a common link. Over the years, we've gotten to know each other. They begin to understand the sacrifices of an army family. But, more importantly, they want me to understand how our family's sacrifice and my father's tour of duty in Vietnam with them, in the jungles, gave them confidence to believe they would make it home alive.

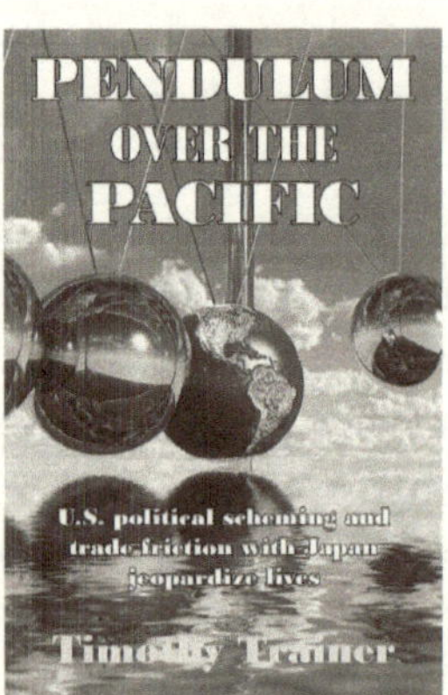

In **Pendulum Over the Pacific**, the President's nephew and advisor goes rogue, teaming with a hawkish U.S. Senator who is scheming to force Japan to lower its trade surplus with the U.S. The senator and nephew see Japan's trade surplus as a threat to the U.S. economy. They decide to manipulate facts and use history to their advantage to force the President to renegotiate an existing U.S.-Japan trade deal. It's the 1980s when Japan was the "bad" trade partner, before China's rise.

About the Author

 **Timothy Trainer** was born in Tokyo, Japan. An Army brat, he grew up on various Army posts then served a tour of enlistment in the Army. He used his military benefits to earn multiple degrees. His advanced studies included a return to Japan to study in Tokyo for sixteen months.

After earning his law degree and passing the bar exam, he moved to the Washington, DC area in 1987. His legal career focused on intellectual property issues with a more specific emphasis on combating international trade in infringing goods. He worked at multiple federal agencies that required extensive travel and consultations with foreign governments. In the private sector, he headed a DC-based trade association resulting in his work with INTERPOL, UN Economic Commission for Europe, and other international organizations. He has testified before congressional committees on several occasions. He was a private-sector advisor with a clearance to the US Department of Commerce from 2000-2020.

Joshua Tree Publishing published two prior books authored by Mr. Trainer. *The Fortunate Son: Top, Through the Eyes of Others* was published in 2017 and the novel, *Pendulum Over the Pacific*, in 2019. Mr. Trainer has authored numerous professional articles and co-authored a legal treatise for fifteen years. His book, *Potato Chips to Computer Chips: War on Fake Stuff* was published in 2015 by Thomson Reuters.